'Robert Bryndza's characters are so vividly drawn—even the slightest character—and fully human and uniquely imperfect. His plots are clever and original and cool, and his sense of timing is excruciatingly flawless.'

'An exciting, riveting read from a master storyteller who never disappoints.'

ALSO BY ROBERT BRYNDZA

STANDALONE CRIME THRILLER

Fear The Silence

KATE MARSHALL PRIVATE INVESTIGATOR SERIES

Nine Elms

Shadow Sands

Darkness Falls

Devil's Way

The Lost Victim

DETECTIVE ERIKA FOSTER CRIME THRILLER SERIES

The Girl in the Ice

The Night Stalker

Dark Water

Last Breath

Cold Blood

Deadly Secrets

Fatal Witness

Lethal Vengeance

Chasing Shadows

COCO PINCHARD ROMANTIC COMEDY SERIES

The Not So Secret Emails Of Coco Pinchard

Coco Pinchard's Big Fat Tipsy Wedding

Coco Pinchard, The Consequences of Love and Sex

A Very Coco Christmas

Coco Pinchard's Must-Have Toy Story

The Coco Pinchard Box Set

STANDALONE ROMANTIC COMEDY

Miss Wrong and Mr Right

ROBERT BRYNDZA

A DETECTIVE **ERIKA FOSTER** CRIME THRILLER

CHASING SHADOWS

Cover design by Henry Steadman

eBook ISBN: 978-1-914547-35-5

Paperback ISBN: 978-1-914547-37-9

Hardback ISBN: 978-1-914547-36-2

ALSO AVAILABLE AS AN AUDIOBOOK

For Mia

The night is darkening round me,
The wild winds coldly blow;
But a tyrant spell has bound me,
And I cannot, cannot go.

From *Spellbound* by Emily Brontë

PROLOGUE

Tuesday, July 8, 2014

'What's the hold-up? Over,' said Detective Chief Inspector Erika Foster into the radio on the lapel of her body armour.

'We lost a camera feed,' said the voice through the radio, back at the Surveillance Command Centre.

'Which one?' There was a tense pause. It was sweltering hot in the back of the van, and Erika was crouched with her Armed Response Team from Greater Manchester Police. Her protective gear was sticking to her skin, and the air was thick with the sweat of the five men sitting alongside her. Detective Chris Porter, their surveillance officer, was hunched over a laptop next to the panel separating them from the driver's compartment. Four windows on the screen showed the surveillance cameras around their target, number 17 Chapel Street.

'The camera feed from the back of the property went down for a short while thirty minutes ago,' said Chris. He wore a backward baseball cap with the Star Wars logo, and Erika could see the sweat on his neck.

She scanned the video feeds. A hidden camera in the lamp-post across the road showed a view of number 17 with their van parked outside. The fake sign on the side read 'Paul Berry Plumbing & Heating.' Two cameras showed side views of the house from the left and right. Behind the house was a large derelict building that used to house a printing press, and it led onto a road running down to the canal. A camera had been hidden in a lamp-post by the gates to the disused loading bay of the print-works, and this showed the back of the house. From weeks of surveillance, number 17 was burned into Erika's brain: bare concrete front garden, overflowing wheelie bins, and a gas and electric metre on the wall with its cover ripped off. The back garden was a forest of weeds with the frame of a little lean-to greenhouse against the rear wall.

'This is not the time I want to be blind. Over,' said Erika, hearing her tense jaw in her voice. The Surveillance Command Centre was silent. 'Did we have eyes on the canal the whole time that camera was down? Over?'

'Yes. Over.'

Erika's husband, Detective Inspector Mark Foster, was sitting next to her, sweating profusely in his protective gear. He'd been resting his assault rifle against his leg, and as he shifted on the hard bench, it slipped. He went to grab it, but it landed on the floor of the van with a clatter.

'Christ's sake, Mark,' she snapped. 'It's not an umbrella.'

'I know that, boss,' he replied amiably and picked up the gun. 'It won't keep the rain off.'

'Don't start.'

'Start what?'

'Provoking me.'

'You're my boss. Would you rather I said, *Yes, dear darling wife*?'

'I'd rather you not make stupid jokes . . .' DI Tom Bradbury, or Brad, a thick-set officer with massive arms straining under his protective gear, chuckled. He was sitting on the bench opposite next to DI Jim Black, whose face broke into a huge grin. Jim's nickname was 'Beamer' precisely because of his beaming smile.

'I need focus from everyone,' said Erika. She saw on the camera feed the front door of number 17 open, and a young Chinese woman with a small child came out. The woman had badly bleached hair with an orange tinge.

'Like clockwork,' said Chris, turning his head to Erika. Ginger, as she was known, took her little girl to nursery school every afternoon at 1pm on the dot.

'The kid's out. That's good,' said Detective Inspector Salman Dhumal. Sal was sitting next to Mark, and Erika could hear the note of anxiety in his voice. If the kid hadn't come out of the house, they would have aborted the raid. DI Tim James, or TJ as he was known, was sitting next to Sal, on the end, clutching his assault rifle, and he looked terrified.

The nickname 'Spice Girls' for the five Chinese women who had been trafficking the drugs in and out of 17 Chapel Street wasn't particularly politically correct, but it had stuck. Their targets for today's arrest were Jerome Goodman, a drug dealer who'd been on their radar for the past two years, and his two associates, Danielle Lang and Frank Hobbs. The trio had been involved in the bloody slaying of a significant drug dealer in a pub in Moss Side. In the resulting power vacuum, Jerome and his associates had taken over the supply of heroin and crack cocaine in the north of England. And this baking-hot day, on this run-down street in Rochdale, was the culmination of ten weeks of intense surveillance – Erika's team planned to storm this large terraced house on Chapel Street, one of the trio's strongholds, and arrest them.

They watched on the screen as the woman walked down the path to the small wooden gate, a laundry bag hooked over one arm, the little girl holding her free hand.

'If we lost the feed on camera four for twenty minutes, how can we be sure there aren't any other kids in there? Over,' asked

Erika. Chris pulled up a separate screen with snapshot images of the five women they'd seen going in and out of the house each day, always wearing tracksuits and oversized coats and carrying a checked laundry bag, which they used to move crack cocaine in and out of the house.

There was a long pause on the radio from the Surveillance Command Centre. Finally the voice said, 'We have officers posted on the canal and the road behind the print-works. Over.'

'Why did you lose the feed? Over,' asked Erika.

'Power supply. Over.' The covert cameras at the front and rear ran off the electricity supplied to the municipal street lamps, which enabled them to run twenty-four hours and broadcast the video feed using mobile phone data. 'Woman and child now approaching the end of Chapel Street. Over.' Uniformed officers had set up a discreet police cordon at the end of the road and would take them both into protective custody.

'Any other intel you want to share with us? Over?' asked Erika pointedly.

'No. Over.'

'Don't spook Ginger. Or the kid. We don't need her running back to the house and sounding the alarm. Over,' said Erika. Her back and arse were soaked with sweat, and she could taste it on her lips, salty. This never felt easy. There was always fear. She felt Mark grab her hand and give it a squeeze. Time seemed to hang in the air.

'It's okay,' he said quietly.

'It'll be okay when we know what's inside. I don't like nasty surprises at the eleventh hour.'

He looked over at her and smiled. 'We've got this. Before you know it, it'll be fish and chips for tea.'

She squeezed his hand and let go.

The voice crackled back through the radio. 'Woman and child are now clear of Chapel Street. You now have clearance to proceed. I repeat: clearance to proceed. Over.'

Erika's stomach felt like ice. The smell of metal and sweat seemed to intensify. Brad and Sal, sitting on either side of the van's back doors, moved, ready to open them. Erika looked at her team and nodded. 'We're going in. Over.'

The heat roared up off the tarmac as they jumped out of the van, sweating, clutching their rifles. Erika's legs were cramping, but she gritted her teeth and took the lead as they crossed the road. Chapel Street was empty. The woman had left the small wooden gate open, and they surged down the path, silent in their rubber-soled boots. It was eerily quiet. No birds or traffic. Just the low whirring sound of the disc turning on the electricity metre on the wall by the front door.

Brad moved up front, holding Bertha, the team's metal battering ram. The tendons on his arms strained as he lifted Bertha. The sun glinted off the disc in the metre as it spun, catching in the corner of Erika's eye, and it flashed, matching the thunk of the battering ram. On the third attempt, the wood splintered and the front door burst inwards.

In one of the houses a little further down the street, eight-year-old Carly Thorne was off school sick after an appendix operation. She was looking out her bedroom window as the back doors opened on the plumber's van, and a group of police officers in what looked like black army gear surged out towards the house. She'd seen enough TV shows to know this was a police raid. The front door crumpled like paper under the force of the battering ram, but the police never made it inside. Carly heard a cracking sound like someone letting off a firework, and it was only when one of the windows in number 17 exploded in a shower of glass that she knew it was a gunshot.

One after another, in quick succession, four of the police officers fell to the ground. Carly wanted to shout out and bang on the window, or tell them to use the guns they had over their shoulders, but she was too shocked and scared. One of the officers, and there was something about the way the officer moved which made Carly think it was a woman, collapsed to her knees, facing the road. Her hand was clutching at her neck and she was bleeding through her fingers. The last man standing on the path rushed to her aid. Carly heard a shrill sound of warning before some unseen force knocked him back, and the back of his head exploded in a shower of red.

Everything was very still and quiet, and then Carly heard the approaching sirens, and the road was flooded with police cars and an ambulance, lights flashing. More police with guns arrived, but this time, they were able to access the house. It wasn't until another five minutes had passed that paramedics could tend to the wounded.

And then, quite thrillingly, a helicopter – a real live helicopter – descended from the sky and landed on Chapel Street, little insignificant Chapel Street, where nothing much ever happened. It flattened the grass, stirred up the rubbish, and made the trees bend.

Only two of the police officers in black were rushed away on stretchers. When the helicopter left, Carly watched as paramedics loaded the other four limp figures into body bags.

No one ever saw Carly watching from the window, and no one ever spoke to her during the subsequent investigation.

1

Ten Years Later
Monday, December 2, 2024

It was 8am and Erika Foster was in her car crawling through the morning rush hour traffic in New Cross, South London. Just as she'd left the house, a courier had arrived with an official Met Police letter: her mandatory medical and fitness test was scheduled for December 20. It was bad news all round. Erika was now fifty-two, and she had serious concerns about passing. There was also the matter of the flights she'd booked on December 19 to visit her sister in Slovakia with her partner, Igor.

On the radio, Cliff Richard was approaching the key change in 'Mistletoe and Wine', and she switched it off irritably and stuffed the letter in the glove compartment. It would have to be dealt with, but first, she wanted to get to work and drink a very strong cup of coffee. Or should she? She drank too much coffee and ate too much junk food. She also smoked, slept badly, and stressed about her job. She'd seen battle throughout her career and still bore a scar on her neck from being shot during the drug raid, and then six years ago, she'd cracked two ribs and broken both legs below the knee in a car accident. And then there were the psychological tests. The deaths of her husband, Mark, and her four colleagues in Manchester still haunted her, but she'd avoided attending therapy, trying, unsuccessfully at times, to keep a lid on her emotions and bury herself in work. There was a high chance she would fail the physical and be consigned to a desk job – or worse, she'd be forced to take early retirement.

A call on her police radio jolted her out of her thoughts.

'Any units close to Amersham Road, SE14, New Cross? Code 5. Over.'

Erika glanced up and saw, just beyond the traffic lights, the sign for Amersham Road on the corner of the grubby brick wall. 'Code 5' meant dead body. And this was a rough area, with the kind of flats and bed-sits where you wiped your feet on the way out. It was either fate she was so close or bad luck. She guessed the latter.

'This is Erika Foster,' she said, hearing how weary her voice sounded. 'I'm right by it. Over.'

Silence. The lights turned green, stingy enough for two cars to cross the junction and for the pavement on each side to fill up, and then the lights flicked back to red. Pedestrians hurried over the crossing with their heads down. Stragglers were not being tolerated. The radio silence went on. Had someone beaten her to it?

'DCI Foster, reading you,' intoned the young woman working control. 'It's number 14B Amersham Road. The tenant reporting the dead body is a Sherry Blaze . . . Sahara. Hotel. Echo . . .'

Erika flicked on her sirens and blue lights and pulled out of the waiting line of cars. The commuters halted on the pavement, and the traffic reluctantly parted.

The terraced red-brick houses on Amersham Road were filthy and run-down, but they were still quite imposing Victorian four-storey structures. When Erika pulled up outside 14A, she was surprised to see her colleague Detective Inspector James Peterson waiting on the pavement.

'What are you doing here?' she said, winding down her window and squinting up at him.

'Good morning to you, too. My new house is just up the road. I was in the car when the call came through,' he said. He was smartly dressed in a long black coat and a sharp suit. He looked good.

'Yeah. Of course. Your new house. You settling in?'

'You'd know if you'd come to my house-warming party last week.'

Erika wasn't in the mood to be picked at. She got out of the car, took her long winter jacket from the back seat, and checked to see if she had her notebook.

'I was in court.'

'And too busy to let me know?'

She stopped and looked at him. At six foot one, Peterson was the same height as Erika. And a slender, handsome black man in his early forties. They'd been an item when she first moved down to London – until Erika messed it up. Peterson now had a wife and two small children, but there was still a frisson between them, even if neither of them would ever act on it.

'I'm sorry,' she said with more sincerity. 'Is it now warm?'

'It is. It costs a fortune to heat.'

'I'll get you some thermal long johns as a combined house-warming, arse-warming present.'

They had to move a clump of wheelie bins blocking the gate, and a cracked mosaic-tile path led to the two faded black front doors for 14A and 14B.

Erika went to ring the bell but didn't get the chance. The door was yanked open, and a middle-aged woman with a pale, haggard face and pencil-thin eyebrows peered at them from under a multicoloured character turban. She swallowed a mouthful of something.

'Are you the police?' she said, peering past them warily, taking in the empty street. Erika and Peterson held up their warrant cards.

'Are you Sherry Blaze?' asked Erika.

'Yes,' she said. She looked them up and down, and her eyes lingered appreciatively on Peterson.

'And that's your real name?'

She turned her gaze back to Erika and narrowed her huge saucer eyes. 'Yes.'

'We're responding to your 999 call,' said Peterson. 'You look like you're in shock.'

'I am a bit. You better come in.'

It smelt damp and musty, and Erika could see a small kitchen at the end of the gloomy hallway. A couple of old film posters were framed on the wall, and the glass was covered in a fine layer of plaster dust. Sherry showed them to the first door on the right, leading into the living room. A giant iron radiator lay on its side on the carpet, surrounded by a shower of plaster and wood splinters, and there was a large hole in the ceiling in front of the doorway where the floorboards in the flat above had collapsed.

'What happened?' asked Erika.

'You can see what happened. That radiator came through my bloody ceiling!' Sherry was wearing pink Crocs and a long towelling dressing gown. The thin belt strained against her belly, and Erika noticed a lot of what looked like orange foundation make-up and blotches of mascara on the dressing gown's collar.

'It's okay. We're here to help. When did it happen?' asked Peterson.

Sherry looked up at him with a grateful smile.

'I was in bed in the back bedroom, my bedroom, and heard this terrible thud from above, a groaning, cracking noise, and then a huge crash. The tenant upstairs can be noisy, but this was something else. Then I tasted plaster dust and came out of the bedroom to clouds of the stuff in the air. And this . . . It was twenty minutes ago. It just happened.'

'Your 999 call mentioned a dead body.'

'Yes. Look.' Sherry gingerly tiptoed through the doorway and along the wall to the back of the living room, where a sideboard and a big mirror were on the wall. Erika and Peterson followed. 'Can you see?' She pointed up through the hole. The room in the flat above looked very bare, with grey walls. A single bed was pushed up under the bay window, and the body of a woman with short brown hair lay on it. Erika could see from her pale, sunken face and waxy skin that she could have been dead for some time. 'I thought at first she was asleep. But who would sleep through that? I shouted at her, but nothing. Is she dead?' She burst into tears and, reaching out, gripped Peterson's arm, twisting the material on the sleeve of his coat. Sherry had long pink acrylic stick-on fingernails, and the one on the index finger of her right hand was missing. She seemed to be expecting a hug. Erika saw Peterson recoil a little.

'Do you have a key for your neighbour's flat above?' asked Erika.

'What? No. No. I don't.'

'It's okay,' said Peterson, gently placing his hand over hers and lifting it off his arm. He took a pack of tissues out of his pocket, pulled one out, and handed it to her.

'Do you know your neighbour's name?'

'Marie or Mary, something like that,' said Sherry as she blew her nose extravagantly on the tissue. Peterson pulled another out of the pack, and Erika had to suppress a smile as he attempted unsuccessfully to give it to her without touching her hand. 'She moved in a few weeks ago. I've only seen her a few times, coming and going,' said Sherry. 'Look at this. Everything is ruined. I can't afford building work.'

Erika looked around at the living room furniture covered in

dust and lumps of plaster. It didn't look like Sherry was a rich woman. The three-piece suite was old and chintzy, and she had an ancient hulking television in a unit next to the bay window, with a video recorder underneath and piles of VHS tapes stacked around it. She saw through the grimy front room window to where a police car was pulling up outside.

2

They left Sherry sitting in her kitchen with a policewoman, and Erika and Peterson came back outside. Two uniformed officers were unspooling a taped cordon on the pavement around the building. Peterson rubbed at his coat sleeve and sniffed it gingerly.

'It's bloody marmalade,' he said, looking up at Erika. 'She had her mucky marmalade hands on my new coat.'

'I can think of worse things to have smeared on your coat.'

'She said she woke up to the radiator crashing through the ceiling and then phoned the police.'

'And then she made some toast,' said Erika.

'At least it wasn't Nutella,' he said, scrubbing it with one of his tissues. 'Do you know what a nightmare that is?'

'What?'

'Nutella. Kyle dropped some on a new cushion, and it was impossible to get it out.'

'Oh, to have your problems,' said Erika. She crouched and looked through the letterbox of 14B. A blank, grimy hallway stared back at her, but it smelt clean. Lemony-fresh clean. She stood up and pushed against the door. After plenty of experience shouldering doors, Erika could now tell, with a bit of pushing, whether a door was sturdy, had one lock or two, or a deadbolt.

She gave it a brisk shove with her shoulder, and the door opened with a crack. The flimsy Yale lock had busted easily and hung off the doorframe.

She looked across at Peterson, and he nodded. They stepped into a dark hallway. The flat had a strange atmosphere. As if time were standing still. The walls were painted deep blue, and the light couldn't quite make it inside.

'Not much security for someone who lives in New Cross,' said Peterson, and his voice echoed on the bare floorboards. The walls were completely empty. No pictures or coat hooks.

The flat above had the same layout as below: a kitchen at the back, painted in the same blue and containing some ancient appliances; a bathroom with a faded pink suite of toilet, bath, and sink; and another blue room that was completely empty with bare floorboards and no curtains. A small window looked down onto a yard, which Erika presumed belonged to Sherry's flat below, and an alley ran behind. When they were sure the place was empty, Erika and Peterson came back to the body in the front room.

'It looks like the radiator was here,' said Erika, standing next to the hole in the floor where a huge chunk of plaster was ripped out of the wall. A piece of thin metal pipe hung off the wall, and the end was twisted and broken off.

'That thing must weigh a tonne,' said Peterson, stepping close to the hole and peering down to where it lay in Sherry's living room. Erika eyed the piece of broken pipe.

'The water must be switched off, or Sherry would have a water feature to go with the hole in her ceiling.' A small single bed was parked neatly under the bay window, and Erika and Peterson went to the body.

The dead woman wore a chocolate-brown tracksuit and white socks with dirt on the soles. Her brown hair was wavy and cut in a short, almost mullet-like bob. A thin gold chain with a gold crucifix was around her neck. She lay on her side with her legs drawn up and a blanket neatly folded under her feet. Her mouth hung open.

It was so quiet. The air seemed to hum with silence, and the smell of cleaning products, and Erika felt the urge to open a window. What if the woman's spirit was still inside and they had to let it out? She shook the silly thought away.

She pulled on a pair of latex gloves, reached out, and touched her fingers to the woman's neck. Her skin was ice cold and hard, like wax.

Peterson was silent, looking around the room, taking it in. Erika followed his gaze over the wooden night table with a lamp. A Bible was placed neatly next to it, along with a rosary and a small statue of the Virgin Mary. Erika noticed a small wooden cross high up on the wall above the door.

A rectangular blue rug next to the bed looked new, and there was a cheap NOKIA phone plugged in and placed on the floor next to a small radio.

'That strong smell,' said Peterson, putting his hand over his nose.

'Yeah. Cleaning products. Lemon. It might be run-down, but this whole place smells like it's been scrubbed,' said Erika. 'And I could smell bleach in the kitchen and bathroom.'

'"Cleanliness is next to godliness", as my mum always says.'

Did she die in her sleep? Was it an overdose? Erika thought. *Was she smothered?* But there was nothing on or around the bed to show a struggle, no drug paraphernalia. There was something very creepy about the room.

'How old do you think she is?' asked Peterson.

'Difficult to tell . . . Shoes.'

'What about them?'

'Where are her shoes?' said Erika, looking around the room and crouching down to look underneath the bed. The floor was neatly swept, but there was nothing. 'No shoes or slippers. Did you see any when we came in?'

'No.' Peterson opened the wardrobe. There were a few outfits hanging up, but no shoes. 'I'll check the hall.'

Erika turned her attention to the wall. Stepping carefully around the hole in the floor she examined the plaster, running her hands over it.

'I can't find any shoes. There's a cupboard in the hallway full of cleaning products,' he said. He came over to Erika.

'Look, this plaster in the wall is soaking wet, and you can see the wood is all rotted at the base of the wall.'

Peterson reached over and pushed at the plaster, which crumbled away in wet chunks.

'A slow leak?' he said, peering at the broken exposed pipe. 'This is all wet.'

'And that's a heavy radiator,' said Erika, looking back down through the hole. It looked like a great chunk of iron had fallen from a plane.

When Erika and Peterson came back downstairs, Sherry was sitting at her kitchen table with the policewoman and now dressed in jeans and a thick woollen jumper.

'Is she dead?' asked Sherry.

'Yes,' replied Erika.

'Bloody hell. Poor thing.' She shook her head, and an odd silence fell over the room. Erika pulled out her notebook to take a statement from Sherry, but one of the young policemen working the police cordon outside tapped at the kitchen door.

'Ma'am. The forensics team has just arrived,' he said. 'They've asked that the downstairs flat here is also vacated 'cos of the hole in the ceiling there.'

'Right,' said Erika, putting away her notebook. 'Is the police support van here?'

The officer shifted awkwardly. 'Er. No, ma'am. I've been told there isn't one available.'

'For how long?'

'Not available at all. It's a busy day. You know two of the vans recently had to be retired.'

Erika put up her hand to silence him. 'I know, I know.'

'I have to leave my flat?' said Sherry.

'Yes, I'm afraid so,' he said.

'For how long?'

The officer looked to Erika for guidance.

'It will probably take a little while,' said Erika.

'Bloody hell,' muttered Sherry. 'I've got things to do.' She pushed her chair back with a terrible scraping sound and went to the kitchen counter, where she unplugged her iPhone and shoved it into a grubby leather handbag with a cracked handle. 'I have to phone the insurance company. I don't know how I'm going to fix that hole in my ceiling.'

'Let's get you outside, and we'll work something out,' said the policewoman brightly.

It was freezing cold outside, and it had started to drizzle. The two flats, 14A and 14B, sat at the end of the terraced row on the corner of Amersham Road, and on the pavement on the corner was a small bank of parcel lockers.

'We can't cordon off the parcel lockers,' said Erika, seeing where the tape had been pulled around the side of the building. The young policeman nodded and went off to adjust the tape.

'I have to leave now,' said the policewoman.

'I thought you were the family liaison officer?' said Erika.

'No. I'm on duty. I just had another call. A family liaison officer has been called, but we don't have an ETA.' She gave them an irritated smile and hurried off.

The black forensics van was parked on the pavement next to

Erika's car. She could see Sherry was shivering, despite her long coat, and she was hunched down, scrolling on her phone.

'We could go up to my house,' said Peterson quietly.

'No. That's not a good idea,' said Erika in a low voice. 'We don't know this woman.'

'We're all frozen. I can't face the bloody traffic to the station. No one's home.'

Erika looked at him. The way he said *no one's home* made it sound like he was worried to bump into Fran, his wife.

'Fine. Let's go,' she said.

3

It was only a short walk up the hill, but as with many places in London, it took only turning a corner to feel like you were in a different world. The scabby flats and bed-sits with wheelie bins lined up outside were replaced with smart townhouses.

'Tea or coffee?' asked Peterson when they were inside and out of the rain.

'Do you have lapsang souchong?' asked Sherry.

'No.'

'Camomile?'

'I'll have a look,' he said, opening a cupboard above the kettle.

'Coffee, black, please,' said Erika. Peterson's substantial open-plan kitchen looked out over a beautifully manicured garden with a steep incline, so from the house, they could see over the tops of the trees and straight down into central London. The houses and buildings stretched out like a carpet of red brick, dark roofs, and cranes to the skyscrapers of Canary Wharf and the Shard, which seemed to spike directly into the grey clouds. 'Kyle's so tall,' she said, seeing the framed photos on the chest of drawers of Peterson, his son, his wife, Fran, and their baby daughter, Ruby. Kyle was now up to Peterson's shoulder.

'He's just had a big growth spurt and is eating us out of house and home. And Ruby is now walking.'

He opened the door of a vast metal fridge and took out a bottle of milk. Erika noticed the old baby scans, which were still fixed to the door with a magnet from Venice. There had been a brief moment where Erika thought they might become serious enough for her to consider having a baby before it was too late, which it now was.

'How's Igor?'

Erika glanced over at Sherry, who was absorbed in sending a text message, her face scrunched in concentration.

'Great. Well, good. He's got the whole of Christmas off.'

'Lucky bastard. Tube drivers get an insane amount of holiday.'

'I think it's partly compensation for all the people who fling themselves on the tracks.'

'You're off to Slovakia, aren't you?'

'Er. Yeah,' said Erika, remembering that she had that letter in her glove compartment. She noticed Sherry was now hovering by the table and watching them.

'Right. Let's take a statement from you,' said Erika, returning to her brisk police mode.

'Have a seat,' said Peterson, clearing away some of the baby toys from the table. Sherry took the chair at the head. When Peterson made their drinks, they came to sit on either side of her. 'What do you do for work?'

'I host a cabaret night in a club near London Bridge. Bryson's. Do you know it?' Erika and Peterson both shook their heads. 'It's well known. I'm the compère. We have comedians and magicians. I'm a trained singer, too. You should both check it out. We have quite a crowd. We're one of the most popular cabaret nights in London on Tripadvisor.'

'When did you last see your neighbour?' asked Erika. Sherry bristled a little that Erika didn't seem interested in hearing more about Bryson's.

'What's today? Monday. I last saw her . . . Saturday afternoon, passing the front window.'

'What was she doing?'

'I just said, she was passing the front window. She was carrying some shopping bags and a little vanity case.'

'A vanity case for make-up?' asked Erika.

'Yes. That's what a vanity case is for.'

'Can you remember what time that was?'

'I don't know . . . around 2pm.'

'Have you spoken to her much? You said she only moved in recently?'

'Yes. We met on the street a few weeks ago, and I'd introduced myself. That's where she said her name was Marie or Mary . . . I take it you, as the police, will be able to find her full name. I'd told her about Bryson's and even offered to comp her, but she was rather blunt and dismissive.'

'"Comp", as in complimentary ticket?' asked Erika.

'Yes. I offered to give her a free ticket if she brought some friends. Maybe she thought I was being a bit forward, but I'm a hustler. And we always need bums on seats at the club.'

There was a pause as Erika wrote this down. Sherry picked up a Rubik's Cube which was perched on the edge of the large fruit bowl. She turned it over idly, and then tried to pick off one of the coloured stickers. She only seemed to notice now, for the first time, that the pink acrylic nail on her right index finger was missing. Peterson smiled and took the Rubik's Cube from her, placing it on the shelf behind him.

'Do you know how old Mary or Marie was?' asked Erika.

'I'd guess . . . early forties? When she moved in, she looked like a real scruff bag, a bit dishevelled. But she looked like she'd pulled herself together and lost a bit of weight when I saw her on Saturday. Although, I don't like to judge people based on their appearance,' she added piously, blowing on her tea and admiring the smart china mug.

'Did you notice anyone suspicious around your flat in the last few days?' asked Peterson.

'I don't know. This is London. Well, at least down my end of the street,' she said, casting her eye around disdainfully, as if Peterson were somehow living it up a little too much in his nice house. 'Plenty of people walk past my window, a lot of odd people. Nonconformists. Mentally ill people who can't find a hospital bed. Homeless. Doesn't mean they're criminals.'

'Any particular weirdos who've caught your eye?' asked Peterson.

'I don't like that word.'

'What would you call them?' asked Erika.

'I'm not here to ask the questions.' She blew on her tea again, and took a sip.

'We can't really ask if you've seen any criminals, can we? Have you seen anyone acting strangely?'

Sherry thought about this for a moment. 'No. Nothing out of the ordinary.'

'Have you heard any strange noises upstairs in the last couple of days? Bangs, shouts, screaming?' asked Erika.

'Saturday night into Sunday morning was very noisy. I got back late from my gig at 2am and it went on until the early hours. But as I said, this is London . . .'

'What kind of noise?'

'Furniture being moved. A vacuum cleaner, water running. And drilling.'

'What kind of drilling?'

'I don't know, maybe she was putting up pictures.'

Erika looked over at Peterson. There were no pictures on the wall in 14B.

'Did you complain about the noise?' asked Peterson.

'No . . . Have you got double glazing?' asked Sherry, looking around.

'Triple,' said Peterson.

'And you heard this noise in the early hours of Sunday morning?' asked Erika.

'Yes.'

'When did it stop?'

'Maybe around four in the morning.'

'And what about the rest of Sunday? Any other noise?'

'No. All was quiet . . . Do you think she's been dead a couple of days?'

'We don't know.'

"Cos the first noise I heard this morning was the radiator coming through the ceiling.' Sherry dabbed at her eyes with a tissue. 'Oh Lord. It's such a mess. And it's going to cost me money I don't have.'

'What's the name of your landlord?'

'I own my flat,' Sherry snapped. 'I'm insured, but you know how insurance companies try to screw you.'

'Do you know the name of the landlord for the upstairs?'

'No . . . When can I get back into my flat?'

'It shouldn't be too long,' said Erika.

'Can you let me know as soon as possible, *please*, when I can get back inside? I have a gig tonight, and I need to get ready.'

Erika's phone buzzed with a message, and she pulled it out.

'My colleagues have managed to find us a police support van. It's parked outside your flat, so we can take you to wait in there.' Erika looked up at Peterson. 'And I have a message from Isaac Strong. Forensics are ready for us.'

4

Erika and Peterson left Sherry with a family liaison officer in the police support van. Isaac Strong, the forensic pathologist, was waiting for them in the upstairs flat. A tall, skinny man in his early fifties with dark features and pencil-thin eyebrows, he was a trusted colleague and a close friend to Erika. He was assisted by Martha and Ian, two scene-of-crime officers Erika already knew, and a handsome young crime scene photographer. Ian was dusting for fingerprints, and Martha was crouched in the corner of the room, taking swabs from the wall. They'd set up bright lights, and the woman lying on the bed looked more like a waxwork under the bright glare.

'Cause of death?' asked Erika, getting straight to the point as always.

'I don't know,' said Isaac, looking down at the dead woman. 'There's nothing to indicate violence or self-harm. If it wasn't for her surroundings, I would hazard a guess that she had a heart attack in her sleep.'

'We can't find any shoes or even slippers belonging to her,' said Erika. 'And the whole place stinks of cleaning products.'

'I think the whole place has been wiped down, deep cleaned,' said Martha, her knees cracking as she stood up, and placed a swab in a clear test tube. 'There are no hairs, no dust or dirt. And the deceased is dark-haired. I'd expect some hairs in the bathroom. The plug hole or in the bath, but there's nothing . . . And the water has been switched off. We're going to have a look at the drains shortly to see if we can find anything. I've taken swabs, but I'll need to return to the lab to test for any DNA.'

'The neighbour downstairs said she heard noises, water running, like someone cleaning, and drilling in the early hours of Sunday morning,' said Erika. Martha raised her eyebrows.

'There's no sign of anything being drilled. No pictures on the wall. There could have been some drilling work done on this damp patch of plaster.'

'I've been fingerprinting this room, the bathroom, and the kitchen,' said Ian, turning with his small brush. He indicated the deposits of silvery dust on the bedside table, door handles, bay windows, and light switch. 'I haven't found one print, not even a partial, anywhere inside this flat. Not even on the stopcock for the water supply. Very odd . . . Did either of you touch anything?'

'I touched the wardrobe and the wet plaster there, above the hole,' said Peterson. He looked over at Erika.

'I touched her neck, and the plaster in the same place.' They stepped out of the way so the crime scene photographer could photograph the woman from the back. As he held his camera facing away from the window, the bright light from the flash pulsed. 'Hang on, there's something on her back,' said Erika. She moved closer and indicated a flat black disc of plastic stuck to the back of the woman's tracksuit bottoms, just below the waistband. She stepped back, and Isaac gently flipped the waistband over, reversing the fabric.

'It's a shop security tag,' he said. The back of the tag had a big plastic lump where the pin was fixing it through the fabric.

'Wouldn't you notice that, poking into your back?' asked Erika.

'What if she shoplifted it?' said Peterson.

'She could have, but most shoplifters remove the tags. And how did she go shoplifting without shoes? She must have been wearing shoes when the neighbour, Sherry, saw her coming back on Saturday, so who took them?'

Isaac let go of the waistband and took a step back. 'As I always say, that's for you to work out.'

'What about the time of death? You worked that out yet?' asked Erika.

Isaac raised one of his immaculately shaped eyebrows as if to say, *Touché*.

'This one is tricky. It's very cold in here, and the heating is off. The effects of rigor mortis have subsided, which would put us beyond twenty-four hours, but if this lady died of natural causes, then I won't know more until I do the post-mortem.' He sighed and looked around. 'If the flat looked more lived-in and normal, I might not even think we need to do a post-mortem, but a lot here gives me cause for concern. A lot that could make this a crime scene rather than a sad final resting place.' Isaac looked over at the hole in the floor.

'We think there was a slow water leak behind the radiator. That's what caused it to fall off the wall and go crashing through the floor,' said Peterson.

'There's a lot of dampness in the wall, and the floorboards are rotten away,' said Martha. 'We've requested a structural engineer to come in and take a look.'

'Good. Thank you,' said Erika. 'And if you could let us have that security tag, we might be able to trace it back to the shop where it came from.' She took another look around the room, and her eyes came to rest on the Bible, rosary, and statue of the Virgin Mary. It all looked staged. But staged by whom?

Erika and Peterson arrived at Lewisham Row police station just before lunch. Erika's murder investigation team was based in a large open-plan office in the basement, which buzzed with activity. Despite the packed office, it was freezing cold. Detective Inspector Moss stood by the bank of printers at the door, wearing her coat and fingerless gloves.

'What's going on with the heating?' asked Erika.

'Gas boiler is on the blink. It's affecting the first three floors in the building,' she said, sorting through a handful of papers as they came out of the printer. Moss was a short, stout woman with flame-red hair that hung past her shoulders. Her pale face was a mass of freckles.

Erika's other colleagues, Detective McGorry, a dark-haired man in his late twenties, and Sergeant Crane, a gangly, balding man with sandy wisps of hair, were also working at their desks in their coats.

'It'll be fixed by this afternoon, apparently,' said Crane, not looking up from his computer. 'And we'll all be basking on sun loungers.'

A new management company had taken over running the huge ancient police station building, and this was the second time in as many months that the heating had failed.

'Can someone request a space heater?' said Erika, moving to her desk.

'Or at the very least, a three-bar electric fire,' said Moss, coming over. 'Boss. I'm just updating the case files. You just came from a code 5 at 14B Amersham Road?'

'Yeah, me and Peterson. Forensics are still there. I also saw Peterson's new house. Very nice.'

'Yes. You missed his house-warming party. The canapés were delicious, but he has the worst taste in music,' said Moss, looking over at Peterson with a smile. 'There was a lot of Enya.'

'Fran did the music. And what's wrong with Enya?' said

Peterson, shrugging off his coat at his desk. Clearly thinking better of doing so, he pulled it back on.

'Nothing. She's a lovely, mysterious Irish lady, but you can't really dance to Enya.'

'Can you even dance?' asked Peterson.

'I'll have you know, I took ballet lessons,' said Moss with mock indignation. 'I could have been a prima ballerina.'

'What happened?'

'I discovered chips. That's what happened.' Moss tapped a blue scribble on the back of her hand. 'Marie Collins. That's the name of the deceased tenant in Amersham Road.'

'Marie, not Mary?' asked Erika.

'Yes.'

'Where did you get the ID?'

'Probation records linked to the address,' said Moss, raising an eyebrow. 'Marie Collins is forty and recently released from HMP Holloway, where she served six months for insurance fraud.'

'Any other convictions?'

'No.'

'Was she out on licence?'

'Yeah. I have the name of her probation officer.'

'That makes this a little more interesting,' said Peterson.

'Yes. I think I need to brief the team on this one,' said Erika.

5

The afternoon went quickly, a blur of paperwork and meetings, and Erika arrived back home just after 7pm, realising she would have to tell Igor about the letter she'd received about her police physical.

George, her cat, was waiting for her in the hallway. He greeted her, purring softly and winding himself through her legs. She picked him up and rubbed her face in his shiny black fur.

'Hello, little monkey boy,' she said. She held him up to face her. 'You had a good day?' George had the most expressive large green eyes and regarded her thoughtfully before miaowing, which Erika was convinced meant 'yes'. She heard voices in the living room and carried him through.

Igor was standing on a stepladder next to a real Christmas tree, and his eighteen-year-old son, Tom, held the base of the ladder, squinting at the decorated tree. It looked very tasteful. All silver and red.

'Hello. What's all this?' asked Erika. 'A tree, already?'

'On the way home from work, I saw they're selling real trees at the garden centre in Greenwich,' said Igor. 'You wanted a real tree?'

'I did. I do.'

'I saw all these posts on Instagram that you should buy a real tree early 'cos they dry out,' said Tom.

'Well, if it's on Instagram, it must be true,' she replied with a smile.

'You're just in time for the switching-on ceremony,' said Igor. He reached behind Erika and flicked off the living room lights. 'Do you want to do the honours?'

'No. You decorated it, you should.'

Tom leaned down and switched on the fairy lights. The room was flooded with a violent blue flashing. George made a loud miaowing sound, jumped out of Erika's arms, and ran out of the living room.

'Not the most festive reaction,' she said.

'What? We bought white ones!' said Tom. Igor switched the main lights back on. He picked up the box with the picture of the snow-covered tree with white lights. 'Look. Look. White.'

He sounded really disappointed.

'I can see,' said Igor. 'But these look like the lights on the top of Erika's squad car.' Tom leaned down and turned them off. Bright blue dots lingered in Erika's vision. He picked up the carrier bag containing some bits of tinsel and emptied it on the sofa.

'Bloody hell. I didn't keep the receipt.'

'I can check the police station,' said Erika.

'For more blue lights?' said Igor with a smile. Tom scowled and tossed the empty box back on the sofa.

'Tom. Ignore your dad,' said Erika. 'There are tons of Christmas lights in the storeroom. Someone buys new ones every year and forgets. I can liberate some for our tree.'

'Ok. Thanks,' said Tom. Igor rested his chin on Erika's shoulder. She felt the bristles of his beard on her neck.

'I know we're going away for Christmas,' he said. 'But it'll be nice to have a tree in the run-up.'

'Yes,' said Erika, her stomach sinking at the thought that she was going to have to upend their plans. Igor had bought a flat around the corner in Blackheath Village, but now that Tom was studying at the Guildhall School of Music, Igor had moved in with Erika, and Tom was living at the flat. So far, the arrangement had been working well.

'Are you hungry?' Igor asked Erika.

'A little. I had a late lunch.'

'I made chilli. There's loads left.'

Her phone rang, and she saw it was Crane. She debated letting it go to voicemail, and then she looked around at the living room where Tom was moodily sorting through the mess of Christmas lights and decorations across the sofa. She grabbed the distraction with both hands.

'Hello,' she said, answering it and coming out into the hallway.

'Sorry to call late, but you said you wanted updates on the deceased woman found at Amersham Road,' he said.

'Of course.'

'It's to do with forensics. They still haven't found a single fingerprint or any DNA evidence in the flat. They checked the drains, and then went as far as swabbing the ceiling to see if they could get anything. There were no prints or DNA, but the ceiling above where the body was found was coated in a fine residue of cocaine.'

'That's an interesting twist.'

'They say the only way that it could have ended up there is if a large amount of coke was somehow discharged in the room. Like if a sizeable bag of the stuff exploded.'

'Drug-dealer size?' asked Erika.

'Yeah.'

'Was any cocaine found anywhere else?'

'A tiny, tiny trace on the floor, but it looks like someone did a deep clean but didn't think about the ceiling. Forensics wants to send a couple of scent dogs this evening to see if there's anything else hidden. Before they think about tearing the place apart.'

Erika checked her watch. 'Okay. What time?'

'Within the hour.'

'Do you know what's happening with the neighbour who lives downstairs? Sherry.'

'I can find out.'

'It's okay. Tell the crime scene manager I'm leaving my house now, and I should be there in the next forty minutes.'

6

When Erika pulled up outside the flat on Amersham Road, the street was busy with police cars, and two uniformed officers were door-knocking on the residents opposite to ask if anyone had seen anything suspicious in the last twenty-four hours.

The van with the scent dogs had just arrived and was parked next to a large grey police support van.

'It's the flat on the second floor,' said Erika to the two dog handlers, Abby and Max, whom she had met on several occasions and knew were excellent. 'A section of the floor has collapsed in the first room to the right of the hall, so be careful.'

The dogs were two powerful German shepherds with soft brown eyes. She saw their names, Roxi and Reggie, written on their high-visibility jackets.

Sherry Blaze came out of the police support van, accompanied by her family liaison officer.

'Detective Gloucester,' she said when she saw Erika. 'This is *beyond* a joke. I've been sitting in that van all day waiting to get back in my flat.'

'It's Foster. Detective Chief Inspector,' said Erika. The two scent dogs, with their handlers, went off up the steps to the front door of 14B.

'I have had to cancel my gig. And lose my seventy-pounds fee. Which is small potatoes in comparison to my professional reputation.'

'Why is she out of the van?' Erika asked the family liaison officer, a sour-faced woman called Fiona, who always seemed to talk out of the right corner of her mouth.

'Excuse me, don't talk about me like I'm not here!' cried Sherry.

'She got a text message saying there was a package for 'er in the locker on the corner. And she wanted some fresh air,' said Fiona. 'It's outside the crime scene, and it's very hot in that van. I thought it might stop 'er playing up.'

'Yes, it's very hot, and I haven't been "playing up",' said Sherry. 'And I shouldn't be expected to eat nothing but Family Circle fucking biscuits all day.'

'I offered to get you some sandwiches,' said Fiona.

'I don't eat bread, and I don't eat petrol station cuisine,' said Sherry. Fiona gave Erika the side-eye. 'Now, can I go to get my mail?'

Erika nodded.

'Go with her,' she said to Fiona. They went off, and Erika stood outside on the pavement in the cold air, waiting for the handlers to finish with the scent dogs. She felt a little ashamed that she'd skipped off again without talking to Igor. Nothing good would come from avoiding the subject. When she'd eaten her lunch at her desk, she'd checked online to see if she could buy another flight to Bratislava on the twenty-first of December, but there was nothing available until after Christmas. All the flights were sold out.

The two scent dogs emerged from the front door of 14B and padded down the steps towards Erika, straining at their harnesses.

'Anything?' Erika asked.

'They didn't pick anything up in the rooms, just the cocaine residue on the ceiling,' said Abby. 'They sit down when they detect drugs, and they kept moving around and sniffing up and sitting, up and down all across the floor.'

Roxi and Reggie approached Erika, and she leaned down to stroke them, her hands vanishing into their thick, warm fur. Max gave each of the dogs a treat that smelt strongly of roast beef, and it was only when the smell hit her nostrils that Erika realised she'd missed dinner.

'I was hoping for them to find something in a wall or under the floorboards,' said Erika. 'It would have given this case some grounding and motive.'

'If there was something, they would have found it. They're our best,' said Max.

Sherry came back around the corner with Fiona. She was carrying a square parcel in her hand, and when she came close, the two dogs sat up, alert, and lurched towards her, sniffing.

'Ooh. I don't like dogs!' Sherry cried, wincing and holding the parcel to her chest. Roxi and Reggie lifted their long noses and sniffed, and they both plonked their bottoms down at her feet. Abby and Max looked at Sherry.

'They're trained to sit when they think drugs are present,' said Max carefully. For a moment, Sherry was too worked up about the presence of the two big dogs to register what he was saying.

'It looks like they've detected something. What's in that package?' asked Abby.

Sherry hesitated, opened and closed her mouth, and looked at everyone staring. 'I just picked this up from the parcel locker,' she said. She turned to Fiona. 'You saw me, didn't you?'

Fiona raised an eyebrow. 'Yeah. But what's in the package?' she asked.

Sherry looked at everyone watching her.

'It's not drugs,' she said, looking at the scent dogs sitting obediently at her feet.

'Okay, but what is it?' asked Erika.

'It's . . . depilatory cream, if you must know. I ordered it from Amazon.'

'Can we check it, please?' asked Erika.

'If you must,' said Sherry, handing it over.

It was bright in the street, but Erika took out her phone and activated the torch, shining it over the box. It had a label showing from an Amazon warehouse and addressed to Sherry Blaze.

'Oh for God's sake! I'm expecting this package,' said Sherry, grabbing the cardboard flap and tearing it open. 'Here. Look.' She held up the box, and inside, Erika could see a bottle of Veet cream with a packing slip. Sherry unscrewed the bottle and saw it was sealed with the little silver foil circle. She ripped it off and held the bottle up for Erika to smell.

'It's Veet. Do you use Veet? Smell.'

Erika took the bottle. It smelt genuine. And she saw that the packing slip looked genuine, too.

'How long have these package lockers been here on the corner?' asked Erika, turning to give them her full attention for the first time. The lockers were attached to the end-of-terrace wall where Parkfield Road met Amersham Road.

'I'm not sure, maybe eighteen months,' said Sherry.

'Can we get the dogs to check them out?'

Roxi and Reggie were still sitting obediently. Abby made a clicking noise, and she and Max took the dogs around the corner of the building. They all followed. The two dogs went straight to one of the waist-high locker doors, sat down instantly, and stayed put.

'Which door did you get your package from?' Erika asked Sherry.

'The one next to it, I think,' she said, peering at the small plastic doors of the locker.

'In the past month, the dogs have been called out twice to check suspect package lockers being used for drugs,' said Max.

Erika turned to Fiona. 'Can you get someone to open this locker?'

One of the uniformed officers from the support van made quick work of the door and got it open. Inside was a small square cardboard package. There was no address label on it.

Erika pulled on a pair of latex gloves and picked it up. She estimated it weighed a half a kilo or more. One of the uniformed police officers accompanied her back into the police support van. She cleared the plastic cups of tea and the box of biscuits off the small table and laid a thin plastic sheet on the Formica surface. Using a knife, Erika carefully slit open the packing tape and slowly opened out the cardboard flaps. There was another box inside, made of thicker cardboard. This second box was lined with thick black plastic, and packed inside was a large clear plastic bag filled with white powder.

Erika looked up at the uniformed officer.

'Can we do a test on this, right away?'

7

Erika's alarm woke her at six thirty, drenched in sweat from a familiar nightmare: gunshots ringing around her ears, and Mark collapsing to the ground. She switched it off and lay in the silence, trying to catch her breath. The bedroom was dark, and she could feel George's hot little body against hers.

When she turned on the bedside light, she saw that Igor had already left for work. It was sweltering hot, and Igor always felt cold. She got out of bed and went to the window, feeling the radiator underneath pumping out heat. Dawn was just beginning to break above the houses, and there were ice crystals on the glass outside.

When Erika sat back on the bed, George turned his head to look at her and gave a grumpy little moan. She scratched his furry head and then took a long drink of water. She thought of the drugs they'd found in the parcel locker the night before. Drug dealers were the scum of the earth as far as Erika was concerned. But there was something outrageous about them using regular courier companies to transport cocaine. Outrageous and terrifying. Erika hated the expression 'the war on drugs'. It was accurate, but it had been hijacked by too many politicians over the years. But now, this discovery felt like another act of war. How many postal lockers were there in London? It was too depressing to think about.

When Erika put her glass back on the bedside table, she saw that Igor had left her a Post-it note:

Have a great day at work. Fancy fish and chips tonight? Love you x

He'd been asleep when she got home late last night. She didn't wake him up because he had to leave for work at five.

'I have to tell him,' she said out loud. 'I have to tell him, don't I?' she added, turning to George, who was staring up at her with his intense green eyes. 'Okay. I'll switch off the light,' she said, flicking it off.

Erika was showered, dressed, and drinking her second cup of coffee with some toast when Crane called.

'Morning, boss,' he said, sounding weary.

'Morning,' said Erika, seeing it was now seven thirty.

'I've been going through last night's duty log. We've found more info about this postal locker on the corner of Amersham Road. It's owned by a company called Ciao Bellissima Limited.'

'Okay. So it's real?'

'Yeah.'

'I did wonder about its authenticity, as it's not branded by one of the big companies.'

'I've checked UK Companies House. This company is seemingly legit; it's registered as having "other business activities". They have this postal locker in SE14 and a couple of other ones in South London.'

'More than one?'

'Yup.'

'Shit. We found 550 grammes of coke in a package inside.'

'And I bet it's not the first.'

'What about company directors?' asked Erika, emptying the dregs of her coffee into the sink and loading her empty mug into the dishwasher.

'This is where it gets murkier. It looks like the company, Ciao Bellissima L-t-d, is operating through another L-t-d, which is linked to a small chain of nail salons in West London. Tania Hogarth is the name of the controlling shareholder in the company. The registered address is in West London. No phone number.'

'Can you send me that address?'

Tania Hogarth lived in a detached house buried deep in the warren of streets off Chiswick High Road in West London. Erika and Moss arrived just after 10am and walked down the long path to the front door. They rang the bell, and it jangled deep inside.

'This place must be worth a fortune,' said Moss, peering around. 'She's living in London with a front garden, set back from the road. Mossy walls.'

'What?' asked Erika.

'The brick walls around the front garden are covered in moss. And she has creepy Gothic statues.'

Erika looked at a row of lichen-covered statues around an ornamental pond.

She didn't get to reply because the front door opened, and a petite blonde woman of indeterminate age stood in the doorway. Her face was taut and pulled with the cat-like eyes of several surgeries, and she had a lusty mane of blonde highlighted and lowlighted hair.

'Yes. Can I help you?' she said, speaking with both perfect enunciation and a strong cockney accent.

'Could we speak to Tania Hogarth?' asked Erika.

'That's me. Who are you?'

'I'm Detective Chief Inspector Erika Foster. This is my colleague, Detective Inspector Moss.'

Tania leaned in and squinted at their warrant cards, a movement which seemed to pull the skin up from the lower part of her face. 'I'm just getting ready to go out.'

Erika noted she was wearing a baggy but expensive-looking pink tracksuit with blindingly white trainers. 'This won't take a moment. We need to ask you about a parcel-collection locker on Amersham Road in South London. It's registered to Ciao Bellissima Limited. You are the sole director?'

Tania rolled her eyes.

'I don't have nothing to do with the day-to-day running of them lockers. What's happened?'

'We've encountered some illegal activity. Can we come inside to talk?'

'My boyfriend, Kieron, deals with the parcel lockers.'

'But you are the person with significant control?'

She didn't say anything and just stared back at them coolly.

'Is your boyfriend in? We could talk to him?' asked Moss. Tania sighed and sized them both up. She nodded and stood to one side to let them in. 'Take off your shoes, please. Kieron!' she yelled. 'There's two old ladies here want to talk to you.' She turned and shuffled off down the dimly lit hallway. Erika and Moss exchanged a look and then stepped inside, pulling off their shoes.

'*Two old ladies?* Cheeky cow,' said Moss in a very low murmur. Erika grinned.

The hallway had a very high ceiling, and was bare. Stark. Black marble floors and walls, but the floor was toasty warm on Erika's stockinged feet as they shuffled past a black marble staircase with no banister. The steps were free-standing and jutted out of the wall until they vanished into the gloom above. The kitchen was dominated by a huge island, a continuous dark marble slab with a white vein running through. Windows looked out over a large back garden with tall, ancient trees that both cloaked it from the surrounding houses and made the room dingy.

'We understand you run a chain of nail salons?' asked Erika, breaking the silence.

Tania pulled a face as if she smelt dog shit.

'I prefer the term "beauty salon",' she said, picking up an iPad, the only item on the surface of the vast empty kitchen island. She swiped the screen with a long, manicured finger. 'There you are. I was about to FaceTime you,' she said, looking up at the door behind Erika. 'This is the police.'

When Erika turned and saw the man standing in the doorway, her breath caught in her throat.

'What can I do for you?' he said, speaking in a Liverpool accent. She felt herself stumble back and had to grab hold of the marble.

8

Erika was unable to speak. Ten years ago, when she'd last seen Jerome Goodman, he'd been tall and wiry, in his early thirties. Now, in his forties, he was filled out and muscular, with massive arms bulging out from the short sleeves of his T-shirt. His hair was bleached blond, and he had a neatly trimmed dark beard, but his face was unmistakable. A large hooked nose and a high forehead. Black eyes and small, sharp ears. It was Jerome Goodman, the man responsible for killing Mark and her four colleagues.

'It's the police, Kieron,' said Tania.

'Oh yeah?' he replied in his scouse accent. He stuffed his hands in his pockets and puffed up his chest, remaining in the doorway. He was barefoot. 'And do the police have ID?'

'Yeah. I checked.'

'Perhaps we can check again?'

Moss looked to Erika, who was still staring at him in shock.

'I'm Detective Inspector Moss, and this is my colleague, Detective Chief Inspector Erika Foster. And you are, Kieron?'

'Bagshaw. Kieron Bagshaw,' he said. Erika swallowed and

tried to compose herself. Despite the tanned skin, cropped blond hair, muscles, and this bizarre house, this man wasn't called Kieron Bagshaw. He was Jerome Goodman. And he was now staring at her.

Moss held up her warrant card, and he went over to her and crouched down to peer at it.

'Right, lovely, thank you,' he said as if *he* were inspecting *them*. 'And you, love?' he said, turning his gaze back on Erika. She fumbled for her warrant card and held it out, pulling her hand back against her chest when she saw it was shaking.

He took a step closer to her and put his right hand up to scratch his ear. There was a tattoo on his wrist, like a skinny twist of rope or twine. In that pale-blue tattoo ink. Photorealistic. As if she could slip her finger underneath it. He looked down at it and then back up to her face. If he recognised her, he didn't show it. Erika thought back to the case file on Jerome Goodman. What did she remember? She'd watched hours of surveillance video of him in Rochdale. Jerome shopping. Jerome driving his car. Jerome sitting with his associates, Danielle Lang and Frank Hobbs, in a greasy spoon café. All of them drinking coffee. Was this just someone who really looked like him?

'Good morning,' said Erika, pulling herself together. She tucked her warrant card back in her coat pocket, and felt the cold metal of her handcuffs. 'Is this your husband? Or partner?' she said to Tania.

'I told you. He's my boyfriend,' she said, scrolling at her iPad and not looking up. 'Kieron. They want to ask about one of them parcel lockers in South London.'

He put his right hand to his temple, touching behind his ear. Jerome Goodman had long dark hair back in 2014. She remembered one particular surveillance video in which Frank Hobbs had challenged Jerome during a meeting at a garden centre on the outskirts of Manchester. Jerome had the habit of tucking his hair behind his ears when he was nervous. She saw him then, amongst the herb bushes and the fake water features. Kieron was trying to do the same thing now but couldn't with short blond hair.

'Have you recently cut your hair?' asked Erika.

'What?' he said.

'Your hair. Have you recently cut it?'

Erika could see Moss was really concerned, trying to catch her eye.

'What's that got to do with anything?' he said, his face changing. Was it anger or fear?

'And is that your natural hair colour?'

He looked at Tania and laughed. 'Is she talking to me or you, Tan? 'Cos look at her. I can tell you that the curtains don't match the carpet.'

'Kieron, stop it,' said Tania, looking up from her iPad with a tone of embarrassment.

Erika looked at Moss and saw her colleague searching her face to determine what was wrong.

'We're here for a routine chat about these parcel lockers, the one in particular on Amersham Road, South London SE14,' said Moss, trying to steer the conversation back. 'Tania said you deal with them?'

'Oh, did she?' said Kieron.

'Can I see some ID?' Erika heard herself say. Kieron turned to look at Erika. *Just ask him!* A voice was screaming in her head, *Are you Jerome Goodman?*

'Why do you want to know about his hair colour? And then you ask to see his ID?' said Tania, putting down her iPad. They now had her attention.

'I'd like to see your ID, too,' said Erika. 'It shouldn't be a problem to confirm your identity,' she added. 'Unless you have something to hide.'

Kieron laughed.

'Nothing to hide.' He pulled down the waistband of his trousers and showed Erika the top of his pubic hair, which was black. 'See. Yeah. I dye me hair. You want to check my balls, too?'

'That won't be necessary,' said Moss.

'Go on, Tan, show them.'

'What?' she said, suddenly looking scared.

'Your driving licence.'

'Oh, yeah.'

She picked up a white designer handbag from a chair at the table, took out a driving licence, and held it out. Erika kept her eyes on Kieron, so Moss reached out and took it.

'What about you? Passport or driving licence?' said Erika. Kieron reached into his back pocket to retrieve his wallet. Their fingers touched as he handed Erika his driving licence photo card.

She felt her heart pound as she turned it over in her hand. It said his name was Kieron Bagshaw, and he was forty. The photo showed him with short brown hair. Erika held it up to the light, tilting it. The hologram below his photo moved, and the watermarks were all there – it looked legit.

Moss came over to Erika with Tania's driving licence, her eyes boring into Erika's, saying, *"What's going on?"* But Erika ignored her, pulled out her radio, and called in to control with the names and dates of birth of Kieron Bagshaw and Tania Hogarth. A moment later, the voice confirmed that the names and address were valid, and neither of them had a criminal record.

Erika's mouth was dry as she handed back his driving licence. Kieron was smirking.

'See. Look at that. Everything's in order,' he said. Tania tucked her driving licence back into her Birkin bag. Kieron kept hold of his driving licence and pointed it at Erika.

'You know, you look familiar. Erika Foster. You've got a bit of Manc in your accent, with what? Eastern Europe?'

'Yes.'

'*Yeah.* Weren't you a copper, back, I don't know . . . ten years ago?' said Kieron, emphasising his point with the driver's licence between his thumb and index fingers. He was grinning. A nasty Cheshire cat grin. Erika thought back to all those months they had him under surveillance. He'd come from nowhere. A young upstart drug dealer, very low down in the chain, and suddenly he was a major dealer of crack cocaine in Greater Manchester. He rose so fast they could barely keep up with him. 'Weren't you involved in some drug bust gone wrong? All went tits up. A load of police officers ended up on the slab?'

He looked surprised when Erika moved so quickly, the flash of silver as she took out her handcuffs and clicked one over his left hand. He was a big man, but he didn't fight her as she twisted his arm around and cuffed his right.

'I don't believe your real name is Kieron Bagshaw. I believe that you are living under a different name. Your real name is Jerome Goodman, and I'm arresting you for the murders of Detective Inspectors Tom Bradbury, Tim James, Salman Dhumal, Jim Black . . .' Erika heard her voice tremble. 'And.' She swallowed. 'The murder of Detective Inspector Mark Foster.'

'What the fuck is this?' shrilled Tania. 'Kieron?'

Moss's head had snapped around when she heard 'Detective Inspector Mark Foster', and she raised her hands in a motion to calm Erika down.

'Erika. What's going on—'

'You do not have to say anything.'

'Erika,' said Moss, her eyes now flashing between Kieron and Tania.

'You can't just come in 'ere!' cried Tania, but Erika kept talking.

'But it may harm your defence if you do not mention when

questioned something which you later rely on in court. Anything you do say may be given in evidence.'

Kieron turned his head to look at Erika, who was now behind him, with her Taser deployed.

'Think very carefully,' he said, his eyes like deep pools of ink. 'I really wouldn't do this if I were you.'

9

Twenty-One Years Prior
November 2003

'I'll have a pint of your strongest, cheapest wine with ice and a straw,' said Danielle Lang to the waiter.

Jerome Goodman sat opposite her with two men she hadn't yet been introduced to. A grungy-looking, young blond man, wearing jeans, a Pink Floyd T-shirt, and a duffel coat. And a chubby guy with spiky black hair who wore a shiny suit. He had strange freckles on his face, like ink blotches. And his skin was greasy.

They were sitting on two large cracked leather sofas in Whisperz, a tacky bar off Cardiff city centre's high street. On this quiet Wednesday morning, they were the only patrons.

Danielle took out the pay-as-you-go mobile phone and placed it on the table. 'I have two hundred and thirty quid to my name till my next Giro. This phone cost me two hundred. This job better be worth it.'

'You'll make over a grand a week. Basic. I promise this will be worth it,' said Jerome.

Danielle was only twenty, and her show of confidence masked her fear and grief. She was still reeling from the deaths of her husband and her parents in quick succession. The waiter came back with her pint of wine. It had a dank purplish colour under the condensation on the glass. Danielle ran her fingers through her long dark hair. She took a deep pull on her wine, the straw in the corner of her mouth, all the time watching the three men. Even in her grief and without make-up, she knew she looked good.

'Who are you two?' she asked with an incline of her head. The wine was freezing cold, which made it taste okay. The alcohol hit her empty stomach immediately, and she felt the fear loosen its grip.

'This is Frank,' said Jerome, indicating the blond man.

'All right. Good to meet you,' said Frank with a nod.

'And this is Hugh.'

'It's good to meet you,' said Hugh. He held out a clammy hand and they shook. There was something icy about Hugh's eyes. *Dead behind the eyes* was the phrase that came to mind.

'You're posh,' said Danielle, wiping her hand on her jeans.

'I have the same accent as Jerome,' Hugh replied, bristling.

'Jerome has style with it,' said Danielle. She was good at reading people and situations. She knew that Jerome was in charge, Frank was his trusted friend, but the jury was still out on Hugh. She wondered what he brought to the table, apart from his greasy face and shiny, cheap suit. Danielle and Jerome had been at school together. He was a bad boy then, a bad boy with charm and good looks.

'Did you hear that, lads?' said Jerome. 'I have style.'

'I'm not sleeping with you.' She fixed him with a stare. Jerome put up his hands. 'I'm not sleeping with any of you lads.'

Frank kept his face neutral, but Hugh got flustered.

'Of course not,' he said.

Frank leaned forward and tapped her new phone in its box.

'This is good business. We need people who can talk up a good story. Jerome tells us you've got the gift of the gab. And you need the money.'

'You don't know nothing about me.'

'I know that your husband, Clive, died in an explosion at the gasworks, and they're not paying you compensation. And your mam and dad have also popped their clogs and left you with Provident loans up to your eyeballs. You've inherited their house, and their mortgage, which you can't afford.'

'Fuck off,' she said to Frank. 'What the fuck is this, Jerome?'

Jerome put his hand on Frank's shoulder.

'Sorry. We had to do our due diligence. Frank can sometimes be a little analytical, but he doesn't mean anything personal. Do you?'

'Nothing personal, just being analytical,' repeated Frank. He smiled, and it seemed genuine.

Danielle bit her lip and ordered herself not to cry. She took another slug of the nasty, tart wine and looked Jerome up and down. He wore Tommy Hilfiger jeans, an Armani jacket, and expensive trainers. When she'd bumped into him at Rossi's café the previous day, he'd paid for their tea and fry-ups, pulling out a wad of pinkies – fifty-pound notes – fastened with a silver clip. She'd thought it was a chance meeting, but now, she wasn't so sure.

'This job. Is this legit?' Danielle asked, picking up the phone she'd just bought. It had a green case. Green was her favourite colour.

'It's real money,' said Jerome, his jaw set and his brown eyes dancing. Twinkling. 'Cash in hand. You won't have to worry about making ends meet.' *You're not sleeping with him,* said the voice in her head.

'If you are the boss, then what do these two do?' asked Danielle, indicating Frank and Hugh.

'Frank is finance. Hugh here is personnel. He runs the office. Dot's the *t*'s and crosses the *i*'s.'

'Er. I think it's the other way around?' said Hugh.

'That was a joke,' said Jerome, his face deadpan.

'Right. Yes. Very funny,' he said nervously, flashing a set of yellow teeth in a smile. 'Right. Danielle. This meeting today is also your training session.'

Danielle looked between Jerome and Frank, they looked back at her, and an understanding passed between them. Hugh was the front man of the operation.

'Training session?' she asked sceptically.

'Yes. Perhaps you might like something to soak up the wine? Maybe we can get you some crisps or peanuts?'

'Are you saying I'm drunk, Hugh? Is he saying I'm drunk?'

'No. He's not saying that. Are you, Hugh?' said Jerome.

'No. Of course not.' He flashed his nervous yellow rabbit teeth again, and Danielle suppressed a shudder.

'Do you like pork scratchings?' asked Frank.

'Yes, I do.'

'Not a lot of people like them these days. Who got you into them?'

'When I was born, my mum's milk dried up, so they moved me onto solids early.'

Jerome and Frank smiled, but Hugh stared at her. 'I'm kidding, Hugh. Maybe you can get me the pork scratchings?' She raised an eyebrow at Jerome, and he nodded at Hugh. He got up reluctantly and went to the bar. Danielle waited until he was out of earshot. 'Quick. Train me before he gets back.'

Frank and Jerome smiled.

'Okay. Get a big piece of lined paper and write out a list crunching backward or forward from your number,' said Jerome, tapping the phone number on the back of the box above the barcode. 'Changing the last digit on the end up or down, 767, 768, 769. That gives you a list of contact phone numbers to ring.'

'What am I ringing about?'

'Mobile phone insurance,' said Frank. 'You tell 'em you've heard from their mobile phone provider that they're eligible for a specially discounted insurance policy for their phone.'

'And how do I know that?'

Jerome leaned closer and smiled. 'You don't. It's bollocks. You'll have a credit card terminal. You ask them to make the payment over the phone.'

Danielle took out a packet of cigarettes and lit up. 'And people pay?'

'You'd be surprised how many people pay,' said Frank. 'Mobile phones are expensive, especially if they have a contract. You need to scare them into buying our insurance. Old people. Businesspeople. Lonely housewives. Foreigners whose mobile phones are their only link to home.'

'If they sound foreign, we put the payment through twice,' added Jerome.

'How much is the payment?' asked Danielle.

'Thirty quid.'

'How much of that do I get?'

'You'll get thirty per cent of every card transaction.'

'How risky is it?'

'Much less risky than defaulting on your mortgage and losing your only home,' said Jerome.

'I need an advance on my first week's wages. Now. Today.'

Danielle sat back and took a drag of her cigarette, and kept eye contact with them. She knew she was taking a risk, but there was an energy, a chemistry, between the three of them. It wasn't sexual, but something told her she would gain their respect if she had her own terms.

'We pay weekly.'

'Yeah. I'll be worth it.'

Hugh came back with a packet of pork scratchings.

'Here we go. Where are we?' he asked, sitting down and patting his legs.

A tinny ringtone playing 'New York, New York' emanated from the inside of Frank's jacket, and he pulled out his phone. He held it up and grinned. 'I have to go. Welcome to Secure Phone, Danielle.'

He left the bar.

'Danielle is starting with us tomorrow. And we're advancing her a week's wages,' said Jerome.

Hugh stared at her with his dead eyes. 'Why?'

"Cos I said so,' replied Jerome. He nodded. Hugh sighed, reached into his jacket, and took out a brown envelope, teased out a thick stack of fifty-pound notes, counted them, and held out the money to him. 'You're advancing Danielle, not me.'

The sight of so many pinkies made Danielle's heart beat faster. This was a lifeline she hadn't dared think possible, but with people like this, she had to play it cool. When she went to take the money, Hugh gripped her fingers and closed the notes around her hand.

'This is an advance. A loan,' he said. His horrible blank eyes bored into hers. 'I'm the money. I pay you. You have a debt. In one week, your debt will be called in. No extensions. Understand?'

'I know how it works,' said Danielle. She took the money and stuffed it into the pocket of her jeans.

'I hope so. For your sake.'

Jerome smiled.

'Welcome to Secure Phone.'

10

Tuesday, December 3, 2024

Erika was still shaking as she waited with Moss in the reception area of the custody suite at Lewisham Row Station.

'As soon as his brief arrives, there's going to be trouble,' said PC Waller, the police officer working on the front desk. He was sweating, his bald forehead shining under the bright lights. 'He's requested Paul Slater. Not the kind of solicitor you want to mess around with.'

Erika wanted to tell him to grow a pair of balls, but she settled with asking, 'You've printed him?'

'Yes. I told you. Nothing. He's got no record,' said Waller, indicating the touchpad where fingerprints were digitally scanned when suspects were processed in the custody suite.

'No. His name is Jerome Goodman. Check IDENT1 and NDNAD.'

'I did.'

'Check. Again.'

'Erika. I'm not your lackey.'

She stared him down across the desk. 'I'm your senior officer. Do it.'

'We've just come from a stressful arrest,' said Moss, trying to ease the situation. 'Could you please check against the name Jerome Goodman?'

Waller's face was impassive as he ran through checks on the two police databases, which stored fingerprint and DNA information for past convictions. Moss was looking over at Erika, her face deeply concerned.

'Okay. Jerome Goodman . . . I have two hits—'

'That's more like it,' Erika interrupted.

Waller's face broke into a nasty smirk. 'One is an IC2 code, white south European, aged seventy-four. He's currently serving a life sentence for murder in HMP Parkhurst . . . on the Isle of Wight.'

'I know where it is.'

'The second hit is for a seventeen-year-old male. With an IC code.' He gave a dry chuckle. 'IC3. Black. His ethnicity is black.'

There was a nasty silence.

'What if he's in witness protection?' asked Erika.

'What if he is? Do you think it's going to show up on my computer? Just admit you're a hothead. You got it wrong,' he said.

'Okay, okay. Easy,' said Moss.

'No!' Erika cried, slamming her hand down on the desk. 'It's him. I know it!'

She felt Moss's hand on her arm. 'Can I have a word?' she said, her voice deliberately low and calm. Moss beckoned for her to move away from the desk.

Erika was breathing heavily, and her heart was thumping. The rage she felt was frightening. They moved away to the chairs lining the back wall.

'Sorry.'

'Don't be sorry,' said Moss. 'Let's just take a step back. Look at this situation.' Erika had been in a cold sweat all the way back from Chiswick. Thankfully, they'd been following a police squad car, in the back of which Kieron Bagshaw was handcuffed. Moss had questioned Erika very carefully as they drove, and she'd explained as much as she could. But when it came down to it, it was Erika's word against everything in the police computer systems. 'Can you remember when Jerome Goodman was arrested and what he was charged with?'

The fluorescent lights seemed to hum, and Erika's eyes hurt in the glare. It was a good question.

'He was arrested once on suspicion of being involved in the murder of local gang members in Rochdale. Drug gang members. He had to be released because there wasn't enough evidence to charge him, we had an eyewitness, but she was shot before we could get her in with an e-fit artist.' As Erika heard this, she realised something. 'Shit.'

'What?'

'He was arrested and charged but not ultimately convicted. The charges were dropped, which means . . .'

'Any DNA evidence taken at his arrest would have been deleted from the system after three years,' finished Moss.

'He was arrested in 2012, or maybe early 2013, when I was on the drug squad in Manchester. It was what triggered my – our – investigation and surveillance into him.'

Moss looked over at Waller. He was staring at them, talking in their low voices. She turned back to Erika.

'We arrested Kieron Bagshaw because you believe he is Jerome Goodman. But according to two of the police national databases, it's not him. We're going to have to release him,' said Moss. 'And we need to do it fast.'

'Kieron Bagshaw's brief is kicking up a stink already,' shouted Waller, putting the phone down. 'Do you have any other accusations you'd like to hold him in custody for? Shooting JFK?'

'Waller. I understand that you have to do your job. Just do it without the sarcasm,' said Moss, raising her voice. Erika felt grateful that Moss was still on her side, even after what had happened. 'Look. Erika. We release him without charge. No harm done. His brief might try to kick up a fuss and threaten to sue us, but you know how things roll. Tomorrow there'll be another scandal, another complaint. Yesterday's chip paper.'

'But it's him!'

'But we have no proof.'

The door opened behind them, and Tania burst into the custody suite with Paul Slater, a solicitor Erika had encountered before. Tania looked furious, her face pinched and eyes wide.

'Alright, Christian,' said Paul chirpily to PC Waller.

'Afternoon,' said Waller. He looked uncomfortable at being addressed on first-name terms. Erika and Moss got up and joined them all at the desk.

'You need to release Kieron,' said Tania, jabbing one of her long, manicured nails on the shiny surface of the desk.

'Alright, Tan. Let me do the talking,' said Paul. He reeked of cologne and money, and his thin black hair was scraped from his forehead. His suit was beautifully cut. Even Erika, who knew nothing about fashion, could see this, and he had on expensive, soft leather shoes. His hands were small, and he was carrying a giant smartphone.

'Which of you lovely ladies is, er, Erika Foster?' he said, emphasising each word and spitting them through his straight white teeth.

'That's me,' said Erika.

'And who's she?' he said, looking down at Moss.

'She is not the cat's mother,' said Moss, bristling. 'I'm Detective Inspector Moss.' She held up her warrant card.

Paul peered at it. 'Kate Moss,' he read. 'Ha ha. Bet that's fun for you.'

Moss ignored him and looked at Erika.

'There has . . . been an error,' said Erika. It was hard to get the words out, but she was smart enough to know to say this with the situation that was unfolding. 'And we're prepared to release Kieron Bagshaw.'

'Wow. "Prepared"? That's nice of you. But hold your horses. I'm not going to stand for that. We need to have a little chat about what's gone down here,' said Paul, fixing her with a nasty stare. He had to look up at her. He wasn't a tall man, but he had the confidence of a scrappy little dog. 'Trespassing on private property. Unlawful arrest with Kate Moss here, and deploying a Taser when there was no risk of violence. Assault.'

'We knocked on the door and were invited in. And assault?' repeated Erika.

'Yeah, assault. They was very rough when they handcuffed him,' said Tania, pursing her oversized lips. 'I want damages. Emotional distress.'

Waller was watching this with his eyes wide, and then his eyes flicked over to the doorway. Superintendent Melanie Hudson appeared from the stairs and approached the desk.

'Good afternoon, ma'am,' he said, his eyes growing wider with alarm.

Melanie looked at Paul standing with Tania and gave them a nod. 'Good afternoon, Mr Slater. Miss?'

'Hogarth,' said Tania.

'Erika. Could you come up to my office? Moss, if you could accompany her?'

Melanie's face was hard to read, and Erika wasn't sure how she knew about this and why she'd decided to come down to the custody suite.

'Are you aware of this situation?' said Erika. 'I just arrested a man who I believe to be Jerome Goodman. A man I had under surveillance for organised crime when I was with the Greater Manchester Police. I believe he's living under a different identity in the name of Kieron Bagshaw . . .' Erika's voice trailed off when she saw Paul smirking.

'Bloody hell. You just told me thirty seconds ago you'd made a mistake. You should get your head checked, love. My client, Kieron Bagshaw, doesn't have a criminal record. Did you run his prints through your computer, Christian?'

'It's PC Waller, and yes, I did.'

'And what did you find, PC Waller? Diddly-squat?'

'That's not the exact correct term,' Waller said, flustered. 'We found no criminal record.'

'Exactly. Now. Who's going to pull their finger out of their bum hole and get my client out?'

Melanie kept her face a professional mask of serenity. 'Erika, Kate, please. I need you to both go up to my office, now,' she repeated.

'Go on. Off you pop,' said Paul, waving with a small pudgy hand.

Erika opened her mouth to say something else.

'Go. Now. That's an order,' said Melanie.

11

'We never got the chance to ask them about the package locker on Amersham Road,' said Moss. For the first time, Erika could hear exasperation in her voice.

'I know. Sorry,' said Erika.

Moss hunched down in her chair and folded her arms. They were sitting on chairs outside Melanie's office like two naughty schoolgirls.

'That's Jerome Goodman. I know it.'

'What if you're wrong? I know that's hard to hear.'

She could see Moss was torn between wanting to be loyal and being a realist. Erika got up and started to pace the carpet. It had to be him, but why would he be living under a different name? In London? She stopped at the window, where she had a clear view of the station entrance and the car park below. A moment later, Melanie came out of the main doors, followed by Kieron Bagshaw, Tania Hogarth, and the solicitor, Paul Slater. Her heart sank. They were leaving, not only leaving but leaving through the main entrance.

Melanie was talking to them and smiling. That really got to Erika. How could she be bloody smiling, as if they were police donors who'd been to visit, and then she shook their hands one by one as they got into a large black 4x4, waiting to close the door.

'They're leaving . . .' said Erika, feeling panic. 'Jerome's leaving.'

'Which is what we expected,' said Moss.

'You're annoyed with me?'

'No. You just don't do yourself any favours.' She sounded disappointed.

Erika came and sat back down. A few minutes later, Melanie entered the waiting room.

'Right. Moss, can I speak to you first?' she said.

'Yes, ma'am,' said Moss, and without looking at Erika, she followed Melanie into her office.

Erika paced up and down outside for a very long ten minutes before Moss emerged from the office.

'What happened?' asked Erika.

Moss sighed. She looked sad. Or was it disappointed? Erika couldn't tell.

'I'll see you downstairs, Melanie said to go in,' she said, and to Erika's surprise, she left.

Melanie was sitting at her desk and looking at Erika with concern when she came into the office. No. *Studying* her with concern.

'Erika, please sit down.'

'That man is Jerome Goodman,' said Erika, remaining standing.

'He's not.'

'He is.'

'Please, take a seat.'

Erika perched on the chair opposite. 'It's not just about how he looks. I studied Jerome Goodman for months. The body language. The rhythm of how he speaks. And he recognised me.'

'Erika, in the course of doing our jobs as police officers,

mistakes are made. Applying the law isn't easy. It isn't always smooth sailing.'

Erika put up her hand. 'Please don't give me the corporate talk. Is he in the witness protection programme and living under a new identity? Is that what this is?'

'If Jerome Goodman was in the witness protection programme, his cover would now be blown, and I'd have to alert the team who deal with relocating witnesses, so no. There is nothing on file about Jerome Goodman being involved in a criminal case where he was required to give evidence as a police informant.'

'We need to do a deep dive into his background and find out what he's been doing for the past ten years. If I can put surveillance on him, I can . . .'

'Erika. Jerome Goodman is dead,' said Melanie.

'What? No.'

'Jerome Goodman is dead,' she repeated. She handed Erika a piece of paper. 'This is his death certificate.' Erika took it and scanned the details. His date of birth was correct. And the location where he was born in Wales. 'He was killed in an automobile accident in July 2016.'

'No.'

Melanie looked down at a folder open in front of her. 'It was in Wales. Just outside of Aberystwyth.'

'That's where he was living?'

'He was of no fixed abode at the time of his death.'

'Which would be consistent with him being on the run. That would have been two years after he vanished in Rochdale.'

'Yes, Jerome Goodman was still a suspect in the deaths of your husband and your colleagues. And yes, it's consistent with him going to ground. There's this small clipping from the newspaper.'

Melanie passed it across the desk. It was dated July 28, 2016, and Erika read:

A Machynlleth man is dead following a single-car accident on the A489. Ceredigion police responded to a phone call from an anonymous witness in the area near Clarach Bay Holiday Village. After a brief search, a damaged blue Mercedes-Benz was found buried in low undergrowth. They found the body of the driver, 38-year-old Jerome Goodman, of no fixed abode. He was pronounced dead at the scene. A crane was used to bring the car out of the woods and back onto the roadway. A post-mortem found Jerome Goodman was six times over the legal limit for alcohol and lost control of his vehicle. The coroner ruled death by misadventure.

'Where is this from?' she asked, looking up at Melanie in shock for the second time that morning.

'It's from the *Ceredigion News.*'

'No one told me,' she said, looking back at the news report. 'This was eight years ago.'

'I only found this after I'd searched for details of "Goodman" in our database.'

'No . . . No,' said Erika, reeling with confusion. 'I'm talking about the people I worked with in Manchester. My former colleagues who are still alive . . . One of the officers who died, his wife, she still works in the force. She's a civilian support officer. Or she was the last time I heard . . . Michelle is her name. She's the wife of Beamer. His name was Jim. He was one of our friends, me and Mark.' Erika's mind was racing. The past was flooding back to her. All the people she no longer spoke to. Not only had she lost the friends who died but their dependents had refused to talk to her after the raid.

'Maybe she doesn't know,' said Melanie after a long silence. 'This was a small byline in a local paper.' There was now a look of pity on her face that Erika didn't like. Melanie sighed and held up a thick folder. 'Erika, this brings me to your HR file. You'll note, ten times as thick as most officers' files.' She opened it and started to flick through. 'Five times in as many years, you have been flagged up for rude conduct, disobeying orders, insulting members of the public, going against police procedure. And every time I have had your back, and sometimes, as you probably know, Commander Marsh has stepped in.' Erika knew Commander Paul Marsh from her days as a rookie police officer in Manchester. They'd trained together and been beat officers. Their paths had diverged when Marsh had been promoted, and he was now one of the most senior police officers in the Met. 'Last week, I had another memo from HR asking if you had attended the counselling sessions recommended two years ago. Counselling sessions I have repeatedly asked you to attend for your post-traumatic stress disorder. I intended to write again and tell them it had been advised and was a private matter, but after this—'

'After what? Me arresting a wanted criminal? I was doing my job.'

'Erika. What happened today worries me. What if you start seeing Jerome Goodman in other people?'

'That's not fair. Are you questioning my sanity?'

'No. I just question why you thought it was wise to arrest someone who "looks like" a suspect from a previous case. One who has been dead for eight years.'

'I didn't know he was dead.' Erika stared at Melanie and knew then that her boss was no longer in her corner. 'I'd just like to remind you, ma'am, I have an active caseload of seventeen murder cases. I've successfully resolved another fourteen murder cases this year. I've made possibly, probably, thousands of arrests over the years, and very few have been in error.'

Melanie's eyes took on a steely glint.

'I'd like you to take some of your annual leave.'

'What?'

'You have a physical and psychological evaluation in two and a half weeks. You should have received a letter? I think you would benefit from taking some personal time in advance of this.'

'You're suspending me?'

'No. I'm not. If you voluntarily take leave, then we can keep this informal.'

'But I have to take a physical and psychological evaluation to return to work?'

'As would any other officer at your level of service.'

Erika almost laughed at Melanie's bullshit use of the word 'service'. There was silver service and service dogs; you could go to a funeral service and could have your car or yourself serviced. And then, of course, there was self-service for the shitty restaurants who don't want to pay waitstaff.

'Is this your decision?' Erika asked.

'Yes.' Melanie got up, went to the window, and looked out for a moment. 'There are people in the Met and higher up who have you on their radar. I'm sure you know this?'

'I've been fighting against it for years.'

Melanie turned back to her.

'You ruffle feathers. You can't be swayed from your course when a case gets sensitive. It makes you a bloody good police officer but also puts a target on your back. I'm saying this as a boss, and as a friend. Take the next couple of weeks as annual leave. You have plenty left. Do the tests. I know you'll pass. And then I can let you get on with doing your job without things potentially getting more difficult.'

'Difficult for who? You or me?'

'Remember. I'm one of the few friends you have left,' said Melanie, her voice now icy cold. There was a knock at the door. 'Come in.' PC Waller entered.

Erika looked between them. 'You're having me escorted from the premises?'

'I need your warrant card.'

'A police officer taking annual leave doesn't have to turn in their warrant card.'

'Erika. Don't embarrass yourself.'

Waller put out his arm to indicate the door. There was a nasty little look of triumph on his face.

Erika wished she had a witty or elegant comeback, but the only thing she could think of was 'go fuck yourself', which she refrained from saying out loud. She took out the leather wallet containing her warrant card, placed it on the desk, and looked Melanie in the eye.

'That man is Jerome Goodman. And I'm going to prove it.'

12

May 2004

Danielle Lang had been working at Secure Phone for six months and was thriving. Lonely but thriving. She worked overtime six days a week, billing way more than the other girls on the phones. She'd paid off her parents' debts and was up to date on the mortgage. It wasn't that the money made her lonely. It was her change in circumstances. She no longer saw the world like the wives of her husband's colleagues did. The world was a hard place. A rotten, mean place. And her only option now was to be hard and mean. She wanted to be hard and mean so that she would never feel loss again.

Danielle knew the police would find out about the fraud at Secure Phone, but she didn't expect it to happen so soon.

One Sunday in early May, on a rare day she wasn't working, Danielle finally got around to visiting the local rubbish tip after clearing a load of old stuff from her dad's shed. The tip was on the outskirts of town, and when she arrived, it was deserted. Just after dumping the last box in a vast container reached by a tall ladder, she noticed a car parked in the corner of the yard. Sitting inside was Hugh with a police officer she recognised as Detective Michael Saunders. They were deep in conversation; it looked heated, and Hugh seemed to be giving the policeman a piece of his mind.

Danielle knew Detective Michael Saunders. He had been the police officer who'd headed the investigation into her husband's death at the gasworks, and he'd made little effort to hide the fact the police came down on the company's side. She knew a bent copper when she saw one.

The next day, Danielle saw Jerome in the corridor on his way out to the yard, holding a pack of cigarettes.

'Can I join you for a smoke?' she asked.

'If you're not on the clock?'

'I'm on my break. I need to talk to you about something.'

He looked at her intensely. Then he took one of the cigarettes out of the packet and pushed it up his nose. He moved his hand to his ear and pulled it out. He was odd like this, coming across as menacing most of the time and then having these odd moments of bad comedy. He offered it to her.

'I'm not smoking that one. Who knows where you shoved it when I wasn't looking?'

His face broke into a grin. When he smiled, it was wide, alarmingly so, and he had straight white teeth.

'Come on,' he said. Danielle followed him out to the yard. It was empty, and his smart black BMW was parked by the gate. It was a sunny spring day, with a slight chill to add to the brightness. He lit two cigarettes and handed her one, inviting her to sit under an awning on one of the old office chairs with foam poking through the material.

'The job's still good?'

She'd decided long ago she'd feel no guilt. After all, it was only thirty quid each person was losing.

'Yeah. Still good.'

He nodded. 'You're my top earner.'

'I know.'

Her confidence always surprised him. This time, it seemed to irritate him.

'What do you want to tell me?' he asked.

Danielle looked around. The fire door was closed, and the yard wasn't overlooked by windows. 'It's Hugh.'

'What about him?'

'Do you trust him?' she asked, holding his stare.

'Yes.'

'I figured that if I talk to you, I'm not a grass. I'd only be a grass if I talked to someone else.'

Jerome's eyes were now wide. On alert.

'Okay. What about Hugh?' he said, his voice lower. Danielle could see he was very wary, but there was something there. Doubt. Fear. He didn't trust Hugh. She quickly told him that she'd seen him in what she assumed was a clandestine meeting with a police officer.

'Did Hugh see you?' asked Jerome.

'I don't think so. The yard at the rubbish tip is huge, and they were deep in conversation. This Detective Michael Saunders – he's a cunt,' she said. 'I know from experience. Now, if he's the type of cunt who's on your side, I won't say anything more, and we never spoke, but if he's the type of cunt Hugh is *squealing to*, I thought you'd want to know.'

'That's a lot of the C-word for a Monday afternoon.'

'Needs must.'

'And you're absolutely sure it was Hugh, and absolutely sure this was a police officer? We're not playing here.'

'Yes. I'm absolutely sure.'

Jerome stared at her long and hard, and for a moment, she thought he was about to flip out and fire her. But he stood up and stubbed out his cigarette.

'Thanks for letting me know. Your break's over. You should get back to work.'

13

Moss had returned to the incident room, waiting for Erika to come out of the meeting with Melanie. Ten minutes passed, then thirty, and then an hour. She called Melanie's office and was told Erika had already left the station and would be taking annual leave.

'I'd like you to take over running the murder investigation team in her absence,' Melanie said.

'How long will she be on leave?' asked Moss. She was itching to ask how readily Erika had agreed to this, if at all, but she now shared Erika's wariness of Superintendent Hudson.

'I'd schedule the work rota without Erika until the first week of January, to be sure.'

'What about Kieron Bagshaw? We have him as a person of interest in the Amersham Road case.'

'How?'

'What do you mean, how?'

'How is he a person of interest? I understand that you found half a kilo of cocaine in the parcel lockers adjacent to 14 Amersham Road, and those parcel lockers are owned by Tania Hogarth through her limited company. She's the sole controlling party in the company.'

'Yes. But when we spoke to Tania this morning, she indicated that Kieron was in charge of those parcel lockers.'

Melanie gave a sigh of impatience. 'First of all, I don't see how your investigation into a potentially suspicious death at 14B Amersham Road is linked to the parcel locker?'

'It's linked by cocaine,' said Moss. 'Cocaine found all over the ceiling of number 14B. The rest of the flat had been scrubbed down. And this kilo of cocaine was sitting in a plain box in the parcel locker on the side of the building.'

'I know the details. But the owner of a parcel locker doesn't have liability when it comes to the items delivered to that parcel locker.' Moss could hear the annoyance in Melanie's voice. 'I'll say it again. Tania Hogarth is the sole controlling interest in the company that owns the lockers. Not Kieron Bagshaw. So he shouldn't be any part of your investigation. Do you hear?'

'Do I hear? Yes, ma'am. You've put me in charge of the murder investigation team, and whilst you can give me guidance and feedback, I don't have to take it. I need to explore every avenue within the law.'

'Don't be stupid, Moss. Is that clear?'

'Crystal,' said Moss, and she put down the phone.

The morgue at Lewisham Hospital was cold. Erika had been buzzed in at the main entrance and the long corridor leading down to Isaac Strong's office.

The door was open, and Isaac was working on his laptop at his desk. He wore a thick pullover, jeans, and furry Ugg boots.

His dark hair was dramatically swept away from his high forehead, and even in casual clothes, he looked like a handsome orchestra conductor. As usual, he projected an aura of calm and order compared to how frazzled Erika felt. The grey December light poured in through a window high on the wall. The room was lined with bookshelves, which were crammed with medical textbooks.

'Knock knock,' said Erika, leaning on the doorframe.

Isaac looked up and smiled. 'Hi. Did we have a meeting scheduled?'

'No. I bumped into Jerome Goodman this morning. I arrested him, but it turns out he's not Jerome Goodman anymore. He's been released, and I've been put on gardening leave.'

Erika wiped her tears away with the back of her hand. There was a long pause while Isaac took this in.

'Bloody hell, sounds like a horribly busy morning,' he said. He got up, put his arm around her, and led her to the sofa. He cleared off a pile of textbooks and a gym bag so she could sit. He closed the door, and she told him in more detail what had happened.

'Do you want a drink?' he asked. Erika was now shivering, and she nodded. Isaac got up and went to the bookshelves, picking up a bottle of Chivas whisky and two glasses.

'I was thinking a drink of water,' she said. Isaac went to the water cooler beside the sofa and poured her a glass.

'Here. Have it as a mixer,' he said, placing the whisky and water on the table beside her. Erika picked up the glass and swirled the whisky. The warm alcohol fumes hit her nostrils, and she took a sip.

'How sure are you he was Jerome Goodman?' he asked.

Erika looked up at him and had to stop herself from breaking down completely.

'It's him. "Officially" Jerome Goodman died in a car accident eight years ago.' She pulled out her phone, found the article from the *Ceredigion News*, and handed it to him.

'Did you know he was in Wales?' asked Isaac, scrolling through the article.

'No. And no one told me he'd been dead for eight years. Nothing has been updated in the case files. As far as I know, knew, Goodman vanished after the raid in July 2014.'

'Was the case, the murder of Mark and your colleagues, kept open?'

'Yeah. That's the case I'm talking about. I've checked it regularly over the years.'

'Do you know the officer it's assigned to?'

'No. It's been passed around a lot.'

Isaac turned to his computer and started to search. Erika took another sip, enjoying how the alcohol on her empty stomach helped her feel a little removed from the situation. It took Isaac a few minutes to find what he was looking for.

'Okay. I have a copy of the post-mortem report,' he said.

Erika got up and perched on the desk beside him. 'And he's dead?'

'As a doornail. Eight years ago.'

'Do you know who did the post-mortem?'

'I don't recognise the name, but I can find out.' He looked back at the screen. 'If Jerome Goodman wanted to hide out somewhere, I suppose the Welsh mountains would have been a good place?'

'Yeah. You can get lost in the country out there. I thought he had gone into hiding abroad, and remained in control of his empire. I don't know.'

'What about his associates?'

'He only trusted a couple of people, or so we knew from our intel. Frank Hobbs was the finance man of the operation, and Jerome's right hand was a woman, Danielle Lang.'

'What happened to them?'

'They vanished in a puff of smoke, just like he did. And neither of them were ever charged with anything.'

Isaac scrolled down, reading the screen.

'The post-mortem report says that Jerome Goodman was over six times the legal limit of alcohol. His car left the road at speed and went down an embankment fifty metres before colliding with a tree. He died instantly from a front collision. Fatal injuries to the head, neck, thorax, and abdomen . . . Fracture to the skull, and there were glass fragments present, which figures . . .'

'He went through the windscreen?'

'Yes. The post-mortem examination revealed no clear oblique bruising of the chest or horizontal bruising across the abdomen, which means he wasn't wearing a seat belt. There were no bruising or lacerations to the face, indicating that the airbags didn't deploy.'

'Does it say who ID'd the body?'

Isaac scrolled down the page a little.

'No. But it's not up to a forensic pathologist to ID a body if the police have already done so. Unless identification isn't forthcoming or disputed and we're asked to compare, dental records, for example. In this case it doesn't look like it was disputed.'

'Does anything about this post-mortem report seem odd?'

Isaac sighed. He looked back at the screen. 'No . . . Sorry.'

Erika nodded and wiped her eyes. She got up and put her hand on his shoulder. 'Have you done the post-mortem on Marie Collins?'

'I'm due to do it in the next couple of days.'

'Any idea of time of death?'

'No, not until I've investigated further.'

'I presume Moss or Peterson will be taking over the case, if there is a case, so you'll hear from them.'

Isaac nodded. 'What are you going to do?'

'I don't know. Go home. I have a lot to tell Igor.' She closed her eyes at the thought.

'Call me if you need anything.'

Erika left the morgue, doubting herself. Doubting her future. Doubting that Kieron Bagshaw was Jerome Goodman.

14

June 2004

For a couple of weeks, Jerome said nothing more to Danielle about Hugh being seen with a police officer. Then, one Monday evening, Jerome stopped her on her way out of the office building.

'Busy tonight?' he asked.

'It's a Monday. It's a school night.'

'You want to get a drink?' He tucked a long strand of his shiny black hair behind his ear. 'Or are you washing your hair?'

'No. My hair is squeaky clean. Like yours.'

'Perhaps we use the same shampoo,' he said.

'Perhaps. Is it just a drink?'

'We can get pork scratchings too.'

'I told you before, I'm not sleeping with you.'

'How did we get from pork scratchings to you sleeping with me?'

'You'd be sleeping with me, I think. Not the other way around.'

'Is that how it would be?'

'Yeah. It would. I'm out of your league.'

Jerome smiled. 'Listen. This is, sort of, work related.'

'You offering me a promotion?' He hesitated. He now looked serious.

'I can pick you up at eight?'

'See you then,' she said.

When Jerome knocked on the door, Danielle was ready. She'd tried on ten outfits, eventually settling on a summer dress and heels with her hair down. Something about Jerome made her feel brave and confident. Whenever she was around him, he seemed to challenge her, and the only option was to rise to that challenge; otherwise, he'd lose respect. She looked at her reflection – was the dress and heels too tarty? He'd want to do more than just respect her. Fuck it. She wasn't going to dress down for anyone.

'Alright?' he said when she opened the front door. He was wearing black: black jeans, a hoodie, a long black coat, and heavy boots.

'Why are you dressed for winter?' she asked.

'I feel the cold.'

They drove in silence without any music playing, towards the outskirts of town. After ten minutes, Danielle asked where they were going.

'Our meeting is a little bit out of the way,' he said. They were now on a long stretch of empty road running alongside fields. The sun was setting in a blaze of melancholy gold.

'Who are we meeting?'

'Frank.'

There was a thump from the back of the car. Danielle looked across at Jerome. He didn't react.

'What was that?'

'Shit. Did I run over a rabbit?' he asked, checking his rearview mirror but unconcerned.

'I didn't see a rabbit,' she said as the road seemed to spool out in front of them.

'You ever eaten rabbit?'

'No. I think the Easter Bunny should deliver the chocolate, and not be on the menu.'

Jerome smiled. The last tip of the blazing red sun dipped below the horizon, and he flicked on the headlights. The thump came again, but he kept his eyes on the road. Danielle worked hard to keep the unease she was feeling away from her face. They drove for another half an hour as twilight faded to pitch black.

'We're just . . . here,' said Jerome. A security light flicked on from under the eaves of a bungalow which sat alone on the road. He indicated and turned into the driveway. The lights were out in the windows, and the whole front garden was paved in red brick. Jerome did a big U-turn, backing his car up to a white garage door. He switched off the engine, and Danielle jumped as he put his hand on hers.

'Jeez. It's okay. Seriously.'

'I'm fine,' she replied. Hating to lose her cool.

'I won't be a sec. Stay in the car, and all will be revealed.' When he closed the door, the car's interior light stayed on for a moment, and Danielle saw her pale, scared face staring back in the window's reflection. The light went out, and she was plunged into darkness.

Only one small security light was fixed to the front of the house, so just a tiny amount of light spilt into the driveway.

Danielle watched as Jerome knocked on the front door, and Frank answered. What was this place? As far as she knew, Frank lived in the city.

He was wearing what looked like painter's overalls, and his long, pale-blond hair flowed out from under a beanie hat.

Jerome leaned in and seemed to be summarising some kind of info. Frank looked over at the car and waved. Danielle waved back.

If they were going to end her, would he be waving?

'Don't be fucking stupid,' Danielle said to her gloomy silhouette in the mirror. 'They're not going to end you. You make them so much money. You've proved your loyalty.'

But was it a lot of money? They had another fifteen girls in the office. In the grand scheme of things, it wasn't going to break the bank if she stopped working for them.

She thought back to Hugh. He hadn't been in the office much since she grassed. However she looked at it, that was what she'd done. Grassed on him. Fuck.

Danielle swallowed. Her mouth was dry. There was another thump. She turned to look through the back window and saw the car rock.

She jumped as Jerome and Frank appeared at the rear window and opened the boot, obscuring her view, and the car bounced and lurched. Danielle was pleased to be in the shadows. She switched her attention to the passenger mirror and saw the white garage door rolling up, and a bright white light flooded out. It was empty inside, with a bare concrete floor. A metal chair sat on a square of tarpaulin. Jerome and Frank appeared in view, carrying a long shape rolled up in something black. It took a moment for her to realise that it was a body bag. But the body inside was thrashing around. They were having trouble keeping hold of each end.

When the two men were inside the garage, they swung the body bag and then let go. It landed on the hard concrete, and she heard a cry of pain. The bag was still moving, writhing and curling, across the floor like it, or whoever was inside, was trying to escape.

Her door opened, and Jerome peered down at her. 'You ready?'

'For what?' she asked. She felt really scared now.

'Our business meeting.'

Danielle got out of the car and came around to the garage. Jerome and Frank unzipped the body bag. Hugh's face appeared. Masking tape was wound tightly around his mouth, compressing his plump face. His hair was dishevelled and he had a bloody gash above his left eye. He writhed and moaned, and his eyes registered surprise to see her. Frank and Jerome pulled him out of the bag. His arms and legs were bound, and they tied him to the chair with blue bungee cords with hooks on each end.

Danielle had grown up in a rough area of Cardiff, where she'd heard about retribution. Her late husband had some mates who were dodgy, and there had been stories about sorting stuff out without involving the police. But this . . . She was in this now. Part of it. Just being here meant she had crossed a line. There was a flash of a silver blade as Jerome slid the tip of a bowie knife under the tape around Hugh's mouth and sliced it off.

'Oh God, Danielle, help me!' Hugh cried. He looked terrified, his waxy face pale.

'You were right,' said Jerome, mildly, looking over at Danielle, holding the knife. 'He was about to cut a deal with the police.'

'All of us in exchange for his immunity in prosecution,' added Frank. He had his arms folded.

Danielle stared at Hugh.

'Please! You don't understand. I had no choice but to talk to the police. You saw me?'

'How did you confirm it? Or is it just based on my word?' Danielle said to Jerome and Frank.

'No. We paid Detective Michael Saunders a visit,' said Frank. 'You were right. He is a cunt. But cunts like him can be bought.'

'Bought?' repeated Danielle. She was looking around the

garage. She saw another knife, a hacksaw, and some plastic bags lined up on the tarpaulin.

'Yeah. We figured we could turn a bad situation into a good investment,' said Jerome. 'We got him on record, accepting our offer, and taking our money. And no copper wants to go down. You know what they do to bent coppers inside?'

'I've heard,' said Danielle.

'Hey . . . Hey! We are partners. Why are you talking to this bitch?' Hugh cried, his face now twisted in a clammy mask of hate. Frank took a run-up and punched Hugh in the face. His head snapped back, and the chair rocked back onto two legs, almost toppling over. When it rocked forward, Hugh spat out blood and a tooth, and it skittered along the tarpaulin.

'Everything is in my name,' Hugh raged. 'You are both fucked. Fucked!' He twisted against his bonds.

Jerome took a handgun from inside his coat, and the temperature in the garage seemed to drop. He slowly turned it to face Hugh.

'No. Oh, God, no!' cried Hugh. 'Please. This has gone too far. This doesn't have to happen.'

'Wait,' said Danielle.

'Wait?' repeated Jerome, turning to her, along with Frank.

'Yes. Wait. Does this house belong to you?'

'What's that got to do with anything?' asked Frank. Jerome ignored him and eyed Danielle.

'It's rented, belongs to a friend.'

'What does your friend use it for?' A look passed between Jerome and Frank. 'You can be vague.'

'Porn,' said Jerome quietly.

Danielle did some quick thinking. The line had been crossed. Jerome and Frank had brought her into this. She could be scared later. She needed to be smart. *They* needed to be smart.

'Don't shoot him.'

'Yes! Listen to her,' said Hugh. 'Thank you, Danielle. I'm sorry. I'm sorry. I didn't mean it.'

'Did you take him from his house?' Danielle asked, ignoring Hugh. Frank nodded. 'Did anyone see you?'

'I parked in his garage. Took him through the house.'

'Did you make a mess inside?'

Jerome looked over at Frank, who shook his head.

'Put one of those plastic bags over his head,' said Danielle.

'I've got a gun!' said Jerome, with a flash of anger.

'Do you watch cop shows?'

'No.'

'If you did, you'd know all about DNA. If you use that . . . What is that gun?'

'It's Jerome's baby. A Stoeger semi-automatic pistol,' said Frank.

'Please don't kill me,' said Hugh, his voice now thick from his swollen lip. 'I can make it up to you.'

'If you shoot him, there will be blood and God knows what all over the walls,' said Danielle.

'But I really want to fucking shoot him!' cried Jerome with a sudden flash of rage. 'He was going to fuck us all!'

'I know. But be smart. Put one of those plastic bags over his head, it'll be much cleaner and leave no trace,' repeated Danielle. She looked down at her dress and heels. An hour ago, she was expecting to go for a pint of cheap wine, and now . . . It disturbed her how much she got a kick out of this. Being in control gave her a high.

Danielle and Jerome watched as Frank opened out one of the thick, clear plastic bags, and stood behind Hugh.

'No, no, no, please!' Hugh screamed, but his voice was muffled as Frank hooked it over his head.

Hugh fought hard, but as Frank tightened the plastic, it moulded to his head, and his mouth sucked uselessly at the plastic, his eyes bulging. Hugh watched them as he died.

Fighting. Writhing. And Jerome and Danielle kept their eyes on his face until he stopped moving and went limp.

There was a terrible silence when the life left Hugh's body, and Danielle moved closer and studied his face through the tight plastic. It happened so fast – Hugh went from being a person to a waxwork.

It helped her to process what had happened and not see him as a person. He was a waxwork dummy.

'Okay, genius girl, what do we do now?' asked Jerome. He still seemed annoyed that he didn't get to fire his gun.

'We passed Mortha Quarry on the way here. All kinds of rubbish gets chucked in there. Let's wrap him up, weigh him down, and dump his body.'

15

Tuesday, December 3, 2024

It felt strange for Erika to be home at 4pm. When she opened the front door, it was still light. She found George snoozing on the sofa in the weak afternoon sunlight, and he looked up at her as if to say, *"Why are you here?"*

Erika made herself a cup of tea and returned to the living room. The sun was just sinking down over the heath, casting the still-frosty grass in a burnt-orange glow. She felt sick and a stab of fear when she heard the key in the lock, and Igor was home.

'Hey. What are you doing here?' Igor asked when he entered the living room. George jumped down and went to him. Igor was wearing his work uniform, and with his greying hair glinting in the last of the setting sun, he looked old and tired.

'I need to talk to you.'

He put his bag down. 'Are you sick?'

Erika hadn't expected this. 'No. What made you think that?'

'You look terrible.' Without warning, Erika suddenly felt a sob emerge from her chest, and she broke down in tears. The kind of crying where you can't catch your breath and your chest heaves. Igor came over to the sofa and sat down, scooping her into his arms. 'Sorry. I didn't mean it like that.' She leaned her head against the scratchy material of his blue Transport for London sweater, smelling his sweat and the faint smell of the tube: damp, newsprint, and smog.

It took a few minutes before she could compose herself and talk. She told him everything. About the letter. Having to cancel their trip. And then the call-out to 14 Amersham Road which led to her coming face-to-face with Jerome Goodman.

'And you've been suspended? For arresting a drug dealer and murderer?' said Igor when she was finished. He grabbed a tissue from the box on the table and handed her one.

Erika smiled, his reaction boosting her fragile emotions. 'According to official records, he's not Jerome Goodman. And officially I'm not suspended. I'm on enforced leave.'

'It must have been a horrible shock to see him. And he's living in bloody London? That's ballsy.'

Erika looked up at Igor, grateful that he was taking her seriously. 'Yeah. But I suppose you get confident if you've been dead for eight years.'

'And you're really sure it's him?'

'Really sure. His looks. His body language. The way he looked at me. He knew I recognised him, and he knew there was nothing I could do about it.'

Erika rubbed her hands together. Her hands looked bloodless, and her fingernails had a blue tinge.

'Are you cold?'

'Yeah.'

'I'll make a fire, get us some drinks.'

Igor came back with two big glasses of red wine. He handed her one and she took a sip, savouring the taste. It was a huge comfort, as he drew the curtains on the darkening sky. She switched off her phone and breathed for the first time in what felt like hours.

Igor cleared the previous day's ash from the wood-burning stove, and Erika grabbed some kindling and old newspaper from the box by the hearth. They built a new fire together, with George purring and criss-crossing through their legs. When it was ready Igor touched a match to the pile, which quickly caught light, filling the living room with a warming glow. Erika sat back and sipped at her drink, and it calmed her. The fire quickly grew from a small licking petal to a blaze, and she felt it hot against her face and legs. Igor threw on two larger logs and closed the stove door.

'Right,' he said, sitting back on his heels and gripping his glass. 'First. Don't worry about us going to Slovakia for Christmas. We'll cross that bridge when we get there. We'll cancel, or go by road?'

'By road?'

'Yeah. Drive, or go by a coach . . .' He saw Erika's face at the mention of a coach journey. 'Maybe not a coach. I did that journey years ago from Bratislava to London. Before you could fly to London.'

'When I first came to England to work as an au pair in Manchester, I came by coach. Thirty-five hours. And the toilet was broken.'

'I wonder how much an Uber would be?' he said with a smile.

'Igor. I don't know if I can cope for two weeks with my sister and her family at Christmas. You go if you want – you and Tom were going to stay with your parents anyway.'

Igor drained his wine. He reached up to get the bottle and topped up their glasses. 'Let's put that to one side for now. What do you want to do? About Jerome Goodman.'

'I want to find out everything I can. Whose body was in the car crash? It wasn't his. And where are his associates? They vanished along with him. And I don't know . . . Can I persuade my team to keep investigating in my absence? And put surveillance on Jerome – or Kieron Bagshaw, as he's calling himself.'

Igor nodded. 'Do you think they would?'

Erika shook her head. 'It would be a risk. Melanie told me point-blank to my face that Kieron Bagshaw isn't Jerome Goodman.'

Igor looked thoughtful for a moment. 'What do you think is happening?'

'What do you mean?'

'How has he ended up changing his identity?'

Erika took a deep breath. This was what she loved about Igor. He always asked direct questions. He had the talent of taking a problem that seemed overwhelming and breaking it down, working things out piece by piece.

'Well. It's actually not that hard in the UK to change your identity. Most simply, you can change it by deed poll.'

'That sounds an easier way than dying in a car crash?'

Erika nodded. 'A lot of people don't know that you can change your identity just by writing out a specific text, which you can find online, stating that you want to change your name, and have it signed by two witnesses. Or you can go the more official route through court. Where it gets tricky is if you have a criminal record. You have to inform the police.'

'What if you don't have a criminal record?'

'Then it's much easier, and it's harder for the authorities to find out your previous name.'

'Does Jerome Goodman have a criminal record?'

'No. He's never been charged with anything, but I was under the impression that there was a warrant out on him, and has been for the past ten years, but now I hear he's been dead eight of those years. Jesus, he died when I first came to London. Fucking hell.'

'I read that you can buy a new passport on the dark web. What if he's done that?' asked Igor.

'Yeah. You can buy fake digital documents, or a new original UK passport, which costs thousands. It doesn't explain his death. There was an official post-mortem.'

'How do people make such good fake passports these days?' asked Igor, taking another slug of his wine.

'Good fakes are rare. Very hard to reproduce with the holograms in the document, the watermarking, and the biometric data. The problem we often have in law enforcement is that there are corrupt people working at the passport office – very few corrupt people, but they are the ones who are taking bribes to print real passports in fake names. So they're hard to trace once they're out in the world.'

'So Jerome Goodman could have done that? Faked his death and bought a new identity?'

Erika nodded.

'So why is no one at the police, your bosses, taking this seriously?'

Erika took a long drink of her wine. It tasted very good and she was now toasty warm. 'I don't know. It worries me. It's as if my boss, Melanie, has been compromised.'

'How much does it cost to bribe a police superintendent?'

Erika looked at him. 'I don't want to think about that. And Melanie hasn't been bribed directly. She was always straight down the line . . . but lately, I don't know. I'd like to think that it's something beyond her, more murky.'

'Someone higher up?'

'Or someone on the outside? The illegal drug trade is worth billions. There are some terrifying people with friends in high places. One of my last murder suspects was a young woman who was a sex worker who had killed some of her clients. We knew she did it, but she had a dossier of photos with rich and famous men in, er, compromising situations.'

'She's the one whose murder trial collapsed?'

Erika nodded. 'And that was, again, powerful people of

influence pulling the strings. I told you about the guy who showed up at the back gate when I was getting wood from the shed. I don't know if he worked for the government. I don't know who he was, but he warned me off. I ignored him, but . . .'

Igor looked down at his drink. 'Are you scared?'

Erika shrugged. 'I'd be scared to walk away from it. And I'd be scared to think I could have done something, but I didn't. It's very hard to go against the grain. Defy people in charge of you. Would you be scared if I pursued this?'

Igor looked up at her and thought for a moment.

'I'd be scared if you didn't. If this Jerome is alive and wanted for the murder of Mark and your colleagues, and he's still trafficking drugs, then you have to try and stop him.' Erika smiled and put her hand over his. Igor noticed the fire was dying down, so he opened the door and threw on another piece of wood. 'Listen.'

'I'm listening.'

'I've got holiday I can take, extra holiday. If you want me to come with you?'

'Where? Slovakia?' she asked.

'No. You said you wanted to find out about Jerome Goodman faking his death. If you've no warrant card, we could travel to Wales together – you won't stand out as much. We could be two Slovaks on holiday.'

Erika was about to laugh but stopped. 'That's not a bad idea. A woman travelling alone always stands out like a sore thumb. If we went as a couple, then we might be able to find out more. Maybe Moss and the team could help with database stuff on the sly.'

'Wouldn't you be putting them in a difficult position?' asked Igor.

'I'd do the same for them,' said Erika after a pause.

'It could be interesting to go undercover with you.'

Erika put up her hands.

'We wouldn't be going undercover. I have details of how he died, where it happened. People live in closer-knit communities in small towns. We need to find a way to ask questions without alerting too much suspicion.'

'What if we're looking for a holiday home, or an investment property to rent out. We could ask around about the area without it being too weird?'

Erika considered this for a moment. 'That's not a bad idea . . .'

'So we're really doing this?' asked Igor, topping up his glass and pouring a generous measure into Erika's. He clinked his glass against hers, and she felt a stab of fear. What if this was a good idea now but would seem silly in the morning? No. She wasn't drunk.

'Let's have a think,' said Erika, clinking her glass against his. They both drank. Sometimes, the craziest plans lead to a breakthrough.

16

June 2004

The day after they disposed of Hugh's body, Jerome, Danielle, and Frank went into an empty office in a high-rise building with a view of Cardiff High Street, and they watched the police raid Secure Phone.

Danielle moved to the window. The Secure Phone office was set back from Cardiff High Street. There was a large white van outside and two police cars, and as she moved the binoculars back up to look at the yard, she saw two police officers wearing latex gloves carrying piles of paperwork. Another had the wireless payment terminals packet in a clear plastic bag.

Danielle closed her eyes for a moment. A clear plastic bag. She thought of Hugh, and how they dumped his body in a quarry a few miles outside Cardiff. It had been very dark and cold. They'd tied a concrete block to his ankles with a long rope and dropped him into the freezing water. There was no way back from this now. She had been instrumental in Hugh's death and the disposal of his body. It had made her feel powerful. Deciding his fate. It frightened her, but she could see it all so clearly now.

It was so simple. Like it or not, this was how the world worked; you either seized power or you were powerless. Did she want to be a victim or the aggressor? She knew the answer.

Danielle opened her eyes again and looked over at Jerome and Frank, watching through their binoculars.

'Those idiot police officers,' said Jerome, laughing. Danielle saw an officer in uniform carrying a computer hard drive, again wrapped in plastic.

'They think they're the ones in control,' said Frank.

Danielle watched for a few more minutes with them in silence. She had insisted that all the other girls were told not to show up to work, and not to say anything. There was very little about the business that existed on paper. No employment contracts, no payroll. The only person connected to anything official was Hugh.

The police had been tipped off when to arrive, and that the doors and the safe would be open. They were also given the passcodes to access the computers.

'We brought you here to make you an offer,' said Jerome as they watched the officers' progress.

'What kind of offer?' asked Danielle.

'Secure Phone is now burned to the ground. The police think Hugh has vanished because of the raid.'

'It's genius,' said Frank. 'The police think he's done a runner. They'll be looking for him in all the wrong places, and by the time they do find him . . .'

'The fish will have eaten him to the bones,' finished Jerome.

Danielle saw another police van was arriving with 'DOG UNIT' written on the side. She put her binoculars down on the table. She'd seen enough.

'What's the offer?' she asked.

'People trust women, but for some men, it's hard to find a woman you can trust,' said Jerome.

'And you are that rare animal that ticks both boxes,' added Frank.

'What are you two, a double act? Cut to the chase.'

'How would you like to get out of Cardiff and earn a hundred times more than you're earning right now?' asked Jerome.

Danielle looked at them both. They were serious.

'And how would I earn so much? Hike up the prices for fake insurance policies?'

'No. We make it snow all year round,' said Frank. Danielle stared at him for a moment.

'Drugs?'

'Yeah. Cocaine. Heroin. Crack cocaine. Pills.'

'And then we all go down for the rest of our lives?'

Jerome and Frank both shook their heads.

'No. We have a plan,' said Jerome. 'We get in. We get rich. And we get out.'

Danielle laughed. 'You guys have balls, I'll give you that. It's one thing to scam some old dear for thirty quid a pop . . .'

'You've done a lot more than scam a few old ladies, Danielle,' said Jerome, moving closer to her. 'You're a murderer, now. We all are.'

Danielle stared back at Frank and Jerome. She balled her fists to keep her hands from shaking.

'I don't want to deal drugs. That's a whole other level of risky shit.'

'Riskier than murder?'

'You know what I mean.'

'Listen. We don't want to *deal*,' said Jerome. 'You're right. That's risky, low-level shit. We want to be suppliers – bring the stuff into the country in bulk. Take over big supply chains and stay far away from the skag dealers on the street.'

'And who do you know that's going to take you to that level?' asked Danielle.

Jerome came over to her and placed his binoculars over her eyes, then gently tilted her head so she could see the office where the raid was taking place.

'The police,' he said. 'That's who we know.'

17

Tuesday, December 3, 2024

Moss never took work home with her. It was a deal she had with her wife, Celia. Work was work. Home was family time. However, the day's events had shaken Moss. She knew Erika to be compulsive and stubborn, but Erika always worked with possession of the full facts. If Erika thought that Kieron Bagshaw was Jerome Goodman, then, well, he must be Jerome Goodman. But according to every police database, his name was Kieron Bagshaw.

Moss needed to try and make sense of things, so she'd requested the Jerome Goodman case file, and a copy had been handed to her at the end of the day.

'What are you reading?' asked Celia, laying out plates and bowls of grated cheese and salsa on the kitchen table. It was taco night in the Moss-Grainger household. Moss turned the page and looked up.

'Kate, you can't be serious. At the dinner table?'

Moss followed Celia's horrified face and looked down at the page at a black-and-white, and quite grainy, photograph showing two dead men who'd been shot in the head, lying in pools of blood.

'Sorry, I didn't know that was there,' said Moss, snapping shut the case file just as their twelve-year-old son, Jacob, came into the kitchen.

'Didn't know what was where?' asked Jacob, going to the fridge and opening the door.

'Dinner will be in ten minutes,' said Celia.

He sighed and shut the door. 'What's that?' he repeated. He eyed the folder. 'Is that a police case file?'

Moss sighed. 'Yes.'

'A *murder* case file?'

Moss looked at Celia, spooning steaming chilli from a pan into a bowl.

'Yes.'

'Kate!' cried Celia.

'He'll be thirteen in a few months. I don't want to lie.'

'What kind of murder?' asked Jacob, opening the fridge again.

'What did I say about dinner?' said Celia.

'I'm getting a can of Coke. Which I'm actually allowed to have, with tacos, if you remember our agreement?' Moss thought about how he sounded like a little lawyer and suppressed a smile.

'Use a glass. No drinking it out of the can,' said Celia. 'Why are you bringing case files home? And reading one here in our kitchen?'

'It's the case file about Erika, when her husband . . . you know.'

Celia put the bowl on the table.

'When her husband and all her colleagues were blown away by that drug dealer?' asked Jacob.

'How do you know about that?' asked Moss.

'One of the guys at school asked me about it.'

'Asked you what?'

'Asked if I knew anything. I said no. He then said that Erika tracked down this drug dealer to a crack house, and they went to arrest him, but it all went wrong and the drug dealers opened fire on Erika and her colleagues, and then he got away. Her colleagues died, including her husband. Is that true?'

Moss nodded her head.

Celia shook hers in disapproval. 'Did he make you look at any photos?' she asked.

'He had them on his phone, but I didn't want to look,' said Jacob. 'I like Erika, and it would feel weird.'

'He's twelve,' said Celia.

'I'm almost thirteen!'

'You shouldn't be bringing this into the house.' Celia reached out and grabbed the file. 'I'm putting this in the safe.'

She left the kitchen, and Jacob came to sit at the table.

'She's a bit emotional,' he said.

'Hey. *She* is the cat's mother.'

'She's my mother, not that cat's,' said Jacob.

Moss had to suppress a smile. 'It's only 'cos she cares.'

'I know.' They heard the floorboards creaking above. 'I also know the combination for the safe,' he said, carefully pouring his Coke into a highball glass.

'What is it? I've forgotten.'

'4291,' said Jacob. Moss had to think about this for a moment.

'Oh, yes. That's Victor Meldrew's phone number in *One Foot in the Grave*,' she said. Jacob nodded. Moss listened for Celia's footsteps on the stairs. 'Tell me the truth. Did you see any of the photos?'

Jacob shook his head. 'I hate blood and guts.'

'Me too. Promise me something?'

'What?'

'Stop growing up so quickly.'

'Yeah, like I can do that.'

Celia came back into the kitchen. 'Who's hungry?'

'We are. *Always*,' said Jacob, smiling at Moss.

After dinner, Moss retrieved the case file from the safe and took it to the tiny spare room they used as an office. They lived in an old terraced house which had a fireplace in every room. Moss lit a fire in the tiny grate and settled in her favourite armchair with a glass of wine. As she read, Moss was ashamed that this was the first time she was reading the complete case files on the Jerome Goodman investigation. In the years since Erika had transferred to the Met Police back in the winter of 2015, Moss had been a loyal colleague who had always had her boss's back, tuning out all the gossip about Erika being responsible for the deaths of her husband and colleagues. But she wished she'd read the facts.

The Jerome Goodman case file started with a multiple murder at the Swann Pub in Rochdale in August 2012. This was two years before Erika's raid on Jerome Goodman's property at 17 Chapel Street.

Wayne "Bimbo" Chance had been a high-profile drug dealer and distributor running operations in the north of England, and he'd used the basement of the Swann Pub to store and distribute large amounts of cocaine. Bimbo and two of his associates were shot dead at the Swann by masked intruders in broad daylight. The landlord of the pub and a barmaid working that day had been gunned down as well. Another member of the bar staff, Bella Mackinson, had witnessed the massacre and identified two men and a woman as the attackers. Erika's team had gone to lengths to try and keep Bella safe, going as far as drawing up plans to put her into the witness protection scheme. But before they could get Bella to go on record, a sniper shot her in the head in her back garden. Police were unable to find out who or where the gunman was.

After the shoot-out, Jerome Goodman and his associates took over the drug distribution previously managed by Wayne "Bimbo" Chance. As Moss read on, she saw that Erika and her team had managed to pinpoint a great deal of the drug activity as centred around a terraced house on 17 Chapel Street in Rochdale. Rooms in the house were being let out to a group of Chinese women who worked at several local launderettes. As Erika built her surveillance case, her team worked out that this hub of local launderettes was being used to deliver and distribute crack cocaine to a broader network of dealers around Manchester, Liverpool, and the surrounding areas.

Moss had forgotten about her glass of wine, and the tiny fire in the grate had burned down, but she carried on reading.

Born in Manchester, Jerome Goodman had been an only child. His mother worked in a bakery, and his father worked as a car mechanic. Jerome left school in 1996, when he was eighteen. He moved to London later that year, and there was a photo of him in the case file from when he worked at a pub in Covent Garden in London. It looked like it was from one of those 'cool' pubs which cropped up in the late nineties, when Britpop was huge and pubs would take Polaroid photos of parties and events and make a collage of them on the wall. In this photo, Jerome had short hair and was posing with a pretty young girl, resting her head on his shoulder.

Jerome Goodman had next popped up back in Cardiff when he claimed unemployment benefits for six months in 1998. There was a passport application in 2000, when he was aged twenty-two, and it had been renewed once, ten years later in 2010, when he was thirty-two. Erika's team had raided 17 Chapel Street in 2014, and Jerome Goodman had disappeared, along with Frank Hobbs and Danielle Lang. There had been an addition to the file, added earlier that day. A newspaper clipping from the *Ceredigion News*, with the details of Jerome Goodman's death. Moss re-read the last two lines: *"A post-mortem found*

Jerome Goodman was six times over the legal limit for alcohol and lost control of his vehicle. The coroner ruled death by misadventure."

And then she found the post-mortem report had been added to the case file along with the newspaper clipping. There was no photo of the body. And the coroner had scrawled at the bottom of the form:

Death by misadventure

A coroner's handwriting always creeped her out. So many of them had bad, even childlike, penmanship. Their scrawl always seemed so at odds with the official-looking print. She peered at the signature and the name, but she didn't recognise either.

Moss sat back in her chair. Jerome would be forty-six years old now, the same age as Kieron Bagshaw. She turned the page in the case file back to the photo of him, aged eighteen, working in the pub in Covent Garden. He had short hair, a similar cut to the one Kieron Bagshaw was sporting when they'd been to Chiswick that morning. Moss felt unnerved. The likeness was uncanny, down to the slightly crooked hooked nose, the piercing eyes, and even the shape of his forehead. Kieron was a little fatter than the lithe eighteen-year-old staring back at her, but . . .

'Bloody hell,' she said. 'That's either a doppelgänger, or Kieron Bagshaw is Jerome Goodman.'

18

Erika and Igor stayed up late, talking. They planned to visit Wales the next day, after Igor had requested his holiday, and after a few glasses of wine, Erika confided in him that before they left, she wanted to visit Tania Hogarth again in Chiswick to see if she could talk to Jerome Goodman. Igor didn't like this idea. Not one bit.

Igor had to get up at six for work. Just before he left the house at six thirty, he came to say goodbye.

'Are you serious about what you said last night? You're going to pay Jerome Goodman a visit?'

Erika sat up in bed, her eyes still bleary with sleep. 'I have to talk to him.'

'And say what?'

'I don't know, exactly. I want to look him in the eye. He might not admit anything to me, but I need to . . .'

'See the whites of his eyes?' Igor finished.

'Yeah.'

'It's dangerous.'

'If Jerome has gone to the trouble of getting a new identity, and he's somehow got enough clout to have me taken off the case, then what else can he do? He's not going to mess it all up and shoot me.'

There was a long silence.

'You're going to do it, whatever I say, aren't you?' said Igor with a sigh.

'Yeah.'

'Keep your phone on. Text me when you arrive. Text me when you leave. If I don't hear from you, I'm calling Moss.'

'Of course.'

'And do you still want me to take holiday and come with you to Wales?'

'Of course. Yes.'

When Igor left for work, it felt like they'd been so close the night before and now there was a distance. Was it coming from her? Was she deliberately pushing him away?

Erika got up, showered and dressed, and got in her car. She was in Chiswick and ringing Tania Hogarth's bell just after 8am. It was just getting light, and there was a layer of frost on the tall mossy walls surrounding the property.

The intercom clicked, and there was a long silence.

'Tania? Hi. It's Detective . . .'

'I can see you on the camera,' said Tania, whose voice sounded as if she had a cold.

'Listen, I'm here on my own. Off duty. May I speak with you and Kieron off the record? I can meet you around the corner—'

'He's gone.'

'Who's gone?'

'Kieron. Skipped off in the night. Packed his stuff. Moved out.'

Erika stared at the tiny lens of the security camera on the gatepost, trying not to let her feelings of triumph show in her face. *If he's run away, he must be guilty. And if he's guilty, he's Jerome Goodman.*

'Can I come in?'

There was another long pause, and then the gate buzzed and clicked open.

Tania stood in the doorway in a fluffy pink dressing gown and matching slippers. An Alice band pulled back her long hair, and her taut face was scrubbed clean.

'Do you want coffee?'

'Yeah. I could drink coffee.'

'I was going to phone you. It was weird that you showed up outside. Like fate or something,' said Tania a few minutes later. They were in her kitchen, and she was making Erika a coffee from an expensive-looking silver coffee machine. There were cream boxes of paperwork all over the black marble counter-top. Some had the lids off, and Erika could see they contained bank statements. There was also an overpowering stench of cleaning products, and Erika saw that one of the big glass panel doors had been pulled back, and cold air from the garden was flooding in.

'Thanks,' said Erika, taking a tiny glass containing a strong double shot. 'I've been removed from the case. Just so you know.'

'What is the case, exactly? Them parcel lockers?'

'That's a part of it.'

'I've nothing to do with them. Kieron asked me to guarantee the deposit to set it up. They're very lucrative.'

'So it's legitimate?'

'Yeah. Kieron gets the money from the post office every month. "Passive income", he calls it.'

Erika took a sip of the coffee, which was very strong. She placed the glass down on the counter-top. 'What's his business, exactly?' she asked.

'I thought you were off the case?'

'I am.'

Tania downed the rest of her coffee, keeping her eyes on Erika even as she tipped back the glass. 'Investments.'

'Investments in what?'

Tania shrugged. 'That's all I know. He invests money, plays the stock market.'

'Does Kieron know anyone in South London?'

'I don't know. Kieron knows lots of people.'

'Does he have access to the lockers?'

'The owner has a master key. However, it should only be used in cooperation with the post office or the authorities. You lot.'

'Did he ever go to the lockers after they were up and running? Or did you ever go with him?'

'We weren't joined at the hip. I have my businesses to run. I haven't been to South London for years. Wouldn't want to go back either.'

Erika nodded and looked around at the paperwork. 'What happened after yesterday morning?'

Tania went to the tap and filled two glasses of water. 'We got home just after three, and he went off with Paul Slater.'

'Off where?'

'I dunno.' Tania put a glass of water in front of Erika and took a long drink from her own. Erika noticed a white residue on the marble, as if a soggy cloth had been pushed over it, leaving a milky sheen. 'Kieron got back at five. And I had it out with him, asking him if any of it was true. *You* seemed pretty convinced.' This surprised Erika. Tania had seemed impenetrable the day before. Although the Botox was probably impairing her ability to project emotions. 'We had a big row, then he said he was sorry and did I want a cuppa tea, so we could talk sensibly. I said yes. He made the tea. I drank it. Next thing I know, it's five o'clock in the morning, and I'm lying on the carpet in the bedroom. No recollection of how I got there or how long I'd been there.'

Erika put down her glass. 'You think he drugged you?'

Tania sighed. 'I don't know. He could have. But I take . . . pills for, stuff. Depression. And when I can't sleep.'

'Do you normally pass out in the early evening after a cup of tea?'

Tania sighed. 'No.'

'Did he assault you?'

'No. God, no. I was still dressed in the same clothes from yesterday. I think Kieron was far too busy getting out of here. When I looked this morning, his side of the wardrobe was empty. He'd been through all my paperwork and emptied his stuff from the safe, he had twenty thousand in cash there. I also think he'd wiped down the whole place. The bathrooms stink of bleach and cleaning products, and this marble – well, look, it's fucked.'

She rubbed at the smears of white residue on the huge kitchen island, her long acrylic fingernails clicking on the marble surface.

'Was anything else stolen?'

Tania shrugged. 'I don't think so. No.'

'What else do you have in your safe?'

'I have my jewellery. Some cash. He didn't take any of it.'

'Do you want to report this?'

'Report *what*?' Tania stared out of the window for a moment at the garden. The sun was coming up over the wall and melting a strip of the frost on the grass. 'I also had a message from Paul Slater this morning.' She held out her phone.

> With immediate effect, I can no longer represent you in any legal matters. Best P.

Erika handed the phone back. 'Interesting timing.'

'I was introduced to him through Kieron . . . Do you really think Kieron has been using a fake name?'

'Yes, I do. But Jerome Goodman died in a car accident eight years ago. Do you know anything about that?'

'What? No. And he was involved in drugs?'

'Yeah. High up in the pecking order. Drug distribution. Murder.'

'Who do you think he murdered?' asked Tania, her face

working hard to match her surprise. It was making her difficult to read.

'Rival drug dealers, and some innocent bystanders during a raid on a pub. My colleagues. My husband,' said Erika, studying Tania's slack, pale face. 'I was investigating Kieron, or Jerome, ten years ago. Had him under surveillance. Watched him for a long time. I know there are people who say they never forget a face, but it's hard to forget a face like his when you've studied it for so long. Can I ask how you met him?'

'I met him in a club in Chiswick over the summer. Malone's, a members-only club tucked away off the high street. Very exclusive. It costs twenty-five grand to become a member, and they screen people, so you have to be introduced by someone to join. It kind of stops you from asking so many questions.'

'Questions?'

'I come from money. My dad is a very wealthy hedge fund manager. When you're the daughter of someone like that, you have to be careful about relationships.'

'And I suppose if you meet a man in a place like Malone's, you know they're well off and they've gone through some screening?'

'Yeah. You'd think. I just assumed Kieron was rich and well-connected enough to be there. He always paid for everything. He lived here with me, but he paid the bills. He told me he moved to Spain with his parents when he was a teenager. His mum and dad are now dead. They were both teachers. He studied in Spain and worked in hotels in his twenties, and then some posh hotel out there hired him to work in their art gallery. That's when he met a bloke in the city who introduced him to the world of finance.'

'Have you met any of his friends?'

'No.'

'When exactly did you meet him?'

'End of July. He moved in here a month later, and he went away a lot.'

'He moved in after you'd known him for just a month?'

Without warning, Tania's face suddenly crumpled, and she broke down in tears. Erika got up and moved around the kitchen island, which was a considerable journey, and she went to put her arm around her shoulder.

'Do you think he'll come back?' she sobbed.

'I don't know. Will you phone me if he does?'

Tania abruptly shrugged Erika's arm off and fixed her with a taut gaze. 'You're wrong. I'm telling you. He might be crooked in his work, but Kieron has been good to me. An angel.'

Erika wanted to say, *Do angels drug you and then leave in the night?* But she kept that to herself. Tania could be good for information in the future.

19

After she met with Tania, Erika called Moss and Peterson and asked if they could meet.

'This is a bit off the beaten track,' said Peterson when they arrived at the greasy spoon café opposite the Catford Broadway Market.

'They do a cracking fry-up,' said Erika, pleased they had both made time to see her. 'And it's my treat.'

The café was cheap and cheerfully decorated, with red Formica tables, tinsel strung over pictures on the wall, a clock, and even a blue bug zapper above the kitchen hatch. A clatter of plates added to the cosy noise of the other customers talking. The radio was on in the background, playing 'Last Christmas' by Wham! Erika was dressed casually in jeans and a pullover, but Moss and Peterson were in their suits, and they stood out a little amongst the homeless-looking guys and the young, thin-faced mothers with babies. A teenage waitress appeared at the table with her pad.

'Cup of tea, and a full English, please,' said Moss. 'Have you got black pudding?'

'Yeah. And you?' asked the waitress, glancing at Peterson as she scribbled on her pad.

'I don't have any black pudding,' said Peterson.

Her face broke into a flirty smile. 'No. I mean, what do you want to eat?'

'I'll have what she's having.'

'And you?' asked the waitress, her face turning back to the stern mask for Erika.

'Fried egg roll. And tea.'

The waitress hurried off and cleared away a load of plates from the booth behind them.

'Oh, to be a man,' said Moss, looking over at Erika, who nodded.

'I was just joking,' said Peterson.

'I bet you fifty pence she'll give you more baked beans because she fancies you.'

'Is giving someone *more* baked beans the best way to flirt?' asked Erika.

Moss laughed. 'Good point. And the windows don't open in the incident room.'

Peterson smiled and rolled his eyes. The waitress returned with three steaming mugs of tea. Erika took a sip and was pleased that nothing had changed with her colleagues.

'So? What's going on?' asked Erika.

'Melanie put Moss in charge,' said Peterson, spooning sugar into his mug.

'What happened after you spoke to Melanie? I thought you'd come back down to the incident room before you left,' said Moss, blowing on her tea.

'She had me shown off the premises by Waller.'

'Seriously? Bloody hell. She came down to the incident room and gave us all a talk about the thresholds and procedures for arresting suspects.'

'Like teaching your grandma to suck eggs,' said Peterson.

Erika had never entirely understood the logic of this saying in English, but she could see their frustration.

'I can't work out what's happening with Melanie,' said Erika.

'You think top brass have given her a talking to?' asked Moss.

'I don't know. It could be murkier. The men in grey suits could be at it again.'

A look passed between Moss and Peterson.

'You think the secret service is interested in Jerome Goodman?' asked Moss.

'Not necessarily the secret service. The world of illegal drug dealing is high stakes. Vast sums of money are involved. Someone influential could be protecting Goodman and his associates. They've managed to vanish for so many years.'

'We ran a check on Frank Hobbs and Danielle Lang,' said Peterson. 'There's nothing. Neither of them has a criminal record. And, like Jerome, they haven't been registered at any address since 2014. Haven't paid taxes. No credit history. They all vanished.'

The waitress came back with their plates.

'Here we go,' she said, placing them on the table.

'Thank you,' said Moss. 'I read the Jerome Goodman case last night,' she added when the waitress had gone.

'Me too,' said Peterson. Erika could see the sadness in their eyes.

'We didn't know all the details. Of course, we knew about the whole thing, but I've never seen the details.'

Moss and Peterson started to eat, but when Erika took a bite of her egg roll, her hunger had gone. The bread stuck to the roof of her mouth, and the runny yolk tasted metallic and almost made her heave. She put the roll back on her plate and washed the mouthful down with some hot tea.

'I went to visit Tania Hogarth,' said Erika. Moss and Peterson hesitated eating and looked up at her. 'When they got home from the police station yesterday, Kieron Bagshaw, or should I say

Jerome Goodman, put something in her tea. When she woke up this morning, all his stuff was gone, and he'd wiped down the whole house, taking twenty-grand cash from the safe.'

'If he's taken cash from her, we can put out a warrant on him,' said Peterson.

Erika shook her head. 'Tania says he took his own cash.'

'Pity.'

'Why wipe everything down?' said Moss. 'We printed him yesterday.'

'The prints we took will have to be destroyed. They're probably already deleted from the system. It was a wrongful arrest,' said Erika.

As Moss and Peterson ate, Erika filled them in on everything else Tania had told her.

'He plays the stock market . . . He's spent his childhood in Spain? It's all very vague,' said Peterson.

'She seemed quite vulnerable when we went there yesterday,' said Moss. 'Way too much plastic surgery for someone so young. How old is she?'

'Only in her early forties,' said Peterson. 'She's minted. She could easily fall prey to guys wanting her money.'

'Aren't we being a bit judgemental?' asked Moss.

'We're investigating,' replied Erika. 'We need to ask these questions. But as far as her being vulnerable to men preying on her for money, "Kieron" had the goods to back himself up. Tania said he paid for everything. Expensive club memberships. And he had twenty grand in her safe.' Erika picked up her egg roll again but still had no appetite. She put it back down on the plate. 'These parcel lockers are still bothering me. He got Tania to have them in her name, and they've been used to courier drugs. And there is a drug connection to this dead woman.'

Moss put her knife and fork together on her plate. 'Marie Collins,' she said.

'Yes. The cocaine on the ceiling, but the rest of the flat had been wiped down. Have you got any further on her?'

'I've got a meeting with her probation officer tomorrow,' said Moss. 'She's been working with Marie since she was released from prison. And I'm hoping she can give me more background. We're still waiting on Isaac for his final post-mortem and the toxicology.'

'What about the security tag that was still on the back of her trousers?' asked Erika.

'The outfit is Primark branded and mass produced. I've got Crane working trying to track down where it was bought from. If we have the correct location, we could find the exact time it was bought, and then potentially match this to their CCTV, but it's going to take time,' said Moss.

'Why leave the tag in?' asked Erika. 'It doesn't make any sense. What about results from a door-to-door on Amersham Road?'

'Nothing. The people who live across who we've managed to track down were at work. It's all bed-sits, so there are people we still haven't got the chance to talk to,' said Peterson.

The waitress came to the table. 'Anything else?' she asked, stacking their empty plates in the crook of her arm.

'No. We should get the bill,' said Moss, checking her watch. Peterson pulled out his phone to do the same.

The café was starting to empty out, and even though it was mid-afternoon, the light was beginning to fade, casting blue shadows outside the windows. Moss's phone began to vibrate on the table and she muted the call. Erika could see they were making noises to leave, and she felt a sudden pang of hopelessness and fear. She had no job to rush back to.

'Listen,' said Erika. 'Before you go. I'm going to go crazy if I have to sit at home for the next two weeks. I don't want to put you two in a bad position, but I'm planning to go to Wales to try and find out some more information about Jerome Goodman's death. I'm going to go with Igor, so on the face of it, it looks like a mini-break.' When she said it out loud, it sounded a little sad and embarrassing. 'Anyway. I wanted to ask – if I need to call on you for information, can you help me, on the sly?'

'Of course,' said Moss, glancing over at Peterson, and he nodded.

'Just be careful only to speak to the two of us,' he added. 'I think Melanie's speech to the team scared everyone.'

Erika nodded. 'Okay, thank you.'

Moss's phone began to ring again, and she picked it up and peered at the screen.

'This is Crane. I need to talk to him. He's preparing a meeting for me to have about Erika's caseload,' she said to Peterson.

'Okay, we'd better go,' he said.

'Yes. Go. I told you it was my treat. I'll get the bill,' said Erika. Moss and Peterson said their goodbyes, and she was left in the booth, waiting for the waitress to bring back the bill.

It was getting dark outside, and the window reflected the almost empty café back at Erika, sitting alone in the corner.

20

August 2012

Bella Mackinson pulled pints at the Swann Pub near Rochdale as a summer job while studying at university.

It was a rough pub, although all the pubs in the area where she grew up were rough. At least this one had a beer garden with a slide, putting it slightly above the rest.

It was a sleepy Wednesday afternoon in August, and the only customers in the pub had been an elderly couple who came in for a ploughman's lunch, which they'd shared. Bella went for her break at two. The sun was scorching hot, so she went to the back office filled with old beer crates and the long, thin desk where they kept the delivery paperwork. The pub was built into a hillside, and the little admin office was cool in the summer. She'd looked forward to eating her sandwiches with a good book.

She had half an hour for lunch. The clock was next to the CCTV monitor on the wall, which showed a clear view of the pub's interior from behind the bar.

Jerome, Frank, and Danielle were parked further down from the Swann in a dirty white van, blending in with three other dirty white vans behind the row of crummy houses on the residential street.

Danielle had been worried about people being in their gardens on such a nice summer day, but the gardens behind the houses were so overgrown, or used for dumping, that all was quiet. The silence was broken by a far-off ice cream truck, tinkling its little tune. The tune got louder.

'No, no, no,' said Jerome, lifting a set of tiny binoculars to his face and peering down the long street to the main road at the end. 'We don't want the place crawling with kiddie-winks.'

The van drove past the junction, and the jangling tune reached its peak and then receded.

Danielle didn't want to think about how crazy and audacious this was. A getaway car, three guns, and a balaclava each – was it really all they needed?

'Here we go,' said Jerome. Frank looked over at Danielle and Jerome up front from his spot in the back seat. A big black Mercedes SUV drew up outside the Swann, its paintwork glistening.

They watched as three men got out. Two were tall and muscly, wearing jeans and leather jackets despite the heat. The third man, Wayne Chance, was short and squat. His nickname was 'Bimbo' due to his sickly pale skin. He had no eyebrows or facial hair, and he'd suffered from alopecia since he was a small boy. Bimbo wore a black trilby, dark glasses, and a long black leather jacket.

'He's left his security detail in the car,' said Jerome. They waited until Bimbo and his associates had gone into the pub. 'Okay, you're up,' he added to Danielle.

She walked towards the SUV in her tight jeans and top, her long dark hair flowing out behind her. When she came up to the tinted window, she saw her reflection: sex on a stick. She tapped on the glass, and a moment later, the window slid down. Bimbo's two hulking security men were in the front and passenger seats, smoking. They were both packing handguns in their pockets. She could see the bulges in the side of their sweatpants. They looked at her like she was a piece of fresh meat, ready to be devoured.

'Sorry, boys. I'm looking for Knight Street?' she said, with a smile. She knew 14 Knight Street was the site of a local strip club.

The meathead in the driver's seat had a toothpick in his mouth, and he rolled it around his gums, looking her up and down. 'Where on Knight Street?'

'The Shadow Lounge.'

'You're way out,' he said, talking to her breasts. 'You need to go down the end here and then take a right.'

'Hang on, I've got a map,' she said, reaching into her bag. She felt the cold steel of her handgun, and using the pretence of rummaging for the map, she brought the gun up, concealed inside the bag, and shot them both in the head in quick succession.

Thwap.

Thwap.

The silencer swallowed the shots, but their clatter still echoed in the empty street.

'Oh. Oh, my God,' she said out loud, her hands shaking. She'd practised the movements over and over, shooting through the bag.

The two men lay slumped forward, the backs of their heads blown out and decorating the rear leather seats. She heard the roar of the van's engine as Jerome and Frank sped up to the pub.

Bella was glad she was taking her lunch break. She'd seen Bimbo and his goons enter the bar on the CCTV. They came once a week, had a drink, and then went off to the cellar with Mick. Bella never saw anything, but the rumour was drugs.

The Swann was the kind of place where you took a job because you needed it. Bella needed money for college. The other bar staff had dependents, so no one was prepared to risk everything to find out what was going on.

Bella watched the two goons drink their beers, and Bimbo sipped his Liebfraumilch. There was something hideously delicate about him. He took off his trilby and scratched his head with large sausage fingers. The glare from the black-and-white CCTV seemed to shimmer off his big bald head. He replaced the hat delicately as he sipped his wine, pinkie finger in the air.

Bella looked at her book and sandwich. There were seventeen minutes left of her break, and she hoped they'd all be gone by the time it finished. She was relieved to see Mick enter the bar. His mouth moved soundlessly as they made small talk. Mick was a big, tall man, but in the presence of Bimbo and his cronies, he always stood subserviently, like in those period dramas when the butler is called upstairs to speak to the lord of the manor. Never offered a seat and always forced to stand.

Bella's book had almost reeled her back in when she saw three black-clad figures rush into the bar, carrying shotguns. She heard the crack as shots were fired, like bubble wrap popping, and a millisecond later, she saw the guns fired on the screen. Bimbo crumpled to the floor, along with the two gangly guys and then Mick. Bella wondered what the black stains were on the floor, and then she understood. It was blood.

Helen was the other barmaid working that day, and Bella saw the glasses stacked behind her explode as her head snapped back.

It had all happened in the space of a few seconds, and Bella watched the three figures in balaclavas move behind the bar and head for the door leading up the stairs to the office. She stood, her sandwich falling to the floor. Apart from going back down the stairs to the bar, there was no way out. She looked around and opened the cupboard under the desk. It was deep and wide, and the bottom was lined with packets of inkjet printer paper. She stuffed her sandwich back in her bag and clambered into the cupboard, her feet slipping on the packets of paper. At the last second, she reached out, and grabbed her half-eaten sandwich off the floor, and she'd only just got the cupboard door closed when she heard footsteps and the door opened. There was a gap between the doors, and she could see the three figures staring at the CCTV screen above the desk. Could they see her through the gap? She could feel one of the printer paper packets shifting under where she crouched.

The three figures pulled up their balaclavas, and Bella was shocked to see that one was a woman.

'Jerome. Where are the tapes?' asked the woman as they searched the office. The tall, dark-haired man found the CCTV. Bella heard the VHS tape being ejected.

'This CCTV footage will send out a message. Change of management,' he said.

'This is just the admin office,' said the other man, who had long blond hair tied at the nape of his neck. 'We need the loading bay.'

Bella held her breath. Her heart was pounding, and she was sweating. Her leg was slipping, but the packets of paper under her could push the doors open if she moved. The woman approached the cupboard doors. Her long dark hair was tied back, and she had such strong, dark features. She had scary eyes – scarier than the men's. She reached out to open the door.

'Come on, Danielle. We need to empty out and get the fuck out,' said the blond-haired man.

Abruptly, the woman turned, and they all left.

The pub cellar was filled with beer barrels and taps, and pipes hung from the ceiling. Bimbo had kept the key for the trapdoor around his neck. They'd found the trapdoor at the back of the cellar and Jerome inserted the key.

A ladder led down to a large dry storeroom, unlike the damp of the cellar. Frank flicked on the lights and whistled.

The space was lined with six square cages. Three contained what looked like white bricks stacked in piles a few feet high. Two of the other cages contained money. More money than Danielle had ever seen. Bricks of money so vast they were just blurs of blue and green, brown, and pink.

Jerome was now whooping and clapping. 'Fuck. Fuck FUUUUUUCK!' he shouted, grabbing a bag of the cash and holding it up. His eyes were shining. 'We fucking did it!'

'We need to get this out of here. We're working in broad daylight, Jerome,' said Danielle. Even though the van was parked right outside, they had to be fast.

'Frank! Fucking hell, can you believe it?' said Jerome.

Frank had been very still as he stared.

'There's enough in here to buy the world. To start a war,' he said quietly.

21

Wednesday, December 4, 2024

After lunch, Moss went to visit Tricia Hern, the probation officer who had been working with Marie Collins. When she pulled up outside the probation offices in Sydenham, Moss saw Tricia outside, having a smoke.

She was a small, rotund woman, rugged up against the cold in an oversized red puffer jacket, furry Ugg boots, and a black beanie hat pulled down low over her blonde hair. She stubbed her cigarette out on the special bin on the wall and deposited the butt inside.

'I'm the only one now who smokes in this whole building,' said Tricia.

'Must be lonely,' said Moss.

'I miss the smokers. Most of 'em here are a good crowd, but it's nice to go for a drink and a cig,' she said, breaking into a cackling, phlegmy laugh. Moss followed her inside, and once they got through security, they went up to an open-plan office. The staff all wore casual clothes, and there was a huge board on the wall with all the cases they were dealing with. A big Christmas tree twinkled in the corner. The light was fading outside, and the windows were steamed up, which gave the office a cosy feel.

An older mixed-race man with a greying beard was working at the desk beside Trish's computer.

'Alan, this is DI Kate Moss from Lewisham Row. Here to talk to me about Marie Collins, who died,' said Tricia. Moss leaned over, and they shook hands. Tricia took off her coat and hat. Moss noticed that her blonde hair started to come with the hat, and Tricia put up her hand to catch it and readjust what was clearly a wig. Alan gave Moss a sharp look, as if to dare her to mention it.

'She was quite a character, Marie, very funny, relatable,' said Alan. He spoke with a deep vibrato, and his voice seemed more suited to performing Shakespeare than working in a probation office. 'Not your typical Catholic.'

'Is three free?' asked Tricia, picking up a thick grey folder.

'Yes. Nice to meet you, Kate,' said Alan.

Conference room three had frosted glass and another small Christmas tree in the corner.

'Alan just said something about Marie not being a typical Catholic?' asked Moss as they sat down at the table.

'Yeah.'

'She attended church?'

'Yes, she would go to mass every morning and evening.'

'Where?'

Tricia looked up from her folder, clearly not expecting the question.

'Er, church . . .' She chuckled and then saw how serious Moss looked. 'I think it was . . . in New Cross.'

Moss sat back in her chair and thought of the Bible, rosary, and statue of the Virgin Mary they'd found in the flat. 'And she went twice a day?'

Tricia nodded. 'My mum called it eating the altar rails, people who go to church that much, but each to their own. Marie said she found God when she was in Holloway Prison.'

'God moves in mysterious ways.'

'Yeah, apparently, he also spends time in Holloway. Right. What else did you want to know?'

Moss could see she had the thick file open.

'I just need some background, apart from the churchgoing. How long did you know her?'

Tricia sat back and chewed her lip for a moment, thinking. 'I first met her two months before she finished her sentence. So that would be September. We like to form a relationship in the time leading up to their release to better understand their needs on the outside.'

'And she was inside for financial fraud?'

'Yeah, falsely claiming insurance on a car which had previously been claimed as a write-off.'

'And she owned the car?'

'She'd told the police it had been stolen, when it wasn't.'

'And didn't realise the previous owner had done the same thing?'

'Yeah, but Marie said herself, she was desperate for money.'

'Did she have any problems with drugs or alcohol?'

'No. Never failed a drug test when she was inside. She was never in any trouble. Model prisoner. I think it was a scandal she got time in the first place – it was her first offence.'

'Did she ever deal drugs, or did you have any worries that she might be dealing?'

Tricia pulled a face, as if Moss were speaking out of left field. 'Marie? Good Lord, no.'

'Her flat had been scrubbed down when we found her body.'

'She was very clean and tidy. Minimalist. Looked after herself. Always had her nails done.'

'Did you visit her flat?'

'Yes.'

'What do you remember about the interior?'

'She didn't have much. She'd only just come out of the nick. She said she'd lost her stuff. She owed rent to a friend she was staying with, and this friend sold it all off when Marie was inside.'

'Do you know the name or address of the friend?'

'No.'

'There was a large residue of cocaine found on the ceiling inside Marie's flat. A fine dust.'

'Really?' said Tricia, visibly shocked. 'Marie had only been there a couple of weeks. I had her in a halfway house for three weeks after she left prison, and then we got her set up in Amersham Road. Could the cocaine have already been there?'

'Possibly. Where was the halfway house?'

'Near Shirley, not far from Lewisham.'

'Can you put me in touch with someone there?'

"Course.'

'How did you find the flat for Marie?'

'I didn't. She found it herself. I think it was advertised in one of the cafés in Brockley, near where she was doing voluntary work in a charity shop.'

'Can you also give the details of the charity shop?'

Tricia nodded.

'Before she went to prison, was Marie married? Did she have a boyfriend or a girlfriend on the outside?'

'Not that I know of.'

'Did she have any children?'

'No.'

'Dependents?'

'Marie's parents both died when she was a teenager.'

'Brothers or sisters?'

Tricia opened the folder and flicked through. 'I don't have

exhaustive information in here, but I don't think she had any siblings. She never mentioned any. We were working more on her plan for the future.'

'What was her plan for the future?' asked Moss.

'Marie wanted to get her life on track. She expressed an interest in doing social work; however, with her criminal record, she couldn't work for the local authority as a social worker. She was volunteering at the charity shop in Brockley, and they were very impressed with her work ethic and how she conducted herself. She was also forging links with the church. If she could get some qualifications in care and social work, the church would probably be a better avenue for work.'

'So the church would be happy to hire someone with a criminal record to work with vulnerable people?' asked Moss.

Tricia gave a nervous laugh.

'No. Well, I don't know, but church is all about forgiveness, isn't it? A few days before she died, Marie said she had made some serious enquiries about taking the veil and becoming a nun.'

Moss stared at Tricia for a moment, thinking this was a joke. 'Really? Taking the veil?'

'Yeah. The week before Marie died, they scheduled a meeting at the job centre with her at the same time as our usual fortnightly meeting, so she asked me if I would come with her and we could have a coffee afterwards.'

'Is it usual for a probation officer to go to the job centre with a client?'

Tricia smiled.

'No, but I like to be unorthodox. And it helps to make sure that things are all working correctly. I have so many cases where ex-offenders have their benefits cut, and it's their only income, so they fall into arrears on rent and they're often forced to reoffend – shoplifting, drugs, prostitution – to make ends meet.'

'And at this job centre meeting, Marie told her advisor that she was looking for work, as a nun?'

'Pretty much.'

'And what did they say in response?'

'They thought she was taking the piss, but she was deadly serious. The only problem is that it can take years to become a nun and join a convent, so she would need to find a way to support herself until then. The job centre suggested she try to get paid work in her charity shop or another charity shop.'

'What did she do before prison? She had no significant other that you know of. How did she support herself?'

'Shop work, bar work, anything she could get hold of.'

Moss sighed with frustration. Again, this was all so vague.

'Do you know of any address where she lived before prison?'

'No. She'd lost her flat a couple of years before in the midlands and she was sofa surfing, as she said, staying with friends, renting rooms off friends. But money was tight, and that's how she wound up doing the insurance fraud.'

'Would you say she was depressed?'

'Depressed? No way. I know you don't know what is happening in someone's head, but she seemed so happy. She'd found God; she was out of prison and single. Marie seemed to be on the threshold of something wonderful, finding a new life for herself, and becoming a nun.'

Moss looked at Tricia, and thought about the wig she was wearing. Tricia looked like she had lost a lot of weight.

'Did you ever go to church with her?'

'No. I was planning to, though. Marie told me she'd lit a candle for me.'

'I didn't know you were religious?'

'I'm not, but Marie raved about the church. We'd made a plan to go on Sunday, but then, she died.' There was a long silence and Tricia's eyes grew moist; she blinked back her tears. 'I always have a policy of not getting close to the people on probation who I look after, but maybe I'm getting older, maybe I let my guard down . . . I can tell you, though, Marie was a good woman. A good woman trying to move on from the mistakes she'd made in the past.'

22

Erika and Igor left a frosty-cold London just before nine the next morning. The traffic was bad on the M25 and then the M4, and by the time they crossed the border and were driving through the Welsh mountains, the light was fading and Erika had no mobile phone signal.

A storm hit about ten miles outside Aberystwyth, and when they arrived in town, it was dark and the rain was lashing down. Everything felt wrong. Losing the case. Driving away from London. She was on a wild-goose chase with no badge and no authority.

Igor had managed to find a nice hotel right on Aberystwyth promenade with a sea view, but there was no parking out front, so they spent another twenty minutes with the rain roaring down on the roof of the car bickering as they navigated through one-way streets, around to the back of the building and the car park.

They got drenched on the short run inside with their bags. The hotel was clean but seemed dingy, and their room was at the top of two very steep staircases. They ate in an empty dining room, where a clock ticked and a Christmas tree flashed its lights in time to the second hand.

After dinner, they went back up to their room. A large bay window looked out over the sea, where the storm was still in full flow. Lightning forked across the sky and lit up the rolling expanse of black water.

'I've never got used to seeing the sea,' said Igor, leaning his arm on the window frame and pressing his face close to the glass. Erika joined him. The floorboards creaked. They could see all the way along the seafront promenade to the pier. The Christmas lights strung along the lamp-posts waved wildly in the gale.

'How much are we paying for this room?' she asked, pressing her foot on the carpet, where the floorboards underneath had a worrying amount of give.

'It's cheaper than London.'

'And a dump.'

'I think it has charm.'

'What is it they say about charm? The English disease.'

'Well. We're in Wales.' He looked over at her and smiled. Erika could see he was refusing to entertain her bad mood, and it made her all the more grumpy. 'Do you fancy a drink?'

'There's no mini-bar, and I can't face all those steps back down.'

'I brought Jablkovica,' he said, pulling a small bottle of the clear, apple-flavoured spirit from his bag.

'You are such a Slovak.' Erika heaved her rucksack onto the bed and undid the straps.

'You brought a printer?' said Igor as she pulled out the printer from home. She placed it on the bed and searched behind the bedside table for a plug socket. '*Why* did you bring a printer?'

'To print. We're going to have to switch sides. My side of the bed doesn't have a plug socket.' Erika pulled out her phone. The battery was very low, and more disappointingly, Moss and Peterson hadn't called.

Igor went into the small bathroom and grabbed two glass tumblers. He poured them each a half centimetre of the Jablkovica, and held out one of them.

'No. I want to keep a clear head. Why is there one fucking plug socket for the whole room?' she said, finding a plug behind the bedside table on the other side. She yanked it out and the room went dark. Igor switched on the main light, and Erika winced. 'Ugh. That's awful. Like the light in Isaac's morgue.'

The printer whirred and hummed on the bed.

'Come on, have a drink. We both just ate duck pâté and pork medallions on a bed of rice. This will help with digestion.'

'Why are you acting like we're on holiday?'

'We're away on a break.'

'No. This is work. We're here to find out about Jerome Goodman!' she shouted. Igor stood staring at her. She took a deep breath. 'Sorry. It's hard. Being chucked off the case at such a crucial point. I thought I might hear from Moss.'

'She's probably busy, which is good.'

Erika nodded. 'I just wish I could be busy with her, with my team.'

Igor held the glass closer and she took it. They clinked and then downed them.

'Wow,' said Igor, his eyes watering. He coughed.

'That's strong,' agreed Erika. She could feel her throat burning, but a delicious, calming warmth was spreading out in her chest. She took a carrier bag out of her coat with a packet of inkjet photo paper.

Igor came over with their glasses, which he'd refreshed, and perched on the end of the bed.

'What are you printing?'

'I want a stack of photos of Goodman. I can show them to people, and they can keep them. I'll put my number on the back.

Sometimes people take a while to recall things.' She got the packet of photo paper open and slotted it into the printer. 'Okay. Jerome Goodman's car came off the road just before Clarach Bay, which is a couple of miles outside the town. I want us to get up early and go there. Ask some questions.'

'And who are we?'

'You've only had one shot of that stuff. I'm Erika. You are Igor.'

'No. I mean tomorrow. Who are we? Are you DCI Erika Foster and I'm your other half with you on a mini-break? Or are we two civilians on holiday, or private detectives?'

Erika looked up at him. 'We are *not* private detectives.'

'What's wrong with private detectives?'

'They're meddlers who should leave detective work to the police.'

Igor raised an eyebrow and took a sip of his drink. 'Okay. But this happened quite a while ago. Isn't it going to be odd that we're here eight years later asking questions?'

Erika took the second glass from him. 'I thought we could say we're journalists writing a book about the drug trade, and we're wanting to do something about the area.'

With a crash of thunder, all of the lights went out and they were plunged into darkness with just the glow of Erika's laptop. Lighting strobed outside and Igor moved to the window, where his silhouette was tall and thin. Erika went to join him. The lights were out in the whole town. The promenade had vanished into a pool of black, and the cars, road, and beach were just shadowy outlines.

'Erika. Do you really think people will want to open up about drug problems in their area?' asked Igor.

'You don't have a background in investigating,' said Erika, feeling her hackles rising.

'I don't. But you've always been a policewoman with

authority and a badge to back you up, presumably even when you've been undercover. Yes?'

'Of course.'

'And right now you don't have a badge. You can't really say who you are. We need to be inventive.'

'Do I ever tell you how to do your job?'

'I'm not telling you how to do your job. I just think we're in Wales two weeks before Christmas, pretending to be on holiday?'

'You're not listening. We're pretending to be two investigative journalists.'

'Do we have business cards? What are our names? What's our back story? Who do we work for? Because whoever we talk to will want to google us straight afterwards, especially if this is a historical case.'

It annoyed her to acknowledge it, but he was right. Erika was glad they were in the dark – she could feel her cheeks flushing with embarrassment.

'Okay, Mr Know-it-all, what do you think we should do?' she snapped. 'How are we going to ask around about Jerome Goodman without people being suspicious?'

'Static caravans,' said Igor.

'What?'

'Where Jerome Goodman's car came off the road, there's a big static caravan site right nearby. The whole area is really popular in the summer with holidaymakers, people who love to surf. There are some really big beaches around. I checked online and there is a static caravan for sale on that site. We say we're interested to buy it.'

Erika stared at his silhouette. It wasn't a bad idea.

'There's a bar and restaurant open all year round on the site. We can legitimately ask about the local area. We can talk to people. And we don't have to make up a bullshit back story. I can be Igor the train driver. You can be Erika the civil servant. That's not too much of a stretch. We can be a Slovak couple. We can talk about wanting to come on holiday with our families. And it's an investment.'

Igor pulled out his phone, found the page advertising the caravan, and showed it to Erika. The lights came back on. They both winced, suddenly thrust back into the glare. The streetlights outside flickered on a moment later.

'It's not the worst idea.'

Igor grinned. 'Wow. DCI Erika Foster likes my idea.'

Despite herself, Erika smiled. 'It's the best worst idea.'

23

Moss arrived very early on Thursday at Lewisham Row's incident room. Peterson was already there, bleary-eyed, switching everything on, including the Christmas tree lights. He was just coming back from the kitchen with two steaming cups of tea when Moss received an email containing the bank account statements and phone records for Sherry Blaze.

'I thought Crane had made a fast-track request for these?' said Peterson, perching on the corner of the desk as Moss opened the first attachment.

'I did. Morning,' said Crane, who was just coming into the incident room, rugged up in an oversized coat, woolly gloves, and his winter hat with ear flaps. He came over to the computer, peeling them off. 'They've got a huge backlog.'

'Sherry Blaze seems to have more outgoings than incomings,' said Moss, scrolling through. 'She's living on credit cards, with a large overdraft and a mortgage.'

Her phone rang; it was Isaac.

'Morning. I heard you've taken over the Marie Collins case,' he said.

'Not through choice. Have you spoken with Erika?'

'I did.' They both paused, not wanting to say too much else over the phone. 'I've just done the post-mortem and had the toxicology report back on Marie Collins. Can you come to the morgue?'

'Can we do this over the phone?' said Moss, looking at her computer screen, which was a mess of opened files.

'Sorry. No. I don't want to talk about it over the phone.'

Moss and Peterson arrived at Lewisham morgue twenty minutes later. Issac was waiting for them in a clean set of scrubs.

'I was hoping we're going to talk in your office?' said Peterson. Moss looked over at him; even after all these years, he was still squeamish about viewing dead bodies.

'No. Sorry. I'm afraid I have to show you the body,' said Isaac. They followed him through to the end of the corridor, and then they reached a steel door, where he input a code. The door beeped and popped open. The room inside was freezing, with no windows. Stainless steel refrigeration units lined one wall, and four post-mortem tables glinted under the fluorescent light in the centre of the room. On the one closest to the door, Moss could see the shape of a body under a blue sheet.

Isaac went to the bench running along the edge of the room and picked up a file. He opened it and handed it to Moss, then moved to the table and gently folded the sheet to expose Marie Collins's head and shoulders.

Her face was pasty and sunken, her dark hair was scraped back from her high forehead, and she looked like a peaceful waxwork. Moss looked down at the file, and Peterson moved around to see over her shoulder. There was an ID photo of Marie taken for her passport application. There was another photo beside it, taken with Marie in prison garb. She had thin features in both images, although she looked plumper in the passport application photo.

'What's this, Isaac?' asked Moss.

'That is two different people,' he said, coming around to join them and tapping his finger on the paper.

'What do you mean, two different people?' asked Peterson sharply.

'I did the post-mortem, and two troubling things came up,' said Isaac, indicating the body on the table. 'The first thing I discovered is that Marie Collins had a condition called situs inversus, in which the major organs are reversed or mirrored from their normal positions. So the heart is on the right, along with the other visceral organs, which are mirrored from their usual positions. It's found in around one in ten thousand people. But you can live with it, with no problems, no symptoms, and often it only comes to light when a person has to see the doctor or have a scan or X-ray.'

'Okay,' said Moss. 'And let me guess?'

Isaac nodded. 'Yes. Marie Collins had a rather nasty chest infection when she was in prison, and it necessitated an X-ray.' He went to his computer on the bench. Moss and Peterson followed. 'As part of the post-mortem, I was sent Marie Collins's medical records. This is her X-ray,' he said, flashing up a scan that showed her heart and lungs and ribs. 'And this is an X-ray of our victim here.' He clicked on another X-ray, then flicked between the two. 'You see the different placement of the organs?'

'Yes, completely different,' said Moss. Her throat suddenly felt dry.

'So, who is that on the slab?' asked Peterson. They turned to look at the woman.

'I don't know. Whoever it is shares a similar age, and she has strikingly similar features. Same height. Similar weight. Eye colour.'

He went on: 'I then looked at these two different ID photos, the one of Marie from prison and the passport photo, and when you really look, there are subtle differences between the two. I put it down to weight loss at first, but you'll see Marie's nose is slightly more pointed in the first prison photo, and the forehead is higher. That's not the case in the passport application photo.'

'So we've misidentified the body,' said Moss.

'If it hadn't been for this rare condition, the situs inversus, I might not have picked up on this,' said Isaac. 'This woman – whoever she is – her DNA isn't in the system. And I'm already on it. I've requested a search through dental records. I'll find out who she is.'

'Hang on, you said there were two things?' asked Peterson.

Isaac nodded. 'Yes. As far as the toxicology report goes, there was no alcohol in her system or any of the conventional drugs you might expect, like cocaine, heroin, et cetera. But. There was a high concentration of tetrahydrozoline.'

'Never heard of it,' said Peterson, looking to Moss, who shook her head.

'Tetrahydrozoline is a form of a medicine called imidazoline.'

'Still doesn't ring any bells.'

'It's found in eye drops. For example, the whitening eye drops you would use if you have red eyes. I use them myself, occasionally, when I want to be bright-eyed and bushy-tailed after a poor night's sleep. Tetrahydrozoline poisoning occurs when someone ingests a large amount.'

'Is it hard to get on prescription?' asked Moss. 'Hang on, no. It's not.'

'Yes. That's the thing,' said Isaac. 'It's an over-the-counter medication. You don't need a prescription for it. If you just use it properly, a couple of drops in the eye, it's fine. But when it's consumed orally, it passes quickly through the gastrointestinal tract, rapidly reaching the blood and the central nervous system.

An overdose can lead to drowsiness, slow heartbeat, hypothermia, and even a coma. There have been a few cases, including one quite high-profile one in the States, where a woman put tetrahydrozoline eye drops into her husband's coffee over a period of three days, and he died.'

'How much did Marie Collins, or this person, have in her system?'

'A very high concentration. One small bottle of tetrahydrozoline eye drops contains 15 to 30 millilitres of solution, and the amount she had in her blood was consistent with her ingesting two or three bottles.'

'Could it be suicide?' asked Peterson.

'Possibly. Or it could have been added to something she drank, without her knowledge.'

'Suicide or murder, and this isn't Marie Collins, bloody hell,' said Moss.

'Is this method of poisoning something that someone would use to try and get away with murder?' asked Peterson.

Isaac shook his head. 'No. The previous cases of tetrahydrozoline poisoning have been easily detected post-mortem. It's very easy to procure. And unlike other poisons, it's odourless and has no flavour, so it can be put into a drink quite easily without anyone detecting it. As you know, anti-freeze is incredibly toxic, but the commercial anti-freezes you can buy have a bitter flavour added. Tetrahydrozoline eye drops are easy to buy and easy to conceal and dispose of the evidence.'

Moss looked at Peterson and shook her head.

'This is all we need,' she said.

'We need to look back over the crime scene forensics,' said Peterson. 'If they found eye drops containing tetrahydrozoline in Marie Collins's flat or her rubbish bins.'

'There's no bruising, minor or major on her body,' said Isaac. 'No other injuries.'

'Great,' said Moss. 'We now have a missing person. An unidentified body, who may have been murdered, and the poison used is something we all have in our bathroom cabinets that you can buy from any pharmacy.'

24

Erika slept better than she expected, her exposure to the sea air seeming to dampen her thoughts and fears. She'd checked her phone at 4am, when she got up to pee, and again when she woke up, but there was no email or text from Moss or Peterson.

The hotel dining room looked much better with the sunshine streaming through the bay windows. After a good breakfast, Erika and Igor drove to Clarach Bay and arrived just before nine so they could have some time to get coffee and orientate themselves before the meeting at ten.

They parked next to a restaurant at the bottom of the caravan site, close to the beach.

The restaurant inside had the feel of a works canteen with rows of white tables and chairs on a bare wooden floor. A tall, broad woman in her late forties was emptying a dishwasher behind the bar, and a short, brooding bald man was working at a laptop on one of the empty tables.

'Are you open for coffee?' Igor asked the woman.

'I suppose so,' she said, wiping her hands on her white apron.

'Do you make cappuccino?'

''Course we do,' she said, a little defensively.

'Two, please.'

Erika took a table near the window, looking out over the empty beach. The sunshine had been brief, and a low bank of dark clouds was rolling in from the horizon, giving the light a steely edge. As Igor came over with their cappuccinos, another woman came into the restaurant wearing a long raincoat and a clear plastic rain hood tied tight under her bulging chin. Erika recognised her from her Facebook profile as Sharon, the owner of the static caravan, who they were due to meet a little later.

'Morning, Anwen,' she said cheerily. 'Milky coffee when you've got a mo.'

Anwen seemed impervious to Sharon's cheer and nodded as she slammed down the crockery. Erika noted that the man in the corner was watching.

Erika indicated Sharon to Igor.

'Hello. Are you Sharon?' he asked. 'We're due to meet you about the caravan for sale this morning.'

Erika's heart sank. She'd wanted more time to discuss with Igor what they were going to say, and how they were going to do things. Sharon had been struggling to untie her rain hood and managed to get it off, smiling triumphantly.

'Igor, is it? Nice to meet you.' She came over to their table. Erika could see why she wore the rain hood. She had a magnificent corona of white-blonde curls set quite tightly in place. She looked to be in her sixties, maybe younger. 'Mind if I join you? We can go over a few things in the warm.'

'Yes, of course,' said Erika, trying not to let her annoyance show. She felt she was on the back foot.

When they were settled with coffee, Sharon got a clear plastic folder out of her handbag. Igor spent the first few minutes chatting about their fictitious caravanning exploits in Slovakia, and how much they loved the sea.

'It's very nice around here. It can get a bit busy in the

summer, but when the sun shines, I think we give the Costa del Sol a run for its money,' said Sharon.

'Is insurance expensive?' said Erika, giving Igor a look she hoped he would pick up on as "let me take the lead".

'No. I can put you in touch with our provider. I think I have details here,' she said, opening the plastic folder.

'Does the site have round-the-clock security?'

'We went online and checked the local crime statistics,' Igor blurted out.

Sharon looked up sharply from sorting paperwork in the folder. 'Over in Aber, they have a lot of trouble. And I tell you, that's the students. Here in Clarach, we're very quiet. Nice people. People who don't want no trouble.'

'We're just concerned about the CCTV,' said Erika, glaring at Igor.

'We don't have CCTV covering the whole park, but there are cameras at the entrance and exit,' said Sharon. Erika could see she was getting worried they wouldn't want to see the van, and the weather outside looked like it was going to turn.

'It's amazing what you can find online and how every area has crime statistics,' said Igor, blundering on. 'We're in London, and if you look at our area, God, you wouldn't want to go out again.' He laughed and Sharon joined him. Erika smiled, and was about to steer the conversation back to the caravan park when Igor said, 'We read about this accident a few years back. Some guy drove his car off the road in the summer of 2016 and was killed.'

Erika felt her stomach crawl. Igor was making it sound so obvious. Sharon's smile faltered, and she fiddled nervously with her necklace.

'Really? I think I heard something about that . . .'

Erika could see that the man working at his computer was subtly listening, and Anwen had even turned down the radio in between songs, but when they saw Erika take notice, they busied themselves again with work.

'I think we should . . .' Erika started to say.

'Was he young? The guy who was killed in the car accident?' asked Igor.

'It was a long time ago, maybe he was in his thirties . . . I really don't remember much. It was quite a while ago.'

'But it stands out, because this place is so quiet. Very little happens.'

Sharon looked between them and nodded.

'He was a local?' asked Erika, deciding that the conversation had now definitely shifted, so she might as well try to salvage things.

'I don't know.'

'Do you know if he had any children?'

'I really don't know. Listen. Do you want to see the van or not? I have to be back in town shortly,' said Sharon. She now had a brittle smile plastered onto her face.

Erika was frustrated and felt Igor had blown it. Their questions had created an atmosphere – a nervous undercurrent – and she doubted they would get much more out of Sharon. And then Igor abruptly said he needed to use the loo, and he got up and went to find them.

The toilets were out the back of the building, along a freezing-cold corridor. It was an old-school urinal, a metal trough that stank. Igor unzipped and started to pee. A moment later, the man who had been working at his laptop in the corner came into the toilets and stood at the other end. He unzipped and started to pee.

'Is that your girlfriend with you?' he asked, turning to Igor.

'Yeah.'

'She's a copper?'

Igor hesitated. 'Why do you ask?'

'I can tell a copper a mile off,' he said. He zipped up his fly and went to the sink. 'Why did she say she was a civil servant?'

'Sometimes people get funny when you tell them you work for the police,' said Igor.

'Are you a copper?'

'No.'

'No, you're not, I can tell,' said the man, grabbing a handful of paper towels. Igor zipped up and debated not washing his hands and getting out of the bathroom. 'Whatever you've got going on, I'd stop asking questions.' He dried his hands and then pitched the paper into the wire basket by the door.

'Questions about the campsite?'

'Don't shit a shitter. I know what you're asking.' Igor felt the colour drain from his face, and the man noticed. 'Yeah. You're not a copper, you've got no game face.'

'What do you know about Jerome Goodman?' asked Igor, swallowing and trying to regain his composure.

The man whistled. 'You've got balls, boyo. And if you go around asking questions like that, you might end up with them chopped off and shoved down your throat.'

'I'm not here to cause trouble.'

'Oh. No, course not,' he said with a nasty smile, which displayed a gold front tooth. 'And I'm not here to threaten you.'

'The body in that car – who was it?' asked Igor.

The man's face seemed to freeze and grow tense.

'Are you fucking even listening to me?' he said, taking a step towards Igor, who stood his ground. Igor could see the man was shaking now, with anger or was it fear? He couldn't tell. 'Get the fuck out. Go on. While you've still got two legs to walk on.'

25

The sky was gloomy when Moss and Peterson arrived at 14A Amersham Road, and many of the bay windows in the surrounding flats and bed-sits had their Christmas lights on.

The curtains had been removed in Sherry's window, so they could see right into the front room. It had been emptied out completely, and two guys in overalls were hammering panels of chipboard over the hole in the ceiling.

Sherry answered the door and wasn't too pleased to see them.

'Yes, can I help you?' she said.

'We need to have a word. May we come in?' asked Moss.

Sherry sighed. 'I've given you a statement: I saw nothing, and only heard some noises. You had me stuck in a van outside the other day, deliberately wasting my time. I don't have to let you in.'

'You can let us in, or we come back with a search warrant,' said Moss.

'Why would you need a search warrant?'

'Do you want to wait and find out?'

Sherry adjusted her pea-green character turban. 'I can give you ten minutes.' She stood to one side, and they stepped into the hall. The living room door was closed and the loud banging erupted from behind it. 'I'm having a temporary ceiling put in place. The insurance company won't cough up for the building work until the new year.'

'Is there somewhere we can sit down?' asked Peterson, having to raise his voice.

'Come through to the kitchen.' They passed another two rooms. The first was a small, dingy bedroom with a window looking out onto the small grey yard, and the next room was bigger but equally dingy. It was filled with bookshelves and boxes.

Moss and Peterson sat down at the kitchen table. A long, glittery jacket in plastic hung off the handle of a cupboard.

Sherry followed their gaze to the jacket. 'I have a gig tonight, so I don't have much time.'

'It's still early,' said Moss.

'I have to supervise the lighting, set list, and bar. It's not just a case of rocking up half an hour before the doors open.'

The banging started up again, and Sherry closed the kitchen door, muffling the noise.

'Do you use eye drops regularly?' asked Peterson.

Sherry looked genuinely surprised at the question.

'I beg your pardon?'

'Whitening eye drops, for red eyes.'

'Yes. Why?'

'Do you have bottles in your bathroom cabinet?'

'I just told you. Yes.'

Peterson took a plastic evidence bag from his pocket. It contained three small bottles of eye drops.

'When our forensics officers were here investigating, they found these eye drops in the green recycling box in your backyard,' said Peterson. He placed the bag on the table. Sherry's large eyes seemed to grow even bigger.

'Why were they in my backyard? The lady's body was found upstairs.'

'Did you put these bottles in the green recycling box outside?'

She peered at the bottles. 'I . . . I use eye drops because I don't sleep well, and I don't want to have bloodshot eyes when I'm performing.'

'We've had the post-mortem results back from Marie Collins's death. There was a high level of tetrahydrozoline in her blood. Three of these bottles' worth,' said Moss, tapping the evidence bag. 'Tetrahydrozoline is the main ingredient in these eye drops. If large amounts are ingested, it can lead to death.'

'I didn't throw three bottles out at once, so I didn't put these in my recycling box,' said Sherry. She now looked very scared.

'So, who put them there? The only way to access your backyard is through the kitchen,' said Peterson.

'Someone could climb down from the window above,' replied Sherry, regaining a little of her composure.

'Who?' Moss shot back.

'That's not up to me to prove.'

'Do you have a receipt for your eye drops?'

'No. I get them from the supermarket. And I think I only have one or two bottles here. Someone could have climbed over the side wall facing the street and got into my garden. Do you know how many times someone has actually done that and tried to break in?'

'No,' said Peterson.

'Well, you should have it in your neighbourhood crime statistics. And it might be worth taking a look, especially now you've moved in up the road,' said Sherry, her titanic confidence seeming to surge back. 'I've reported six intruders in as many years. *Six.* Thankfully, no one broke in, because I've got bars on the windows and door. Where were you when I reported all those people trespassing on my property? And now you're showing up here to interrogate me about stuff in my recycling box? A recycling box that I haven't emptied in a long while. And if my neighbour was killed by someone giving her these drops, whoever gave them to her could have chucked them in my recycling bin.'

Moss sighed and looked over at Peterson. 'Can I ask . . .'

'Are you now going to lecture me about not recycling?'

'No. I wanted to ask if you go to church?'

Sherry laughed dryly. 'No. Why?'

'Your neighbour was a regular churchgoer.'

'Was she? I didn't know.'

'Do you know much about the local Catholic church?'

'I've no idea. I get the local Jehovah's Witnesses knocking every few months, but we don't see much about religion around here.' Moss nodded, took a folder out of her bag, and placed it on the table. 'Oh. There's more, is there?'

Moss opened the folder and took out the two photos Isaac had given them. There was the ID photo of Marie taken for her passport application and another photo beside it, of Marie in prison garb.

'You mentioned to our colleague Erika Foster that you saw Marie Collins last Saturday, 30 November, around 2pm; she was going up to her flat carrying a vanity case?'

'Yes.'

'And you said that she looked different. We'd like you to look at these two photos,' said Moss, placing the passport application photo on the table next to the photo of Marie from prison. 'Did the woman you saw on Saturday look like either of these?'

Moss watched Sherry study the photos. This was a difficult one; they didn't want to lead her as a witness, but they needed to know if Sherry had noticed a difference.

'I only said she looked different because she seemed to have cleaned herself up, lost a bit of weight. I don't know. She looked much less bedraggled. Like she'd had a makeover or had her hair and make-up done,' said Sherry. 'These are both photos of Marie.'

'Can you please tell us which photo most matched Marie's appearance from when you saw her on Saturday?' asked Peterson, tapping the two photos.

'They look the same to me.'

'No. Marie's nose is slightly more pointed here in the first prison photo, and the forehead is higher. In the passport application photo, can you see, her face is rounder and her nose softer? Her hairline is slightly different. She looks more polished.'

'Which you might expect if one photo was taken inside prison and the other outside,' said Sherry.

'Yes. But based on what you saw on Saturday, which photo looks most like Marie?' said Moss, trying not to lose her temper.

Sherry studied the two photos for a long moment.

'It could have been the second one,' she said finally.

Moss and Peterson exchanged a triumphant glance over Sherry's head.

'Thank you,' said Moss.

26

It was raining as Igor drove them back to Aberystwyth.

'You seem pissed off,' he said, breaking the silence.

'Of course, I'm pissed off. What the hell were you doing back there?'

'I was asking questions.'

'No, you blew it.'

Igor stared at the road for a long moment. His jaw clenched.

'She still showed us the caravan.'

'That wasn't our goal,' said Erika, thinking back to the sad, musty little box. 'Sharon either thought we were mad, or the worst kind of undercover police officers. I'd hope it was the former, because that's not how I do my job.'

'You're not doing your job, you've been signed off sick. I was here to help you.'

'Fat lot of good you were. Blundering around.'

Igor stared ahead at the road for a long moment as the rain began to ease.

'When I went to the loo, the guy from the restaurant followed me, and he threatened me,' he said.

'What did he say?'

'He correctly guessed you were a copper.'

'Only because of you!'

'He told me to stop asking questions. That's when I just went for it.'

Erika turned to him. 'What do you mean, you went for it?'

'I think I pushed it a bit far. I named Jerome. I figured at that point there was nothing to lose.'

'How did he react?'

'His reaction was extreme. Scared. Angry.' Igor looked over at her.

'You definitely named Jerome Goodman?'

'Yes. And I asked him who the body in the car belonged to.'

'Bloody hell, Igor. And then what exactly did he say?'

'He threatened to chop my balls off and shove them down my throat. And told me to get out of here while I still have two working legs to walk on.' Erika stared out of the window at the fields and hills rolling past. Even if it was cack-handedly done, they were on the right track. Poking the bear sometimes worked. 'Did I do the right thing? You saw the reaction of that Sharon woman when you mentioned the car coming off the road. And now this guy comes sidling up when I'm pissing to make threats. Shit.'

'What? Was there something else?' asked Erika.

'We told Sharon where we were staying when we sat down for coffee. And he was listening.'

'We don't know if he was listening to everything.'

'Sharon has my Facebook profile. My name.'

'Listen. I'm a police officer,' said Erika, putting her hand on his arm. 'I've lost count of the people who have tried to intimidate me. If I'd have run away every time that happened—'

'I'm not suggesting we run away. But I quite like my life, Erika. Our life.'

'Calm down.'

'Do you know how many years I've heard about Jerome

Goodman, how he killed Mark and your colleagues, how he managed to be on the most wanted list for almost ten years, and how the police never caught him? This guy is seriously dangerous. And if he's killed so many other people and got away with it, who's to say he won't do the same to you, to me.'

'Why are you only realising this now? You offered to come here with me. You were the one blundering around back there, shooting off your mouth.'

'What about Tom? They can very easily find out about him through my fucking Facebook. Jesus, why do we give away so much information? I'm going to delete my profile.'

'How many times have I warned you about posting all your private information? This is why I don't have Facebook,' snapped Erika, regretting it a second later.

'Oh, well, good for you. I'm glad you're going to be okay.'

Erika could see that Igor was spinning out of control. They were now back in town. They pulled into the empty car park behind the hotel and came to a screeching halt. Igor switched off the engine and let go of the steering wheel, flexing his fingers. Erika could see he'd been gripping it tightly.

'I'm going to pack my things, we should check out, and leave, get out of here,' he said, his voice dangerously quiet. 'Are you coming with me?'

'Look. Let's calm down and find a pub in town where we can sit down and talk this through. There might be something more I can do. Someone else I can talk—'

'What about Tom? They can find him through my Facebook profile.'

'Igor, calm down.'

'You're something else,' he said, unclipping his seat belt and opening the door. 'I'm leaving, even if I have to walk back to London.'

Erika got out of the car and followed him up the steps to the rear entrance of the hotel. Just as they reached the top, her phone rang. She took it out of her pocket and saw the caller ID.

'Who is it?'

'It's okay. It's Moss.' He turned around and glowered at her. 'I have to take it. I'll be up in five minutes.'

'You better be, or I'm going without you.'

They were now at the bottom of the stairs in the hallway outside the dining room. Erika answered the call and hurried through to the front entrance of the hotel.

'Moss. Hi.'

'Where are you? You sound out of breath,' said Moss. Erika came out of the front door, crossed the road, and took the steps down onto the beach. The tide was out, and it felt good to get a bit of distance from everything.

'Still in Aberystwyth.'

'How's it going?'

'Not great. We've been asking questions about Jerome Goodman and one of the locals has been a bit threatening at the mention of his name, but nothing tangible.'

'Sorry, Erika, I haven't got long. I wanted to quickly bring you up to speed with developments.'

Erika listened as Moss outlined the discovery that the body in the flat wasn't Marie Collins and that whoever it was had potentially been poisoned. It began to rain again. The beach was empty, apart from a lone dog picking its way through a pile of driftwood in front of its owner. Erika pulled up the hood of her jacket.

'Think about the crime scene. That radiator,' she said. 'If it hadn't fallen through the floor, there might have been a much less dramatic discovery of this woman's body. Maybe she would have lain there for days or even weeks decomposing, and her identity might not have been questioned – apart from this situs inversus.'

'And whoever killed her might not have known about the situs inversus.'

'But why use eye drops to poison her? A dead body found in that way, even a decomposed dead body, would arouse suspicion and lead to a post-mortem and toxicology. The room was so clean and empty. Wiped down. It was almost like the body was staged to look innocent.'

'What if the eye drops were just used as a covert quick, clean method of killing?' said Moss. 'They're easy to get hold of. Don't have a strong taste, and can be slipped into someone's drink surreptitiously. They were used more to incapacitate the victim quickly.'

'Then what's the motive?'

'I have no idea.' Erika could hear the frustration in Moss's voice. Her phone began to beep with call waiting, and she saw Igor was calling. She looked up at the window to their room but couldn't see him.

'What if, whoever killed this woman, wanted to throw a spanner in the works, and cast doubt on Sherry Blaze? You said forensics found the eye drops in Sherry's recycling box. What if someone planted them there, knowing we'd suspect Sherry? It sounds cack-handed, but you've been and questioned her about the eye drops. It's given the real Marie Collins extra time to, I don't know, run away?' Her phone beeped, and she saw Igor trying to ring her again.

'I never really thought Sherry was a suspect. She's got no prior criminal record. She's a struggling actress, compère, okay, her finances are in a mess, but where is the motive to murder her penniless neighbour who has no possessions apart from a Bible, a rosary, and the clothes she was lying down in?' said Moss.

'And no shoes,' added Erika.

'That's still something we're trying to work out too.'

Erika was quiet for a moment, and her phone began to beep again. Igor was calling for the third time.

'Listen. Igor keeps calling me. I'd better go, but I'll call you back.'

Erika ended the call and answered Igor.

'Christ, Erika. I've been trying to ring you.'

'I know.'

'Glad you could pick up.'

'I was talking to Moss.'

'Someone's vandalised your car.'

27

Erika hurried through the hotel and out to the car park at the back. Igor was standing by the rear passenger window of Erika's car, which had been smashed.

'What happened?'

'I don't know. I came down with our cases, and the window was broken,' Igor said. Erika moved around and peered inside the car. Broken glass lay all over the back seat. She hurried across the car park to the narrow road running behind the houses and looked up and down; it was empty.

'Did you see anyone?' she asked, coming back to the car.

'No.'

She studied the broken glass. There were green fibres and a larger piece of material snagged on the broken edge of the frame.

'It looks like someone smashed this with their hand, with some kind of material wrapped around it,' said Erika. 'Has anything been stolen?'

'I don't know. I just got here, and then I phoned you.'

'Let's look,' she snapped. Igor went to open the passenger door, but the car alarm began to shrill. 'It's still locked, why didn't you say?'

'You didn't know it was locked either,' he said.

'But you have the keys. You were driving.'

Igor searched his pockets and found the car keys, deactivating the central locking. Erika went around to the boot and opened it. There was nothing much of value inside, but she checked that the spare wheel and her small toolkit were still there.

'What the fuck?' she heard Igor say. Erika came around to the passenger side of the car. He had the glove compartment open. Inside was a clear plastic bag filled with small yellowish lumps wrapped roughly in cling film and another bag filled with white pills. 'What's this?' he said, picking up the bag with the small white wraps inside.

'I don't know,' said Erika. 'But it looks like crack cocaine, and the pills could be anything.'

'What's it doing here? It wasn't here when we left this morning. I put my sunglasses back in the glove compartment when we left the hotel.' Igor's face was white as a sheet.

'It's okay. Let me see.' Erika always kept a pair of latex gloves in her pocket, and she slipped them on and picked up the two bags and examined them. The off-white lumps were hard, chalky crystals. She took one out of the bag and felt it, then put it to her nose. It emitted a chemical smell like a solvent mixed with motor oil.

'I think this is crack cocaine.'

'Crack cocaine? Jeez, Erika. There's so much of it.'

Erika suddenly felt a heightened sense of danger – or was it instinct? She heard the sound of a car approaching. She dropped down so the car shielded her from the road. There was a drain with a wide grate next to the front wheel of the car, and she quickly dropped the two bags through the grate. She heard a splash. By the time she stood up again, slipped off her latex gloves and stuffed them into her pocket, a police squad car was pulling into the car park.

'Don't mention what we found under any circumstances,' muttered Erika. She closed the door and walked around her car. A young female police officer, who looked to be in her early thirties, was getting out of the squad car. She wore a large anti-stab vest with a high-visibility raincoat on top. A younger male officer with jet-black hair got out from the other side.

'Afternoon. You've got a broken window,' said the woman, pointing to the glass lying on the tarmac.

'Yes,' said Erika. 'Did someone call you?'

'Nope. Just on a routine drive around town. Is this your car?'

'Yes. It's my police car. I'm also a police officer.' She turned to look at the male officer, but he didn't react. 'I'm Detective Chief Inspector Erika Foster. I work for the Met Police in London. This is my partner, Igor Mak.'

The woman was already pulling on a pair of latex gloves.

'What are you doing?' asked Erika.

'If you can stand back, I need to observe and gather forensic information,' she said self-importantly. As if Erika were a moron who didn't know police procedure.

'Could you show me your warrant card?' Erika asked.

She raised an eyebrow. 'It's here on display.' She tapped her lapel, where a warrant card showed she was Detective Marsha Hall.

'Good to meet you, Detective Hall. Who is your colleague?'

'That's Detective Matt Parker,' said Marsha. Matt had returned to the squad car and was talking on his radio.

'Her name checks out. But she's on leave from the Met,' said Matt, coming back around to join them.

'Are you able to show me your warrant card?'

'I have other ID,' said Erika.

'It's not necessary,' said Marsha, waving Erika and Igor out of the way. She went straight to the front passenger seat, opened the door, crouched down, and opened the glove compartment. Erika watched Marsha and saw her flash of surprise when it was empty apart from the logbook. She lifted it and looked underneath. *Bloody hell,* thought Erika. *Someone planted those drugs for her to find.* It was now raining harder, and she could hear the gurgling sounds of the water in the gutters and running down into the drains. She hoped that the two plastic bags weren't visible by looking down through the grate.

'What are you looking for?' asked Erika.

'Forensic evidence.'

'Right. Considering that the back window was broken, I'd have thought you should start there?'

Erika kept her voice light. She could see Marsha was momentarily thrown. Matt then joined her, and they opened the car doors and started to search through the car. Erika didn't dare look at Igor, fearing he would give something away. She was also worried that something else had been planted in the car, but after fifteen minutes of searching, they found nothing else out of the ordinary.

'I'll have to give you a crime number, but I'm sure you know the score,' said Marsha, barely able to hide her annoyance. She cast her eyes around the car park and walked around the car. She stopped over the drain, and for a horrible moment, Erika thought she'd seen something, but she pulled out a form and quickly filled it in.

'You don't want to take prints?' Erika asked Matt.

'The chance of finding the perpetrator is very slim,' he said.

'Yes, and you've established he's not hiding in the car – you both had a very thorough look,' said Erika. She pulled out her phone. 'And just so *I* have a record, I'm taking a photo of your warrant card and ID number, Matt. And yours too, Marsha.' She snapped photos of them both.

'And you are entirely within your rights to do so,' said Marsha, angrily tearing off the completed form with the crime number and thrusting it at Erika.

'Oh my God, that was close,' said Igor, when the squad car had gone.

'It was,' said Erika, feeling shaken.

'What would have happened if they found the drugs in the car?'

'Nothing good,' said Erika, not wishing to go into detail. 'Did you check us out?'

He shook his head. 'I just got the bags.'

'Okay. You load them in. I'll settle the bill, and let's go.'

'Do you still want to stop in a pub and talk?' asked Igor. Erika could see his hands were shaking and he was very pale.

'No. We're getting the fuck out of here.'

28

Shortly after Moss spoke to Erika on the phone, she noticed Melanie had arrived in the incident room, and was talking with McGorry next to the photos of the Marie Collins case on the whiteboard. Peterson was sitting at his desk on the phone with his feet up, and he clocked Melanie at the same time. He took them off the desk and sat up straight. She hadn't announced herself, and Moss wasn't sure how long she'd been there when she saw her.

Melanie then moved over to speak to the two new civilian support workers, Frieda and Ryan, who were working at the desks. There was something patronising about the way she crouched down to talk to them, with her hands on her knees, as if they were two children.

Like Erika, Moss had noticed a change in Melanie over the past few months. It used to feel like she was much more accessible as a superintendent. Her door would often be open, and Melanie would come down to the staff room to have a cuppa and chat. And she would always call ahead if she came down to the incident room. Now she was popping up without warning, and always suspicious of her officers, guarded, and short tempered. And you had to schedule a meeting to talk to her – unless you were summoned.

One of the last big cases they'd worked on, involving the sex worker with links to the establishment, had marked the change, for the worse, in Melanie. Erika, Moss, and Peterson had privately discussed this, wondering whether Melanie had been visited by one of the men in grey suits, telling her to keep an eye on Erika and her team.

That was Erika's problem – she was too straight down the line. Incorruptible. She didn't have kids, or many friends, and she didn't care what people thought of her, which made her more challenging to control.

Moss felt a nervous cramp in her belly. She was now the head of the murder investigation team – a temporary head, but still. Did she possess the same stubborn confidence to do the right thing? She took a deep breath, slipped her shoes back on (she liked to work at her desk in her socks), got up, and went over to Frieda and Ryan.

'Afternoon, ma'am, everything okay?'

Melanie turned. She looked tired and drawn, thought Moss. Her pale-blonde hair had grey at the temples.

'Kate. Hello. How is this case coming along? Marie Collins. Ryan was just telling me that he's been working on tracing the security tag found on the back of the victim's trousers.'

'I'm just putting the updates in a report for you to read.'

'Why don't you just tell me now?'

Moss was a little taken aback by her tone. 'Well. She didn't die of natural causes.'

A look of alarm flashed across Melanie's face.

Moss told her about the toxicology report. 'And the body we found isn't Marie Collins.'

'Why has it taken so long to discover the mistake?'

As Moss carried on explaining, the officers and support workers in the incident room behind them fell silent, and she could feel them listening. Melanie moved along the wall, studying the photos of the collapsed ceiling, the mess in Sherry Blaze's living room, and Marie Collins's – or the person they'd *thought* was Marie Collins's – body, lying neatly on the bare mattress.

'Can you *conclusively* prove this was murder?' asked Melanie.

'That's what we're investigating.'

'Don't be opaque. You know what I mean.'

'Well. The presence of such high levels of tetrahydrozoline—'

'Could indicate suicide?' finished Melanie.

'Possibly, but we're concerned – I'm concerned – that we have a woman who looks like the victim, in the victim's place. That, in itself, is suspicious.'

'But that's also conjecture. Isn't it? Kate. You are now running the murder investigation team. Not the suicide investigation team. Your caseload is vast, unlike our resources, and all I seem to see people doing here is working on the Marie Collins case. Which sounds very much like suicide.'

They had now worked their way around the room to Moss's desk, and a vein was throbbing in Melanie's temple.

'It's only today I've heard this news from Dr Strong,' said Moss.

'I would think that someone who is suicidal could find it very easy to use eye drops to take their own life. Tetrahydrozoline is colourless and odourless. A quick Google search would show that death from this method is fairly painless. Dizziness, vomiting, and then unconsciousness.'

Sounds like a great night out, Moss wanted to say, but Melanie was really pissed and getting herself more worked up by the minute. Moss had never understood before why Erika allowed herself to get so prickly and angry when dealing with top brass, but now she did.

'I've just been putting together everything on Marie and

checking the other lines of enquiry we need to pursue,' said Peterson, getting up from behind his desk to join them.

'And if you are unable to prove that this was murder, which I don't think you are, I would urge you to hand this over to the drug squad,' said Melanie. Moss's phone began vibrating on her desk, and 'ERIKA FOSTER' flashed up on the screen. Melanie saw it, and there was a nasty silence. 'I also hope that Kieron Bagshaw isn't part of your investigation?'

Peterson looked at Moss.

'We received some information the day after we arrested him,' said Moss as her phone continued to vibrate. She picked it up and cancelled the call from Erika. 'Kieron drugged his girlfriend, Tania Hogarth, and when she woke up, he'd taken twenty thousand pounds in cash from her safe. He also potentially could have sexually assaulted her.'

Moss saw Peterson give her a subtle look. This was stretching the truth.

'*Potentially?*' repeated Melanie sharply.

'Again. This is another line of enquiry into a case which has become complex,' said Moss. Her phone began to vibrate again in her hand, and she stuffed it into her pocket.

'Listen, both of you. Erika has been signed off from work pending a medical evaluation. Now, if she passes, then great. If not . . . Well. I *had* been lining both of you up for a promotion. We're looking at expanding the murder investigation team into two teams. Just make sure that Erika isn't still trying to steer from the back seat, or you'll both find yourself disciplined. Or worse, signed off with her.'

'Disciplined?' said Peterson, bristling.

'That's what I said. Erika is currently a civilian, and I'm sure you wouldn't dream of sharing confidential details of a police investigation with a civilian?'

Moss didn't like that Melanie was making no effort to lower

her voice in front of the team. Something in her tone made Moss feel like a child being threatened with a smacked bottom.

'Of course not,' said Moss, keeping her voice even.

Melanie turned to Peterson and looked up at him.

'No, ma'am.'

'And steer clear of Kieron Bagshaw. There is no connection to him and this *murd* – and this case. Understood?' Moss and Peterson nodded. 'Good. I expect you now to rapidly and robustly investigate whether Marie Collins's death was murder or suicide and if, as I expect, it's suicide, I would want to see this all wrapped up and sent over to the drug squad within the next twenty-four hours. I'm sure you've got plenty of other cases to deal with.'

29

'Did these two police officers say why they wanted to search your car?' asked Moss, opening the ketchup bottle and squirting a generous blob on the corner of her plate.

'They were looking for the drugs,' said Igor.

'But how did they know there were drugs in the glove compartment?' said Erika. 'We didn't say anything. And the officers didn't give a reason.'

Erika and Igor had made good time driving back from Wales, arriving back in London the previous evening. It was now the following afternoon, and Moss had come over to Erika's house for lunch to talk through what was happening with the case. They were all sitting in the kitchen having fish and chips from the chippy around the corner.

'What about body cams?' asked Moss.

Erika shook her head. 'Nope. They weren't wearing them.'

'The hotel might have CCTV?' said Igor.

'What would I get from it?' said Erika. 'The drugs were probably planted in the glove compartment by some low-level drug dealer who had no idea why he was doing it. And if I'm right, the person was probably quite savvy and wore a cap or a face mask. And on what authority would we request the CCTV footage? And I don't want to poke the bear any more than I need to.'

'Who do you think is the bear?' asked Moss, swallowing and taking a sip of her Coke.

'Someone who doesn't want me asking questions about Jerome Goodman's fake death.'

'The man who came to talk to me in the toilets at the campsite was quite scary. Well. He was scary, and he seemed scared,' said Igor.

'And this was after you mentioned the car accident?' asked Moss.

'Yeah.'

George came into the kitchen with a miaow. Igor finished his last chip and got up.

'I know you need to discuss work things, so I'll go and watch some TV with this furball,' he said, picking up George. 'Has Tom been feeding you again? You feel heavy,' he added, kissing the cat on the top of his head. George purred and shook his ears.

'Thanks, Igor,' said Moss. When he'd gone, Erika closed the kitchen door and came and sat back down, topping up their glasses with Coke.

'I was officially warned off yesterday by Melanie,' said Moss.

'Warned off Jerome?'

'Kieron Bagshaw. And you rang whilst she was warning me. She saw your name on my phone.'

'Shit, sorry.'

'It's okay. I've not been in your position much, heading up cases. And this Marie Collins case, or whoever the body belongs to. Melanie wants it closed, ruled as a suicide.'

'What has Isaac said?'

'I haven't had the chance to talk to him.'

'He was suspended during our last big case when he refused to rule a suspicious death as suicide,' said Erika.

'I think this time the onus is more on me.'

Erika sat back for a moment and studied Moss. She looked exhausted and pale, quite unlike her usual buoyant self.

'I would never condone leaning on someone to alter the course of a case.'

'You're thinking about Tania Hogarth?'

Erika nodded. 'If Tania was assaulted, or if there was something taken from her house, maybe something she hadn't noticed before that was missing? Then you could legitimately put out a warrant for Kieron Bagshaw's arrest.'

'Why would she agree to that?' asked Moss.

'I don't know. Maybe Tania doesn't know enough about Kieron's past. Maybe you could go to her and fill in the gaps. Tania also could have forgotten that the twenty thousand in her safe belonged to her. That amount of cash stolen would mean an arrest warrant would be automatic.'

'You think he's going to try and leave the country?'

'If he hasn't already.' Erika sighed. This was exhausting. Not being in control. Not knowing who she could trust. And that someone like Jerome Goodman had the power or the luck to get away with it for so long. 'A UK arrest warrant could trigger an international arrest warrant.'

'I don't know,' said Moss, who sounded equally weary and depressed. 'This is getting too murky for my liking.'

'So where do you think you stand with the Marie Collins murder? I'm calling it that.'

'Good question. Where do we stand? Okay, well, we have Marie Collins in prison for insurance fraud. She served six months. Before her incarceration, she seems to have very little in the way of a life, at least on paper, no partner and no children, no property, very little financials. Her parents died when she was young. Worked low-paid jobs, seemingly cash in hand because she doesn't have much of a financial history . . . and she wanted to become a nun and started going to church. But none of this matters, in a way, because we have no clue who the body is. Marie Collins had no past, and this body has no ID.' Moss sighed. 'I also think that her probation officer was emotionally involved, which is never good.'

'Who is it?'

'Tricia Hearn.'

'I haven't come across her.'

'I don't know her that well. I think, well, I'm pretty sure she has cancer. She's lost a lot of weight. She's trying to hide that she's wearing a wig. Of course, no crime in that. But I feel like Marie going to church and her wanting to become a nun . . . It's awakened the whole religious side of things. I feel like Tricia idolised her.'

'You think she's covering up for her?'

'No. I do think that Tricia thought Marie was a saint. Which could have made her miss the details, if you know what I mean?'

Erika nodded. 'Yeah. The little details that give people away. The sideways glance, the slip-up in the conversation. I suppose if someone wants to become a nun and is toting the Bible and rosary, you look at them in a different light. What about the security tag on her clothes?'

'We know the tracksuit bottoms are from Primark, but the security tag only tells us the price, and that they're from the store in Oxford Street,' said Moss.

'That doesn't narrow it down much. That place is always crazy busy. It's the first place my sister always wants to go to when she comes over from Slovakia.'

'What do you want to do?'

'How do you mean?'

'You're off work for two weeks. I'm going to have to be very careful about us communicating. I will, of course, but I think Melanie is getting serious with me and Peterson.'

'I'm going to go back up north, to Rochdale,' said Erika. 'It's the place where Jerome Goodman spent a good chunk of his time. I want to talk to my ex-colleagues. Face up to my demons. I just have this feeling that I could get somewhere with some good old-fashioned investigating.'

She saw the look of surprise on Moss's face.

'Are you sure?'

Erika nodded. 'I've avoided it all for so long. Maybe it's time to go and face the past. It might open the door to a breakthrough.'

30

'Are you sure you don't want me to come with you? Give Jerome Goodman a good kicking if you find him?' asked Igor. It was 5am on Monday morning, and Erika was on the doorstep, saying goodbye. It was still dark, and the air was biting cold. The pavements glittered with ice and a thick hoar-frost covered the grass on the heath opposite.

'No. You have work. And I think I need to go on my own. I need to face some things I've been putting off for a long time.'

Igor nodded.

'I'm here if you need me.'

'I know. Thank you. That means the world to me.' She gave him a kiss. Erika picked up George and looked into his beautiful green eyes. 'And you, you little shit-head. Look after Igor and the house.'

George licked his lips and fixed her with a green-eyed stare, as if to say, *That's what I always do.*

The icy roads were quiet, and she got out of London just on the cusp of the rush hour. At 6am, the sky began to grow light, as she passed the huge sign reading 'THE NORTH' on the M1.

Erika had been back to her former home a few times since

she moved down south, to visit Mark's ailing father, Edward, in Slaithwaite. Each time she'd gone back, a rumbling terror had gripped her stomach, the fear she might see someone or something connected to Mark. She'd avoided going back to their house in Altringham. The police station where she'd spent fifteen years as a police officer. The bars, restaurants, cinema, theatre. All the places she used to go before that fateful day in July, when she was a 'normal' person. Jerome Goodman had taken so much from her that day. And she'd never got it back. She loved Igor, but he seemed to fit in around her job and the new 'normal' she'd created for herself in the last ten years. They didn't have 'couple' friends. They didn't really have any friends in London, beyond their work colleagues.

Erika broke her journey at the Watford Gap service station. She was pleased to feel hungry and devoured a McDonald's breakfast and a bag of mini doughnuts washed down with strong coffee. It felt good to have the warmth of a full belly.

She reached the outskirts of Rochdale just before 9am, and the traffic was slow as she got caught up in the rush hour on the main road leading into the town.

She'd programmed Chapel Street into her GPS. Even the act of doing that felt momentous. And as she drew close, she felt nervous and afraid, but there was something right about her coming back now. It was as if this had been the date when she would return – she didn't know it until now, but it felt right. Erika wasn't superstitious, but there was a strange electricity in the air.

Chapel Street seemed like it had been upscaled to HD. The sun was shining on the cold morning, and there seemed a lot more colour than she remembered from that hot July day. The red postbox, brightly coloured cars. The doors on the street, which had looked run-down, were now painted in bright pastel blues and greens. The road had recently been resurfaced with a smooth river of black tarmac, and the pavement's crooked slabs had been replaced with neat slate squares. Erika wasn't prepared for the shock of seeing number 17 Chapel Street. For so many years it had been burned into her memory, the overgrown front garden and dirty windows. The peeling paint on the front door, and the electricity metre with the cover ripped off.

She parked outside, without realising she was parking in the exact same spot where they'd sat in the surveillance van on that fateful day. Two tiny children dressed in thick coats were being ferried up the front path by their parents, and a sign for *Buzzy Bees Nursery* hung above the front door. The windows were all painted a bright blue, and surrounded by fairy lights, which were faintly shining against the sun. Huge renderings of the Hungry Caterpillar and the Gruffalo, both several metres high, were stuck to the brickwork on the facade, and the front garden now had a small pond with a net, some trees. It looked and felt so utterly different on this crisp winter morning. How was it possible that the house of such death and destruction, which existed in Erika's mind, was so utterly changed?

A young woman emerged from the front door. She was accompanied by a tiny older lady with long jet-black dyed hair, a huge fur coat, and a vape around her neck on a chain. They greeted the two small children and their parents, and came out of the gate. They passed Erika as they crossed the street, and it was only when the young woman reappeared at her shoulder that Erika realised she must look odd, standing in the middle of the road, staring with her mouth agape.

'Are you okay? Can I help you?' she said. There was concern in her voice, and not necessarily for Erika.

'Sorry. How long has this been here?' Erika said, pointing at the house. She could hear the emotion in her voice.

'The nursery?'

'Yes.'

The older lady came to join them, and seemed to shrink

down in her huge coat against the cold. She eyed Erika beadily, sucking on her vape.

'About four years,' said the young woman. 'Do you want to enrol your kids?' she added, and it sounded like she hoped Erika would say yes, answering her curiosity.

'It ain't cheap, love,' croaked the older lady through a mouthful of vape.

They both had Manchester accents, and Erika remembered how much more friendly and chatty people could be compared to London. 'You got kids? Or grandkids – I don't want to judge.'

'No. No kids. I used to live round here.'

'Did yer?' said the older lady, and she and the young woman exchanged a glance.

'Not here on Chapel Street.'

Another car arrived and parked with a screech on brakes. A flustered young man got out, scooped up a little girl dressed in a fairy costume, and hurried up the front path with her under his arm.

'Hiya, Robbie,' said the young woman to the guy.

'Hey, Carly, Loretta,' he shouted over his shoulder.

'So why are you just standing here staring at a kids' nursery?' said Loretta, her voice taking on a harder tone. *'Well?'*

'Gran,' said Carly, but she was also staring at Erika, her brow creased.

'Sorry. I'm actually a police officer,' said Erika. She patted her coat and took out the scan she'd printed off of her warrant card. She'd packed it hoping it might suffice.

'Why you carrying a photocopy? I've seen *Line of Duty*. You're meant to show a card. A warrant card,' said Loretta, sucking on her vape.

'I'm . . .' Erika felt her eyes begin to water, and hoped they'd think it was the cold. She took a deep breath.

'Is everything alright?' asked Carly.

'Yes. I'm off duty. I've been signed off sick.'

'I hope it's nothing contagious,' said Loretta, taking a step back and pulling at Carly.

'No. Injury. And nothing is wrong here. In fact, this place looks so happy now.' Erika turned to them. 'This may sound like an odd question, but have you lived here long?' She directed it more to Loretta, as she could see Carly was in her late teens or early twenties.

'I've lived here all my life,' said Carly.

'The nursery . . .' Erika tried to say through her tears. 'It wasn't always here. Before, it was . . .'

'I think we should go,' said Loretta in a low voice, grabbing at Carly's arm. 'Come on, you left that thing in the oven.'

'What thing?'

'The thing. That potato.'

Loretta didn't seem to like the idea of an off-duty copper, who might be contagious, welling up in the middle of the street.

'Before, it was drug dealers,' said Carly, turning back to Erika. 'It was bad news for the street. Is something going on again?'

Erika turned back to the house and took deep breaths of the cold air. 'No.'

Carly hesitated. 'Your warrant card. Erika Foster. You were one of the police officers that day?'

Erika looked back at her in surprise. 'How did you know that?'

'For gawd's sake, Carly, come on,' said Loretta, her voice now sharp.

'I saw it all, from my window up there,' said Carly, pointing to the house across the street.

'Saw what?' croaked Loretta, looking back at the window, as if it might show her the answer.

'The police raid. I was off school, after my appendix operation . . . Your husband and colleagues died.' They were silent for a moment.

'Erika. Would you like to come inside for a cup of coffee?'

31

It was cosy in Carly's tiny back kitchen looking out over the garden. The windows were steamed from the cold. She made them each a mug of instant coffee, and they settled at the table.

'I never knew you saw the raid. I don't remember anything in the police report about a young witness,' said Erika. 'Not that I continued on the case after . . . Did any police officers come and ask questions?'

'People round here don't want to talk to the police, no offence,' said Loretta.

Erika remembered this often being said when she worked in Greater Manchester.

'No one from the police ever spoke to me,' said Carly. 'But I was a child. And everyone was out when the raid happened. Mum was at the shops. Dad was at work. A police officer came to the door that evening and spoke to my dad, I think, but they were more concerned if a stray bullet had flown across the street.'

'Did any?'

'Did any what?'

'Stray bullets fly across the street?'

'I remember seeing forensics people in white overalls, lined up in a row on the road and pavement. Doing some kind of search.'

'A fingertip search.'

'Yeah. They looked outside our house on the driveway, the neighbours' houses. Number 17 was crawling with them.'

Erika had been taken to hospital, and she'd been taken off the case. She'd never been back to the crime scene, until now. 'I'm really sorry about your husband and your colleagues,' Carly added.

'Thank you. I'm sorry you had to see it. And you were only eight.'

They were silent for a moment. Loretta watched them beadily, still puffing on her vape, which had an aroma of cherries.

'My daughter sleeps in the back bedroom. It's a bit damp, but I don't want to let her sleep in that room. Silly, really. This street is so different now.'

'How old is your daughter?' asked Erika.

'Two. Going on twenty-two. A right little madam.'

'Carly got a place to study at university,' said Loretta, her mouth curling sourly.

'But I ruined my life getting pregnant? That's what you want to say?'

'No! Carly. No, and not in front of company.' She rolled her tongue over her teeth and sat back, puffing on the vape.

'You had a plumber's van for surveillance, didn't you? A fake plumber's van,' said Carly. 'I saw you all come out of it. That was your first mistake. Sorry. I didn't mean it to sound like that.'

'What was the mistake?'

'My dad's a plumber. His van's always parked outside – well, it was back then. You also had some guy sitting in the front reading a newspaper, which most plumbers don't have time to do. And also, you just had one person's name on the side. One-man-band plumbers don't have such big vans. Sorry.'

For a split-second Erika was transported back to the van. The sweat and the smell. There was a roaring in her ears. She swallowed and took a deep breath.

'Did you see anything else that might have given us away?' The question felt so defeatist, but Erika had to ask.

'No.'

Erika didn't know how much she should share, but Carly might have seen something else, however small.

'The old couple who lived opposite number 17 had their driveway resurfaced a few weeks before the raid. When the builders were digging up the path outside, we managed to get a small surveillance camera placed in the lamp-post in front of their wall. We also had cameras on either side of number 17 and in another lamp-post at the old print-works behind.'

Carly looked surprised. 'I never saw any of that. Just saw the plumber's van.'

'What about you?' Erika asked Loretta.

'What about me?'

'Did you see anything?'

'I wasn't here that day. I did hear about it. Although, I didn't know you'd seen it all, Carly.'

'In the weeks leading up to the raid, we had five Chinese women under surveillance going in and out of number 17. One of them had a little girl. Did you ever come across them?' asked Erika.

Loretta nodded. 'Only that I remember them. Rumours was they was prozzies. Prostitutes. But I only ever saw them a few times with launderette bags.'

'Did you ever talk to the young girl? Or did your parents use any launderettes around?' Erika asked Carly.

'No.'

'Carly's mum and dad always had a washing machine,' said

Loretta. As if using a launderette were some kind of low behaviour.

Erika had some small printouts of Jerome Goodman, Danielle Lang, and Frank Hobbs, and she took one of each out and laid them on the table. 'This was the group we had under surveillance. Do you recognise any of them?'

Erika watched Carly and Loretta as they looked, but they took their time and then shook their heads.

'He was the main person we had under surveillance. Jerome Goodman,' said Erika, tapping his photo. 'He only ever went in through the front door, twice. The first time was five weeks before the raid. The second time was on July 14, the morning of the raid. The only person who should have been in that house was Jerome Goodman. We never got in there. And no one knows how he got out. But we believe he was the one who fired the shots at us. At my team of police officers.'

'Could he have gone out the back?' asked Loretta.

Erika shook her head. 'Every angle was covered.'

'You don't sound too sure, love?' said Loretta, not unsympathetically. Erika thought back to the problem with the surveillance camera behind the house going down, but this had been before the raid, and police surveillance on all sides hadn't seen anything.

'I know.'

'And you knew for sure that the house was being used to deal drugs?' asked Carly.

'Yes. It was being used to cook and distribute a large amount of crack cocaine. The Chinese women who lived there worked at local launderettes. They would go back and forth from the house to the launderettes with those huge washing bags. We believed they were using the bags to move the drugs.'

'Jesus,' said Loretta.

'We had police officers doing covert surveillance in three

launderettes. They saw activity where drugs were changing hands,' said Erika.

'Why didn't they arrest anyone in the launderette?'

Erika sighed. 'We knew that the whole operation would vanish if one of them got arrested.' She shook her head. 'I didn't like it any more than you that drugs were continuing to flood into the local community. It's something that's weighed on my mind over the years.' Carly put down her mug, and her brow furrowed. Erika could see she was thinking, and the wheels were turning fast. 'What?'

'Shit.'

'Carly. Language,' said Loretta.

'I didn't know all of the facts before of the case.' Erika saw Carly's face glimmering with a thought. 'Listen, I know the couple who took over the lease on number 17 – they run the nursery . . . I think I might know something about how Jerome Goodman was getting in and out of the house without you seeing him.'

32

St Agnes was a traditional Catholic church with a spire and stained glass windows, and was tucked away in a rough area of terraced houses between New Cross and New Cross Gate Station. When Moss and Peterson arrived, the afternoon mass was in full flow, and they took a pew at the back.

The congregation was around thirty strong, and as atheists and lapsed Catholics, they sat, watching. It was like entering another world from the rough, dirty streets – the pews were polished, and the blond stone floor seemed to absorb and radiate the soft candlelight. The high stained glass windows were beautiful depictions of the crucifixion and resurrection of Jesus Christ and cast with vivid blues, greens, reds, and purples. The priest was a very young and charismatic black man. His sonorous voice echoed throughout the church and mixed in with the smells of incense, and the soft lighting made Moss feel drowsy.

After the service, they waited for the rest of the worshippers to leave, and then Peterson went up to the priest. Moss hung back a little to watch. His name was Father Clarence. He wore a beautiful emerald-green robe and fashionable thick-framed glasses. Peterson introduced himself and gave the priest a little background on his mother, who attended the Catholic church in Sydenham. Moss wondered how difficult it was for Peterson to step back into a church. His sister had been abused by a Catholic priest when she was younger, and she'd taken her own life. It wasn't something that Peterson talked about much, but Moss knew the church always loomed like a long shadow in the background of his life.

'And this is my colleague, Detective Inspector Moss,' said Peterson, turning and bringing her into the conversation.

'Afternoon,' said Moss.

'Good afternoon,' he said, offering his hand. His inquisitive eyes seemed to settle on her and see right into her mind. She looked down at his hand and saw his nails were beautifully shaped and manicured, and he had several gold rings – although none on his wedding finger. Was his intense gaze judgement or curiosity? Or was it just Moss's defence mechanisms that were up in the presence of clergy? This man seemed very nice, and his attitude appeared inclusive, but being a happily married lesbian with a son still attracted some prejudice, even in London. 'And how may I help my fellow public servants?' he said with a smile.

'We're here to ask you about a member, or should we say a former member of your congregation, Marie Collins?' said Moss.

Father Clarence adjusted his glasses and nodded sagely. 'Yes. We were very sad to hear of Marie's passing. I've been speaking with one of our assistant priests, Father Michael. I believe he is liaising with the funeral home.'

Moss looked over at Peterson for a moment. 'Does Father Michael know something that we don't? The body is being held at the morgue for the time being due to the suspicious nature of her death.'

'Suspicious? Really?' His face registered an almost comic alarm.

'Yes. As we would expect with an ongoing investigation.'

'Of course, officers. We were just hoping that we would be able to give Marie the funeral service she laid out in her last wishes,' said Father Clarence.

'Marie had last wishes? She was only a young woman,' said Moss.

Father Clarence smiled.

'I don't think that death was something that loomed large with Marie, but it is something she discussed with Father Michael. He has taken confession with her.'

'Can we ask you about Marie's wish to become a nun?' said Moss.

'What do you want to know?' Father Clarence glanced over at the altar, where an elderly priest was clearing away the communion wine, aided by another younger man in red robes, who was extinguishing candles with a metal snuffer.

'When did Marie first attend the church here?' asked Peterson.

'She's been a relatively new member of the congregation,' said Father Clarence. 'I think it would have been a few weeks ago. But Marie had been a regular worshipper for the months she was incarcerated. And I know that she had her confirmation when she was in prison. She's been working towards taking the veil and becoming a nun.'

'And she was a devout Catholic?' asked Moss.

'Is that in doubt?' asked Father Clarence, showing a flash of steel in his smile for the first time. 'How do we prove our love for God?'

'Did you ever visit Marie at home?'

'No. I know that Marie has been helpful to Father Michael, assisting him with his shopping, and he interacted with her outside of the church confines. He lives locally.'

'Is Father Michael here?' asked Peterson.

'Yes, I think he is,' said Father Clarence. He put his hand into his robes, pulled out his phone, and typed a quick text message.

The electronic whoosh as it sent echoed in the church. He smiled at them both, and there was an awkward beat of silence in the quiet church, and then a small, grey-haired priest with a neatly trimmed goatee appeared from behind a pillar. He wore tiny round glasses and black robes and had a stocky, compact little body.

'You wanted to see me?' he said, eyeing them beadily. Father Clarence quickly explained who Moss and Peterson were, and that they were investigating the death of Marie Collins.

'Yes. It was terrible to hear. She was such a nice lady,' he said. He spoke meekly, with a Kentish twang to his accent.

'We understand from Father Clarence that you've been liaising with the morgue about Marie Collins's funeral?' said Moss.

Father Michael's eyes darted between them. 'Well, I've . . . yes, I was in contact with them . . .'

'Did Father Michael do something wrong?' asked Father Clarence.

Moss wanted to ask them to sit down, but somehow it didn't seem right to ask two priests to sit down in their own church, so they all stayed standing next to one of the huge stone pillars.

'No, you didn't,' said Moss. 'There's no way to say this without sounding blunt. The body found in 14B Amersham Road isn't Marie.'

A look of confusion passed between the two priests.

'I'm sorry? I don't understand,' said Father Clarence.

'We conducted a post-mortem and the body doesn't belong to Marie Collins,' said Peterson.

'Oh. And who is this poor woman?' asked Father Clarence.

'We don't know. What's puzzling is that she looks remarkably similar to Marie Collins.'

'Have you done a DNA test on this other woman?' asked Father Michael.

'Yes. There's nothing on any database. We are looking at dental records, but this could take time.'

'And you believe Marie is still alive?' asked Father Clarence.

'We don't know.'

Moss took out the two photos of Marie in prison and also the woman in Marie's passport application, and she explained the situation.

'Father Michael also works as a prison chaplain in several prisons around the London area,' said Father Clarence. 'Michael, you can confirm that the photo of Marie in prison is really her?'

'Of course, yes, yes,' he said, nodding so enthusiastically that his jowls wobbled.

'Did you have much contact with Marie when she was in prison?' asked Moss.

'Only through religion. She attended the chapel at Holloway Prison. She came to me for confession.'

'And what did she confess?' asked Peterson.

'Ah. That I can't tell you, but I can assure you that it's nothing I would need to contact the authorities about.'

'When did you last see Marie?'

'It would have been at church last Sunday.'

'This Sunday just gone?' asked Moss, glancing over at Peterson.

'No. It was the previous Sunday, it would have been the 24 November,' said Father Clarence. 'We noted her absence last Sunday.'

'Yes,' Father Michael nodded in agreement.

'Father Clarence mentioned that Marie helped you with your shopping?' Moss said to Father Michael.

'She did. I have a bad back which flares up sometimes. She offered to help me with heavy bags.'

'When was the last time Marie helped you with your shopping?'

'A couple of weeks ago,' he said. Both of the priests kept fixed smiles on their faces.

Moss took out her card. 'Thank you. Both of you. Can we ask that if Marie does get in contact with you, you let us know right away? Also if you have anything else you can think of.'

'Absolutely,' said Father Clarence, taking her card. 'And we will be praying for Marie and, of course, this poor woman.'

33

Erika had never expected to walk up the path to number 17 again, and she paused at the gate. Carly was halfway up the path when she looked around.

'Are you okay?'

Back in 2014, the garden had been paved over roughly with uneven slabs and weeds poking through the cracks. Now there was the small pond with grass and trees. Erika stopped at the bench. It was made of iron and painted light blue. Carly came back down the path.

'This is where Mark – my husband, Mark – died.' It was difficult to feel like this was the same place; Erika was struggling to see it again. The grass edges were neatly cut. She saw a glimpse of gold in the pond where a net was stretched across the water. The trees were much taller on the house opposite. A flock of blackbirds wheeled across the grey sky.

'Do you need a minute?'

Erika had expected to feel a darkness, a fear, in the front garden, but it felt as if the horror had gone. It only remained in her mind.

'No.'

She followed Carly to the front door, where the younger woman buzzed the intercom.

'Laura, have you got a minute? It's Carly.' She looked up, and Erika followed her gaze to a camera mounted above the door. There was a click, and the door popped open. The hallway was bright with white walls and a blond wood floor. The space had been widened on the left, and there was now a small room where the kids' coats and shoes were hung. Each peg had a cartoon picture of an animal or a Disney character above it. Erika could hear the sound of children floating down the corridor and music playing, and there was also a delicious aroma of home-cooked food.

'Smells good, doesn't it?' said Carly. 'They have a chef.'

Carly knocked on a door to the right, and it was also on a locking mechanism, which made Erika realise that this might be a different time, but they still had to be very careful about the kids' safety and security. The office inside was bright and modern, with a wall of books and folders and a big squishy sofa. A woman with long curly hair tied back sat behind a desk. A thin man with long black hair tucked behind his ears and olive skin came out of a doorway leading to a kitchen; he was carrying two steaming mugs of coffee.

'This is Detective Chief Inspector Erika Foster,' said Carly. Both of their heads snapped up, alert.

'I'm not on duty, hello,' said Erika, trying to conjure up a smile. She put out her hand, but this did nothing to dispel the alert on the woman's face.

'I'm Laura,' she said.

'I'm Stephen,' said the man, speaking with a strong Spanish accent. He smiled broadly and shook Erika's hand.

'Can you spare a few minutes? I think this is important,' asked Carly.

Laura remained in her chair, while Stephen perched on the

edge of the desk. Erika briefly outlined her role in the drug raid ten years ago.

Laura and Stephen looked increasingly uncomfortable.

'Did you know about this?' Erika asked when she'd finished.

'We'd heard bits and pieces,' said Laura. 'But we were assured it was in the past.' She raised an eyebrow at Carly.

'I'm so sorry this happened to you,' said Stephen, giving Erika a sympathetic smile. 'We're sorry,' he added.

'Of course,' said Laura. 'But this is now our business. I'm not sure why you're here.'

'Stephen, you said that when you were renovating the house, you found some kind of hidden cellar?' asked Carly. Erika felt her stomach lurching.

'Yes. In what was the back bedroom, which we now use as the dance studio.'

'What kind of hidden cellar? There is a small cellar, isn't there?' asked Erika, thinking back to the plans of the house.

'Yes. There's a small one accessed in the hallway opposite. This is another underground cellar at the back of the house.'

'How was it hidden?'

'It was a disused wine cellar,' said Laura. 'There's nothing there to see, apart from bricks and dirt.'

'Did you know about a second cellar?' asked Carly. Erika shook her head.

'I can show you,' said Stephen. Laura glared at him. 'It's just bricks and dirt, as you said.'

'Yes, please,' said Erika.

'Well. I have to stay in the office,' said Laura. 'I've got a call with the council.'

They followed Stephen out of the office and along the corridor, passing a door with windows into a big, airy room where children were playing in groups.

'This is the original cellar,' said Stephen, stopping at a heavy door painted dark blue. It had no door handle. 'We use it for storage.'

Erika was struggling to remember the house's old layout. Just past the door to the cellar, at the back, there had been a grotty kitchen and a small bedroom, but now this had all been knocked into one to make a big room with a parquet floor. Chairs were set up for lunch. An extension had been added onto the back of the building, and Erika could see through a hatch where three women were working in a large kitchen with stainless steel counters. A large window, slightly steamed up, looked out over a small patch of garden and red-brick walls. Stephen glanced up at the clock. It was coming up to midday.

'I'm sorry to take up your time, but this is important,' said Erika. 'We had the blueprints for the house for surveillance, and there was nothing about another cellar.'

'It's here,' said Stephen, leading them to a big brick-surrounded fireplace with a wide mantelpiece. A Christmas tree was lit with coloured lights and decorations made by the children. 'Due to safety regulations, we keep it locked.'

'This was the kitchen in the old house,' said Erika, looking around. Again, she was struggling to orient herself in the space.

'They've done a lovely job with renovating,' said Carly.

Stephen was now crouching by the fireplace and pulling out the small wrapped presents that had been piled in the hearth. A clanking, crashing sound came through the kitchen hatch.

'When did you take over the lease on the property?' asked Erika.

'We bought the place six years ago. It was owned by the council, but they didn't own the lease, so they put the whole thing up for sale,' said Stephen.

'There had been some dodgy types after . . . and then some homeless people started breaking in. There was a small fire one night, and then it was boarded up and empty for eighteen months,' said Carly.

'Okay,' said Stephen, crouching beside the empty fireplace. 'This is now a steel trapdoor. We put it in when we found the second cellar, but it used to be bricks.' Erika noted that the fireplace was quite large inside, a metre wide at most. There was a padlock on the steel trapdoor. Stephen took out a bunch of keys and opened it.

'Can you make sure the main door is closed? Thanks,' he said, and Carly went and closed the door leading from the corridor. Stephen stepped out of the fireplace and lifted the big metal panel towards them on a hinge.

It revealed a dark, gaping hole. Carly came back, and Stephen took out his phone and activated the torch. Erika did the same. She could see down a few feet, where some bricks had been pushed into the earth to make four steps. Cobwebs hung in fronds around the brick-lined walls, and they moved in the draft.

'Can you feel the cold air?' asked Stephen with a smile. It smelt damp.

'Where's the draft coming from?' asked Erika.

'You want to go down and take a look?'

'Of course.'

The door opened, and Laura came into the room.

'Stephen. Lunch is in ten minutes. We can't have that open,' she said.

'We'll be done by then,' he said. He seemed keen to show Erika. He was quite a small man, and he climbed down into the hole with ease. Erika had to crouch almost double, clinging to the damp walls as she climbed down the four steep steps. Carly and Laura didn't follow them, and very quickly they were insulated from the sounds of the kitchen and the house. Stephen flicked on a light switch. It was cool and dry, and the space widened out to a thin brick-lined corridor with a smooth vaulted ceiling. The floor was made of compacted earth, and Erika could feel a light breeze, which made her shiver. What surprised her was how far the passage went, and the end seemed to be bathed in shadows.

34

'How far does this cellar go?' asked Erika.

'Ten metres,' said Stephen, as they came up against a roughly built brick wall at the end.

'Are we still underneath the house?'

'No, we're now under the garden, up to the boundary wall.'

Erika shone her torch around. This wasn't a cellar. It looked like a passage. 'This wasn't on the deeds of the house when you bought it?'

'No.'

'How did you find it?'

'Do you know the film *The Goonies*? From the 1980s.'

'Is that the one with the little fluffy thing that can't eat after midnight?'

'No, that's *Gremlins*. The Goonies are the kids who follow the treasure map.'

'What's that got to do with this?'

'When we were cleaning out the house before renovating, I pulled out the old kitchen units, a pipe burst and we had a huge water leak. The water was running down through the bricks in the fireplace like there was a drain. When the plumber came,

Carly's dad, he saw that the bricks all had, like, a fake mortar. They fit together like a jigsaw puzzle – you could just lift them out. And this cellar was underneath.'

Erika shone her phone torch on the bricks at the end of the tunnel. She knocked with her fist, but it felt cold and solid. 'Have you ever thought that this might be a wall, and not just the end of the passage?'

'It's a cellar. We had to get a structural engineer in to find out if it could collapse. That cost a lot, and thankfully he said that it was well made. You see that the roof is curved, like you would have in a wine cellar.'

Erika angled her torch up and saw that the ceiling of the passage was lined with bricks like the walls. 'That doesn't answer my question.'

Stephen was silent for a long moment. 'It's a solid brick wall.'

'And the structural engineer confirmed this?'

'Er, yeah. Well, that wasn't even a question,' he said, now sounding uneasy.

'Why didn't you fill this cellar in?'

'We kept it for storage, if we ever need more storage. Do you know how much it would cost to fill this in? We would need tons of soil and an earthmover. The engineer said that it was sound, and he thought that it might be some kind of priest hole.'

Erika turned back to him. 'This is Chapel Street, and the church is over . . .' She had to think for a moment to get her bearings.

'It's north, just a couple of streets back from the canal.'

'So, if it were a priest hole, logically it could lead to the chapel?'

Stephen's face was in shadow, but she could tell by his body language, his outline in the shadows, that he didn't like this line of questioning.

'I don't know . . . We never asked. Laura doesn't like the church much, and we put so much money into this place . . .'

Suddenly his enthusiasm for showing her the passage evaporated. "Please don't tell me that you want to investigate this? I showed you this as a courtesy.'

Erika hesitated. She tried to think back on the exact details of that day: Jerome Goodman had been inside the house, but no one knew how he'd left. The original theory was that he managed to get out when one of the surveillance cameras failed for a short time. But if this was a passage which went to the church . . . It would explain.

'Did the structural engineer you brought in use ground-penetrating radar?'

'I don't know.'

'Did they give you any idea of when this was built?'

'No.'

Erika took photos with her phone. Whoever had built this had done a very good job. It was built to last. Stephen was wearing only a thin top, and she could see he was shivering.

'Where's that draft coming from?' she said. She started to feel around the bricks, and as she crouched down, she could feel air rushing through a gap at the bottom, like a draft coming under a door. 'This could definitely lead somewhere.'

Stephen ignored her. 'We better get back. The lunch bell's going to ring any minute.'

Erika heard Laura and Carly talking when they came back up the steps in the fireplace, but they stopped when they saw her. The dining room was warm in comparison. Laura was staring, stony-faced.

'Everything okay?' asked Carly.

'This passage . . .'

'It's a cellar,' snapped Laura, watching Stephen as he closed the steel door and reattached the padlock.

'It leads under here, and halfway across the garden,' said Erika. 'Carly, how long have you known about this?'

She looked awkwardly between Stephen and Laura. 'Stephen told me about the leak.'

'Didn't you think to go to the police?'

'And say what? They got in a structural engineer, and he thought it was some kind of ancient priest's hiding place. Isn't that right?'

'Priest hole,' corrected Laura. 'They thought it could date back a few hundred years. There are priest holes all over the country in old buildings.'

'When we did our original investigation, we got the deeds for this property. It was built as a merchant's house,' said Erika. 'This whole row of terraces dates back to the turn of the century, which was well after the fifteen hundreds, when the Catholics were persecuted. If this was a priest hole, it would have been on the original deeds.'

Carly looked at Laura, shaking her head. The dinner bell suddenly trilled out, reverberating off the wooden floors.

'Carly, you saw the drug raid, and you didn't think to go to the police when you knew about this?' said Erika.

A gaggle of voices announced the children filing into the dining room, and suddenly the room was alive with chatter.

'I was a young kid when the raid happened. It was only when you came here today and we talked that I put the pieces together.'

They had to stand to one side as one of the teachers brought over a group of children.

'We need to leave and let the children eat,' said Laura, whose face now looked like thunder. 'And there are no pieces to put together. This is a priest hole. It's something that we have had checked and signed off by a structural engineer. We have building permissions and all permits and insurance to run our business within the law. Now. We've been very courteous and indulging, but we have work to do.'

She held out her arm towards the door, and Erika knew it was time to leave.

35

'The house in Chapel Street . . . There's a hidden cellar in the back room – or what was the back room. I think it's been bricked up, and it could run for longer with an exit. Jerome Goodman could have used it to access the house without us knowing,' said Erika, speaking on the phone to Moss back in London. She'd left Carly and was sitting on a cold bench outside the Catholic church behind Chapel Street. An elderly couple rugged up in winter coats walked past. They regarded her curiously as she spoke animatedly on the phone, stumbling over her words in the excitement.

'How did you find this hidden passage?' asked Moss.

Erika went on to explain exactly what had happened. 'It might not be a passage. But there's air coming in from an external source. We need to get a structural engineer, ground-penetrating radar. This could be a major breakthrough.' Moss was quiet on the end of the phone. 'Are you still there?'

'Yes. I am. And this is fantastic, but, Erika. What case?'

'What do you mean, what case? I just told you.'

'Yes, but we work on the murder investigation team down here in London. You're on leave.'

'Moss. This is Jerome Goodman, who we know is Kieron Bagshaw.'

'Yes, and when we met for lunch, we talked about this. We've been warned off Kieron Bagshaw *and* Jerome Goodman. Unless we can find some compelling evidence that forces him into our investigation.'

'Did you hear me? I could have found a passage leading to the house he used to distribute crack cocaine.'

'And this could be an amazing breakthrough, but I can't do anything until we have something solid.'

'And if I don't get someone in to investigate number 17, then we won't have anything solid.'

They were both silent on the phone.

'Catch-22 situation,' said Moss. 'Look. I'm meeting Tania Hogarth later this afternoon, and I'm going to press her about the safe. If anything was stolen. And if it was, we have a chance at getting a warrant out for Jerome Goodman's arrest. And the whole team is working away here, but you've made a breakthrough on a case which is out of our jurisdiction.' The adrenaline was coursing through Erika's body, and it was particularly disappointing that she was having this kind of conversation with Moss. Finding the passage, even if she didn't know where it went, was a revelation. For the past ten years, Erika had lived with the guilt that she'd screwed up the surveillance before the raid on Chapel Street. That she'd missed something, and that was why her team and her husband were ambushed and killed. 'Erika. I want nothing more than to pursue this. But think. Think how crucial it is that you, we, get this right. If we can get Goodman, then I'm with you one hundred percent, but you know how the CPS and the courts work with these scumbags. We have to do it by the book and be sure that we've followed due process.'

Erika sat back on the bench, and her stomach dropped.

'Shit,' she said, staring gloomily at the water in the canal. She could see the dirt particles floating by, old pieces of trash, and sticks, and the air had a sharp smell of cold and pollution. 'If I could get ground-penetrating radar out here and just see what this is, that could be enough to go further.'

'What about Commander Marsh?' asked Moss. 'You've known him since you were at Hendon. He was a beat officer with you and Mark in Manchester. He must be able to pull some strings. Especially with the personal connection to you and Mark.'

'No. He'd already been with the Met for years by the time I headed up the drug squad in Manchester. And I only have a finite amount of goodwill with Marsh at the best of times. We're always in that awkward place between being old friends and him being a boss way above my rank. And right now I'm supposed to be on annual leave, aren't I?'

'Supposed to,' said Moss. She laughed. 'Bloody good work, though. You only left London this morning.'

Erika could hear the sounds of her colleagues in the background working in the incident room, and she suddenly missed them all. She missed her job, and the ability to lose herself in work.

'Can you look on the system and tell me who the officer is who's now leading the case?' asked Erika. She hated that she was sitting on a bench out in the cold, both physically and metaphorically, and didn't have access to any of the computer systems.

'Sure, hang on. Okay, the officer in charge is . . . Detective Chief Inspector Rafe Grainger, Rafe actually spelt R-a-f-e, not like Ralph Fiennes, who makes us all think he's a Rafe when he's a Ralph.'

'And he's based out of Altringham Central Police Station?'

'Yes. Are you okay?'

"Course. I'm fine.'

'It must be tough being back up there after so long away, especially if everyone . . .'

'Especially if everyone hates me? Well, the only person I've met is an eight-year-old girl who saw . . .' Erika took a deep breath, feeling a sob suddenly emerging in her chest. 'Sorry. She saw the shoot-out.'

'Everyone doesn't hate you,' said Moss.

'The raid was my responsibility. I took the blame for it going wrong, which I had to do. And then today I make this discovery. It's handed to me like a ray of hope. What if I didn't fuck up?'

'What if you come back to London, and we could find a way for both of us to go up there together, officially. Or Peterson might be able to come up north.'

'Thank you. I'll let you know. But I'm here now, and perhaps I should stick around for a bit. There's some personal stuff I need to do first,' said Erika.

36

An hour later, Erika sat in the waiting room at Altringham Central Police Station. Like Chapel Street, she hadn't been back since the raid, but it had been her nick for the best part of fifteen years. It felt emotional to be back and see that nothing much had changed inside. She didn't recognise the young officer wearing the hijab with her Greater Manchester Police uniform, and the young woman didn't seem to recognise her when she asked to speak to Michelle Black.

The young woman had told her Michelle was at work, and that she would be down shortly, but thirty minutes had passed. Like Lewisham Row, police officers and support workers used a side entrance to the reception. And the door buzzed and opened and a small woman with long grey hair and big brown eyes wearing a blue trouser suit stood staring at her.

It was the first time Erika had seen Michelle since the funerals of Mark and their colleagues, including her husband, Detective Inspector Jim Black. Michelle stepped into the waiting room area and the door closed behind her and clicked shut, but she didn't take a step closer; she just stared.

Erika stood. 'Thank you for seeing me.'

She could see Michelle's hands were shaking.

'I always promised myself if I saw you again, I'd slap you in the face,' said Michelle. She had a Liverpool accent, and Erika hadn't forgotten how lyrical and eloquent her voice was. It had a slightly lower register than Erika remembered, which, along with her grey hair, marked the passing years.

'That's why I thought it best to meet you in a police station,' said Erika with a feeble attempt at a joke. Michelle didn't laugh. She breathed out. Her hands were shaking too. 'Can we talk?'

'And say what?'

'I found Jerome Goodman. He's living under a different name. And I think I know how he escaped from our surveillance.'

'It was *your* surveillance. It was *your* case. *Your* call. You have no right to come here and talk about this.' Michelle's voice echoed in the reception area, and the young woman on the desk looked up from her computer.

'Is everything okay?' she asked. Michelle put out her hand, as if to calm herself, or the situation, Erika didn't know.

'Michelle. Will you meet me at the Stockpot? I wouldn't come here unless I had something really serious to talk to you about.'

Michelle went back to the door. As she swiped her card to open, the young woman indicated that Erika should leave.

A few minutes later, Erika stood in front of the Everything's a Quid! shop, where racks of cheap Christmas decorations were lined up amongst racks of Tupperware and kitchen equipment. This had been the Stockpot Café, where Erika and her team had met for lunch and coffee. She felt a loss. A loss so deep that it shocked her. It was just a café. And in the grand scheme of things, she'd lost far more. She moved to the bench opposite, sat down, and lit a cigarette. The Stockpot had been such a warm, comforting place, and to see this gone and replaced with a fucking pound shop was too much.

Erika didn't know how long she sat there, smoking. She didn't notice the cold, until she felt a warm hand on her arm. She flinched and turned to see Michelle sitting next to her on the bench, wearing a big coat and a woolly hat.

'Hi,' she said.

'Hello,' said Michelle.

'I was about to give up and go. Can't get coffee here,' said Erika.

'It felt wrong that you didn't know. It went bust during the pandemic. You remember Wally, the owner?'

'Yeah. The twinkly-eyed homosexual. What happened? He didn't die of Covid?'

'No. He moved to Florida, with a gay Republican. They own a bar out there.'

'A gay Republican, Publican . . .'

Erika blew her nose and glanced sideways at Michelle, who despite everything, laughed. How was it that they'd fallen back into their friendship in the space of twenty seconds?

'Wally still sends me a Christmas card,' said Michelle.

'He doesn't send me one.'

'How do you know? You up and left, no forwarding address.'

Erika turned to her. 'You really wanted me to send you a forwarding address?'

'It would have been nice to have the option.'

'I wanted to send you a Christmas card, the past few years.'

'I probably would have ripped it up.' Michelle sighed and looked down the half-empty street. 'Fuck you, Erika. Why is it good to see you? I shouldn't feel this way, but I'm exhausted being mad at you.' Erika didn't know what to say and just nodded, feeling tears prick her eyes. 'You said you found Jerome Goodman?'

'Yeah.'

Michelle shivered and looked up and down the street. 'There's a Starbucks further up. Do you want a coffee?'

'If you do?'

'I can't promise that I won't get mad at you again and storm off.' Her face was hard again, and Erika could see that she would have to step carefully.

They found a table and ordered coffee. Michelle sat with her handbag and coat on her lap, and Erika briefly outlined everything that had happened in London and her visit to Chapel Street earlier that morning.

Michelle was quiet for a long moment after Erika finished. 'How did he look? Jerome Goodman?'

'He looked well. Not a care in the world.'

'Bastard. What do you need?'

Erika had to think – this wasn't something she'd factored in happening so quickly. 'I've been signed off from work.'

'Why?'

'I arrested him, Jerome Goodman. Or Kieron Bagshaw, as he's calling himself. He's got an expensive London brief and some kind of hold over top brass.'

'And your super showed you evidence that Goodman was dead?'

'Yeah, showed me a newspaper article that reported Jerome Goodman died in a car accident in Wales.' Michelle snorted. 'I got a colleague, a forensic pathologist, to pull the post-mortem report. I also went to Wales, asked around.' Erika told her about the reaction of one of the locals after being asked about Jerome and the car accident, and the attempt to plant drugs in her car.

'When was the car accident?'

'Eight years ago.'

Michelle raised an eyebrow. 'What? I heard nothing about this. Rafe Grainger would have told me if he knew.'

'When I arrested Jerome, he knew who I was. He gloated.'

'I would have stubbed my fucking cigarette out in his eyes,' said Michelle with a flash of anger. She glanced at Erika almost accusingly, as if to say, *Why didn't you do that?*

Erika looked down at her coffee for a moment. 'This cellar under 17 Chapel Street. I need to find out where it goes, if it goes anywhere. It could go all the way to the church. The canal. And if so, it would have been an escape route, and it could have been how he was moving the drugs.'

'What about the launderettes, and the Chinese ladies? I thought that was how he was doing it?'

'What if they were a decoy? What if they were using an underground passage?'

Michelle looked out the window. The sky was darkening for a rainstorm, like a vicious dark bruise. The pathetic Christmas lights flashed on in the high street – or what was left of the high street. 'You got your badge?'

'No.'

'Got an old badge? Very few people actually check the validity of a police officer's badge. You just flash it and it does the trick.'

Erika looked down at her coffee. 'I don't have anything with me.'

'I can put you in contact with Rafe, but if I know you, you're not going to want to work under him. If he can be persuaded.'

'The quickest way would be to get ground-penetrating radar out to 17 Chapel Street, and see if that cellar goes any further. What if there's a gas leak, or something else municipal. You could call in a favour from one of your council contacts. We bypass having to deal with Rafe? And police at this stage?'

Michelle stared back at her with the years of sadness and fear in her eyes, and Erika knew she was on board.

37

Erika spent the night in a travel inn just outside Rochdale and slept decently for the first time in several days. Michelle phoned her at 7am.

'I managed to swing it,' she said, without saying hello. 'Meet me at the print-works behind 17 Chapel Street in an hour.' There was a click as she hung up.

Chapel Street intersected with Gordon Crescent just after number 20. Gordon Crescent was a short cul-de-sac leading down to the canal. The old print-works dominated a half acre of land down to the canal and behind 17, 18, 19, and 20 Chapel Street.

A giant moulding wooden fence topped with razor wire surrounded the print-works, a squat, low building. Michelle was already waiting outside with a man in blue overalls when Erika arrived at 8am.

'This is Ted Farmer. He's a private contractor, working in ground-penetrating radar,' said Michelle when she introduced him.

'Nice to meet you,' he said, speaking with a Yorkshire accent which reminded Erika a little of how Mark used to speak. Ted had a thick beard with greying patches and wore a flat cap with his thick winter coat and wellies.

'Morning,' said Erika.

When they shook hands, he noticed she wasn't wearing gloves. 'It's not going to get much above freezing all day,' he said, indicating the thick frost covering the road and the roofs of the surrounding houses. Erika felt around in her pockets and found a pair of gloves and slipped them on.

Michelle had a cigarette on the go and clamped it between her teeth as she unlocked the padlock on the huge gate. The three of them had to push hard to get it to move, and it slid a couple of metres to the right and then stuck in the overgrown weeds behind.

'I don't have to get the van inside, just the radar box,' said Ted. He went to the boot of his van parked opposite.

'How did you swing this?' Erika asked Michelle.

'Environmental. I called in a favour with the council. The print-works is now owned by them, and they had a call about a sewage leak. Potential collapse of a septic tank.'

'But that's not true?'

''Course it's not true. My mate at the council has given us access and funded Ted, here, with his ground-penetrating radar for an hour to check it out.'

'Is anyone coming from the council?' asked Erika, looking back to where Ted was unpacking a small contraption that looked like a very square lawn-mower.

'No,' Michelle said.

'Thank you for doing this.'

'You can thank me if we find something,' said Michelle, and she followed Ted pushing his lawn-mower contraption, which was now on wheels, through the gap in the gate.

The print-works had already been long abandoned back in

2014. The windows and doors had been boarded up, and the loading bay behind was a mess of weeds growing through the cracks on the concrete. However, ten years on, nature had reclaimed the loading bay. Thick grass grew everywhere, so deep that Erika's feet broke the crust of frost and sank into the freezing wet soil. Several thin trees grew amongst the grass, and pieces of torn plastic and trash were stuck between the bare branches. She caught up with Michelle and Ted, who in addition to his scanning machine had an iPad, and he was swiping through a screen.

Erika looked up at the lamp-post on the corner of the loading bay, facing the back of number 17, where they'd managed to place a surveillance camera. The undergrowth had now grown so tall it nixed a clear view of 17. Michelle noticed where Erika was looking.

'The roof collapsed on the main building. It's full of wildlife. If they want to demolish it now, they'd have to spend a fortune rehoming a load of bats who've taken up residence,' she said.

'Where do you want me to start?' Ted asked, turning to Erika. She looked over at the tall wall that separated the print-works from the garden of 17.

'The cellar starts under the fireplace at the back of the house, and runs up to the boundary wall here,' said Erika.

'I usually have someone working with me, but his wife went into labour last night,' said Ted apologetically. He set up the scanner against the wall by the gate leading into the loading bay, and pushed the scanner across the frosty grass and vegetation, following the line of the boundary wall, and then doubled back, much like mowing stripes in a lawn. When he'd doubled back and forth twice, he stopped and looked at the results on the iPad.

'Good Lord,' he said, peering at the iPad and pinching his fingers to zoom in. Erika's legs, ears, and face were now numb from the cold. When Erika and Michelle joined him at the screen, she saw the depth in metres written down on one side of the image. The scan of the earth below was represented in grey waves.

'What is it?' asked Erika.

'There's a very deep and wide sewage pipe, or . . .' said Ted.

'Could it be a tunnel?' asked Erika.

'Yes, the passage runs under the wall here, and then diagonally to the right, crossing the bottom corner of this old loading bay, and then it looks like it carries on under the wall on the right boundary line.' They were standing against the high wall next to a pile of rubbish frozen into the thick frost on the tall grass. 'It's about four metres underground, and it looks like, if it remains on the same trajectory . . .'

'It would run down towards the canal?' asked Erika.

'Possibly. Yes.'

'Does what you've found look like a passageway, or is it just an old sewage pipe?'

'Looking at the size and depth, and taking into account what you explained you saw at number 17, I think that this is a passageway four metres underground and with a height of maybe two metres.'

Erika and Michelle decamped to a café a couple of miles away in Rochdale town centre, and Erika was grateful to be out of the cold. Michelle grabbed a table in the corner, and Erika went up to the counter to order. It was busy, so she had to wait a few minutes for their cappuccinos. When Erika returned to the table with their coffee, she saw Michelle glance up at the door, where a tall man with short curly brown hair had just entered with a young Asian woman with her hair cropped in a pixie cut. They approached the table.

'Michelle, thanks for your call,' he said.

'Your call about what?' asked Erika.

'This is Detective Inspector Rafe Grainger, and Detective Inspector Suzanne Franco,' said Michelle. 'They're heading up the Jerome Goodman case.'

38

It was dark when Erika and Michelle returned to 17 Chapel Street with Detective Inspector Rafe Grainger and Detective Inspector Suzanne Franco. They'd brought with them a structural engineer, a young guy called Tiger Jones. He didn't seem long out of his teens, and he wore a pair of huge ear expanders that made Erika feel a little queasy.

Erika was pleased to be returning with the officers currently heading up the Jerome Goodman case, but she was very much aware they were letting her tag along.

Rafe rang the intercom bell on the front door, and stepped back to peer up at the huge Gruffalo and the Hungry Caterpillar, which were now lit up on the building's front wall. Erika couldn't see or hear if any of the kids were still there. It was close to 6pm, and they'd left it late to deliberately avoid upsetting the nursery's programme.

'Yes?' said Laura's voice through the intercom after a long pause. Rafe explained who they were, and that they needed access to the cellar in the fireplace in the dining room. 'What if I say no?' Laura snapped, her voice crisp and metallic through the intercom.

'Then we'd have to look at something more official,' said Rafe, his voice both untroubled and authoritarian. 'We'd pursue a search warrant, which we'd get no problem. And I can't promise it won't be in the middle of a busy day. I assume that police officers arriving with children on the premises wouldn't be great for business.'

There was another long pause, and then Laura buzzed them in. The rest happened quickly. Stephen met them in the corridor, and walked them through. The kitchen was closed for the night, and the tables and chairs were all stacked against the wall. He opened up the steel trapdoor over the fireplace. Rafe, Suzanne, and Tiger went down into the small space.

'Do you want to see?' Erika asked Michelle.

'No. I'll wait here,' she said.

Stephen fixed Erika with a stare, as if she had betrayed him. 'How long will you be?' he asked.

'As long as it takes.'

Erika followed down into the hole. Rafe and Suzanne were inspecting the low brick ceiling with Tiger, holding up a powerful torch.

'What did you say this was, a wine cellar?' asked Tiger.

'I don't think it was built as one,' said Erika.

'It's good workmanship, this,' he said. He swung the torch around to the back wall.

Rafe had the printout from the GPR scan. 'And you think there's something beyond this wall?'

'Yes. The passage carries on.'

They all moved to the back wall. Tiger shone the torch closer.

'Can you feel the breeze, coming under here?' Erika asked, crouching down.

'There's a steel supporting beam running along the ceiling here. You can just see glimpses of it through the mortar,' said Tiger, crouching down and placing his upturned hand on the floor. 'Yeah. Air's coming in.'

Erika ran her fingers along the ceiling and her fingers brushed against the patches of steel poking through the mortar.

'Does the steel support mean there's a tunnel?' asked Suzanne.

'It could mean that this isn't necessarily a supporting wall, and it can be knocked down without the tunnel collapsing.'

Tiger had brought a tool bag with him, and he hefted out a big mallet with what looked like a crowbar.

'Here, hold this,' he said, handing Erika the torch.

'Hang on. What are you doing?' asked Rafe.

Tiger squinted up at him. 'You want to know if this is a passage?'

'Yes. But. Is it safe structurally?' asked Rafe with a note of fear in his voice.

Tiger peered up with a grimace, weighing things up. 'As I see it. You've got a slight vaulting on the ceiling in here, and brick walls. This place looks well built. You've also got some serious steel supports on the back wall. If I try and bang out a brick or two, it won't hurt.'

Rafe looked at Suzanne, who nodded. Tiger held the long metal spike against a piece of grouting three bricks up from the floor and gave it a sharp bang with the mallet. On the third strike, two bricks made a hollow cracking sound and fell through a hole.

Erika's heart began to beat faster.

'Gimme that torch.' He took it from Erika and shone through. 'It's a recess, or a tunnel, alright,' he added, looking up at them with his eager face covered in brick dust. 'Want me to carry on?'

Rafe nodded. It took only a couple of minutes for Tiger to bash out a space ample enough to crawl through. Tiger waved the dust away, and then he crouched down with the torch. Erika wasn't going to wait to be told what she could or couldn't do. She switched on her phone torch, knelt down, and squeezed through the gap.

'Erika, wait, we don't know if it's safe! You don't have hard hats!' Rafe shouted from behind. She ignored him. It was very dark inside, and smelt of damp. She held the torch on her camera and moved aside to let Tiger through the gap. He shone his torch around above them. They were in a passage. He whistled and it echoed around them.

'This looks like cement walls, and there's steel supports every few feet,' he said, slowly standing up. He started to move further along the passage. Erika stood up and followed. It grew damp and colder, and their footsteps echoed as the floor began to slope downwards. Erika's heart was beating faster, and she was both freezing cold and sweating. Cobwebs strung on the ceiling moved softly in the breeze, then the ceiling dropped down dramatically, and a few feet later, a wall of black suddenly seemed to loom in front of them. Tiger stopped abruptly.

'What is it?' asked Erika.

'Dead end.' He tapped at the wall in front of him with the metal spike. 'Well, looky here,' he added, directing the torch above his head.

There was another shout behind, and Rafe and Suzanne caught up with them. Rafe was taller than Erika, and she could see the dust in his hair.

'What are you doing? We're breaking every rule!' he said. He saw where Tiger was shining the torch, and he trained his phone light in the same place.

'That looks like the underside of a drain lid,' said Erika. There were two huge screws embedded on each side of the circle. Tiger knocked on the metal, and it gave a dull thud. They watched as he ran his fingers, which were surprisingly smooth and clean, over the screws.

'Can you get it open?' asked Erika.

'Now, let's just hang on a moment,' said Rafe, trying to edge his way past Suzanne and Erika in the crowded space. 'We don't know where this leads. Maybe we should try and find municipal records or blueprints from the house.'

Erika turned to Rafe and squinted as his bright phone light shone on her face. 'How long have you been assigned to this case?' she asked.

'Excuse me?'

'It's not a trick question.'

Everyone fell silent.

'I'd say around two years.'

'We do have a large caseload,' said Suzanne, her voice now a little hostile.

'That should never be an excuse,' said Erika. 'If you knew the basics of this case, then you'd know that we *did* acquire the blueprints for number 17 Chapel Street. It was built in 1899, and the print-works were built in 1955. We also requested municipal records of the sewage works and any other electrical and gasworks in this area. There was no tunnel listed on any official documents,' said Erika. 'This is a major breakthrough. We need to open this.'

'Hang on. I'm the officer in charge here,' said Rafe.

'My husband and my colleagues died on July 8, 2014, and I was blamed, because my colleagues and top brass thought I authorised the raid on 17 without knowing who was inside. This passageway proves that there was another way into the house. I'm not on the case anymore. You are. This is teed up for you to take the credit.'

Rafe sighed and then nodded at Tiger. 'See if you can get that open.'

Tiger went back to his tool bag to fetch a drill, and it was an awkward few minutes until he returned. With a powerful whirr, he reached up with the drill and got both of the bolts undone. He now had on thick gloves, and as he felt around the edges of the metal, he managed to push up the lid. A cold breeze and the smell of dampness blew into the tunnel. The lid flipped over and landed somewhere above with a clang.

'Here, give me a leg up,' said Tiger to Rafe. He heaved himself up through the hole. Erika stepped into where he had been standing and she looked up.

She saw the night sky, stars, and orange light pollution. Tiger's head reappeared above her, and he offered her his hand.

'Come up and have a look. The passage leads right down to the canal bank.'

39

'I didn't appreciate you pulling rank on me there,' said Rafe. They had all climbed out of the drain hole and were standing on the narrow footpath next to the canal. Michelle had joined them. The temperature had dropped dramatically. The canal path was lit sporadically with orange streetlights, so great swathes were in shadow and the water glistened like ink. Erika was still in shock. If Jerome Goodman had direct access to the canal, this changed everything. 'Did you hear me?' Rafe repeated.

'That's all you have to say?' said Erika, holding up her arms to emphasise where they were. 'I've spent my whole career having to push for results. And what's this? It blows the whole case open. Yes?' Suzanne was standing with her shoulders hunched against the cold, and her seeming lack of interest made Erika want to slap her. 'Suzanne. I assume you've read the Jerome Goodman case?'

'Of course I have,' she said.

Rafe looked over at Tiger, who was working on his phone.

Michelle was peering down into the manhole.

'And this goes all the way back up to the house?' she asked.

'Yes,' said Erika.

Michelle looked as shocked as she did. Erika wanted to put her arm around her old friend and colleague, but something stopped her.

'Okay. There's nothing on the municipal council database for a storm drain right here,' said Tiger, kicking the manhole lid with the toe of his shoe. 'There's two other manhole lids here that are for gas and water.'

'So it's been hidden amongst real drain . . . manholes?' asked Erika. Tiger looked up at them all and gave a dry laugh, like he didn't want to be the one to confirm or deny this. 'Could it have been something classified – I don't know, a tunnel built during the Second World War?'

'If it was classified, the destination, 17 Chapel Street, would be a government building. It wouldn't be in private hands.'

'And if it had previously been classified and then declassified, it would be marked on these maps, so we would know,' said Rafe.

Erika looked at Suzanne, who had remained silent.

'What do you want me to say?' she snapped.

'You don't have questions? This is your case,' said Erika.

'Is it usual for something like this to be left off municipal council or national maps?' asked Michelle, still staring with a grey face at the open hole.

Tiger looked up at her. 'If it was a new drain, then there would be a lag between it being dug and updated on maps, but this looks like it's been here a long time,' he said. 'The grouting around the lid has moss and mildew. And as for the drain cover, Rochdale council stopped using these heavy cast iron ones a few years ago. Now there would be a metal grate.'

'It's a fake drain lid?'

Rafe put out his hand in a placating gesture.

'You don't need to answer that,' he said to Tiger.

'What do you mean?' said Erika. 'He's not under oath. We're just trying to solve the puzzle here. Detective work and all that.'

Erika turned back to Tiger. 'Listen. I know it's cold, and you probably want to clock off, but let me give you some background: Number 17, up there on Chapel Street, was rented by a known drug dealer who used it to distribute crack cocaine. In 2014, I was involved in a police raid to arrest him, but he escaped. He killed my husband, my colleagues . . .' Erika indicated Michelle, and wanted to mention Jim, but her eyes were wide and she looked like she was still trying to process it all. 'Jerome Goodman vanished,' said Erika, continuing. 'For years, I never knew how he got away until we found this passageway. I, we, just need to know if somehow someone could have dug this passage down to the canal to use as a secret back channel for moving large volumes of drugs.'

Tiger raised his eyebrows.

'Jeez. Sorry. I don't know about the whole back channel for drugs stuff. But. If you're going to start digging tunnels, you'd need to know a bit about the landscape and the type of soil. And on a practical level, you'd need to make sure you were going straight or in the right direction.'

'Okay. If you knew how to do all of that, it's feasible that a tunnel could have been dug from Chapel Street down to the canal bank without anyone knowing?'

'There would have been a huge amount of soil which needed to be got rid of. And whoever dug it used bricks and metal supports, cement . . . But if it was done over a longer period of time, then I suppose the waste soil could have been disguised as refuse, rubbish,' said Tiger. 'And this print-works has a huge amount of scrub-land. The soil, or some of it, could have been offloaded onto it.'

'And when it came to constructing this manhole drain cover – who would be the ones in charge of this canal bank, or who would not have to notice?' asked Erika. Michelle was watching this all with wide-eyed panic.

'The inland waterways association maintain all of the canal

banks in Great Britain,' said Tiger. 'Each region is either maintained by a port authority, a local council, or in some cases a charity association.'

'What about here in Rochdale?'

'You'd have to check,' said Tiger.

'Could a manhole be put in without their knowledge?'

Erika could now see that everyone was cold and feeling uncomfortable with where this was going. The canal path and the water were deserted, and it felt like everything was about to freeze.

Tiger shrugged. 'People are pretty sharp. They notice things, especially on the canal. My dad has a canal boat, and it's the kind of place where people get to know each other. It's like trainspotters. They notice stuff.'

'Maybe they didn't notice,' said Erika, feeling frustrated. Tiger didn't want to commit to an opinion. He looked like he wanted to leave. Erika turned back to Rafe. 'What do you want to do next?'

'We need to write this up. And then, of course, we will pursue this robustly,' he said. 'We need to replace this lid and retrieve our things from the house. Tiger, thank you for your help. We will need your discretion on this, er, matter.'

'You don't have to tell me twice,' said Tiger.

'What do you think?' Erika asked Michelle when they had parted company with everyone and were back at the car.

'I don't think you should have given Rafe such a hard time. He's a good officer.'

'That's all you can say? After all that. Don't you want to know more? This could be the answer we've been waiting for. For years.'

Michelle now had tears in her eyes. Angry, hot tears. 'Is it,

Erika?! It might give us more insight into what happened, but nothing is going to change the fact that your Mark, my Jim, Brad, Sal, and TJ all died 'cos no one looked close enough!'

'That's not fair. How could I have known about this?'

Michelle stared ahead and wiped her eyes. 'Do you think it will bring them back?'

'Of course not. But wouldn't you like to see Jerome Goodman behind bars?' Michelle was silent. 'Michelle! Don't you want justice?'

'Erika. Can't you see? It could be dangerous messing with this. Whoever Jerome Goodman is, he must have had help from influential people. If he built this passageway, how has it gone under the radar for so many years? You know what it's like – the council are all over everyone. If you let a tree get too big, or if you build a wall beside your house that's a few centimetres too tall, or if you don't follow planning laws, they're onto you. Do you think Jerome Goodman did this alone?' Erika shook her head, astonished at Michelle's reaction. The sound of defeat in her voice. 'I've heard rumours over the years that people high up in the police know where Goodman is.'

'Who told you that?'

'I've heard. You know how these things work. The drug trade generates billions. You don't think there are a few coppers here and there taking backhanders and bribes to let stuff keep going under our noses? Who do you think tried to plant those drugs in your car?'

'Let me get this straight. You're happy to blame me, but you're also alluding to some kind of cover-up?' Michelle shook her head, tears running down her cheeks. 'If we keep running away, it will never stop. Are you saying you know how Jerome Goodman has managed to stay under the radar and get a new identity?'

'Of course I don't.'

'Michelle, we can't give up.'

'I'm not giving up. But I know when to stop poking the wound. Pushing. You *push*, Erika. You push everyone too far! You push them away!'

'At least I try and do something.'

They sat there in the silence. Erika shaking.

Michelle wiped her eyes. 'Do you want me to drop you back at your hotel?'

Erika watched as Michelle put her keys in the ignition and started the engine. 'That's it?'

'Yeah. That's it. I've done what you asked.'

Erika looked at her former friend and knew that things were over. When they'd met the day before at the coffee shop, she'd had wild ideas about them rekindling their friendship, solving this, and moving on from all the horror. Now she knew that wouldn't happen. Michelle was comfortable keeping her head in the sand.

Erika opened the passenger door and got out.

'I'll make my own way back,' she said.

40

Tuesday, October 25, 2011

It was midnight on the stretch of the canal behind 17 Chapel Street. It had been one of those damp, gloomy afternoons when the clouds seemed to descend and draw the light out of the world. As night fell, so did the clouds, and a thick mist now hung over the water.

A longboat cut through the mist, swirling it as it moved slowly with its lights out. It came to a stop, bumping against the concrete wall on the section of the canal bank with the newly minted drain cover.

Frank and Danielle secured the longboat and stepped onto the canal path, each carrying a black holdall bag. The air was sharp and cold and smelt brackish. The path was empty, and they listened for a moment to the roar of the far-off traffic and an owl hooting before they moved to the drain cover. Frank pulled it up using a crowbar, and Danielle went first, dropping her bag inside. It seemed a long way down when she heard it hit the earth. She dropped down on top of it, feeling her ankles burn when she landed.

It was surprisingly warm inside the tunnel, the air thick and clammy. As Danielle waited in the dark, she put her hands up to the sides of the narrow tunnel, feeling the rough concrete.

Frank handed his holdall down to her – its contents were much more valuable than what she had in hers—and then he climbed inside, bracing his body so he could pull the drain cover back over them with a clang before dropping down beside her.

'You okay?' he asked.

'Yeah,' said Danielle. She switched on her torch and came face-to-face with Jerome.

'Jesus! You fucking scared me!' she cried, grabbing her chest.

'Did anyone see you?' he asked.

'No,' said Frank.

'You got the stuff?'

'Yeah.' Frank hitched the holdall carrying the fifteen kilos of cocaine over his shoulder and buckled a little under the weight.

'You've got something on your cheek,' said Danielle, holding the torch up to his face. Jerome winced as she wiped at a spot of dried blood. His face was beaded with sweat. 'Did you have trouble?'

'Nothing we couldn't handle,' said Jerome. He turned, and they followed him. The tunnel banked up steeply from the river, and they trudged in silence, sweating in the warmth. Danielle had read that in the winter months, underground tunnels and caves would leach out the heat stored over the summer. It was like the earthy floor was sweating. Danielle saw Jerome up ahead take a big step, as if he was avoiding standing in something, and she trained her torch on the ground, stopping when she saw the dark glistening patch in the soil. Frank crashed into her with the holdall, and she had to grip the walls to prevent herself from falling over.

'Jerome. Jerome!' she said, her voice echoing in the tunnel. Jerome stopped and doubled back. He saw where Danielle had the torch trained on the dark patch.

'One of them was quicker on his feet than we anticipated,' he said.

'He didn't escape, did he?' said Frank, his voice sounding low and dangerous behind her.

''Course he didn't fucking escape. This was as far as he got.'

There was a coppery tang of blood mixed in with the humidity, and Danielle felt queasy.

'Come on. Think of the bigger picture. It was dealt with. It's over, okay?' said Jerome. He reached out and put his hand on Danielle's shoulder. 'Okay?' he repeated. Danielle swallowed. Her mouth was dry.

'Yeah. Okay.'

'Let's get out of here,' said Jerome. And they carried on.

Finally, they reached the end of the tunnel, where it opened out into the wine cellar. Art, a new associate of theirs, was leaning on a spade next to a large hole in the earth floor. He was stripped to the waist and sweating, standing next to two huge piles of earth which almost reached the ceiling. Five bodies were piled up beside the hole, each tightly bound in a blue tarpaulin. Danielle was glad she couldn't see their faces, but even the blue shapes were undeniably human.

'Evening,' said Art, nodding at Danielle and Frank respectfully. Frank stopped to shake Art's hand, but Danielle merely nodded, stepped around the damp piles of earth, and followed Jerome up the steps. There was something about Art that gave her the chills.

It was a shock to go from the passage and cellar into the tiny back kitchen of 17 Chapel Street. A single bare bulb cast its harsh light over an old gas cooker and a sink filled with filthy pots and pans, and the back window was covered in black plastic. Danielle looked at the fireplace, and she thought about the five men. What had they been thinking when they filed down into the cellar? They'd been told they could leave and were going down to collect the money they were owed.

'Show me where the men slept,' said Danielle.

Jerome took her up the stairs. The two bedrooms were on opposite sides of the hall.

'You got everything you need?' he asked. 'Bleach? Bin liners.'

'And what if I haven't? You gonna run to the corner shop for me?'

'Danielle.'

'I'm not stupid. I'm always prepared.'

'I know this isn't your job description, but we can't risk hiring some cleaner with loose lips.'

'Go. I want to get this over with.'

Jerome left her on the landing, and she went into the room on the right, with three unmade single beds. A small TV sat on a table against one wall, and a bag containing each man's belongings were on the end of each bed.

She worked quickly, unzipping each bag and emptying their clothes into bin liners. She could smell the tang of the dead men's sweat on their T-shirts and the rich aroma of their hair. It wasn't entirely unpleasant, but it was mixed in with the smell of cooking fat and stale cigarette smoke. In the second bag, she found a small plastic first aid kit and feeling curious, she opened it. Inside, on top of the grubby bandage and a few yellowing plasters, were photos of a tiny baby lying swaddled on a blanket, face turned up to the camera, large blue eyes staring innocently into the camera.

Danielle had to sit down. The sorrow hit her like a gut punch, and she sobbed over the child and its father. She didn't know either of their names, but she was burdened with the knowledge that the child's father now lay dead in the basement, along with his fellow countrymen, and no one would know.

The five Polish men had spent the last six weeks at 17 Chapel Street digging and tunnelling. The job had been advertised at the Exchange, an old newsagent near Hammersmith train station in London. The Exchange's grimy front window had become an unofficial employment agency where the Polish community gathered to find work. Every morning at 8am, small white postcards with details of work available, hastily scribbled in Polish, were stuck up in the window, and the men would crowd around to be the first to call the numbers on their mobile phones and secure work.

Art's full name was Artus Szmigiel. He was in his mid-thirties, and he'd been one of the first wave of Polish workers to travel to the UK in 2004, after Poland joined the European Union. He'd recruited the five men in London, writing out the postcard himself for the window, and he'd brought them up to Rochdale in an unmarked van. The men's mobile phones had been taken. They'd been told they would get them back in two weeks when the job was finished, and they would be paid three thousand pounds.

Danielle knew otherwise. Their mobile phone SIM cards had been destroyed the day they arrived. She'd first met Art when he started working as a kitchen boy at the Swann Pub. Jerome had seen something in Art, and slowly, he brought him in on the drug operation. It was a story Art had told him that sparked the idea for the tunnel leading down from 17 Chapel Street to the canal.

Art had told Jerome about his childhood growing up in Zielona Góra, in West Poland, an area known for its wine and vineyards. Art's father had been a builder specialising in piwnica winna, or wine cellars, and taught him everything he knew about building wine cellars, big and small, and all about the tunnelling needed, the type of rock or soil which was safe to cut into, and what could be self-supporting and what might need bricks or iron to support it.

The five Polish men stayed at 17 Chapel Street while they did the job. The men didn't speak English, but they were well fed. When they weren't working, they slept and were kept under curfew, forbidden to leave the house. Their only point of contact was Art, and Jerome had chosen Art, knowing the men would trust him as a fellow Pole. He told them they were digging a drainage system.

Danielle wiped her eyes and looked down at the photo of the tiny baby. So beautiful. She thought of Clive, her husband, and of the day she got the phone call from the gasworks to tell her he'd died in a tragic accident. They'd been trying for a baby; she'd lost her first early in the pregnancy. How had she arrived at this point? Her job was to destroy all evidence that these five men existed. And that included the photo of this tiny baby. Danielle looked up at herself in the mirror on the wall. And she saw how hard she looked. Her face was drawn, and she was thin and had hard edges. This was the life she'd chosen. She was in too deep to have the luxury of thinking otherwise. She was rich and powerful. She didn't have to worry about money. Worry. That was a laugh. Her whole life was now about looking over her shoulder. How long would it be before it all came tumbling down? She repeated the thought. She was in too deep. There was no way back.

Danielle pushed her emotions to one side. And she began to clean. At 10pm, she took a break and went back downstairs to make some tea. The kitchen was hot, and steam was rising from the hole in the fireplace leading down to the cellar.

She heard a sharp crack. It was the sound of Jerome's gun firing with a silencer. The crack came again, and a moment later Frank climbed out of the fireplace, followed by Jerome.

'We got most of the earth filled in before we shot him,' said Frank, and without missing a beat added, 'Are you making tea?'

Jerome put his gun on the table. The plan had always been to shoot Art. He knew too much.

'Yeah. I'm making tea,' she said.

'How close are you to finishing up there?' asked Jerome. 'Did you get everything? There's nothing left of them?'

'No. There's nothing left of them. It's all in the black bags waiting to be burnt,' said Danielle. This wasn't entirely true. She'd kept the photo of the tiny baby with the big blue eyes, it was in her jacket pocket.

And she'd kept it to prove to herself that a part of her was still human.

41

Wednesday, December 11, 2024

'Hello, stranger,' said Erika. 'Long time no see.'

She was standing in the graveyard in Slaithwaite, the Yorkshire town where Mark was buried. It was a crisp, bright morning. The sun had just come up, casting everything in brilliant gold. A thin layer of frost covered the black marble headstone, but Erika remembered the inscription:

IN MEMORY OF
MARK FOSTER
1 AUGUST 1970 – 8 JULY 2014
LOVED AND REMEMBERED ALWAYS

The village of Slaithwaite, and the moors, covered in snow in places, rolled away from the graveyard, which sat high on the hill. Erika had spent a sleepless night in her hotel tossing and turning, and she knew she had to return to London, but before she left, she wanted to visit Mark.

Erika knelt down, cleared away the dead leaves from the

black marble stone's base, opened the carrier bag, and took out a small bunch of flowers.

'I know,' she said, looking up at his name on the headstone. 'They're from a petrol station. Sorry. And they're carnations. Not the most imaginative.' She lifted out the brown bunch of flowers in the small vase and put the fresh ones in.

Then she sat on the carrier bag and took a McDonald's Sausage & Egg McMuffin from the pocket of her jacket, unwrapped it, and took a bite.

'I thought I'd have breakfast with you. Is it against the rules to eat in a graveyard?' She chewed and swallowed before taking another bite and finishing the rest of her sandwich quickly. She wiped her mouth with the back of her hand and balled up the paper, then sat and told Mark everything about Jerome Goodman, and what she'd been doing since her last visit.

She would always love Mark, and she felt the guilt of what had happened weighing heavily on her, but life was for the living, and she had Igor and her cat, George, and her friends and a career – well, the career part was debatable right now, but she had a life in London. As she talked, the sun was obscured by a bank of grey clouds which came rolling in from the surrounding moors. And without the warm sun on her face, she felt the cold creep into her bones. She noticed a few candles flickering on the surrounding gravestones. 'Every time I think I'm close, another barrier goes up. But I'm going to get him. I made that promise, and I'm going to keep it.' Erika heard her voice, clear and strong, in the empty graveyard. She'd learned to speak English in the north, from Mark and her colleagues, and like them, she flattened her vowels, saying 'oop' rather than 'up'.

She stood up, her legs now stiff from the cold. She touched her fingers to her lips and then pressed them against the cold stone.

The weather got worse as Erika drove south, and it was a slow trip with traffic. It was almost four o'clock when she turned into her street in Blackheath. Despite the miserable weather and the fading light, there was something very bright and alive about London, many more houses and shops had Christmas lights in the windows, and it lifted her heart to be back.

George was waiting for her in the hallway when she opened the door, and Igor was making a fire in the living room.

'I didn't know you were coming back?' he said, turning with a big smile on his face. He held his arms open, and she went to him for a hug. 'Are you hungry?'

'I could eat.'

'Sit down and get warm by the fire,' he said. Igor had made chilli with rice, Erika's favourite, and she told him all about her time away.

'You've solved the case after all this time.'

'I haven't solved the case. I've made a breakthrough. I know how Jerome was getting in and out of the house. It also means there could have been much more drugs taken in and out without us knowing. The women who worked in the launderettes could have been a decoy,' said Erika.

'Do you know what happened to the women?'

Erika shook her head. 'Not exactly. I know that in the aftermath of the raid, they couldn't find them at the launderettes. They vanished into thin air.'

'What about the people who owned the launderettes?'

'They said they had no idea any of it was happening. If I remember correctly, we looked at three launderettes, and two of them were owned by an older couple and another was owned by a younger man and his wife.'

'Are they still there?'

'I don't know. I should know . . . It's more pressing that I find out who knew about this tunnel.'

Igor looked concerned. 'You're worrying me,' he said.

'Why? I've been doing this job for years. You've never said that before.'

Igor went to the log-burning stove and opened the door, chucked on another piece of wood, and closed the door with a clang. The fire instantly began to roar.

'I've been thinking about Wales. And how someone tried to plant those drugs in the car. These people are targeting you personally. If they'd found those drugs, you could have gone to prison for ten, twelve years.'

Erika nodded. 'Yes. I would have been out of everyone's way until . . . until I was long past retirement age.'

'What are you going to do?' asked Igor. 'This officer, Rafe. Do you trust him to pursue the investigation?'

'Honestly? No. I don't think he wants to go near it with a barge pole. And I don't know how long it will take for my trip up north to trickle back down to my bosses in London. If it hasn't already.'

Erika got up and grabbed her phone off the table.

Igor followed her into the hallway, where she grabbed her coat and car keys. 'Where are you going?'

'I'm going to see Commander Marsh. He owes me a big favour. One I've never explicitly called in before.'

'Sophie and Mia?'

'Yes. I love you. My phone is on, and I'll be back as soon as I can.'

42

Commander Paul Marsh lived with his wife and daughters in a large terraced house on Hilly Fields Road, a smart neighbourhood in South London. Erika pulled up outside at half six. She had timed it so that she was close enough to dinner time as not to be *too* disruptive, but close enough to know Marsh would be home. He always liked to be home for dinner. The lights were on in the living room, the curtains were open, and the TV was on. A picture-perfect Christmas tree with white lights glowed in the corner.

Erika gave the brass knocker a good hard bang. A moment later, a tall, elegant young woman with long dark hair opened the door, wearing a short tartan skirt and a sweater.

'Erika?' she said, her face breaking into a smile.

Erika was surprised at the warm welcome and confused about the identity of this beautiful young woman. 'Hello.'

'Mia, *darling*, who is it?' asked a voice from the kitchen, which Erika recognised as belonging to Marcie, Marsh's wife.

'Mia? Hi. Bloody hell, you've grown up. How old are you?'

'I knew you didn't recognise me,' she said with a laugh. 'I'm thirteen – I'll be fourteen in a few months.'

Six years ago, Mia and her twin sister, Sophie, had been abducted by Max Kirkham and Nina Hargreaves, who had targeted them specifically for being the daughters of a senior Met Police detective and demanded a ransom for their safe return. It had been Erika who'd headed the investigative team, and who'd found them and brought them safely back to Marsh and Marcie. Erika always maintained that she was doing her job, and she was, but now was the time to call in something in return from Marsh.

'Mia, who is it, darling?' said Marcie, appearing at the end of the hallway. 'Oh, Erika. Good evening.' Like Mia, Marcie was beautiful, slim, with peaches-and-cream skin and an effortless elegance. If Erika was ever pressed to describe Marcie's style, it was the type of outfit Princess Diana might wear for a photo-op in a field of live landmines, or during a visit with Mother Theresa. However, for the first time, she thought Marcie was looking older, with bags under her eyes and a hint of grey roots at her temples.

Erika closed the door behind her, and they stood in the hall for a moment before Marcie embraced her awkwardly. 'Would you like some tea?'

'I was hoping to speak to Paul, is he here?' asked Erika. She saw Mia glance at her mother.

'No,' said Marcie.

'Sophie's out at her dance lesson, but she'll be back at seven,' said Mia.

'Yes. It will be nice to see Sophie,' said Erika. 'Do you know when Paul will be home?'

Marcie put her hands on her hips and fixed Erika with a stern look. 'I thought you knew? We've separated. Paul moved out a couple of months ago. We're, unfortunately, getting a divorce.'

Mia's shoulders sagged a little.

'I'm so sorry, I didn't know,' said Erika.

'Well. Now you do.'

'Where is he living?'

'At our flat on Foxberry Road.'

'The rental flat I lived in when I first moved to London?'

'That's the one,' said Marcie. The temperature in the room had dropped.

'I'm sorry. I can't stay. I really have to speak to him.'

The cold air hit Erika when she came back out onto the street. She passed the living room window just as Marcie yanked the curtains closed. When was the last time Erika had seen Marsh? It had been last week, fleetingly, in the reception at Lewisham Row on one of his rare visits to the station. He hadn't said anything about him and Marcie separating for good. They'd had problems in the past, but this . . . this would have hit him hard.

Foxberry Road was a short drive from Hilly Fields. As Erika passed Brockley Train Station, the platform was lit up dazzlingly and crowded with commuters huddled in their coats. A train streaked out from under a footbridge, clattered past, and rushed on towards central London. She drove past a long row of terraced houses and found the flat down the far end, perched on a corner, where the road led off sharply to the right. There were no free parking spots, and she had to drive a considerable way further through the maze of roads until she could find one. It was residents' parking only, but she took a risk and pulled in. There wouldn't be any parking attendants working on this freezing Wednesday night.

Erika doubled back to Marsh's flat and was both shocked and unsurprised to see that after all these years, the street lamp on the corner was still out.

Erika had to press the intercom twice before Marsh answered and let her in, muttering a 'bloody hell' she wasn't supposed to hear before he replaced the receiver.

It was like time had stood still as she opened the communal

front door against a swish of junk mail into the small, dingy hallway. The hall light was on a timer, and it whirred softly as she climbed the narrow staircase.

When Marsh opened the front door, he wore old jeans and a sweater and looked terrible, bloated, and exhausted.

'What are you doing here?' he asked.

'Hello to you too. I just called at your house. You weren't in.'

He sighed. 'Yeah. Well. It's not my house anymore.'

'When were you going to tell me?'

'Erika. We're not friends. Not friends like that.'

'Yes we are. Or we were, until you had crazy ambitions to head up the Met Police.' Marsh chuckled dryly. 'Are you going to let me in?'

'It's a mess.'

'It was a mess when I lived here.'

He rolled his eyes and stood to one side to let her in. The hallway was lit by an overhead light with a narrow wicker shade, which gave the feeling of being in a tunnel. The first door leading off the hall was the small, stark bathroom. Next to it was a tiny bedroom with a pine double bed and the same wobbly IKEA wardrobe Erika remembered.

At the end of the hall was a combined living room and kitchen, and it was a mess of pizza boxes and dirty plates. A Netflix show about alien abduction was paused. On the table with the pizza crusts was a half-empty bottle of Bell's whisky. Erika noticed a row of empty whisky bottles on the kitchen counter.

'Do you want a drink?' he said, stumbling and putting out his hand to catch himself on the corner of the kitchen work surface.

'Go on then, a small one. I'm driving.'

He waved that statement away with his hand.

'Just put your blue lights on. It always works for me,' he said with a laugh.

'How long have you been here?'

'Today, or in total?' he asked, pouring Erika a large measure of whisky in a highball glass. He topped up his own glass, opened the freezer door, and reached in with one hand, taking out ice. 'My hands are clean,' he added, mistaking Erika's concern at his drinking for disdain at him using bare hands to pick up the ice. He closed the freezer door with his hip and came over unsteadily with the drinks. 'Did you read about that coffee shop where they found human faeces on the ice?'

'Yes, I heard they do a lovely latte,' said Erika, taking one of the glasses from him.

He chuckled. She put out her hand to help him, but he shrugged her away. 'I'm alright. I'm alright.' He sat down heavily on the small sofa next to her. 'I'm not drunk, just exhausted. Meetings all fucking week.' He held up his glass, and they clinked.

'Fucking week, eh? Are you okay?'

'I'd say, on the whole, no. I've been here for a month. It was meant to be a stopgap, but I haven't had time to shop or do my laundry, let alone find a place to live. And it suits me for right now. It's impersonal. Impersonal is perfect for right now.' He took a sip of his drink, and after a pause, he laughed.

'What?' asked Erika, sipping her whisky.

'Do you remember, when we were first on the beat, and there was that case of the university lecturer who went mad at his wife after she spilled coffee over his doctoral thesis, broke her jaw, and put her in the hospital?'

'No. And that's funny why?'

'You were still a bit shaky with your English, do you remember? When we put him in a cell, he went a bit doolally and went on a dirty protest. You wrote up the report and got "thesis" and "faeces" mixed up.' He started to chuckle.

Erika rolled her eyes. 'Okay, yes, I remember.'

Marsh laughed harder. 'You wrote that he smeared his thesis

over the walls of his cell and his wife spilled coffee where he'd been studying his . . .'

'Alright. Yes. Very funny.'

Marsh was now laughing so hard his face was red. Erika thought back to how mortifying that had been. She was glad to see him laugh, though.

He finally stopped and wiped his eyes. 'Oh dear . . . Marcie doesn't love me anymore.'

'Sorry.'

'That art class poofter and her have been dating.'

'Poofter?'

'Oh, fuck off. I can say what I bloody well want in my own bloody home.'

'Some of the younger officers working in the Met would disagree with that statement.'

He rolled his eyes and nodded. 'Mia and Sophie come and see me most days. They haven't been today. Hence the crap everywhere. I'll be fine. Pull myself together.'

'Good.' Erika saw that she'd drunk most of her whisky. She put the glass down on the table, trying to work out how to broach the next subject. 'Paul. I need your help with something.'

'You do?' he said, his interest piqued. 'You're calling me Paul, so I take it it's not work related.'

Erika took a deep breath. 'Er. Sir. I've been put on leave pending a physical exam next week.'

He frowned. 'Are you okay? You seem well.'

'Yes. It's Melanie, Superintendent Hudson. Something odd happened last week.'

And then Erika started to tell him all about finding Jerome Goodman.

43

Marsh listened sagely as Erika told him the whole story, starting with the discovery of the body of the woman in Amersham Road, the parcel locker which led them to Kieron Bagshaw, and Erika then coming face-to-face with Jerome Goodman, who she believed was living under a different identity. Erika was surprised Marsh didn't know about her pseudo suspension. Then, warmed by the second whisky, she told him about her trips to Wales and then Rochdale, and the discovery of the tunnel leading from 17 Chapel Street to the canal bank.

'Ever since I was transferred back down here to London, I've been haunted by not being able to catch Jerome Goodman, and now I feel like I'm so close. And not only that, I think I'm close to cracking the case.'

Marsh looked down at his whisky, his brow furrowed. 'I'd have to refresh my memory with the ins and outs of the case. I often think about Mark and Brad, Beamer, TJ, and Sal.' He sighed and wiped a tear from his eye. 'And I think back to us all working together – we had a lot of fun, didn't we?'

'We did.'

Marsh nodded, and took another slug of his drink.

'What exactly do you want to do? And what do you need from me?'

'We never knew how Jerome Goodman escaped that day. I was blamed for bad intelligence gathering. But if he was coming and going through a tunnel, with access to the canal, then it solves a huge part of the puzzle. It also opens up other lines of enquiry. The guy I spoke to about the drain cover leading onto the canal bank alluded to the fact that Goodman and his gang could have had help from the inside, inside local government, or even the police.' Erika took a deep breath.

'He knows this?'

'No. He was just talking about the process of local government. I need to know if someone high up is still protecting Jerome Goodman. If I can prove, on paper, that Kieron Bagshaw is Jerome Goodman, then I can arrest him. Take him off the streets. Charge him and carry on working to solve the case.'

Marsh got up and started to pace the room. It seemed like he had sobered up.

'Okay, but you're still not being specific. What do you need from me?' he snapped. Erika stared at him and he stopped pacing.

'Sorry. I'm just all worked up about this,' and then he added, more softly, 'What do you need from me?'

'I need you to get me reinstated.'

He stopped pacing and studied her. 'Will you pass your physical?'

'Of course. What's that saying you have? I'm as fit as a butcher's dog.'

Erika could see he was thinking.

'What did Melanie do when you arrested and brought in Kieron Bagshaw?'

'She went out of her way to appease his brief and have him released.'

Marsh came and sat back down. 'This is the one thing I have trouble with, being in such a senior position – there are things I just don't hear about. You know I can't override day-to-day decisions Melanie might make.'

'Yes, that's technically correct. But, come on. You're Commander Marsh.'

'Don't patronise me,' he said, snapping again. 'You come here, asking me for favours.'

'Which you owe me.'

Marsh sat back with his eyebrows raised. 'What?'

'Yeah, Paul. I don't like to bring this up, but you do. I've never tried to call in a favour for saving Sophie and Mia. But this is about my Mark, and our colleagues, and when you were with us, we all looked out for each other. So, yes, just this once I'm telling you, you owe me.' Erika sat back, shaking. Marsh stared at her. 'Right now, I'm on annual leave, which I've agreed to take. I have my physical, and I need to pass it. I'm not worried about the physical part. I'm just worried that there's going to be some funny business, and I'm going to be forced out.'

Marsh nodded.

'Okay. That won't happen. I promise.'

'And you'll see what you can do about Kieron Bagshaw. Even if you just ask around, on the QT?'

He put his hand on hers and he nodded.

'Thank you,' said Erika.

Erika left shortly afterwards and walked back to her car. Over the years, they'd shared a friendship that had been battered by work. He had been her senior officer, and she'd often gone against him, but it was Marsh who had offered her the lifeline after the Jerome Goodman case imploded and she was blamed for everything. Marsh had specifically requested that she come down to London to head up the murder investigation team. She hoped that he would come through for her again. Erika was frozen by the time she reached her car, and she was about to get in when she saw a yellow envelope stuck to her windscreen and a car clamp on her front right wheel.

'Fuck,' she shouted, kicking the wheel. It was a private company who'd clamped her car. The police couldn't do much to help her, so it would involve a trip to East Ham, bloody miles away, to pay the fine and get the clamp removed. She debated calling an Uber, but she didn't fancy that much, so she walked back to Marsh's flat to ask if she could use his car.

When Erika got to the front door, one of Marsh's neighbours, a young man, was just opening the communal front door. He smiled and nodded, and she followed him inside. The young man went to one of the flats on the ground floor and let himself in. Erika went back up the stairs to Marsh's flat, and she was about to knock on his door when she heard Marsh's voice. He sounded urgent and panicked.

'I'm telling you, she knows way more than I ever thought she would . . . I can't do that . . . Listen, Jerome. No, that's risky, beyond risky. We stick to what we agreed. I can get her out of the way.'

Erika couldn't quite believe what she was hearing, and a nasty, cold trickling feeling ran through her body.

Marsh went on: 'We've already shut down any kind of investigation into Kieron Bagshaw. You need to go asap on that passport . . . No. You're not listening to me . . . I have to talk to him. I'm leaving now.'

Erika was still in shock, but she heard footsteps and a rattle of keys being picked up. She was out in the open on the landing, on the top floor of the three-storey house. Erika ran for it, thankful the stairs were carpeted. As she turned the corner of the second-floor banister, she heard Marsh's front door open with a creak, and then he closed it, locking it with a rattle of keys.

Erika could hear Marsh's footsteps on the stairs when she reached the main door. She got it open and closed it behind her, but she knew she didn't have enough time to get down the front path before Marsh would come out behind her. There was a hedge bordering the tiny front garden and the garden of the terraced house next door. Erika moved swiftly and pushed herself into the hedge, crouching in the shadows between the branches. A barbed spike scratched her cheek and the back of her neck, but she stayed still, holding her breath.

Marsh emerged from the front door. Erika could see his outline through the branches. He had his phone clamped to his ear and was swaying on his feet. 'No, of course this isn't my fucking phone . . . Shut up. *Now.* You get yourself back . . .' Marsh stopped level with the place in the hedge where Erika was crouching, and fumbled with his keys. He dropped them on the ground and stooped to pick them up, tucking the phone under his chin. He was so close that Erika could smell the alcohol fumes on his breath. 'I'll deal with Erika Foster. She still trusts me after all these years. No. It's too much of a risk to do things your way. I have plenty of levers to pull.'

Marsh managed to pick up his keys, and went off unsteadily to his car.

44

Erika didn't know how long she crouched in stunned silence, the sharp branches digging into the flesh of her face and neck, but the next thing she knew, she was walking back to her car, numb with shock. She stared at the clamp around her wheel, like some kind of sea creature hanging on to the rubber of the tyre.

Erika found her toolkit in the boot and set to work removing the clamp. The puzzle of doing it focused her mind. Snow started to fall. When she finally got the clamp off, she placed it in the boot. Inside the car, she switched on the heater, and sat for a moment as the snowflakes swirled. Her car sat in a pool of darkness where the streetlight was out and the windows were unlit. Erika watched as the snowflakes began to settle and obscure the windscreen. It was as if she'd never moved on from ten years ago.

Who was Marsh talking to on the phone?

He was *Commander* Marsh.

Four ranks below the head of the Met Police.

He couldn't have been talking to Jerome Goodman, could he?

But he said the name 'Jerome.'

Moss had returned home late, and Celia had left some food on a plate for her to reheat. Jake and Celia sat with her in the kitchen as she ate, telling her about their days. She was just unwinding with a glass of wine when she saw her phone vibrate and the screen light up.

'If that's work,' said Celia with a warning tone.

'It's Erika,' said Moss, glancing at the screen.

'Bloody hell. Just because she never sleeps or has any time off, doesn't mean you shouldn't,' said Celia.

'She's pretty good about not phoning after hours,' said Moss, and ignoring Celia's angry face, she picked up the call. 'Hey.'

'Sorry to call you at home. Can you talk?'

'Yes, I can,' said Moss, getting up from the kitchen table.

'I'm outside the front door.'

Moss glanced at Celia, who was now clearing away the plates. Jake was looking between them as if he were watching a tennis match. Moss got up, closed the kitchen door behind her, and went down the hall to the front door. When she opened it, she was shocked to see Erika with a bloody scratch down her right cheek.

'What happened to your face?'

'Oh,' said Erika, putting her hand on her cheek. 'I didn't notice.'

'Come inside.'

Celia was coming out of the kitchen and looked ready to burst when she saw Erika. In the light of the hall, the cut looked worse, quite deep, and even though the blood was dry, it was still oozing.

'What happened to you?' asked Celia, her tone changing to concern. 'Come through to the kitchen.'

'Run-in with a hawthorn bush,' said Erika, glancing at Moss. She allowed Celia to clean up her face, and then Moss took Erika into the sitting room, where the wood-burner was glowing. She closed the door.

'It was more than a run-in with a hawthorn bush. What is it?'

'I went to visit Marsh this evening.'

'He did this?'

'What? No. No.'

Erika went on to tell her everything that had happened. When she'd finished, Moss sat in silence for a moment.

'Is there any way you misheard this, misconstrued this?' she said finally.

'I've been replaying it in my head. No.'

'Could it have been another Jerome he was calling?'

'Come off it. I don't know of any other Jerome who is connected to me in that way.'

'Do you seriously think he could be involved with Jerome Goodman?' asked Moss.

Erika could hear a little doubt in her voice, and she regretted showing up on Moss's doorstep unannounced with a bloodied cheek.

'I know what I heard on the phone. And when he'd gone, so much started to fall into place. After Mark and my colleagues died, I was investigated, and I almost lost my job through gross negligence. It was Marsh who pushed to have me transferred here, at Lewisham Row, working on the Andrea Douglas Brown case. Why would he do that?'

Erika clutched the piece of tissue Celia had given her to her cheek and looked up at Moss.

'You've known him since you were both coppers on the beat. That's what you always said?'

'Yeah. But we both know I should never have been put on such a high-profile case, after what had happened to me.'

'You solved it. Your track record speaks for itself.'

'But what if Marsh wasn't handing me an olive branch? What if he brought me down to London to keep a closer eye on me?

And until now I've been a good little detective. I've been given plenty of big cases that I've been able to solve – cases that ruffled no feathers . . .'

This last sentence hung in the air for a moment. A log shifted in the stove, and the fire started to crackle.

'Well. Apart from Annabelle Wallis,' said Moss. Their most recent murder investigation involved Annabelle Wallis, a sex worker who had murdered rich and influential men in London. She'd also kept Polaroids of many more affluent and influential men in compromising poses.

'We had every piece of evidence we could to nail her. Then she pled guilty, and evidence went missing, witnesses disappeared, and the trial collapsed,' said Erika. 'What's that got to do with Jerome Goodman?'

'I'm just saying, that was another case that ruffled feathers.'

Erika and Moss were quiet, and they listened to the sound of the fire crackling.

'You know that both me and Isaac were visited by the same man, no badge or rank. He didn't even give us his name, but he was obviously high up in something government related and he warned us off the Annabelle Wallis case,' said Erika.

'Do you want a drink? I feel like I could do with a drink,' said Moss, moving to the sideboard. She took out a bottle of whisky and glasses and poured them each a stiff drink.

'Thanks,' said Erika, taking a glass. Moss could see her hand was shaking. 'What if this is just one of those dark nights where I start finding coincidences where there are none?'

'Are you doubting what you heard from Marsh?'

'No.' Erika took a drink. 'For so many years I've felt like I've always managed to have the upper hand, and to be the kind of police officer I want to be. But what if all along I've just been Marsh's little plaything?' She looked at Moss and felt sudden angst.

'What?' asked Moss.

'Oh, Jesus,' said Erika. She put her glass down on the table. 'I'm going to tell you something else, but please, try not to judge me.'

'Okay,' said Moss, feeling worried about what the next revelation might be.

'When I first came to the UK and started to train at Hendon, I dated Marsh.'

'Yes, I know that, but I always thought that was almost like a late-teenage thing. Couple of dates at the pub and a bit of snogging?'

Erika laughed. 'It was. But there have been a couple of times since, when he made a pass at me and I didn't exactly fight him off.'

'Okay.'

'Not that we had sex. God no, but there's always been this tension of Marsh being attracted to me. And now I'm thinking it was the other way around, for him to keep me close. I do want to add it only happened when him and Marcie were separated. When I was just with him, I got that same vibe, that he was drunk and he wanted something to happen. But then I heard him on the phone, and the way he talked about me, it was like a different person. He sounded like he hated me.'

Moss got up and went to her. 'Erika. Listen. You're a bloody good detective. We need to take the emotion out of this. I know this has been hard for you with Jerome Goodman reappearing, the link to Mark and your colleagues. What I need you to do is take a step back.'

Erika looked up at her. 'And do what?'

'I need to think. And we need more proof.'

'What about round-the-clock surveillance on Marsh?'

Moss sat back in shock. 'That's not a decision to be taken lightly.'

'I know. And right now it would have to be your decision.' It felt odd that Erika was having to ask Moss to authorise this.

'How can I justify surveillance on Marsh?'

'Jerome Goodman murdered my husband and colleagues, and I believe that the commander of the Met Police is assisting him as a fugitive.'

Moss sighed and looked at her empty glass.

'Fuck. When you put it like that . . .' She got up and started to pace the carpet. 'We keep this to a bare minimum of who knows. Just trusted officers, until we have additional evidence. Not even Melanie should know.'

'What should I do?'

'Continue to pretend that you're on leave. I might need you to meet with Marsh again, but I'll keep you posted.'

'Kate . . . this is a huge risk,' said Erika.

'Doing the right thing always carries a risk.'

'Thank you.'

'I'm just doing my job,' replied Moss. She held her glass in both hands, not wanting Erika to see that they were shaking.

45

When Erika crawled into bed late that night, Igor was already asleep. She didn't wake him, but she lay in the dark staring at the ceiling, listening to his soft breathing, and trying to comprehend the night's turn of events.

When she woke up on Thursday morning, Igor had gone to work, but Tom was downstairs. He was wearing his workout gear and making scrambled eggs.

'Morning,' he said. 'I was about to come and knock on your door.'

Erika felt bleary-eyed after the whisky she'd drunk the evening before and the sleepless night she'd just had. 'Morning.'

Tom gave the eggs a stir and looked up at her. 'We're going running, aren't we?' he said.

Erika remembered a conversation she'd had with Igor about her upcoming physical and that Tom had offered to go running with her.

'Of course. Sorry. Yes.'

'I'm making us a healthy breakfast so we can fuel up before we run?'

Erika could see Tom looking at her, and suspected she

seemed far from capable of running up the stairs, let alone around the heath.

'I'm fine. If the eggs can include strong coffee, then great.'

'What happened to your cheek?'

She touched her hand to it. 'I was looking for evidence in a bush – evidence in one of those recycling boxes – and I scratched my cheek.'

'You should put some antiseptic on it.'

'Yeah, I should,' said Erika, peering at her curved reflection in the silver kettle. The scrape was a little red, but it looked much better now that Celia had cleaned the blood off her face.

After some food, Erika felt better and went upstairs to dig out a tracksuit and some trainers. She checked her phone and saw there was nothing from Moss. If she didn't have a scratch on her face, she might have thought she had imagined everything that happened the previous night. She was just sitting on the edge of the bed, lacing up her shoes, when her phone rang.

It was Marsh.

'Erika, you almost ready?' Tom called up from the bottom of the stairs.

'Just a minute,' she shouted. Seeing his name on the caller ID made her feel sick, but she had to pick it up. If she was going to keep up the pretence, she might as well start now.

'Morning,' he said cheerily, as if nothing had happened. It chilled Erika. She swallowed and felt the eggs she'd just eaten shift in her belly.

'Morning,' she said, matching his bonhomie and seeing her reflection in the wardrobe mirror, perched on the bed with a manic smile. 'You'll never believe this, I'm off for a run!'

'Good Lord,' he said, laughing. 'Good luck. Okay. I just wanted to circle back on our conversation last night. I've called in a few favours, and I've got your physical bumped up to tomorrow morning – 8am sharp.'

Erika hesitated. Feeling shocked.

'A thank-you would be nice.'

'Sorry. Thank you. I didn't expect . . .'

'And between you, me, and the garden wall, there should be no problems, barring any serious health issues you might have. Do you have any serious health issues?'

It felt strange to be talking like this with him. He sounded so normal and, well, kind. If he was faking it, he was bloody good.

'No. I don't. Beyond the usual aches and pains of people our age.'

He chuckled. 'Speak for yourself. Be on time. Be nice. And we should have you back on duty by Friday lunchtime.' There was something chillingly authentic about his teasing, hectoring tone, and for a split-second, Erika doubted overhearing him on the phone the previous night.

'Thanks, Paul. I better go.'

'Happy running,' he said, and the line went dead.

It was a crisp, bright morning, and it felt good to run with Tom. Erika was surprised at her stamina, and she managed it to the Whitefield Mount on the common, lagging behind Tom only a little. They sat on the bench, catching their breath as they looked out over the sleepy, cloud-covered views of London and Greenwich Park.

'You ran for fifteen minutes, which is good,' said Tom. Erika nodded and took a long drink of water. 'Is everything okay?'

'Why do you ask?' said Erika, a little more sharply than she intended.

'Dad's worried about you.'

'What did he tell you?'

'He told me someone tried to plant drugs in your car. He said it's to do with this drug dealer from . . . a past case.'

'The drug dealer who killed my husband and colleagues.'

'Yeah.'

'Do you remember when I used to drive you to school, and you were excited to hear about the murder cases I've solved?'

He smiled and nodded. 'I know a bit more about the world now.'

'Hopefully not too much more?'

'No. I didn't mean it like that. I just know a little more how the world works.'

Erika nodded. 'I have to take a physical. Which will decide my future in my job. And I need to get back to work, so I can solve this. I don't want you or your dad to worry. I work with excellent people. And I don't think Jerome Goodman, that's his name, wants to come anywhere near me. He's the one running away from me.'

Tom frowned and Erika didn't know if he believed her. She wasn't sure if she believed it herself.

'You shouldn't have trouble with the physical. You're fit for someone of your age.'

Erika laughed. 'Cheeky.'

'You know what I mean. You're not overweight. Dad says you're the toughest person he knows.'

'Sounds romantic. "I love her because she's a tough old bird."'

Tom looked out across the common, and the wind caught in his long curly hair. 'Do you still enjoy it? Your job.'

Erika was momentarily thrown by the question. It was something she never thought about, the enjoyment. Did she enjoy it? She wasn't sure. It was now akin to a calling.

'I enjoy the feeling when I've caught a bad guy,' she said.

She sighed and scanned the park. A few people were running in the distance, but they were alone on the bench.

'Just make sure you enjoy your life, too. Dad understands what you do, but he wants to enjoy life with you. Christmas. Next year. Holidays. He wants to be with you. Forever. He wants to grow . . .'

'Cabbages?'

Tom smiled. 'I'm being serious. He wants to grow old with you.'

Erika stared out at the heath. Growing old physically didn't terrify her. It was having to retire. And she *would* have to retire at some point. This wasn't a job where you could go on and on.

And then she thought about the previous day's events. Marsh had been someone she thought she knew. They'd been police officers since Erika trained back in her early twenties. She felt she was approaching the end of her career knowing less than when she started.

'I love your dad very much,' said Erika, hoping this would close down the conversation. 'Now how about I race you back?'

When they got home, Tom returned to his flat around the corner to change. Erika had a quick shower, and then her phone rang. It was Moss.

'You've got a back garden, haven't you?' asked Moss.

'Yes,' said Erika, drying her hair and pulling on some clean clothes.

'The one with the blue or green shed?'

'It's brown.'

Erika went to the window, and saw Moss and Peterson standing at the back gate next to the shed.

Moss waved. 'Do you have a hacksaw I can borrow?' she said into her phone. 'I've got this tree in my back garden that needs chopping down.'

'Come inside, out of the cold,' said Erika. She knew it must be something serious if they were sneaking in through the back gate.

46

Erika put on the kettle. Moss and Peterson sat down at the kitchen table.

'I take it Moss filled you in on what happened?' said Erika.

'Yeah. You okay?' he asked.

'No. But I feel better that you two know.'

'I've always thought there was something slimy about Marsh.'

'If he's done this to me, I don't want to think about what else he's done.'

'I also told McGorry and Crane. They're doing surveillance on Marsh,' said Moss.

'You've authorised it. Already?'

'Yeah. If he contacted Jerome Goodman as soon as you left last night and Goodman put pressure on him, who knows what Marsh is going to do. He might meet him.'

Erika came to join them at the table. 'But this is surveillance on a Met Police commander,' she said. 'This is risky for everyone to be involved with.'

'We all believe you and think you're worth the risk,' said Peterson.

'Have you heard from Marsh since last night?' asked Moss.

'He just phoned. He's had my physical moved to 8am tomorrow morning. And he's said I don't have to worry about passing it.' Moss and Peterson exchanged a look. 'What do you think I should do?' The kettle boiled and she got up to make their drinks. She was trying to keep her voice even.

'You need to go to that physical. If we have you back at work, then this gets easier,' said Moss.

'Why do you think he's helping you?' asked Peterson.

'I asked him, and I told him he owed me,' said Erika. 'And he's kept me close for all these years. Maybe he wants to keep tabs on me. Maybe it's easier for me to have an accident if I'm on duty.'

They were silent for a moment.

'That's why we need to be vigilant. The rest of the team at Lewisham Row, support workers, Melanie – especially Melanie – have no idea about this surveillance,' said Moss.

Sergeant Crane had been sitting in his car on Foxberry Road since 6am, a few doors down from Marsh's flat. It was a busy street, and a steady stream of people had passed on their way to the train station.

At 9.30am, he saw Marsh emerge from his front door wearing jeans, a thick blue jacket, and a flat cap.

'He's on the move,' he said into the tiny radio on his lapel. He expected Marsh to walk past where he was parked on his way to the train station, but he started off in the other direction. Crane waited a moment and got out of his car.

He locked it and hurried after Marsh, adjusting the baseball cap he had pulled down on his head. Marsh walked along Brockley High Street, and then he took a left down the steps of Crofton Park Station.

'Looks like he's getting on the train,' said Crane as he followed. The platform at the bottom wasn't very busy, so Crane went to the newsstand and bought a paper and some chocolate. He subtly scanned the handful of commuters waiting on the platform for the next train.

'Which way is he headed?' asked McGorry through the radio.

Crane glanced up. 'The next train is to Blackfriars Station in central London. Hang on, he's meeting someone.'

Crane saw Marsh go up to a tall, dark-haired young woman and kiss her on the cheek. 'He's meeting a girl. They're chatting.' There was a clatter and whoosh as the train appeared further up the tracks and then pulled level with the platform. 'They're getting on.'

'I'm still circling Brockley Road and Honor Oak Park in my car,' said McGorry.

Crane watched as Marsh and the young woman got onto the train, and he boarded the same carriage a door later, sitting further down. It was risky. Crane had worked at Lewisham Row while Marsh was superintendent and then chief super, but he now had a thick beard and a baseball cap pulled down on his head. Marsh sat with his back to him, and Crane had a clear view of the young woman during the journey.

McGorry was in a panic. Doing surveillance in the city was difficult enough. Usually, an operation like this had more than two officers, and it didn't involve following one of the Met's most senior officers. He parked his car close to Brockley Train Station and was just in time to catch one of the regular trains to Charing Cross, which ran every five minutes.

'Crane. I'm headed to Charing Cross. If you keep me in the loop, I can jump on the tube and be in Blackfriars a few minutes after you arrive,' said McGorry.

Crane's train seemed to reach Blackfriars very fast, and he almost lost Marsh and the young woman when they got off at the platform. They headed for the Underground, and Crane followed them down the steps to the Circle Line. He just made it onto a packed tube train going westbound. Two stops later, Marsh and the young woman got off at Embankment, and they walked up towards Charing Cross.

'McGorry, it's busy,' said Crane. 'We're on Charing Cross Road.' He was now on the other side of a crowd of people at a pedestrian crossing.

'My train's stuck just outside London Bridge Station,' said McGorry. 'We've been sitting here for five minutes.'

There were so many people crowded at the crossing, giving Crane good cover.

'I think I can keep following them,' he said. 'It's so busy, and they're deep in conversation.' The lights turned red, and everyone crossed. Crane's phone pinged with a couple of photo messages. He glanced down and saw a screenshot of two Facebook profiles, one for Mia Marsh and the other for Sophie Marsh.

'Okay. Yeah. It's his daughter Mia, jeez she's grown up fast,' said Crane. He followed Marsh and Mia as they passed St Martin's Lane and then walked up to Leicester Square, taking a right at Piccadilly Circus onto Regent Street. It was crowded with people doing their Christmas shopping and Crane struggled to keep them in sight. They took a left onto Vigo Street, and immediately, the crowds thinned. Marsh glanced back, and Crane thought he'd been rumbled, but Marsh was only checking the road so they could cross and go into the Starbucks further down on the right.

'My train's coming into Charing Cross,' said McGorry.

'They're going into the Starbucks on Vigo Street.'

Crane felt exposed and wished there were more of them on the surveillance team. Further down from the Starbucks, there was a small juice bar, and he went inside and ordered a drink.

McGorry hurried up from Charing Cross, and he was just turning into Regent Street when Crane told him over the radio that Marsh and Mia were leaving the Starbucks and heading back to Regent Street.

McGorry picked up the pace and almost blew his cover, running right into Marsh and Mia as they emerged back onto Regent Street. Luckily, a motorbike with a roaring engine zipped past, taking their attention with it.

'Have you got them?' asked Crane.

'Yes,' said McGorry, falling back and slowing his pace. 'They're headed towards Oxford Circus.'

Halfway up Regent Street, Marsh and Mia stopped outside the Apple Store, where another young girl was waiting.

'Okay, looks like Mia is going off shopping with a friend,' said McGorry as he passed the huge glass front entrance. He saw the two girls walking into the store, deep in conversation. Marsh carried on up Regent Street. Just before the next traffic lights, he took an abrupt turn and went into one of the many nondescript doors. McGorry followed and a moment later heard the click of the door locking.

'Crap, he's just gone inside number 132.' He looked up at the tall building. It seemed to loom over him against the grey sky. He heard footsteps behind him, and a DHL courier carrying a small package walked up to the door and buzzed himself in. McGorry followed.

Inside 132 was a small lobby that led directly onto a staircase. No lift. McGorry peered up and saw the iron balustrade winding away up many floors. He followed the DHL courier at a pace, trying to work out where Marsh had gone. He could hear two sets of footsteps above. He passed five landings with closed doors with signs for solicitors, lawyers, and unmarked doors which could have a more sinister purpose. If he ran into Marsh, there was a danger he would be recognised. McGorry rummaged in his bag and found an old face mask from the pandemic and quickly slipped it on. He also pulled down his cap a little. On the sixth floor, the staircase opened out into a long thin landing where there were hundreds of tiny PO Boxes on the wall, each with a little gold number and a keyhole, and piles of junk mail on top of the boxes. Marsh was in the middle and had a box open for number 236, and the DHL courier was knocking on a door at the end of the landing. It was opened by a woman who was eating a sandwich and had a phone under her chin.

McGorry quickly had to think what to do. He grabbed a pile of letters and started to flick through, as if looking for something. Marsh had his flat cap pulled down and McGorry saw him take a white envelope from his inside pocket and place it in the box. He locked it with the key and walked past McGorry without paying him much attention.

'Crane?' said McGorry in a low voice, when Marsh had started back down the stairs. 'You there?'

'I'm in a coffee shop on the other side of the street,' said Crane, his voice muffled slightly by the loud voices around him.

'Marsh is on his way back down the stairs.'

47

McGorry glanced around at the ceiling in the small space. He couldn't see any cameras. The door opened to the small office, and the DHL courier came out holding a piece of paper. He closed the door and went down the stairs. McGorry was left alone in silence. He felt around in his bag, where he kept a set of skeleton keys for picking locks.

'Okay. Marsh is just coming out,' said Crane's voice in his ear. 'Shit. He's coming towards me. He's coming into the coffee shop.'

'Keep your head down, and be thankful you didn't take your wife's advice and shave off that beard.'

Crane laughed.

'He's gone to the counter. I think he's getting a takeaway. I'll stay on him.'

'He put a white envelope in a safety deposit box,' said McGorry. 'What do you think?'

'This is unofficial surveillance. Do we have strong enough evidence to get a warrant, based on what you've seen?'

McGorry considered his options. He didn't know how much longer he would be alone by the PO Boxes.

'I'm going to take a look.'

Keeping his gloves on and glancing around, McGorry took out a pick, holding it like a key. He started to pick the lock on box 236.

'Marsh is waiting for his coffee, and you've got another courier on his way up,' said Crane's voice in his ear.

McGorry felt the lock yield, and he got the door open of box 236 just as the courier rounded the stairs. He walked past McGorry and knocked on the door. This time, when the woman emerged from the office to let the courier in, she noticed McGorry.

'You alright there?' she asked.

'Sí, gracias, sank you,' said McGorry, affecting a Spanish accent. This seemed to do the trick. At the sound of a foreign accent, she lost interest and went back inside the office with the courier. When the door clicked shut, McGorry leaned down to peer inside the box and took out the white envelope. There was nothing else inside.

'How you doing?' asked Crane's voice in his ear. The envelope wasn't sealed, and the flap had been tucked under.

'I'm in.'

'There's a guy who just entered the building downstairs. Looks dodgy to me.'

McGorry heard footsteps on the stairs below. He untucked the flap of the white envelope. Inside was a piece of paper. The footsteps were louder, and the man was now on the landing below. McGorry unfolded the paper, took a picture of the blue handwritten note with his phone, folded it back up, slipped it into the envelope, and then quickly bundled it all back into the box. He just got the box locked and closed as the man rounded the corner and came onto the landing.

Moss was still at Erika's house when her phone rang. It was McGorry.

'I'm here with Erika and Peterson, and you're on speakerphone,' said Moss, answering.

'We followed Marsh to a PO Box on Regent Street. He left an envelope inside one of the boxes. I'm just emailing a photo over now,' he said. Erika grabbed her laptop and opened it, pushing it across the table to Moss.

'You broke into the PO Box?' asked Moss.

'Yeah.'

They were silent as Moss logged into her email.

'I'm in my email. I've got it,' said Moss clicking on the image link. The photo opened, showing McGorry's hand holding a piece of paper. Written in block capitals in blue ink was:

MR ETHAN ROBERT KERSHAW
DATE OF BIRTH: 16.02.1979
(2 passport photos signature on back £8,000)

'And you're sure you saw Marsh put this note in the box?' Erika asked.

'Yes,' said McGorry.

'Is this his handwriting?' Peterson asked Erika. She peered at it. She couldn't be sure.

'I don't know.'

'There's something else,' said McGorry. 'I'm sending a couple more photos. When I was inside, Crane was watching the building from the street when he saw a suspicious-looking man enter. He grabbed a photo of him. This man then came up to the deposit boxes and opened number 236, and he took out the white envelope with the note that Marsh had put in.' McGorry's email appeared in Moss's inbox.

'Did he see you?'

'No, I had cover; a courier and a woman who worked there were also by the PO Boxes, but I clearly saw him open box number 236, take out the envelope, and leave. Crane photographed him again as he was coming out of the building.'

'I'm just opening the attachment,' said Moss.

'Fuck,' said Erika.

'What?' asked Peterson.

'I recognise him.'

'Who is he?' asked McGorry.

Erika stared at the photo of the man. He now had short blond hair, slightly greying at the edges, and his face was fuller, as she would expect. It was ten years since she last saw him.

'It's Frank Hobbs. He was an associate of Jerome Goodman. He was one of the people we had under surveillance.'

'Are you positive?' asked Peterson as Erika zoomed in on the photo. He wore pale-blue jeans, white trainers, and a black bomber jacket.

'We need to get this photo run through the system subtly,' she said.

'Where did Marsh go afterwards?' Peterson asked McGorry.

'Back to his office.'

'What about this guy, Frank?' asked Erika. McGorry hesitated for a moment.

'I'm sorry, it's just Crane and me, and we lost him. He got into an Uber on Marble Arch.'

'Stay on Marsh,' said Moss. 'And good work.'

'Thanks, boss.'

When she came off the phone, they studied the handwritten note some more. Erika was trying to wrap her head around the enormity of it all.

'It's a passport. Marsh is arranging a counterfeit passport for Jerome Goodman,' she said. Peterson whistled.

'He's willing to risk his entire career for eight grand?'

Erika shook her head.

'They must have something on him. Or this isn't the first passport he's brokered.'

'If it is a passport,' said Moss.

'What else would it be?' asked Erika, looking back at the note. 'I just can't believe the fucking balls of it all. Here they are in broad daylight on Regent Street. Marsh and Frank fucking Hobbs.'

'And it's Marsh. One of our own is involved,' finished Moss.

'We need to find out what identity Frank Hobbs is living under,' said Erika, looking back at the photos of Frank Hobbs exiting the building on Regent Street.

'I've got a mate who works in immigration,' said Peterson. 'I can get the name Ethan Kershaw checked out. And I'll send him the photo of this Frank Hobbs and ask him to run it through the RFR.'

Erika knew the Retrospective Facial Recognition database would run the photo against any suspects who were on wanted lists or of interest to the police.

'We also need to keep our eyes on Marsh,' she said. 'And we need surveillance on those PO Boxes.'

48

It seemed to take an age for the next morning to come around for Erika's police physical exam. It was Friday the thirteenth, which on top of everything else, didn't bode well.

She reported to Guy's and St Thomas's Hospital just before eight. It seemed that someone had smoothed the process, because she was ushered into the private wing of the hospital, and it took just over an hour for her to have the physical exam, which tested her heart rate, breathing, and reflexes.

A nurse showed Erika into a conference room afterwards, and she was surprised to see Marsh waiting for her with two police officers she didn't recognise.

'Good morning, Erika. I hope everything has been as painless as possible,' said Marsh, greeting her with a hug.

'Yes. It's been fine,' said Erika, having to force herself not to tense up and to be upbeat and happy to see him.

'Good. Good. This is Superintendent Liz Robson and Superintendent Tim Morgan,' he said, introducing the officers. Erika shook hands with them and took the seat they offered at the head of the table.

'Right, Erika,' said Liz, perching a pair of glasses on her nose and peering at her test results. 'I just want to reassure you that this is a safe space. We're not here to judge you or to make you feel awkward. We just want the best outcome so you can feel comfortable continuing your career in the Met Police.'

Erika couldn't help but watch Marsh as Liz said this. He was flicking through the results. Little did Liz know that her safe space contained a Met Police commander who was working directly with some very dangerous criminals.

The process wasn't as awful as Erika had expected. In fact, it disturbed her to experience such a whitewash – even if, for once, she was the beneficiary. They asked her some basic questions: Did she feel stress at work? Did she feel supported by her senior officer? Marsh had obviously briefed them beforehand, and there was no pressure for her to take early retirement. They did ask about her PTSD after the events of ten years earlier, but her answer that she sought help when needed seemed to be enough.

'That was much smoother going than I thought,' said Erika when she got into the lift with Marsh after the meeting.

'I told you I'd be able to help,' he said, looking up at her with a sly glance.

'Thank you.'

It was warm in the lift, but Erika felt a shiver move across her shoulders.

'Liz Robson will inform Melanie of the results of your medical right away, and recommend that you're fit to continue service, effective immediately.'

'You already know what Liz is going to say?'

Marsh raised an eyebrow.

'Liz is a good egg.'

The lift doors hadn't closed, and Erika was standing by the bank of buttons. He leaned over and pressed the button for the ground floor. She could smell the alcohol on his breath, both stale and fresh, and wondered how much he was drinking every day, and whether anyone was brave enough to tell him. And then she thought about the conversation she'd overheard, and the surveillance drop-off with Frank Hobbs. She could feel the subtext in the air. She was uncomfortable and scared. Did Marsh feel it too? Or was he too numbed by alcohol to notice? Erika thought what she would normally do. Normally she would have mentioned the drinking – his drinking the other night and now smelling of alcohol in the day. She crossed to the other side of the lift and Marsh perched on the guardrail that ran all the way around the inside at waist height. His suit jacket was open, and she could see his shirt was crumpled and a little grubby. There was some kind of food stain on the crotch of his trousers – she hoped it was a food stain, at least.

'What are you thinking?' he said.

'What am I thinking? Jesus, Paul, are we teenagers in a relationship?'

Even though her comment had irritated him, she could see they were on safer, well-trod ground.

'I just meant, are you pleased?'

''Course I'm pleased.'

'And it's Friday the thirteenth!' he quipped.

'Yeah, I thought the same thing.'

The lift slowed, and the doors opened with a soft clang. They got out, passing a group of nurses and a porter with an empty bed. Marsh's phone rang when they reached the lobby, and he pulled out his phone.

'I've got to take this, I'll see you,' he said, swooping in to peck her on the cheek. She tried not to recoil when his dry lips touched her cheek, and she got a stronger whiff of the stale alcohol on his breath, and with that, he quickly vanished down the stairs to the underground car park.

Erika took the train back to Lewisham Row and went straight upstairs.

'Erika. Hello. You've been cleared for service,' said Melanie when they were sitting in her office. She looked across the desk at Erika, unable to hide the look of shock on her face.

'You sound surprised?'

'No.'

'Did you think I'd fail?'

'No. Of course not. I just know that you've had problems.'

'Have I?' Erika cocked her head. This was all very odd. Melanie was acting as if she had been sure Erika would fail the physical.

'You are officially on leave until next Friday,' she said, sifting through the printouts in her folder.

'No, I'm not.' Melanie looked up. 'You advised me to take annual leave until my physical. It was moved up to today, so I'll return to the murder investigation team immediately. The doctor, Superintendent Liz Robson, and Superintendent Tim Morgan all cleared me for immediate return to work.'

'Moss has just taken over your caseload. She should be up to speed.'

'Good. Moss can brief me.' Melanie's brow creased again, and Erika was convinced she saw a flash of fear cross her face, but it quickly passed. 'I hope I'm returning to work with your full support? I know that I can sometimes be a pain in the neck.'

'Is there anything else you want to share with me before you go back to work?' asked Melanie.

'No. But thank you for asking.'

'Very good. Welcome back.'

Erika left the office, not knowing whose side Melanie was on.

49

Erika hesitated at the door to the incident room and could see the team working away through the windows running along the corridor.

When she opened the door, Moss was by the printers, and she unexpectedly broke into a round of applause. The rest of the team followed suit, and Erika felt a lump in her throat.

'Okay, okay, so you've heard you're stuck with me again,' said Erika.

'Great to have you back, boss,' said Moss, patting her on the back. McGorry and Crane came over and gave her a high five, and Peterson came over with a takeaway cup of coffee.

'We got an extra one on the coffee run,' he said.

'It's good to see you back, ma'am,' said a tall young woman with a shock of short blood-red hair and glasses, who was on her way to the whiteboards across the back of the room.

'Who's that?' Erika quietly asked Moss.

'Frieda North. New support worker. Bloody good she is, too. And another young guy, Ryan Waters, also very good.' Erika followed Moss's gaze to a young man with bleached-blond curly hair and nose rings, and he had two considerable rings in each ear. He was talking on the phone and scribbling on a pad. 'Just remember appearances can be deceiving.' He nodded at Moss and waved.

Erika scanned the room and saw that their numbers were depleted. In past cases, she'd had more support workers and police officers, but this investigation was going to spread them thin.

'Where are we with you-know-who?' Erika asked. Moss went over to Crane sitting at his desk, which, as usual, was piled high with folders.

'Afternoon, boss,' he said.

'I didn't get the chance to tell you what good work you did with the surveillance yesterday, and you too, McGorry,' said Erika.

'I just wish we hadn't lost this Frank guy,' said Crane.

'But we got the handwritten note,' said McGorry.

'We've had an official request for surveillance approved,' said Moss, putting her hand on Crane's shoulder. 'And we've just had our video cameras installed with a secure internet connection in number 132 Regent Street. We've got one on the inside of the main entrance, and an angle of the PO Boxes from above the admin office door facing the stairs. We also got permission to put a pinhole camera inside box 236.'

Crane pulled up a screen with the three video feeds on it.

'How did you get this approved?' asked Erika.

'I cited money laundering in connection to another murder case,' said Moss. 'No mention of Marsh.'

'What about the people who work at the PO Box?' asked Erika.

'The building is part of The Crown Estate, and the company it's rented to is part of a global office space rental company, Faron.'

'I've heard of them.'

'Yes. All legit. The office manager is aware that surveillance cameras have been placed inside, but she doesn't know exactly why. It seems like we're not the first police team to request surveillance,' said Moss.

'And the company who administrates these safety deposit boxes? Anything else?'

'The box numbered 236 is rented out by a company called 2squareFormations L-t-d. They paid in cash for two years back in April of this year. 2squareFormations L-t-d is, in turn, connected to another three L-t-d's with the name of an elderly lady, aged ninety, in Newcastle, who is currently in a nursing home. It's going to be hard to track down who actually owns it and if this woman's name has been used fraudulently,' said Moss.

'Okay. How long has surveillance been running?' asked Erika.

'We've had the surveillance up and running since eight this morning.'

'What about the photo of Frank Hobbs?'

'A match came back from the Retrospective Facial Recognition database. As far as official records go, Frank's name is Victor Gill. Age forty-two.'

'Does he have a record?'

'No record. Full passport and driving licence. Registered at an address in Essex.'

'What happened to Frank Hobbs?'

'Last known address is in Rochdale in—'

'Let me guess: 2014?'

'Yeah. Since then he's fallen off the radar. No financials, socials, no vehicle registration.'

Erika took the printout from Peterson with all the details. 'Can you also check out Danielle Lang? Find out where her last known address is?'

'Whoa, boss. We've got something happening here,' said Crane, who still had the 132 Regent Street PO Box video feeds on his screen. He leaned forward and lowered his voice. 'Frank

Hobbs. Or Victor Gill, as he's going by, has just entered the building.'

Crane pulled a screenshot from the live feed and dropped it onto his desktop.

'We don't have live video of the stairs?' said Erika.

'No.'

Crane opened the screenshot. It showed Frank wearing the same jeans-and-jacket combo as the previous visit, entering the front entrance. His coat collar was turned up, but he wasn't wearing a hat or shades.

'He's confident no one's watching,' said Moss.

'Or confident that he's untouchable,' added Erika.

'Okay, here he is coming up to the PO Boxes,' said Crane. No one else was in the lobby, and Frank went straight to box 236. The third blank video feed with the view inside the box suddenly flooded with light as Frank opened the door.

'It's like he's looking right at us,' said Erika with a shudder, as the camera focus adjusted, and they were treated to a perfect close-up of his face staring at them. On the other screen showing the view of the boxes, Frank took a thick brown envelope from his pocket and placed it inside the box. The camera feed went black when he closed the door. He locked the box and then walked back to the stairs down.

'Okay,' said Moss. 'We have an officer on surveillance on the other side of the street above the vacant shop. When Frank is clear, we'll look at what he put inside the box.'

'We need to be careful in case of another tight window between the drop-off and the pickup,' said Erika. 'Have we got Marsh under surveillance?'

'Yes, we followed him from his flat on Foxberry Road to the hospital, where he met with you, then we picked him up again, leaving the hospital, and he went to his office at New Scotland Yard. As far as we know, he's still there, but let me check,' said Moss, moving off to her phone.

'Frank is now clear of the building,' confirmed Crane, who was talking to the surveillance officers on the radio.

'Do we have anyone on him?' asked Erika.

'Yes.'

'Good. See where he goes,' said Erika. Moss returned from her desk.

'Marsh is still at Scotland Yard. He hasn't left the building by any entrance,' she said.

'Okay, this is our officer going inside to check what Frank just put in box 236,' said Crane, tapping his laptop screen with his pen.

They watched as a plain clothes officer in his twenties, dressed in jeans and a T-shirt with a beanie cap, entered the PO Box lobby, which was still empty. He opened box 236, and they saw his face close-up as he took out the envelope.

'It's cash. A stack of fifties, quite a few thousand,' he said, moving to the corner table for people to open their packages. 'And two passport photos. Signed on the backs in blue ink.' They saw him quickly photograph the envelope and the photos, and then flick through the fifty-pound notes. He placed the envelope back in the box and locked it.

A moment later, the photos he'd taken came through to Crane's computer. When Crane opened the image with the two passport photos, Jerome Goodman's face stared back at them.

And the back of each photo was signed: Ethan Kershaw.

50

Erika, Moss, and Peterson came upstairs to Erika's office on the fourth floor to discuss what to do next.

'We could drop the bomb on the passport office,' said Peterson. 'We have a name which we can directly link to Marsh and Jerome Goodman, or Kieron Bagshaw. We could find out if a passport is about to be printed, produced. We could get Marsh, too.'

Erika shook her head.

'No. I don't want to do that yet. We have surveillance in place. We should see what happens next. If Marsh collects the cash we have a stronger case.'

'And Marsh could lead us directly to Jerome Goodman,' said Moss. 'I bet it feels good?'

'What?'

'This validates what you've been saying. We always believed you, didn't we?' Peterson nodded in agreement. 'But this has it justified. Even if no one wants to believe that Jerome Goodman is Kieron Bagshaw, they have to now question why Kieron Bagshaw is having a fake passport made for him, which was potentially arranged by a commander in the Met Police. And we have Frank Hobbs involved, also with a different ID.'

'It still doesn't feel good,' said Erika. 'And there has to be a point where I share what's happening with Melanie.' There was a knock at the door. 'Yeah.'

McGorry poked his head around the door. 'Sorry to butt in. Marsh just left his office at New Scotland Yard and boarded a district line train going northbound.'

'He's on the move again,' said Erika, feeling a jolt of fear and adrenaline. When they returned to the incident room, Crane had all the surveillance images up on his computer screen.

'Marsh just got off the northern line and is headed up to Regent Street.'

The police officer covertly following Marsh had a small camera mounted on the front of his jacket, and they saw how crowded Regent Street was in the late afternoon. The air had a dusky blue quality, and the Christmas decorations were switched on, forming a canopy of glittering light above.

Erika wasn't one for biting her fingernails, but she felt like she could start. Why else would Marsh leave his office in the middle of the afternoon and travel to Regent Street? On foot? She looked over at Peterson and Moss. The rest of the team in the incident room had taken note, and all was quiet.

'Okay, he's just passed Vigo Street,' said the police officer in pursuit, his voice now playing through Crane's computer. His video showed a crowd of people on the pavement waiting to cross, and his view of Marsh was momentarily blocked by a woman carrying bulging Selfridges shopping bags.

'I have him in sight, preparing to take over,' said another officer. A second body cam video feed came up on the screen, this time taken from the opposite side of Regent Street, facing the PO Box storage at number 132. 'He's going inside.'

'Paul. What the hell are you doing?' said Erika quietly, but

Moss heard and looked over with similar concern. Marsh entered the front door of 132.

'Do we have enough people in place to keep up with him?' asked Erika.

'Yeah,' said Crane. 'We've got four officers circling the area on foot and another in a car.'

'If we arrest him, we need to be prepared for Marsh saying he's acting on an official basis,' said Peterson, turning to Erika.

'That's absurd. Marsh wouldn't be involved in operational surveillance at his rank. And on his own?' she said. Marsh had been a beat officer for only a few years before he started to rise the ranks. He was now purely a police officer in a senior managerial capacity. The last time he'd been a beat officer on the street was way back in 1994. But Peterson was right. If they confronted him without proper evidence, he could easily say that he was working in his capacity as a police officer.

They watched as Marsh went to the PO Box and opened it with his key. The camera inside the box clearly showed his face as he took out the envelope with the cash and passport photos, tucked it into his jacket, and then closed it. They watched as he turned and left.

'He's coming back down the stairs,' said Crane to the two officers outside the building. The officer outside across the street picked up surveillance again. 'He could be headed back to the tube.' They watched as Marsh walked back up Regent Street the way he came. It was now almost dark, and as the shop windows swam past, the coloured lights spilled out onto the wet pavements.

The next half an hour passed in silence, as they watched Marsh get on the tube and retrace his journey back to his office.

The officer following him peeled off and stopped just short of the building's entrance.

'I don't like the fact we've got Met Police officers doing covert surveillance on the New Scotland Yard building,' said Erika, as everyone dispersed back to their desks. 'We need to keep watching.'

Frieda came over to Erika with a folder. 'Excuse me, boss. You requested information on a woman called Danielle Lang?'

'Yes.'

'There's very little after 2014, no credit score, financials, or addresses. I did manage to find something dating back to 2004, which wasn't in the system. I had to do some digging online.'

'Thanks,' said Erika, taking the folder. She returned to her desk, cleared some space, and sat down. It was a small clipping from the *Cardiff Herald*, a local paper:

The suspected ringleader of a Cardiff-based gang involved in a mobile phone insurance scam has vanished. Hugh Walters of Cliff Place, Cardiff, was believed to be the mastermind behind the scam, which tricked over 16,000 mobile phone users into purchasing non-existent insurance policies. Police raided Secure Phone's premises on David Street last Monday, after a tip-off, but the offices were empty and Walters had disappeared.

Cardiff Police also arrested three suspects in conjunction with working at Secure Phone, Jerome Goodman, Frank Hobbs, and Danielle Lang, but they were all released without charge, stating that they were unaware the insurance policies being sold were counterfeit.

At a separate hearing, a confiscation order was made in respect of Hugh Walters, totalling £673,980. As we go to press, the location of Walters is unknown.

'Frieda,' said Erika. 'Is there anything else about this insurance scam case in our system?'

Frieda came back over to Erika's desk. 'No. Nothing since 2004. I've included the details there.' Erika flicked past the photocopy of the news clipping and saw a summary of the case dating back to 2004. 'The case remains unsolved. Hugh Walters vanished, and he was the only person who anything could have been pinned on. The £673,980 has never been recovered.'

Erika scanned the details and sighed.

'This sounds like another vanishing act. The police interviewed several young women who had been working at Secure Phone, but none of them had employment contracts. Everything was in Hugh Walters's name. Frieda, can you see if you can find out where this Detective Inspector Michael Saunders is now?'

'Yes, of course.'

Erika heard Crane swearing loudly at the next desk, and he slammed down his fist.

'What is it?' asked Erika, noting that this was out of character for Crane.

'Our surveillance officer just lost Frank Hobbs. He thinks Frank realised he's being followed. Frank led him up to Camden, ducked inside the covered market, and vanished in the crowds.'

'Shit,' said Erika. The covered market in Camden was like a rabbit warren and, on a Friday, would be packed with people. 'Well, let's just keep our eyes peeled. It's all we can do.'

51

It had been a freezing, sleepless night for Erika. Igor was perpetually working, so, again, they were like ships in the night. He was in bed asleep when she arrived home just after midnight, and he was gone when Erika woke at 6.30am.

Just before nine, Erika was pulling into the car park at Lewisham Row when a call came through on her mobile phone. It was Crane.

'Where are you?' he asked.

'Station car park. Why?'

'Okay. I'm in the incident room. Marsh is on the move. He arrived at his office just after eight, but he just left again. He's headed in the other direction, away from the centre of London.'

Peterson pulled up beside Erika in the car park, and she told him what was happening as they hurried inside the station.

'The last update I had was at six thirty this morning,' said Erika as they rushed through the reception area and buzzed into the main part of the station. 'He arrived back at his flat on Foxberry Road at 10pm last night. He received no visitors, no calls apart from his wife, Marcie.' They were now hurrying down the corridor, and Peterson held the door open for them when they reached the stairs. Erika had read the transcript of Marsh and Marcie's conversation. They were moving towards divorce, and they had spoken on the phone about a meeting with their divorce lawyer later that week.

'Do we think that he already has the passport with him?' asked Peterson as they took the stairs two at a time.

'He spent the rest of yesterday at his office. He could have used internal post, or a courier that we wouldn't have known about. Think of how much mail goes in and out of the New Scotland Yard building every day,' said Erika. When they arrived in the incident room, Moss was already there, along with Crane, Frieda, and Ryan, who were huddled around Crane's desk. Erika looked around at the faces when they turned. They looked stressed. 'Where is he?'

'McGorry is part of a team of four officers on the surveillance,' said Crane. And then into his radio, he said, 'McGorry, I've got you on conference in the incident room.'

'Morning, John. I don't have a visual on you?' asked Erika.

'I've been having problems with my body cam,' he said, his voice crackling through the radio. 'Do you have a visual on the other officers?'

'Yes,' said Erika, looking at the screen, which showed four different views of a road she recognised as Shooters Hill on the A205. One of the officers was on foot, the second on a bike, and the third in his car, parked in a lay-by.

'Could he be heading to Woolwich ferry?' asked Frieda.

'Why would he take the ferry?' said Erika. The blank screen with McGorry's body cam video feed came to life, and they saw he was following Marsh's blue Jaguar through the traffic passing the industrial estate.

'John. You know I don't like the fact we have one of our own under investigation. I've known Marsh personally for many years, and we need to tread very carefully on this.'

'You know what else is in Woolwich,' said Peterson to Erika.

She nodded. Paul Gadd operated his import-export business out of Woolwich docks – the legitimate side they knew of.

'He's taken a turn-off towards the docks,' said McGorry. 'I'm following.'

They watched on the screen as Marsh's car was followed down a slip road past the Woolwich ferry entrance.

'I'm going to park up in the ferry car park,' said McGorry, and they saw him turn off and go through the gates to the ferry terminal. 'Detective Cooper is taking over.'

Detective Cooper was dressed as a GLS courier on a motorbike. He accelerated past the ferry terminal entrance and drew close to Marsh's Jaguar as it headed down a road of lockups and empty wastelands running alongside the Thames, which looked grey and bleak on this cold morning.

Marsh indicated as he approached a set of iron gates and went inside, suddenly pulling off the road.

'Shit. I've got to keep going,' said Detective Cooper as he sped past the gates, then turned to give them a view of Marsh driving up towards a tall white building at the end of a yard.

'Who else do we have?' asked Crane.

'Detective Allie Khan,' said a young woman. She'd been circling in a car, and the view of her camera was from the other direction. She was in the passenger seat, and the car pulled up a few feet from the iron gates, and she got out.

'Hang on, what's she going to do?' asked Erika.

'She's dressed as a Royal Mail postwoman,' said Crane.

'Do you want me to go in or just to go past?' asked Allie.

Crane turned to look at Erika. From Allie's body cam, she could see that she was now almost at the gates.

'She should go inside, follow Marsh inside. She's got some dummy post or junk mail?'

Crane nodded. 'Follow him inside if you can,' he said into the radio. The view of Marsh's Jaguar drew closer through her body cam.

'What do you want me to do if I see him hand something over?' she asked. Despite the cold morning, Erika could feel sweat on her forehead. This was all happening too fast. She needed coffee and some time to think.

Erika made a sign for Crane to mute the radio for a moment.

'Listen. If we have Marsh handing what we think is a passport over to someone, do we make an arrest?' she said, looking at Moss and Peterson.

'We have Marsh on camera collecting eight grand, and passport photos with the signatures.'

'And if Marsh hands a passport to a third party in Woolwich Dockyard, it's not exactly legit,' said Moss.

'But that's different to being illegal. Do we have uniform officers in the area?' asked Erika to Crane.

'They're a mile away.'

Erika looked back at the screen. Allie was now level with Marsh's Jaguar, which was parked next to the building's high wall. Allie stopped, and as she leaned over, they saw she was carrying a postbag on her shoulder. She turned her body cam to show two empty parking spaces and another car, a Mercedes, parked at the end. Erika saw Frieda note down the number plate, then move to her computer to look it up.

Erika knew she had to make a decision. She leaned forward and unmuted the microphone. 'Allie. If you see a package or any cash changing hands, then you are cleared to make an arrest.'

'Backup is a quarter of a mile away,' said Crane. 'Should be there in less than thirty seconds.'

'Just to be clear, ma'am, if the target is seen exchanging or handing over a package, or cash, I'm authorised to make an arrest?' Erika could hear the fear in Allie's voice.

'You will first say that you suspect an offence, and you are using stop and search powers, because you suspect him of carrying objects, made or adapted, to commit theft, fraud, or criminal damage. We suspect he has a counterfeit passport in the name of Ethan Kershaw. If he does, you have authorisation to arrest Commander Marsh under the 2010 Identity Documents Act. It is an offence to have possession or control over false identity documents,' said Erika, hoping that she had her facts straight. Arresting such a senior officer had to be done by the book or there could be serious repercussions.

'The black Mercedes in the parking space belongs to a Paul Gadd, registered at an address in Knightsbridge, central London,' said Frieda.

Erika nodded, trying to keep her cool. 'That's what we expected.'

'Allie, you now have uniform backup outside,' said Crane.

Allie was walking towards the door to the white building, which was ajar. She went inside and into a small office piled high with papers on a desk and filing cabinets along the wall. Marsh was in the process of handing over a small padded envelope to a large man sitting behind the desk. Erika recognised the man, Paul Gadd, who had a shock of greying strawberry-blond hair. He looked a little older than he had on that night in 2016 when he'd thrown her out of his mother's wake in The Crown pub in Sydenham.

Both men looked up at Allie, and for a moment, they seemed to think she was a regular postwoman – until four other uniformed police officers burst into the office behind her.

Allie took the padded envelope from Marsh, explaining why, and everyone in the incident room seemed to hold their breath as she tore it open. She pulled out a passport, and when she opened it, she held it up to her body cam.

A collective whoop went up in the incident room. The passport was in the name of Ethan Kershaw, but Jerome Goodman's photo was staring back at them.

'Commander Paul Marsh, you are under arrest for possessing and controlling false identity documents. You do not have to say anything, but anything you do say could be used in court.'

'What?' spluttered Marsh, turning bright red.

Paul Gadd put up his hands and stepped away from his desk as two of the police officers moved in to handcuff Marsh.

'I just want to say for the record,' said Paul Gadd, spotting Allie's body cam and staring straight into the lens. 'That I don't know this man, and I have no knowledge of this document, or what he was about to hand me.'

52

An hour later, Marsh arrived at Lewisham Road Station. Erika, Moss, and Peterson went down to the custody suite. Waller was on duty, and he was sweating and pale, waiting at the desk with another officer.

'Is it true? Commander Marsh is being brought in?' he said.

'Yes,' said Erika. She could see the razor rash on his face and the back of his head were more prominent than usual.

'What do I do about him having legal representation?'

'You offer it to him like any other suspect,' said Peterson.

'And which cell should I put him in?' He glanced back at the door leading to the custody cells. There was a strong smell of disinfectant, and Erika could see the edge of the cleaners' cart.

'You need to treat him like any other suspect,' said Moss. They heard Marsh's loud voice before he entered the doors.

'I am not a risk. I do not need to be cuffed!' Marsh entered, red-faced, escorted by Detective Allie Khan and two of the uniformed officers who had arrived as backup. He stopped when he saw Erika waiting with Moss and Peterson by the desk.

'What are you doing here?' he spat at Erika. Allie put her hand on his arm, indicating that he should approach the desk.

'Get off me,' he snapped, shrugging her hand away. 'I'm not an idiot.'

'You've been read your rights . . . sir?' asked Erika.

'Yes!'

She looked over at Waller and nodded. He jerked into action, even more sweaty and nervous.

'Right, hello, sir. Welcome,' he said, as if Marsh was checking into a nice hotel. He placed the sensor pad on the desk with a shaking hand. 'If you could just give me your fingerprints, here.' Marsh was released from his handcuffs.

'I'm not saying anything until I have my legal representation,' he said haughtily to Erika.

'Naturally.'

There was an almost comical moment where Marsh wasn't placing his fingers properly on the sensitive touchpad, and Waller had to take Marsh's hand and help him.

'There we are, that's the right one,' said Waller.

'If you could please empty out your pockets,' said Erika, placing a plastic tub on the counter.

'Does it really take two DIs and a DCI to process me?' asked Marsh. He was now sweating as much as Waller, and Erika could tell he was scared.

'When it's a very senior officer, yes,' said Moss. 'We want to make sure it's all done by the book.' Peterson nodded along with her. Erika was impressed by how Moss and Peterson stood with her as support.

Allie had some paperwork ready and handed it over to Waller. And then Waller asked Marsh to remove his shoes.

'Thanks, Christian. Can you keep me posted?' said Erika to Waller. He nodded.

'I want to speak to my wife,' said Marsh. He was now in his socks, and he'd handed over his belt and tie. 'Erika, can you call Marcie?'

'No. You have to call Marcie,' said Erika. Marsh suddenly

went pale, as the enormity of his situation clearly began to sink in. Erika, Moss, and Peterson left the custody suite and started back up the stairs. Erika checked her watch. It was coming up to midday, and the start of the twenty-four hours they had to hold Marsh in custody.

Ryan and Frieda met them at the door of the incident room.

'I've got bank statements and phone records for Marsh,' said Ryan. 'Do you want hard copies or it sent to your email?'

'Both. Thank you.'

'Is there anything else you need?'

'Yes. Can you please let Superintendent Hudson know I'm on the way up to her office.'

Melanie was in a meeting, and her secretary didn't want to bother her. It was only when Erika explained that Commander Marsh had just been arrested that the secretary pulled her out of the meeting.

'You can't be serious,' said Melanie, when Erika was in her office and had explained the situation. She looked panicked.

'Deadly serious. We've had Marsh under surveillance for the past few days.'

Her eyes were now wide. Alert. She gripped the edge of her desk. 'What gave you probable cause to put surveillance on a Met Police commander?'

Erika explained the phone call she'd overheard between Marsh and Jerome Goodman.

'Where is Marsh?' asked Melanie.

'Downstairs in the custody suite. He's probably now in a cell,' said Erika, trying not to enjoy this too much.

'Jesus, Erika. And you can show proof at every point in this chain of events that you've been acting by the book?'

'Just about. Yes.'

'Just about?'

'After overhearing the phone call, I had unofficial surveillance placed on Marsh, which we conducted within the team.'

'But you were on leave at the time?'

'Moss had unofficial surveillance placed on Marsh. During this surveillance we followed him to a PO Box office on Regent Street. One of my officers did access the PO Box without a warrant, but we felt that due to the phone call I had overheard, we had probable cause.' Melanie looked at her and raised an eyebrow. 'Nothing was damaged.'

'But you didn't have a warrant?'

'No. When we opened the box, we found Marsh had left an envelope with a written note with the name Ethan Kershaw, a request for two passport photos, and eight thousand pounds in cash. A few minutes later, Frank Hobbs, a named associate of Jerome Goodman, collected the money. Based on this information, we applied for an official warrant so that the PO Box office would cooperate. This is when we set up surveillance cameras in the PO Box office and the box itself.'

'If the box was accessed by us illegally, Marsh dropping off this first envelope with the note would be inadmissible in court.'

Erika almost rolled her eyes at Melanie's use of 'accessed by us illegally'.

'But the note was collected by Frank Hobbs. And two days later Frank Hobbs placed eight thousand in cash and two passport photos, signed with the name Ethan Kershaw, in the PO Box. The two passport photos were of Kieron Bagshaw, the man who I believe is Jerome Goodman. Marsh collected the cash and the passport photos. And today we followed him down to Woolwich, where he attempted to deliver a passport in the name of Ethan Kershaw to Paul Gadd. Who as you know is a rather suspect figure in import-export in South East London. Our surveillance officer recorded the exchange on her body cam, and she arrested him under the 2010 Identity Documents Act for possession or control over false identity documents.'

Melanie was now white as a sheet.

'If it's a legitimate passport, then it's not a false identity document.'

'Yes, but if, as you took great pains to tell me, Kieron Bagshaw's identity is completely legal, we now have Marsh procuring a fake passport using Kieron Bagshaw's photo.'

Melanie looked slightly less grey. 'Okay.' Erika didn't know if she was mistaken, but she could see relief in Melanie's eyes.

'Are you going to take me seriously now when I say I believe Kieron Bagshaw is Jerome Goodman?'

Melanie sighed and put up her hand. 'Let's just deal with one thing at a time.'

Erika could feel her frustration boiling over. 'Please. Listen to me. This whole situation concerns Jerome Goodman and his associates. I identified Frank Hobbs collecting Marsh's instructions and depositing the cash to pay for the passport. However, Frank Hobbs is currently using a passport with the name Victor Gill. I'm still looking into the whereabouts of Danielle Lang . . . There's something going on here with identities being recycled. I believe that Jerome Goodman, Kieron Bagshaw, is planning to leave the country. We've stopped him being able to leave using this new passport. I would like you to authorise me to put out a warrant for Kieron Bagshaw's arrest.'

Melanie crossed her arms and Erika could see she was thinking.

'Okay. Put out a warrant for Kieron Bagshaw's arrest for the murder of Mark and your colleagues. Make a splash.'

Erika felt an enormous sense of relief, and it took a moment to compose herself. 'Thank you.'

'I need to be kept up to date at all times on this case. And I'm going to get a crisis team in place, and prepare a statement about Marsh for the press.'

'No. No press. Not yet.'

'Erika. He's a senior Met Police officer. We might not have a choice in the matter.'

53

Erika could barely hide her elation as her team prepared the arrest warrant to go out for Kieron Bagshaw and Jerome Goodman.

She sat down to write it out herself, a rough draft by hand, and as her pen moved across the paper and she wrote down Mark's name and the names of her four colleagues, she felt like she was moving closer to catching Jerome Goodman and locking him up, after having it snatched away from her the previous week.

She handed the handwritten statement to Frieda, with the photo of Jerome Goodman from the Ethan Kershaw passport.

'I want this to go out on the police database. I also want this out on socials and for you to draft a press release. All channels,' she said.

'Yes, ma'am.'

Erika sat on the edge of the desk and took a drink of water. This was the calm before the storm. The press release would hit social media instantly. She hoped the London press would go hard on it and then prompt the nationals to take notice. Peterson came over to Erika with a fresh cup of coffee.

'You okay?' he asked.

'Thank you. Yes,' she said, taking a deep breath.

'David Doxworth, Marsh's brief, has just arrived. Marsh has also refused to give Waller access to his mobile phone.'

There was a cold silence in the lift as Erika travelled down to the custody suite with David Doxworth. He was definitely dressed like an expensive solicitor, but he was very young and handsome. Erika wondered whether he was cutthroat enough for the fight Marsh was about to have.

As they approached the desk, Waller was just in the process of dipping a chocolate digestive biscuit into a big mug of tea. When he saw them all arrive, his soggy biscuit broke off and plopped into his cup, splashing tea over his paperwork.

'This is David Doxworth, Commander Marsh's solicitor,' said Erika.

'Yes, hello,' said Waller, flustered. He wiped his hand and offered it up.

David shook it unenthusiastically. 'I would like to speak to my client,' he said.

'Of course.'

'I need a quick word, also,' said Erika. Waller led them into the corridor with the cells. It had been modernised a few months previously. The floor was resurfaced and the cell doors were all new, but it hadn't wiped away the lingering smell of sweat, sick, and disinfectant. Waller went to the first door on the right and tapped on it.

'Er, hello, sir?' He opened the hatch. 'Sorry to interrupt.' Marsh was sitting on the bare bench in his trousers, shirt, and socks. His face was pale and eyes were red. 'Your solicitor is here.' Waller opened the door, and David went inside first.

'Hello, Paul,' he said, shaking hands.

'What are you doing here?' Marsh said when he saw Erika.

'Paul. Your solicitor will give you all of the details, but we've just been granted an S49 Ripa notice, an S49 Regulation of Investigatory Powers Act 2000 notice,' she said.

'I know what it is!'

'You have to give us the passcode for your phone.'

Marsh sat back on the bench, and a look of fury crossed his face. He looked up at David.

'Can I speak to you in private? Without her?'

'Yes, we will speak in private,' said David. 'But Paul, I have to tell you. If you don't give them access, you automatically will be in line for a two-year minimum prison sentence.'

Paul was now so grey he looked like he was going to throw up.

'Let me speak to him,' said David. Erika and Waller left the cell, and he closed the door.

'This is a bad business, a bad business,' said Waller.

It was just after eight when Erika arrived home and opened the front door. The windows were dark, and Igor was working a night shift. Even George was out, probably catching mice.

She had wanted to start questioning Marsh in the late afternoon, but his solicitor had insisted that Marsh get some sleep and they would start early the next morning.

Erika's sense of unease was growing. The clock was ticking. The arrest warrant for Kieron Bagshaw was now live, and it had been shared with the media and social media channels, but nothing seemed to be happening.

Erika wasn't hungry, but she went through to the kitchen and opened a can of baked beans. Her phone rang and she scrabbled in her pockets to find it, but she didn't recognise the caller ID number.

'Oh, hello, is this Erika Foster?' said a rather posh, cultured voice.

'Yes.'

'I'm Devlin Newberry-Jones. I'm calling regarding a query from Michelle Black? About the Rochdale Canal? I'm from the Canal and River Trust.'

Erika quickly put her phone on speaker so she could carry on making some food. 'Thank you for calling. Yes, I have a query about a drain.'

'Right. You would need to be more specific.'

'Of course,' said Erika as she opened the bread bin and pulled out a loaf of white speckled with mould. 'Do you work for the council?'

She stepped on the pedal bin and dropped it in, noting that another loaf was lying inside and now looking as furry as a green cushion.

'Good Lord, no. It's quite an unusual quirk in that we are *technically* a charity, but the Canal and River Trust does vital work for public infrastructure. We manage the canals around the Rochdale area through donations and an army of volunteers.'

'Could I please speak in confidence?'

'Yes . . .' he said, his voice sounding wary.

Erika sat down at the kitchen table, and opened her laptop.

'This is regarding a sensitive police investigation, so I'm asking for your confidence and not the other way around. I'm just checking the exact area,' she said, pulling up Chapel Street on Google Maps. 'I'm trying to trace a drain cover, or manhole, on the section of the canal path in Rochdale directly behind the disused print-works on the corner of Chapel Street. This manhole, drainage lid, I've seen it, but there are no records for it on any municipal databases.' Erika got up and went to the microwave, where she'd forgotten about her beans, which were now a boiled mush in the bowl. Devlin was quiet for a long moment. At this stage she didn't want to mention anything about the secret tunnel. 'Hello. Are you still there?'

'Yes. I've just come through to my office, where I keep the maps for our canals. You say you're a policewoman?'

'Yes. I'm a detective chief inspector with the Met Police. I was with the Greater Manchester Police for over ten years before I moved down south . . . for my sins.'

Erika dumped the lump of burnt beans in the bin on top of the mouldy bread, and heard some clanking, clicking sounds on the other end of the phone, as if he were looking through filing cabinets. Then she heard crisp paper unfolding.

'I have that section here. The whole part of the canal bank there comes under our authority. The canals are rather odd in that the council runs the municipal aspect, drainage, and utilities, but we are responsible for maintaining the canal banks and the canal paths. That section behind Chapel Street and the old Markers Print-Works, that's what it was called, does come under our remit. So any work done building a drainage channel, fixing a wall, or repaving the canal path would have been done by us and not the council.'

Erika sat at the table again and stared at the map.

'This drain cover would have been put there around 2010, maybe 2011. I don't suppose you have records going back that far?' she asked, thinking that things at Devlin's end sounded very much paper-based.

'I do have records on my computer. I also perform the role of treasurer to the society, so I have to deal with the finances and keep records going back at least fifteen years. I tell you what, shall I have a look and then call you back?'

'Yes. I'll be here.'

He hung up and Erika sat in the silence for a moment, trying to shake off the paranoia that he wouldn't call back. An urgent hammering on the front door made her jump. She got up, hurried into the hall, and saw a dark outline through the coloured glass.

'Who is it?'

'It's Marcie,' said a choked-up voice.

'*Shit,*' Erika said under her breath.

'I hope you're going to let me in. The number of times you've banged on my door at dinner time!'

54

Erika reluctantly opened the door. Marcie looked dreadful, and quite unlike herself, with red eyes, no make-up, and her hair in disarray.

'Why have you arrested Paul? What's going on?' she said. Erika could hear the fear in her voice.

'Come inside. It's cold.'

Marcie followed her into the living room. She looked around accusingly, and her eyes lingered on the Christmas tree with its glowing lights. 'Where's your boyfriend?'

'He's at work.'

She went to the living room door and peered out. 'What about his son? Doesn't he live with you?'

'He lives around the corner in Igor's flat. He's studying at uni.'

Marcie turned back to Erika. 'Are you his mother now?'

It was such an odd question, delivered in an accusing tone.

'No.'

Marcie sank down into the armchair. 'Our solicitor told me you arrested Paul this morning, and you're going to keep him in custody.' Erika nodded. 'For how long? Don't you have to release him after twenty-four hours?'

'Yes.' Erika didn't tell her that they had already applied to have this extended to thirty-six hours. 'Can I get you some water or tea?'

'Have you got anything stronger?'

'Did you drive here?'

'Yes.'

'Then no.'

Erika went to the kitchen and returned with two cans of cold Coke. She thought they could both do with the sugar. Marcie took the can and held it in her lap.

'What did he do?'

Erika was surprised she didn't know. If she did, she was a good actress. 'What has Paul told you?'

'Nothing, Erika. *Nothing!* I spoke to him on the phone for two minutes. He kept saying that it's some kind of error that will be straightened out, which is utter bullshit, isn't it? I know it. Tell me.'

'For the past few days, we've had Paul under police surveillance. We arrested him for brokering a deal involving a counterfeit passport we believe he'd procured for a known criminal.'

She stared at Erika. *'Procured?'*

'Yes. We believe the criminal is involved in drugs, one of a group of people involved in drugs. We also believe that the man who Paul procured a passport for was Jerome Goodman, the man responsible for the death of my husband, Mark, and the four colleagues I worked with.'

Marcie closed her eyes as if to centre herself. 'He did it for money?'

'Why do you say that?'

Marcie opened her mouth to say something and then

hesitated. 'I've filed for divorce. The house is in my name. We haven't been talking to each other, really, for years.'

'We've pulled all of his financial information, and my team is going through it. But the amount of money he took, it wasn't a lot, in the grand scheme of things. Is there anything you want to tell me? Do you know anything?'

'I don't know anything, Erika.' She opened her can of Coke and took a shaky-handed sip.

'Does the name Jerome Goodman, or Kieron Bagshaw, mean anything to you?' Marcie shook her head. 'Has Paul been acting odd lately?'

'I came to you to answer my questions, Erika. As a friend.'

'Are we friends, Marcie?'

She sipped at her drink thoughtfully. 'My girls like you. I think they have a bond with you . . . *They* think they have a bond with you. When you came round the other day, it was the first time Mia had seen you in years. I'll always be grateful to you, you know? For bringing them back safe.'

Erika nodded. 'I was just doing my job.'

'I know. But your job was saving my girls. So I always will be in your debt,' she snapped. 'I think Paul has always held a candle for you.'

Erika shook her head. 'He's just known me the longest. I've known him since he was a skinny, zit-faced police trainee who used to crap himself when we were on the beat. I think the further you move up the ranks in the police, the less real people you have around you.'

'Do you think *you're* real?' she said with a snarl. Erika ignored the question and opened her can of Coke. 'Why would he be involved with the man who killed your husband and colleagues?'

'That's what I'm trying to find out.'

They both let that hang in the air.

'He's going to go to prison for a long time, isn't he?'

'I don't know, Marcie.'

'I'm the dumb wife who knows nothing. And you know what? After a while, I stopped being interested in what he was up to.'

'Up to?'

'I don't mean anything illegal. I don't know if he had another woman. Or even a man – no, I don't mean that. It's just that he seems to keep so much of himself hidden. I stopped going to those bloody awful police dinners and rotary club fucking bollocks a few years ago.'

'Has Paul ever mentioned a colleague that works at the passport office?'

'No.'

'Anyone in immigration?'

'Oh, for God's sake, Erika. No. I just told you, I don't know. We don't talk about anything.'

'Does he confide in the girls? When he was under surveillance, he went into Charing Cross with Mia.'

'Don't you dare,' said Marcie, suddenly turning on her with a manicured finger. 'You leave the girls out of this. He would never talk to them about something illegal.'

'Okay. Is there anything odd that stands out about his behaviour over the past few months, or even further back?' asked Erika.

Marcie closed her eyes and lay back in the armchair. Her once-clear complexion looked grey and lined under the lights. She blew out her cheeks. 'The only odd thing I can think of is that he said he was going to church.' She opened her eyes and rolled them.

'His parents used to go to church, I think?' said Erika. 'I know he had a confirmation when he was a kid.'

'But he never went to church as an adult. But it was one

Wednesday afternoon, and I'd been shopping at the Sainsbury's in New Cross when I saw him just walking along the pavement. Seeing him there in the middle of the day was so odd. I wound down the window and asked him what he was doing. That's when he said he'd been to church.'

Erika hesitated at the mention of this. 'New Cross?'

'Yeah. That's what I said, near Sainsbury's.'

'Which church?'

Marcie shrugged.

'The one near there? I don't know. He said he'd been to mass, and he'd lit a candle for his parents. He's a bloody police commander in the Met – I can barely get him on the phone when he's at work, he's so busy, and there I am, bumping into him on a Wednesday morning, and he's been to mass. I thought it was bullshit, and he had some fancy woman. I offered him a lift, but he said he was going to get the train.'

Erika thought back to New Cross. St Agnes was the only Catholic church in quite a significant radius.

'Marcie, did he say it was the Church of St Agnes? That's the only Catholic church in the area.'

'No, you're not listening. He was acting shifty. I think the whole church thing was a silly lie. And he's got some old slag on the side.'

'When was this?'

'Three weeks ago.'

'Are you sure?'

'Yes, of course I'm bloody sure! You think I can't remember three weeks ago? I don't know why I came here.' Marcie finished the last of her Coke, and she got up out of her chair. Her demeanour changed back to looking angry. She loomed over Erika and jabbed her finger. 'I'm no longer with him. We have separate finances, Erika, and as of tonight, we have separate solicitors. Okay? He's on his own. You leave me and my girls out of it, you hear me? You really want to speak to me? You'll have to get a warrant or haul me into court. Understand?'

'Marcie, sit down.'

'No. I'm going.'

She picked up her bag and left the room, slamming the front door behind her. Leaving a trail of her perfume in the air. Erika got up and went to the hall. She pulled out her phone and checked Google Maps for the second time that evening. The Church of St Agnes was the only Catholic church within a six-mile radius of the Sainsbury's at New Cross.

Marie Collins had been to St Agnes, and now if Marsh was going there, a week before the body was found in 14B Amersham Road? Erika didn't like that coincidence one bit.

She was about to call the incident room when her phone rang. It was Devlin Newberry-Jones calling her back from the Canal and River Trust.

'Sorry for the delay. I've had to do a bit of digging,' he said. 'I've managed to find the details of work that was undertaken. This was a piece of restoration of the canal bank section you asked about.'

'Yes,' said Erika. 'What I need to know is who authorised the work, specifically the drain covers?'

'Okay, so there was no mention of drains being put in. There are two municipal manholes on that section of the canal bank. One is for electricity and the other is a sewage pipe running along under the canal path. And they've been there since 1991. And it was a volunteer who organised the work resurfacing the path and putting in some new electric lights. His name is Frank Hobbs.'

Erika froze with her phone in her hand.

'Frank Hobbs?' she repeated.

'Yes. He was a member of the Canal Bank Trust for a few years. He had a flurry of activity between 2005 and 2011, being involved in many projects. It says in the notes that he had contacts in the local council.'

'What happened after 2011?' asked Erika.

'There was something in the minutes from that year. He just seemed to vanish. He stopped attending meetings, and no one knows what happened to him.'

55

Erika asked to convene the team very early the next morning, at
7am, and though there were many bleary eyes in the incident
room, everyone arrived on time. She felt nervous for the day she
was about to have. And what she had to do.

'Morning, everyone. Please help yourself to breakfast,' she
said. 'I know it's a Sunday, and the end and the beginning of
another busy week, but we're against the clock on this
investigation. If I don't get the chance later, I just want to say
thank you for all your hard work.' Erika was fighting exhaustion.
She'd been up half the night, preparing to interview Marsh, and
set her alarm at 5am so she could collect a mammoth order of
McDonald's breakfasts, coffee, and doughnuts on her way to the
station, to rally the team. 'We have Marsh in custody for the next
twenty-one hours – this is with an extension to thirty-six hours.
After this, we have to charge him or let him go.'

'What time is his solicitor coming in?' asked McGorry.

'Eight,' said Peterson through a mouthful of Sausage & Egg
McMuffin.

Moss had been working at the photocopier, and she passed
Erika a green A4 folder and gave a subtle nod.

'I also had a conversation last night with Marsh's wife, Marcie,' said Erika, taking the file. 'A few weeks back she saw Marsh walking on the street close to the Sainsbury's in New Cross. It was a Wednesday, a working day, and he said that he'd been to church, which she said was most unlike him. Marsh is, or was, a lapsed Catholic and he specifically said he'd lit a candle for his parents. The only Catholic church close to where she saw him is St Agnes. Now, we have Marsh procuring this new passport for Jerome Goodman, or Kieron Bagshaw, and we could have a potential link between Marsh and Marie Collins, who, it seems, tried to pass off her own death as murder at 14B Amersham Road. We still don't know the whereabouts of Marie, or the identity of the body found in her flat.'

'Father Michael McCall from St Agnes was prison chaplain at HMP Holloway, where Marie Collins was serving her prison sentence,' said Moss. 'He told us that he'd got close to Marie in the weeks leading up until her death, she'd helped him with his shopping, and that he'd taken Marie's confession.'

'I also had a phone call last night with a man from the Canal and River Trust in Rochdale. Frank Hobbs was part of a volunteer group who did reconstruction on the section of canal bank with the drain cover leading up to 17 Chapel Street. This could have been when the false drain cover was fitted. We need to find Frank Hobbs. I know we lost him. That's a big error, but we need to know where he is.' Erika could see a gloom settling over the incident room. 'Look. All is not lost. Just remember what I always say in these briefings. There are no stupid questions. Let's go back to the basics of the case. We started with the body in 14B Amersham Road. And then the parcel locker outside her flat led us to Tania Hogarth, who led us to Kieron Bagshaw. Maybe we've discounted Tania Hogarth in this too early? Have a closer look at her. The same with St Agnes church. Have a look at everyone there. The congregation. Who has seen what? Dig deep. What you think might be the simplest little thing could lead to a breakthrough. Now, Moss is coming with me to question Marsh, and I'm putting Peterson in charge of the rest of the team.'

'I never thought I'd have Paul Marsh in custody, let alone have to question him about Jerome Goodman,' said Erika as she straightened her suit and peered at her reflection in the smoky mirror covering the lift's back wall. She'd applied make-up to try and disguise the exhaustion on her face, but as she stared at her reflection, she had a sudden feeling of standing on the precipice, and she wasn't quite sure what would happen next. She clutched the green folder against her chest, feeling the photos inside. Moss stood beside her with her long red hair neatly tied back, and she was also clutching a pile of folders against her chest.

'Are you sure you should be the one questioning him? I know this one is close to home.'

'Maybe that makes me the best one to question him.'

The lift came to a standstill and they stepped out into the corridor.

Marsh was waiting in the interview room with his solicitor. Erika sat opposite the two of them with Moss on her right.

'It's eight thirty am on Sunday, December 15, 2024,' said Erika, looking up at the video camera recording in the corner of the room. She knew some of the team were watching from the video suite next door. 'I'm Detective Chief Inspector Erika Foster. This is Detective Inspector Kate Moss, and we're joined by the suspect's legal representative, David Doxworth.'

Erika stared at Marsh sitting in front of her. He looked confident and was dressed in jeans and a blue flannel shirt open at the neck. He'd had a shave. He looked ready for work. She placed the green folder on the table.

'Can you confirm your full legal name and rank?'

'You know. It's Paul Marsh,' he said with an impatient tone. 'Commander Paul Marsh,' he added, looking up at the camera.

Erika followed his gaze. 'Something interesting?'

'Who else is watching this interview?' he asked, pointing up at the camera.

'That's not your concern.'

Marsh moved his gaze back to her, his eyes boring into hers.

'As Met commander, it *is* my concern. I can find out. I can find out who is watching,' he said, fixing his gaze on the camera again.

'What if I told you no one's watching? No one really cares about you at work. Just like no one really cares about you at home.'

'What?' Marsh sat back, thrown off his stride. David sat forward.

'Please, Erika. We've all been called in at a very early hour – let's not waste time on subtext,' he said.

'Do you hear that, Paul? He thinks the fact your wife wants a divorce and custody of your two girls is subtext.'

'What are you talking about, custody? They're in their teens.'

'Marcie can sue for custody until they're seventeen. That would still be a lonely few years of not seeing them. She could stop them from coming to see you in prison.'

'Erika. My client is here to answer questions pertaining to his arrest,' said David.

Erika looked at Marsh. She could see she had him a little rattled. *Time to turn up the heat.*

She took a deep breath, and in her head said, *I'm sorry to do this to you all, but I think it's the only way.* She opened the green folder and took out six large colour A4 photos, which she lined up on the desk in front of Marsh. He recoiled.

'What the . . . Erika? What is this?'

The six photos were taken from the shoot-out at 17 Chapel Street on July 8, 2014. The first showed Erika's husband, Mark, lying on the ground. It was a graphic photo of the back of his head blown away, and fragments of skull and brain glistened on the tarmac. The subsequent photos showed TJ (Tim James), Jim Black, Salman Dhumal, and Tom Bradbury. All gunned down, their bodies strewn on the ground, their gaping wounds as fresh as they had been ten years ago. The final photo was of Erika, taken for the tribunal. She sat up in her hospital bed facing the camera with stitches in her neck, with two black eyes and a broken lip.

Moss had agreed with Erika not to react to the photos.

'Erika, what is . . .' David started to say, but Erika went on.

'Paul, we had you under surveillance and recorded you collecting two passport photos of Jerome Goodman and eight thousand pounds in cash from a safety deposit box on Regent Street. Two days later we followed you to Woolwich where you attempted to hand over a passport in the name of Ethan Kershaw. This passport was for a Kieron Bagshaw, who we believe is Jerome Goodman. The man who did this,' she said, tapping the photos.

Marsh stared at her, his eyes wide.

'Look at the photos, Paul.'

'I've seen them before.'

'What's your question, Erika? You're getting sloppy.'

'My first question is how did you get the passport for Jerome Goodman?' She picked up the photo of Mark and held it up to Paul's face.

Marsh sat back. He glanced across at David, who sat forward with his pen in his hands.

'My client believes he was involved in an undercover operation that you don't have sufficient rank to pursue,' he said.

'So, Paul, you believed you were part of an undercover operation?'

Erika placed the photo back down and adjusted the gruesome gallery on the table in front of them.

'Is it really necessary to keep these photos on display?' asked David.

'Yes. It is. A passport would only be issued by the Met Police if Jerome Goodman or Kieron Bagshaw was placed or about to be placed in the witness relocation programme. We put in a request for information on this from the assistant commissioner, and she confirmed that both Jerome Goodman and Kieron Bagshaw are not.'

'I have a coroner's report that says Jerome Goodman is dead,' said David.

Erika ignored this.

'Even if what you say is true, Paul, you wouldn't be procuring any legal documents on behalf of the Met for cash. There are special processes.' Marsh kept his lips pressed together. 'You cowardly little shit,' she spat, deciding to dig in right away. Moss glanced at her. 'Look at the photos. Look at them! No, you can't. You were always weak. Spineless.' Erika slammed her hand down on the table and Marsh jumped.

'Erika, this is not—' David started to say.

'Paul Marsh. *Commander.* His uniform is always so clean. He's safe in his little office. Corrupt. Weak. Spineless.'

'You don't talk to me like that!' he shouted, leaning forward.

'Now look at the camera. Be a man. Everyone is watching – we're beaming this through the whole station. The corrupt, squealing little pig—'

'Erika,' said David, looking across at Marsh, who was now bright red.

'Who sells his friends and fellow officers down the river for cash. Friends and officers who had your back when you were on the beat,' said Erika, picking up the photos again and pushing them in Marsh's face. 'How much did he pay you, Jerome Goodman?'

'Erika!'

'Did you use the blood money to buy toys for Sophie and Mia?'

'ERIKA!' roared David, banging his hands on the desk. Paul jumped but Erika kept her eyes on Marsh, not letting him get away. She kept talking, fast.

'Who has you on their payroll, Paul? Mia and Sophie could be in danger, and Marcie too. You're stuck in here with no friends.'

'I must ask that you—'

Erika could see Marsh was tensing up, and a vein was pulsing in his forehead.

'Look at the photos or look at the camera. Be a man! Did you think it would end like this? Do you know what they do to bent coppers inside? Improvised shanks. Hot water and sugar. And don't bend over in the shower. The weak ones always get fucked in the arse. Who? Who is it? Who?' Erika grabbed Marsh's arm and placed his hands on the photos.

'I had no choice! It goes back to Manchester!' cried Marsh, pulling his arm away. There were now tears running down his face.

'Who in Manchester?'

Erika went to grab Marsh's arm again, but David, now standing, took Erika's hand before she could reach.

'My client will not be subjected to this. Do you hear me, Detective?' he said. His voice was now low and commanding. *'Do you hear me, Detective?'*

'I'm terminating this interview at eight thirty-seven,' said Erika, and both she and Moss got up and left the interview room.

56

It was freezing cold, and Frank Hobbs had spent the last four hours on his motorbike driving down from London.

He rounded the bend of the quiet country lane, and the North Sea and sky appeared grey and choppy through the magnificent ruined arches of St Andrew's Church in Covehithe, in Suffolk. As he drew closer, the fourteenth-century tower seemed to grow, looming beside the row of windowless arches. Frank had been to Covehithe so many times over the years, but the size and the bleak beauty of this place struck him every time.

He'd passed the houses in the small village, and the road stopped abruptly just past the church, and led across a wildlife reserve to the beach. Frank killed the motorbike engine and locked the motorbike against an old railing on a stretch of crumbling wall.

The wildlife reserve was flat and, in December, bleak and otherworldly. The grey light seemed to hold a magic that made you question whether what you were seeing was real, especially when you were alone, and he hadn't seen another soul since he turned off the main road. Frank pulled on a small backpack, and he hopped over the stile. The beach was a twenty-minute walk through trees and gorse, along the sandy path as it banked down towards the sea. He passed several ancient, felled hornbeam trees. Their root structures were tall and round, and the trees themselves were two or three storeys in height.

He disturbed a flock of crows pecking at the sand when he emerged from the undergrowth onto the beach. And he stopped and watched them take flight, black and gleaming. They seemed to move in a pattern as one against the slate sky.

The wind screamed across the sand coming off the water, which was as flat and colourless as the surrounding landscape. The beach was a mixture of white sand shot through with lines of black soil, and he could see a great deal of rubbish strewn along the tide line in long, waving lines. Frank had kept his crash helmet on with the black visor up, in case he saw one of the occasional dog walkers who braved the cold beach, but there wasn't a soul. He'd travelled down from London on the motorbike because it was acceptable to travel with your face covered in a visor. The bike was registered in another name, and there had been no police, none that he'd seen, anyway.

Half a mile along the beach was a small cottage, and as he drew close, he saw a spire of smoke rising from the chimney. He pulled off his helmet and the cold wind hit his face. Just as he reached the front door of the cottage, Jerome opened it and Frank felt the warmth of the tiny front room, where a wood-burning stove glowed. Jerome closed the door behind them and threw a large bolt across. They hugged. They hadn't seen each other in a while.

'You worried about seagulls breaking down the door?' said Frank, shrugging off his thick coat. They went through to the small kitchen, where Jerome poured Frank some tea.

'Did anyone see you?' he asked. Frank thought Jerome looked pale and thin, and uncharacteristically worried.

'No. It was a good run. Quiet. There's no one on the beach.'

'Have you heard from Danielle?'

'She's okay. She's getting ready to leave and come down here,' said Frank.

'You should have brought her with you,' said Jerome. Frank shook his head.

'It was too risky. I told you, I think I was being followed in London. I managed to lose them in Camden Market. I couldn't risk leading them to where she's hiding . . . There's a bike going to pick her up. She's going to bitch about having to ride all the way here in the cold.'

Despite all that had happened, Jerome smiled. Then his black eyes seemed to flare and the smile vanished.

'I can't believe they got the passport,' he said.

'We've got to work on the assumption that my Victor Gill identity is blown. You know it's everywhere.' Frank pulled out his mobile phone and found the Facebook page with the police appeal. The details of the arrest warrant had gone out on the social media profiles of all UK National Police. They were using the Kieron Bagshaw passport photo and the most recent passport photo. 'They arrested Marsh as he was doing the drop-off.'

Jerome took a look and then waved it away.

'I hope Paul Gadd is keeping his mouth shut?'

'Yeah. More for himself.'

Jerome gritted his teeth, and for a moment, Frank thought he was going to hurl his phone against the wall. Jerome always seemed to internalise his anger, and he paced up and down, barefoot in his jeans and woollen sweater, swallowing his anger, drawing it all back into himself to stay calm. Whenever Frank saw this, he wondered how Jerome was still healthy.

'What about Danielle? What do you think they know?'

'They know the body in the flat wasn't her. But they haven't found out who it is. Or where she's hiding.'

They had agreed on minimal contact over the past few weeks, mostly speaking in vague terms or code. It was impossible not to know who was listening.

Jerome went to the small window, which was streaked with salt, and looked at the blurry outline of the horizon beyond the grey ridges of the sea. A gust of wind peppered the glass with sand.

'Are you sure no one followed you?'

'Yeah.'

'I don't like it that we have to wait. Even for a few hours.'

'You want to go? Now? Before the weather gets too bad.'

Jerome turned on him and unleashed a powerful blast of anger. 'We do not leave Danielle. Do you hear me?'

Frank took a step back and put up his hands. 'Okay. I hear you.'

Erika sat across from Marsh. They were back in interview room one, and Erika was regretting pushing him so far in their first interview. In the break he had recovered his nerve and resolve, and he had now clammed up.

'Paul, we have you on surveillance camera,' she said. 'Even without anything else, just for possession or control over false identity documents, you could go down for two years. You'll lose your job.'

Paul sat back, his face slack and impassive. 'Then charge me.'

'We're very close to bringing in Jerome Goodman and Frank Hobbs,' said Erika.

'Are you? I don't think so.'

'Frank Hobbs picked up the note you deposited. We've had him under surveillance since then. We're just waiting to see where he leads us.'

Paul was silent.

'I appreciate you hypothesising with my client, but we'd welcome more constructive questions,' said David. He checked his watch. It was now coming up to lunchtime.

'I have nineteen hours to question your client,' said Erika. Marsh sighed and rolled his eyes. 'Do you remember a lad called Joey Dunbar when we were beat officers in Manchester?'

Marsh sighed. 'No.'

'We'd only been police officers for eighteen months. We caught Joey Dunbar dealing crack. Ran off and dropped his wallet with his library card inside. Library card! With his address. We went round the next morning to his flat on the Culpepper Estate. Rough estate. Remember?'

'Erika, where is this going?' asked David. 'I hope we're not going to spend the next nineteen hours going down memory lane?'

'It's relevant,' she said, and she could see a glimmer of something in Marsh's face.

'So we knock on his door. Joey Dunbar opens it, and he's alone, scared, but he lets us in. He lives at home with his parents, and it looks like a nice flat. There's coats hung up, a piggy bank in the hallway with "HOLIDAY FUND" written on it. We go into the living room and Joey gets very shifty. We give him the name of a local drug dealer we think he could be working for. I forget the name of the dealer, but what I will never forget is what happened next. He bolted for it, into his parents' bedroom, which was off the living room. By the time we got there, he was already out of the sliding doors and standing on the edge of their balcony. You remember, Paul? Do you also remember that he lived on the twenty-first floor? And we watched him just leap over the side . . . Do you remember what his body looked like when it was scraped off the concrete below? And then, we had to tell his parents, who had no idea that their dead son was mixed up in drugs.' Erika leaned forward. 'The death of that kid haunted me. Still does. And it strengthened my resolve to go after the big fish. The drug dealers and distributors. And I did. And here we are. Sitting on opposite sides of this table, but also on opposite sides of the moral spectrum. How long have you been helping Jerome Goodman?'

Marsh was shaking, and a tear emerged from his left eye, pooled on the edge, and then fell, streaking down his cheek.

'I've taken legal advice and chosen not to answer that question,' he said.

57

Peterson pressed the intercom outside Tania Hogarth's house in Chiswick and leaned on it. He stepped back.

'She's not there,' said McGorry, his mobile phone to his head. 'And she's not answering.'

'Good detective work,' said Peterson dourly. He felt annoyed that he'd drawn the short straw, that he and McGorry were so far away from the action at Lewisham Row. Questioning Tania Hogarth again felt like a pointless errand. She didn't know anything.

Peterson looked up and down the empty street, and thought for a moment.

'Where is her nail salon?' he asked.

'It's on the high street. We passed it on the way,' said McGorry.

'Let's take a look. They might know where she is.'

Chiswick high street was busy with traffic, and the shops were crowded. Ciao Bellissima was tucked in between a Starbucks and a small Sainsbury's supermarket.

'There's a Ciao Bellissima nail salon near where we live. My wife goes there.'

'So, it's a proper chain?'

'Yeah.'

Peterson sighed and turned off to park around the corner. From what Erika told them, Tania Hogarth was a spoiled trust-fund type and probably wouldn't even visit her businesses.

When they reached the high street, they saw the nail salon was busy, filled with women and a couple of men having their nails filed by masked technicians. All eyes looked up at them when they went to the front desk, where a small Asian lady with neat black hair sat at a computer wearing a white smock. It was noisy with the high-pitched whirr of the nail files and chatter. Peterson introduced himself, and surreptitiously flashed his warrant card, but he noticed that several of the workers saw him.

'I'm looking for Tania Hogarth?' he said. The warrant card had made the woman uneasy.

'Who?' asked the woman, having to lean closer to hear him over the noise.

'Tania Hogarth,' he said, louder. 'She owns the company.'

The woman looked between him and McGorry and shook her head. 'Abbi, she's our manager, she's not here today.'

'You don't know Tania?'

'What?'

'You don't know Tania?' repeated McGorry, louder.

Peterson turned to look at the rows of nail technicians. They were a mixture of ages and races, and two very young-looking guys who were checking out McGorry.

'What is this concerning?' said the woman.

'Can I speak to Abbi?'

She shook her head and came around the desk.

'Why don't you come to my office,' she said, beckoning them to follow. They went past the rows of nail technicians working on customers and through to a small comfy room with a desk and a sofa. She closed the door and the noise outside muffled.

'My name is Pian. I'm a supervisor here. Has one of our staff done something wrong?' she asked, moving around to the desk.

Peterson was looking around the room, and he noticed a big dry-wipe whiteboard on the wall with three rows of five staff photos. "**SECRET SANTA**" was written above the photos. He noticed one of the women in the middle, and moved closer to examine the photo. She had short brown hair and looked to be in her early forties. She wore a green blouse and her coral lipstick shone.

'This lady,' he said to McGorry. 'That's Marie Collins.'

Pian looked up at where he was pointing. 'No. Her name is Cheryl . . . Is she in trouble?'

Peterson and McGorry looked at each other, and Peterson scrolled through his phone to find the photos they had of Marie Collins. He put his phone next to the picture on the wall.

'This is a woman called Marie Collins,' he said.

Pian got up and came to join them. 'No. That's Cheryl Regan. She's been working here for a couple of years.'

'Where is she?'

'She's not here today. She's taking annual leave. On holiday.'

'When did she go on holiday?'

'Two weeks ago. She's due back today, I think. She's down on the rota for tomorrow.' Pian looked between them, confused.

'How well do you know Cheryl?'

'I'm her supervisor. I don't really know her outside work. Er. Zoot, one of our nail technicians, knows her well. I can ask him to talk to you – he's coming up on his break.'

Zoot was one of the young, slim guys who had eyed up McGorry. He agreed to speak to them in the staff break room next to Pian's office.

'Is Cheryl alright? I haven't heard anything from her since

she went away. I've been getting worried,' he said. Zoot had long pipe cleaner legs, encased in a tight pair of cream tracksuit bottoms, and he wore a black sleeveless T-shirt. His long black hair was poker straight and tucked behind his large ears. He was wearing eyeliner, which somehow seemed to suit him, thought Peterson.

'Where did Cheryl go on holiday?' asked McGorry.

'Alicante. Why?'

'Who did she go with?'

'A customer . . . I know, I thought the same thing. But there was this woman who started to come in and have her nails done a few weeks ago, and she just formed this friendship with Cheryl. Latched on to her. This woman was due to go to Alicante with her boyfriend, to her holiday flat. But then the boyfriend dumped her and she was *distraught*. Somehow, she convinced Cheryl to go with her. Cheryl only had to pay for her plane ticket, and at this time of year, it cost nothing.'

Peterson saw McGorry shake his head.

'She bought plane tickets?'

'Yeah. Cheryl was dead excited. I'm just confused as to why I haven't seen her posting on Instagram.'

'Have you got her Instagram there I can see?' asked Peterson. Zoot got out his phone and found her profile, handing it to him.

He could see that Cheryl liked to post pictures of early-morning walks along the river. It looked as if she lived in Hammersmith. There were pictures of a night out with work friends. Two with Zoot at a coffee shop. And another picture of a flat-pack bookcase she'd put together. It was filled with colour-coordinated books with the caption, 'FOUR HOURS LATER. I HAVE MY BOOKS TIDIED. WINE TIME!'

'Look. She's posted regularly up until 29 November,' Peterson said to McGorry as he scrolled through.

'What was this woman's name?' asked McGorry.

'Danielle something. I don't know her last name.'

Peterson's heart began to beat faster. He looked over at McGorry.

'Do you know if Cheryl was following her on Instagram?' asked Peterson.

'No. That's what was weird . . .' Zoot opened his mouth to say something more, and hesitated.

'Please don't be shy to tell us whatever. It's important. We're worried about Cheryl.'

Peterson handed Zoot his phone back, and Zoot took it, sighing.

'Look. I love Cheryl, but I think she thinks we're closer friends than we actually are,' he said, looking a little ashamed. 'She's nice, but a bit clingy. Bit odd sometimes. I've heard the other women calling her a loser, and a loner. I think she's just lonely, and that can make you desperate for friendship. I know she had a couple of boyfriends who were wrong for her, and she was too clingy. I just thought that this Danielle liked coming to see Cheryl to get her nails done, 'cos Cheryl made her feel better about herself. That's horrible, isn't it?'

'No. I just can't understand how this Danielle went from having her nails done to inviting Cheryl on holiday? Did they meet outside the nail salon?'

Zoot shook his head.

'I don't know. One of the girls joked that Danielle was only taking Cheryl as a drug mule.' He saw the look between them both. 'I think that was a joke. I've never seen Cheryl do drugs. I think we were all trying to find the reason. And the fact they looked so alike.'

58

McGorry was driving and Peterson was on the phone to Crane. They were very close to New Cross, but the Sunday afternoon traffic was busy.

'You need to get in contact with Isaac Strong. We think we have an ID on the body of the woman found at 14B Amersham Road. Her name is Cheryl Regan, she's in her mid-thirties, and her address is 46A Railroad Avenue, Hammersmith. Yes, West London. We need to find out her medical details, if there are any dental records so that Isaac can confirm.' Peterson looked up and saw that they were passing New Cross train station. 'As soon as Erika comes out of her interview with Marsh, you need to tell her. We're just going to talk to Sherry Blaze again.'

Peterson hung up the phone. He had the staff photo of Cheryl Regan from the nail salon in his lap.

'Pull in anywhere you can,' he said as McGorry turned in to Amersham Road.

They jumped out of the car and McGorry hammered on Sherry Blaze's front door. After a long wait, she answered wearing a robe and her pea-green character turban.

'What?' she croaked, peering up at them.

'Please can we come in, we need to talk to you urgently,' said Peterson, flashing his warrant card. McGorry did the same.

'I know who you are. Well, one of you,' she said, eyeing up McGorry. 'It's Sunday.'

'This is important.'

They came into her flat, and saw that the front room had a couple of folding chairs under the boarded-up ceiling. She indicated they should sit.

'You told us that you saw your neighbour arriving home with a vanity case on Saturday, 30 November, around 2pm?' said Peterson.

'Yes.'

'Was this her?' he said, holding up the photo.

'Yes, you know that's her,' said Sherry, taking the staff photo of Cheryl Regan from the nail salon. 'She looks better in this photo. Why is she wearing a tabard?'

'You also said that you heard lots of noise coming from upstairs in the afternoon and evening, particularly in the afternoon, like a high-pitched whirring sound?'

'Yes.'

'You said you thought she was cleaning, but could it have been the noise made by a nail technician's filing drill?' asked Peterson. 'You have your nails done regularly,' he added, looking at her manicure with the false extensions.

'Yes. And yes, that makes sense – it had the same high-pitched dentist's drill sound. And I saw her with another plastic bag when she was going up the stairs with her vanity case.'

'What was in it?'

'There was something long sticking out with a plug on the end. At the time I thought it could have been a pair of hair straighteners, but it could have been a nail technician's drill.'

Peterson and McGorry came back out to the car.

'So we think Cheryl Regan came to the flat to do Danielle's nails, and they were planning to go on holiday?' said Peterson.

'What if she was coming to stay with Danielle the night before, because they were going to go to the airport together?' said McGorry.

They got into the car, and Peterson drummed his fingers on the steering wheel, thinking.

'And then Danielle killed Cheryl and left her body in the flat. Where did she go?'

'The simplest plans are always the best,' said McGorry. 'What if Danielle stayed somewhere close by? Hiding away, until things died down, or until the body was found?'

'What if she used her connection to the church?' said Peterson.

Danielle was sitting at the table in Father Michael McCall's tiny kitchen, staring at the Facebook post on her burner phone, saying Kieron Bagshaw was wanted by the police.

Father Michael lived in a small cottage on the grounds behind the Church of St Agnes, and it had been the ideal hiding place. As a Catholic priest living alone, he didn't get many visitors. Even so, Danielle had felt like a caged animal for the past two weeks. And after their plan seemed to go successfully, the net seemed to be closing.

The curtains were drawn. And when Danielle heard the front door open, she instinctively jumped.

'It's okay. It's me,' said Michael, hurrying into the kitchen, shrugging off his coat. Underneath, he wore his robes and had a gold cross around his neck.

'I've heard from Frank and Jerome. The plan has changed.' Danielle eyed him moodily. She hated that her communications were going through Michael. 'I also got you a coffee and a Danish.' He placed a shopping bag on the kitchen counter, removed a small paper bag, and placed two glistening Danish pastries on a plate each. He placed them in the microwave. They had both gone past mere cabin fever, and she wanted to stab Michael. His fake piousness and his self-importance were driving her crazy.

'Fuck the Danish. What is the plan?'

'I bought you the Danish because you need energy. Frank is sending a bike to collect you and drive you down to the east coast.'

'A motorbike?'

'Yes, Danielle. They're not sending a fucking push bike.'

'When?'

'Within the next half an hour.'

'A bike driven by who?' said Danielle, her mind working fast.

'I don't know. A trusted third party. It's had to be arranged quickly.'

The microwave beeped, and he took the plate out and sat at the small kitchen table. She came to sit opposite him.

He tore off a piece of the Danish and put it in his mouth, flapping his hands in front of his face because it was hot. Danielle stood over him.

'Let me see the text they sent,' she said, holding out her hand. Michael rolled his eyes and rummaged under his cassock, pulled out his phone, unlocked it, and slapped it in her palm.

Danielle scrolled through the text messages and found the one from Frank, written in his short, blunt style.

> Nu-plan Bike4D there in 30. D going 1 way.

Michael had texted back:

> OK.

'And you trust that Frank's phone hasn't been compromised?' said Danielle, looking up from his phone.

Michael went to put another piece of the Danish in his mouth and hesitated.

'I'm just the messenger.'

Danielle put his phone on the table and seized his wrist. 'A well-paid messenger, so I don't need the attitude.'

Michael looked up at her and twisted her fingers off his wrist.

'Danielle. There is only so much I can do.'

'So I don't have a passport, Jerome doesn't. What about Frank?'

He shook his head.

'I don't know. You always planned to get into Europe without a passport. You have friends in Amsterdam. Once you're inside the Schengen Zone, you have options.'

'I know my own plan. I know how it fucking works! Jesus. This has turned into a nightmare. That fucking woman was supposed to lie there dead in the flat and not be discovered for days or longer.'

'Please don't take the Lord's name in vain. And we didn't know the radiator was going to fall through the floor. It was an act of God.'

'Shut up. And you can drop the priest act.'

'It's not an act.'

'You might believe in God, but you've still been flogging gear and fixing stuff for us. Remember who you really work for.'

Michael sat staring at her in his priest's robes. She raised an eyebrow, daring him to contradict her. He shoved another piece of the Danish pastry in his mouth. The plan was for Jerome and Frank to declare themselves at Amsterdam port with their new passports and for Danielle to hide in the boat and sneak through customs. She would then get a Dutch passport in a new name. Then, they had other options. Jerome or Frank could marry her, giving one of them European residency. Either way, they would have all skipped off into the sunset to start new lives.

'Eat your Danish, Danielle. The bike will be here very soon,' said Michael.

There was a knock at the door, and they both froze. Michael pushed out his chair and got up.

'Stay calm. It's probably Clarence or one of the lay clergy.'

'I'm so close to getting out of here,' Danielle hissed through her teeth. He hesitated on the threshold of the kitchen. 'If I don't answer, it will look odd.' He waved her away. 'Go on, hide.'

McGorry and Peterson were about to knock again when Father Michael opened the door.

'Good morning,' he said, giving them the same insipid smile he had when Peterson visited the church the week before.

'Good morning. I don't know if you remember me?'

'Yes. Detective Inspector James Peterson, and who is this?' he said, moving his ethereal smile onto McGorry.

'This is my colleague, Detective Constable McGorry. Listen, we've tried to call in at the church, but the door is locked. And this is a Sunday afternoon?'

'We do have to keep the church locked outside of service hours.'

'Do you know how we can get hold of Father Clarence? We just wanted to ask him some more questions.'

'I think he's doing hospital visits until later,' said Michael.

'Maybe you can help us?'

'I'm sorry to be rude, but Sundays can be very busy for us. I have a Sunday school shortly.'

Peterson exchanged a glance with McGorry. The priest was very nervous and acting shifty. They heard a creak from above.

'Do you live alone?'

'Yes . . . Yes. This is an old cottage. It's always creaking.'

'Could we just come in to talk to you for a moment? We really won't take up much of your time,' said Peterson.

'Of course.'

They stepped into the cramped living room. It was a small cottage with a low ceiling and fairly functional inside.

'Do sit down,' he said. 'Would you like some tea or coffee?'

He hurried off before they could answer. Peterson looked over at McGorry, and they heard another creak from upstairs, this time of someone walking across the floorboards. Peterson got up and went to the doorway, and he saw two plates on the kitchen table with the remains of the Danishes.

Father Michael was furiously typing on his mobile phone and didn't notice him for a moment.

'You said you were alone?' said Peterson. Michael's head snapped up. 'But I can hear the floorboards?' added Peterson, pointing his finger up at the ceiling.

'James! There's a woman climbing out of the upstairs window!' McGorry yelled from the front room. Peterson went running through. The front door was open, and McGorry was running down the path to the gates of the churchyard in pursuit of a brown-haired woman.

She reached the gate and managed to get out, but McGorry caught up with her on the other side. Peterson got through the gate just as McGorry tackled her to the ground.

Danielle fought and kicked, but McGorry got her in handcuffs lightning quick.

'Marie Collins, or should I say, Danielle Lang, I'm placing you under arrest for the murder of Cheryl Regan at 14B Amersham Road.'

'No! You fucking bastards, no!' she cried. Her face was furious.

Peterson hurried back to Father Michael's cottage. He found the priest standing in the middle of the room with his mobile phone. He turned and looked at Peterson.

'Who are you texting?' said Peterson. He lunged at Michael, and in the tussle, he managed to grab the priest's phone and read the text message he'd just sent.

> Polcie arrived and arrested D. Im next. BOat will leave Lowestoft hrbour NOW. Shud be an hour. Thisz number bUrnt.

He scrolled back, Michael having just sent another text a minute before.

> Leave now

'This boat? It's going to meet Jerome Goodman?'

Michael closed his eyes and sighed.

'I'd like to speak to a solicitor,' he said.

Peterson wanted to punch the pious little shit, but he pulled out his phone and made a call to control, keeping his eyes on the priest.

'I need an immediate check on boats leaving Lowestoft Harbour now. Stop anyone leaving and find out where they're going. Lowestoft is a small port, and it's off-season, so it shouldn't be difficult.'

He hung up the phone and put Father Michael in handcuffs.

59

Jerome and Frank stood on the empty beach, staring out at the choppy grey water. The cold salt air was making Frank's eyes water, and he didn't like the thought of having to get in a boat and travel across the North Sea so late in December. Jerome's phone pinged in his pocket and he pulled it out. 'No!' he cried. 'Fuck!'

'What?'

Jerome put his hands up to his face, and Frank grabbed his phone.

'They've just arrested Danielle. They tracked her down to the church. Why is that fuckwit Michael texting the details? Jesus.'

Frank scanned the text message, hurriedly written with typos. He looked back at Jerome. The grey roots were starting to show through his blond hair, and he looked old and scared. It chilled Frank to see him like this.

'Okay. Jerome. *Jerome!* We need to focus,' said Frank. He grabbed him by the shoulders. 'We can still do this. We go without Danielle. We take the money we have. Yeah? The boat can get here fast. The plan was always to start again. It's just going to be harder. Come on. We need to get ready. Now.'

Frank pulled Jerome back across the sand to the cottage. The wind had really picked up, and they walked around to the back, where a large dinghy was parked under a tarpaulin. When Frank started to untie it, Jerome seemed to focus and he started to help on the other side.

Half of the tarp came loose, and it crackled and whipped away in the wind. Frank got the last piece of rope untied, and before he could grab the tarp, the wind took it out of their hands, and it streamed away across the sand. Jerome went to go after it.

'Leave it!' snapped Frank. The dinghy took four people and had an outboard motor. It was sitting on the metal trailer on wheels. They heaved and pulled it out from behind the cottage and rolled it down close to where the waves were breaking.

Just doing this had taken almost fifteen minutes. And in that time the weather had worsened and the waves were getting bigger.

'The tide's going out!' Frank shouted above the screaming wind.

Jerome nodded, his jaw clenched. The diesel-powered fishing boat coming from Lowestoft port was thirteen metres long with an enclosed cabin, communications. It gave them much more chance to weather the crossing. They just had to use the dinghy to get past the breakers and rendezvous in deeper water.

'This is seriously good work,' said Erika to Peterson and McGorry in the corridor at Lewisham Row police station. Danielle Lang had been booked in the custody suite and taken into interview room two, where a duty solicitor had been assigned to her. McGorry and Peterson had briefed Erika on what they'd discovered at the nail salon in Chiswick.

Erika went into the interview room with Moss. Danielle was sitting hunched over in a chair. Her mid-length brown hair was unkempt, but Erika was struck by the resemblance to the deceased woman from 14B Amersham Road, Cheryl Regan. Erika wasn't surprised to see that Danielle's solicitor was Paul Slater.

'Here we are again,' she said to Paul as they sat down. He might have been called in from a day off, but he looked both smart and a little oily in his made-to-measure suit.

'Good morning, Danielle. Or is it Marie Collins?' she asked. Moss sat beside her.

'My client changed her name by deed poll several years ago,' said Paul. 'It's not illegal, and at the time, she had no criminal convictions, so was under no obligation to alert anyone of her name change.'

'That's correct, but you did try to apply for a passport renewal using a photo of Cheryl Regan,' said Erika, taking a photocopy of the application from her folder and laying it on the table.

Danielle glanced at it and back up to Erika. She shrugged.

'Is that a no shrug or a yes shrug?'

'Just a shrug,' she said. 'I can't tell the difference between us.'

'Is that why you decided to kill Cheryl and then pass off her death as your own?'

'No. I got to know Cheryl at Ciao Bellissima nail salon. I felt she was a kindred spirit 'cos we got on so well and we looked alike. I was just out of prison. She was having trouble with her mental health, so I invited her to come and stay at my place while I went away. She came over and did my nails, and I left her the keys to my place. Then she killed herself when I was away.'

'Cheryl's colleague at Ciao Bellissima, he told us Cheryl was going on holiday with you to Spain?'

Danielle shook her head.

'No. He's mistaken.'

'Is he? Cheryl had a plane ticket booked.'

'She must have been confused.'

'Okay. How did she kill herself?' asked Erika.

'Well. I don't know – I only just heard she was dead. And that you'd mistaken her for me.'

'What made you think she'd killed herself?'

'She said she was feeling a bit depressed. I just figured.'

'Where have you been on holiday?'

'I went to see a friend. In Norfolk.'

'Norfolk?'

'Yeah.'

'Can you give us the name of that friend?'

'Her name's Kim.'

'Kim what?'

'Kim Smith. I can't remember her address; she met me at the station. That's where I've been. Then I arrived back and I went to see Father Michael. I go to the church a lot. I stayed the night with him.'

'Why?' asked Erika.

''Cos I did.' Danielle crossed her arms and looked confident.

Erika took out the crime scene photos from 14B Amersham Road, the photos of Cheryl Regan lying on her side on the bed. Her upturned feet in white socks with dirt on the soles.

'Cheryl Regan wasn't wearing any shoes when we found her body. Can you explain that?'

'I told you she was depressed.'

'The whole flat had been scrubbed down with bleach.'

'She was a neat freak. That's not a crime.'

'There was a thin residue of cocaine on the ceiling of the flat.'

'I'd only been living there a couple of weeks. The place was a shit hole when I moved in. I don't do drugs. I got tested all the time inside, and my probation officer gave me two tests in the time after I came out. I was clean.'

'Why did you change your name from Danielle Lang to Marie Collins?'

'I just did. Like Paul says. It's not illegal.'

Erika opened her folder again and took out another sheet of paper. 'Right, Danielle, or Marie – which do you prefer to go by?'

'I'm happy with either. I've got nothing to hide.'

'You worked for a company called Secure Phone between November 2003 and June 2004. Over sixteen thousand people were defrauded.'

Danielle kept her arms crossed. 'None of us knew the insurance policies weren't valid.'

'My client was never charged with a crime in connection to Secure Phone,' said Paul.

'We also had you under surveillance in conjunction with Jerome Goodman, or Kieron Bagshaw, as his passport says.'

'I was Jer—' Danielle looked to Paul and he stared at her, his eyes cold. 'Jerome's girlfriend. I had no idea what he was doing.'

'And what was he doing?'

'Like I just said, I had no idea.'

'Where were you on July 8, 2014?'

Danielle laughed. 'No idea. But I can check.'

'How do you know Frank Hobbs?'

'He's a friend of Jerome's.'

Erika was silent for a moment.

Danielle raised her eyebrows and gave her a cold smile. 'Feeling a bit stumped?' she said.

'Oh, no,' said Erika. She was looking down at the paper, but not seeing the words. She had a horrible sensation of falling. And the feeling that Danielle was going to get away with this.

60

The wind was screaming around their ears as Jerome and Frank wheeled the dinghy down to the breaking waves on the launching frame. They each wore a large, heavy waterproof backpack and a life jacket.

Frank felt the wheels of the launching frame moving smoothly but with resistance across the sand, and then, as they hit the water, a breaking wave quickly rolled in and frothed up around their legs, soaking them in the freezing water.

'Now!' shouted Frank as he saw a big wave coming at them. They both pushed down on the edge of the boat and rolled their legs over just as the wave went under. The dinghy detached from the metal launching frame. Jerome moved to the helm and started to paddle so the outboard motor wouldn't get entangled in the frame underneath.

Frank glanced towards the shore to pull the starter cable on the outboard motor, and when he turned back, he saw they weren't moving forward. The water was rapidly dropping as the wave receded.

'We're stuck on the frame!' yelled Jerome with his oar in his hand. With a thud, the dinghy landed with the back half, the stern, caught on the launching frame, and the bow, the front of the dinghy, dropped down and hit the sand in front. Frank was thrown forward just as another wave hit, and with the dinghy now lying on a downward slope, he was pitched headfirst into the freezing water just as another wave slammed into them.

The water was murky and brown with churned-up sand, and Frank was dragged under the dinghy with the full force of the breaking wave. His head hit the metal launching frame, and he was pulled underneath. Frank gasped, inhaling seawater. He felt the pull of the water, but he was underneath the frame, unable to move. Something was caught, trapping him. Another wave dredged over him, but he remained pinned underneath the frame.

The wave completely submerged Jerome and the dinghy when Frank was thrown out. He thought he was done for, but he clung to the outboard motor as the wave rolled over him. The thick rubber dinghy had surprising buoyancy, and even though it was two-thirds full of water, it floated up and freed itself from the metal launching frame. Jerome choked and spat, gasping at how cold it was and scanned the churning water, but he couldn't see Frank. There was a lull in the breakers, and as the waves began to recede and pull back, Jerome frantically began to bail out the dinghy using a plastic container. He managed to get a great deal of the water out before the next wave hit, and the bow was now high enough, giving the dinghy enough buoyancy so that it pitched up and over the breaking wave. When Jerome looked back, he saw the wave roll away to shore. There was no Frank, and he couldn't see the launching frame. Jerome was now a good fifteen metres out from the beach.

He frantically bailed out more water and searched the beach and the water. It was empty. There wasn't time to wait. Frank was gone. He gave the cable a massive tug, and the outboard motor roared to life. The dinghy shot forward and pitched up and over two massive waves, bouncing around so violently that Jerome almost went over the side, but he clung on for dear life. And then he was past the breakers and speeding towards the darkening horizon.

Erika and Moss came out of interview room two after another forty minutes of questioning Danielle.

'Do you want to have a crack at Marsh again?' asked Moss, checking her watch.

'I need more leverage. How can Danielle have been involved with so much, and there's no tangible evidence to link her to anything?'

They went down to the incident room, where they found Peterson and McGorry.

'I need some good news,' said Erika.

'How about this. The coastguard just stopped a boat going out from Lowestoft Harbour, a thirteen-metre fishing boat loaded up with fuel and supplies. The guy on board told them he'd been paid to take the boat to Covehithe ten miles down the coast, and rendezvous with a dinghy.'

'Who is in the dinghy?'

'Two men.'

'Okay. What's happening now?'

'Local police are on the boat, and they're heading out to the rendezvous spot.'

'Are they armed police?'

'Yes.'

Erika looked at Moss.

'We think it's Jerome Goodman?' asked Moss.

'The last message Father Michael sent on his phone indicates maybe it's Goodman, and it was planned that

Danielle was going to meet with them,' said Peterson. He held up a printout of the message. 'But look. Even in the message, he writes "D". That's the closest to a named person we get. We're never going to get anything on him, or Marsh, or this bitch.'

Ryan approached where Erika was sitting.

'Sorry—'

'Yes, Ryan. I know calling Danielle Lang a bitch could be seen as problematic.'

'No. It's not that. I think I can prove Danielle bought the eye drops.'

'What?'

'Come and look,' said Ryan. They all got up and went over to Ryan's desk in the corner of the incident room. 'You know we've been working on the security tag left on the trousers of who we now know is Cheryl Regan?'

'Yes,' said Erika.

'Okay. So. We found out the trousers were from Primark. The trousers were a new line of product which was only launched on November 30 at 10am, opening time. And what is more brilliant is that they were launched first in the Oxford Circus store, and then rolled out from December 2 in other stores.'

'And if Cheryl Regan died on November 30 . . .' said Erika.

'Time of death was around 6pm. So feasibly, the trousers were bought between 10am and around 4pm. I did shorten the window to between 12pm and 2pm because Sherry Blaze says she saw who she thought was Marie Collins arriving back at her flat at 2pm, carrying a vanity case.'

Erika was listening now. Ryan went on.

'I've been back and forth with Primark. I requested all of the CCTV footage from the Oxford Circus store between 10am and 2pm. Fifteen cameras. I had help from Frieda and Crane, but we went through it all, and we found this video timestamped at 11.30am.'

Ryan turned to his computer and maximised a video screen showing a cash register at Primark.

'Bloody hell, that's Danielle Lang buying them,' said Erika, peering at the clear view of her face as she stood at the cash register.

'Now, the reason I haven't brought this to you sooner is because of the confusion around Danielle Lang's identity and the identity of the woman whose body was found in 14B, Cheryl Regan.'

'Okay,' said Erika.

'But Peterson and McGorry spoke to a guy called Zoot at Ciao Bellissima nail salon in Chiswick. Zoot says that he met Cheryl for coffee on the morning of November 30, before she went off on her holiday. He says they met at 10.30, and she left at 12pm. So, Danielle Lang bought the trousers. But that's not the best bit. Once we had the time code for when Danielle paid for the trousers, we tracked her out of the store and requested CCTV from Oxford Street. The place is full of cameras, as you know. She then went to Superdrug a few doors down, and armed with the time code from the CCTV, and the location of the cash register, we were able to find out what she bought.'

'Oh, please don't tease me. Don't,' said Erika.

'Three bottles of Murine anti-red eye drops. Her face is on the camera, clear as day.'

'No way!' cried Moss.

'Yes,' Ryan said, grinning. 'Now, she paid cash, of course, but I was able to get the product codes for those bottles from Superdrug. The bottles are numbered, and they match the three bottles we found in the recycling box belonging to Sherry Blaze behind 14B.'

'My God. I could kiss you!' cried Erika. 'Can you get all of this information printed out?'

Ryan nodded.

'Brilliant work. Well done, all of you,' said Erika.

61

Jerome sat wet and shivering in the dinghy, bobbing around violently, waiting for the boat. The sea was a churning mass of brown underneath him, and the current and swells were growing. There must have been a small tear in the dinghy when it got stuck on the metal edge of the launching frame, because it was sitting low and taking in water. There was something ominous now about the miles of water which surrounded him. And Frank was gone. Jerome sat in shock. Frank had been like a brother to him. They'd been through so many near misses and close calls, but this couldn't be how it ended? Jerome felt a massive relief when the fishing boat appeared on the right. It was moving very fast. He would soon be warm inside, cramped but warm, on his escape across the North Sea to Amsterdam.

The first thing that went wrong was Jerome heard the sound of a loudhailer as the boat drew close.

'This is the police. Put your hands in the air!' came a tinny voice.

'Fuck!' Jerome cried. His eyes blazed in the fading light. He yanked at the cord for the outboard motor, but it was futile. The cord was slack, and he could hear the motor was flooded.

'Start! You fucker! Start!' Jerome cried, tugging more frantically. The fishing boat was now close and someone aboard it activated a flood-light, which swept across the surface of the waves. The fishing boat drew closer, and then seemed to suddenly loom over him.

Jerome fumbled with his backpack, pulling it off his shoulders and around to his chest. The waves started to rock the dinghy violently.

'Place your hands in the air!' came the tinny voice again through the loudhailer.

Jerome got the straps of his pack open, and found his gun amongst the soaking-wet clothes inside. He had two bullets. He raised the gun and fired, but he couldn't aim with the rocking motion of the dinghy. He fell back, and the first shot whistled up and over the boat.

Bright lights blinded him, and he knew the game was up. It was over. He had one bullet left.

Jerome pushed the muzzle of the gun into his mouth and pulled the trigger.

Later that day, Erika and Moss were back in the interview room with Danielle and her solicitor, Paul.

They both seemed very confident.

'Time is ticking, Erika,' said Paul. 'You've already had my client in custody for ten hours. Time goes by fast when you're having fun.'

Erika smiled thinly.

'How are you, Danielle?' she asked.

'Fine.'

Erika sat back and placed her hands on the table.

'Frank is dead,' said Moss. 'Jerome and Frank were trying to escape in a dinghy and the sea was rough. Frank was washed overboard and drowned.'

Danielle gave a tiny reaction, her eyes seeming to flare open, and then she kept her face even. 'No.'

Erika nodded.

'Yes. Jerome and Frank were in a dinghy out at sea near Covehithe in Suffolk, waiting for a fishing boat from Lowestoft the waves were bad and Frank was swept away. The police commandeered the fishing boat before it left the port.'

Danielle looked across at Paul, who put out his hand and indicated she should remain calm. Erika continued.

'That was your plan, wasn't it? You were going to meet them in Covehithe. Dinghy to fishing boat. Cross the North Sea to Amsterdam. The police found charts, supplies. Jerome and Frank didn't wait. They went without you. Well, Frank didn't make it. His body was found close to shore.'

'What about Jerome?' asked Danielle, seemingly unable to stop herself.

'He fired his gun at the police, and then tried to kill himself, put the gun in his mouth and pulled the trigger, but it jammed. He's still alive. He's in a cell downstairs. It's been a huge benefit to us that he fired a shot, and then the gun jammed on the second bullet, but I'll come to that later.'

Danielle wiped a tear from her eyes.

'Do you need a moment?'

She looked back to Erika and Moss.

'No,' she said.

Moss opened the folder with the CCTV photos of Danielle in Primark and Superdrug.

'We also have proof that you bought the trousers Cheryl Regan was wearing when we found her body in your flat. We also have you on CCTV buying three bottles of Murine eye drops. The bottles match the ones recovered from the recycling box out behind the flats.'

'Let me see that,' snapped Paul. Moss passed the papers across to him.

'With this evidence we can charge you with murder. And I believe we have a strong chance of a whole life sentence. Juries don't look upon female killers with the same sympathy that they do with some men. If we also factor in that this was an evil death by poisoning. We have CCTV evidence. And a clear motive. You befriended Cheryl Regan, who looked remarkably similar to you, so you could fake your own death. We've also got CCTV of you at Ciao Bellissima nail salon with Cheryl.'

Danielle stared at Paul, who was silent for once. He rolled his tongue around his teeth and looked up at Erika.

'Why do I feel there is a deal in the air?' he said, passing the papers back across the table.

'When Jerome was brought in, we were able to test his hands for gunshot residue. You heard of this? It's very effective at linking a gun to a person. Proves he shot the gun. Jerome has quite a unique shooter.' Erika took another printout from her folder. 'A modified Stoeger semi-automatic pistol. And as you know, we can also trace the bullets fired by a gun. The bullets used in the raid on 17 Chapel Street were from a Stoeger semi-automatic pistol. You see this?' said Erika, pulling down the neck of her sweater to show the scar on her neck. 'It's from a bullet from a Stoeger semi-automatic pistol. We're testing the bullets, now we have the gun.'

Danielle sat back, clearly trying to keep calm. Erika leaned forward.

'We know that you and Jerome and Frank have recycled your identities over the years. Jerome became Kieron, you became Marie, and Frank had a passport in the name of Victor Gill. And you've been using bent coppers, bribing them. Commander Marsh is the biggest prize. Although I'm sure you guys lucked out with him. He was just a regular detective when you put him on the payroll?'

'Do you have a direct question, Erika?' asked Paul. He was sitting back now and watching the situation.

'And are you going to ask Jerome about all of this? Because I know nothing,' said Danielle. Erika had left the printouts on the table, and Danielle looked at them and then glanced away.

'I think you know a lot, Danielle. And I want to offer you a plea deal,' said Erika.

'Are you authorised to make an offer?' asked Paul.

'Yes. I am. Danielle would agree to share all information she has about Jerome Goodman and their drug-import operations, past and present. Danielle would also share all information about the raid on the Swann Pub in August 2012 and the raid on 17 Chapel Street in 2014. We would need names, account numbers, and details of the tunnel built from 17 Chapel Street to the canal bank. And any other information that would result in the closure of Jerome Goodman's operations, the recovery of any drugs and money, and also the successful imprisonment of Jerome Goodman. We would also ask for the names of every police officer who has cooperated with them for the past twenty years. Do you have that information? I take it you've seen a lot over the years?'

Erika was watching Danielle. She remained with her arms folded and paused for a long moment.

'And what would I get in return?' said Danielle.

'You would be given a new identity in a new location. You would also be given reasonable funds to start a new life. You would be on licence for the remainder of that new life. If you did anything illegal, you would be recalled to prison, and we would proceed with a trial for the murder of Cheryl Regan. Also, at that stage we would most likely have lots more to charge you with. You would rot in jail. Those are your two options.'

Paul Slater was looking slyly at Erika and Moss. 'This is all very lovely, in theory, but what guarantees do we have that you will follow through on this? That this is not just a bluff?'

Erika opened her folder and removed the final sheet of paper. 'This is everything I have just outlined in an official offer, dependent on the conditions being satisfied, from the assistant commissioner of the Met Police. This is confidential.'

Paul pulled the paper towards him eagerly. 'Well, I never. I've never seen anything like this. This is all very legitimate.'

He passed the letter over to Danielle.

She blinked her large eyes. Looked down and then up again at Erika and Moss. 'Okay. I'll do it. Where do I sign?'

It was late when Erika came out of the interview suite. And she travelled down in the lift to where Marsh was being kept in his cell. She asked Waller if she could speak to Marsh, alone.

He took her to the cell and knocked. When the hatch opened, Erika saw Marsh sitting on the thin bench, staring at the wall.

'Can I talk to you, off the record, as a friend?' she said. He looked at Waller and nodded. Erika stepped inside and waited until he closed the door behind them.

'Erika. I . . .'

She put her hand up. 'Can I please go first?'

'Yes.'

She took a deep breath and moved to the end of the bench. He moved his legs up so she could sit. 'This will probably be the last time I ever speak to you.'

'What? Why?'

'Why? Danielle Lang has just signed a plea bargain. Confessed to all of it. She's cooperating with us and naming you, among others. They kept records of your meetings, Paul. Phone calls. Cash drops. All of it.'

Marsh's face turned grey, and he went to speak.

Erika held up her hand again. 'I know you'll get a good barrister. But I also know there's enough to get you sent down if it's done right. What's bothering me most is the figure. Yes, Danielle could actually recall how much Jerome paid you over the years. Enough to buy a couple of very nice London houses. And I'm just in shock, really. That's all you got from it. You betrayed me. You betrayed your friends. Betrayed your family. And what do you have to show for it? A couple of semi-detached houses in South London. I just wanted to say that I pity you. I'll make sure Mia and Sophie are okay. I'll look out for them because you won't see them grow into young women. And I'll even help Marcie if she needs it. And good luck in prison. I really mean that. You hear so many horrible stories about what they do to senior-ranking officers inside . . .' Erika got up and went and banged on the door and turned back to him. His mouth hung open, and he looked destroyed. 'You weren't a beat officer for very long, but you should remember what they taught us. In a fight, stay on your feet. You might get your face rearranged, but you've got a better chance of walking away from it.'

And with that, Erika walked out of Marsh's cell.

EPILOGUE

Thursday, December 19, 2024

Erika splashed her face with cold water and stood up, wiping her face. The tiles of the women's bathrooms at Lewisham Row station were stark and white, drawing the colour out of her already-pale complexion.

She patted her face dry, adjusted her hair, and pulled on a fresh blouse and black jacket. She rummaged in her wash-bag, found the bottle of anti-red eye drops, and stared at them for a long moment. The irony was not lost on her. It had been a long week, watching the interviews with Jerome Goodman, Danielle Lang, and Marsh. Father Michael had been released on bail, pending further investigation.

The bathroom door squeaked open, and Melanie came in. 'How you doing?'

Erika tipped her head back and applied drops in each eye, feeling the faint sting. She straightened up and checked her reflection one last time.

'I'm ready.'

'I just want to tell you, good work. You're a good police officer. I'm proud to have you here . . . Listen Erika, I want to . . .'

'You don't need to apologise. We're good.'

Melanie smiled and nodded.

'Good. You go and get him.'

Erika hadn't come face-to-face with Jerome Goodman. She hadn't wanted to, preferring to observe him from afar. But now they had concrete evidence. And she wanted to look him in the eye when he was formally charged.

Erika's whole team was waiting in the corridor when she went down to the interview suite. Moss, Peterson, McGorry, Crane, Frieda, and Ryan, and so many of the other support officers patted her on the back as she went past.

'This was a team effort,' she said. 'Each and every one of you have a drink on me later.'

The inside of the interview room had a strange atmosphere, like there was too much static in the air. Jerome Goodman was sitting in a plain sweater and tracksuit. His mid-length blonde hair now had an inch of grey roots. He looked up at her and across at his new solicitor, Carolyn Jones, a woman who didn't quite have the stomach for the case, Erika thought, after the hours of observing them. Paul Slater had chosen his side. The winning side. If you can call witness protection and relocation for Danielle a win.

Erika sat down opposite them. She cleared her throat.

'Good morning, Jerome. I'm here to inform you that you are being charged with the murder of Hugh Walters. Danielle Lang led us to recover his body from the Mortha Quarry in South Wales. His remains were recovered with his skull encased in plastic. And we positively identified two hair strands from inside the plastic that match your DNA.'

Erika watched him, but he kept his dark, impassive eyes on her. She went on, 'Bullets from your gun, a Stoeger semi-automatic pistol, were recovered from the bodies of Detective Inspector Jim Black, Detective Inspector Tom Bradbury, Detective Inspector Tim James, Detective Inspector Salman Dhumal . . .' Erika heard her voice break a little. 'And.' She swallowed. 'Detective Inspector Mark Foster. And you are being charged with their murders. Two days ago, with information gleaned from Danielle Lang, we also recovered the bodies of six men in the cellar of 17 Chapel Street. As with these other murders, bullets were present in their bodies from your Stoeger semi-automatic pistol. We are also preparing charges on the import and sale of controlled illegal substances over a prolonged period of years, organised crime, money laundering, and bribery. You will be remanded in custody to await sentencing.'

Erika sighed and felt a huge weight fall off her shoulders. It was so enormous and yet, at the same time, so anticlimactic. Jerome just sat there impassively.

Maybe he really was a monster? Simple as that. He was just born that way. He sat forward and scratched his nose, fixing his eyes on her.

'Why did you do it all?' asked Erika. She knew that if she didn't ask the question, she would regret it for the rest of her life.

Jerome took a deep breath and exhaled. He leant forward so their faces were close together. Erika stood her ground, she didn't flinch or sit back.

'I did it because I could,' he said.

Erika stared at him, looked deep into his eyes, and she knew he would never tell her the real reason. Maybe he didn't even know himself. Erika got up and left the interview room.

Moss found her in the yard behind the police station shortly afterwards. Snow was starting to fall, and Erika was sobbing. She'd lit a cigarette but had been unable to smoke it as the sobs racked through her body. She cried for her friends who'd died, for her husband and the life with him that she'd lost. And she cried for the victims she would never know.

Moss came and held her for a long time. Just a friend being there for another friend. Eventually, the sobs subsided and Erika felt a calm settling over her.

She took a deep breath and looked around at the custody yard, which had been transformed with a perfect layer of white.

'Sorry,' she said, wiping her eyes.

'It's the best therapy, crying. "Having a good clear-out," that's what my Nan used to say.' Erika noticed her burnt-down cigarette and stubbed it out on the ground. 'You know, this has been a horrible week. How would you feel about me, you, and the whole team heading down the pub? I know that this is all far from over, and there's still much to deal with in the future, but right here, and now, you should celebrate catching Jerome Goodman. We should raise a glass to you and the team, and we should raise a glass to your absent friends and loved ones.'

'Yes,' said Erika, taking a deep breath. 'I'd like that very much.'

A NOTE FROM ROBERT

Thank you for picking up *Chasing Shadows*. I hope you enjoyed reading it as much as I enjoyed writing it. Writing this book was a great escape from a difficult few months of upheaval. Our dog, Lola, had to have an operation on her spine to fix a slipped disc which had left her back legs paralysed. Thankfully, she is now back to full health, but it was a tough time not being able to visit her in intensive care and not being able to explain to our other dog, Riky, where she had gone. At the same time, we moved house, and it all happened before Christmas. So, writing this book was my saviour, along with my husband, Ján, who did a great job keeping everything else from falling apart.

I've wanted to write this particular Detective Erika Foster story for a long time. In fact, as soon as I finished writing the first book, *The Girl in the Ice*, I knew I wanted to go back and discover what happened to Mark and Erika's colleagues. The aftermath of the events in this book will be wide-ranging for Erika, in good and bad ways, and I'm intrigued and excited to see where the series goes next. I have no plans to stop writing the Detective Erika Foster series, and ideas for the next book are already bubbling away in my brain.

Thank you to my excellent editing team, Haley Swann, Kellie Osborne, and Tara Whitaker. Henry Steadman, for another great cover, and Jan Cramer, for her wonderful recording of the English language audiobook edition. Thank you also to my wonderful publishers, editors, and translators around the world.

A big hug and a thank-you, as ever, to my first reader, Janeken-Skywalker, and the rest of Team Bryndza/Raven Street Publishing: Maminko Vierka, Riky, and Lola. I love you all so much, and thank you for keeping me going with your love and support!

If you enjoyed *Chasing Shadows*, please tell your friends and family and consider writing a product review. Word of mouth really is the best way for new readers to find my books. If you'd like to know when my next book will be published, please also consider signing up for my author mailing list.

It's becoming harder for authors to keep in contact with readers when, understandably, people are moving away from social media. Signing up to my mailing list means I can keep in contact with you directly with all my book news. I won't bombard you with emails; I typically only send out 2-4 emails a year, your email will never be shared and you can unsubscribe at any time. So rest assured, when I contact you, it will be worthwhile!

You can sign up using the QR code, or with this link: http://eepurl.com/duluLz

There are lots more books to come, and I hope you stay with me for the ride!

Rob

ABOUT THE AUTHOR

Robert Bryndza is the author of the international #1 bestselling Detective Erika Foster and Kate Marshall Private Investigator series. Robert's books have sold over 7 million copies and have been translated into 30 languages. He is British and lives in Slovakia.

You can find out more about Robert at www.robertbryndza.com

f facebook.com/bryndzarobert
⊙ instagram.com/robertbryndza
BB bookbub.com/profile/robert-bryndza
g goodreads.com/Robert_Bryndza